Athenaeum Inc.

Door Number Three

by

Dan Kemp

Chapter 1

"A day at a time, I 'spose..."
~Omar Little, Baltimore philosopher, when asked how he'd survived for eight or nine years.

Things were a lot simpler back when I was still a normal soldier. Back then, my life was getting drunk in the barracks and maybe puking on the next morning's run before training all day. My nights were spent meeting fascinating girls on the Internet to visit and hopefully screw on my next available weekend. It was a joyful existence, a prolonged and largely blissful martial adolescence with merely adolescent problems. Unfortunately, as time goes on, you get moved up.

Things can go on several ways from there. While your former peers from your days leading teams or squads go upward along the conventional track to being drill sergeants or recruiters, eventually to platoon sergeant slots or higher, you go sideways. Maybe someone pulls you to a weird assignment where uniforms and written duty descriptions become a memory. Sometimes you have two or three different ID cards, at least one with a fake name on it. And when the knees start to pop their last and your back is pretty well wrecked, by then you are carrying the clipboard and moving from player to coach. If you do that well, you move up again while you go even further sideways in 'retirement.' Sometimes it's in the civil service, sometimes with a favored contractor. And then one day, when the old guys who gave you your orders and your gym bags full of operating cash finally go down from heart disease, cancer, or high-velocity lead poisoning, then you are now Management with a capital M. You are now in charge of the team in a competitive league where there is no off-season.

And all I had wanted was to do was hoodrat shit with my friends.

I got the call around 0200, but I had expected it for some time. Nashville is more famous for country musicians than oncologists, but it had some of the best in its several hospitals. This was important, as my employer had spent heavily over the last year and a half trying to cheat the Grim Reaper one last time. When it became clear he wasn't gonna, he accidentally-on-purpose slapped on every fentanyl patch left in the box. He then poured a tall tumbler of twenty-eight year old Laphroaig single malt and took a permanent nap on his couch listening to Pink Floyd's *Dark Side of the Moon* one last time.

I grumbled about that as I drove. I was irrationally pissed off that if Big John was finally going to kill himself, he didn't do it either two days earlier or have the common fucking courtesy to wait until Monday. Leave it to that asshole to fuck up one last weekend for me on the way out.

We had a conference call scheduled at 1500 to deal with the aftermath of John's death. His problems were over, but ours were just beginning. Really, there was a lot to discuss. We who remained had to keep the doors open and the lights on. Most importantly, we had to keep the money coming in to pay for it all. It was either that or we shut down and tried to lead normal lives. Excuse me while I scoff at that. None of us were normal life kind of people.

It wasn't like we were in the normal trades, either. Put vaguely, Athenaeum Incorporated is in the information business. As we shared a name with several libraries and private schools, that was fitting. On one hand, we were a national agencies-level intelligence contracting company, legally rated as a 'disabled veteran-owned small business' for contract award purposes. All management and on-the-books employees had current top secret clearances. Many of our people were former employees of the government agencies with whom we contracted.

Those contracts were how we made our overt and legal living. Income taxes, Medicare, FICA, W-2s, all that normal people stuff. We had low-dollar but broad 'red team' analysis contracts with two of the big ones and took piecework consulting jobs from four more of the government's seventeen intelligence services. We also held a data backup contract with another agency, so there were racks and racks of red-tagged classified hard drives in one of our basements blinking away. Really with the advent of solid-state drives, there was less spinning and grinding every year as the equipment was swapped out for age. We always aced our semiannual contract compliance inspections, our facility exceeded *every* published standard for physical security, more on that in a bit, and we did solid work. Compared to the billions shelled out to the big contractors, we hid in plain sight, and not just because the name was hard to spell until you got used to it. *Athena-eum,* Athena's place, a home for the goddess of wisdom and strategy.

No, I do not know which one of my forebears named the firm. We who work there are shockingly ignorant of our own history much of the time, mainly since this business attracts grumpy old men who keep secrets a little too well. Even Googling the company was an exercise in frustration, though we liked it that way. You'd get everything from the Athenaeum faculty club at the California Institute of Technology to the student newspaper at West-by God-Virginia University. There is a theater in Indianapolis, a very renowned scientific and literary club in London, and an even older club in Liverpool. Even Gilbert Stuart's portrait of George Washington anyone would recognize from the one dollar bill would come up in the results, since the unfinished painting went to the Boston library of that name when Stuart died. We didn't care. If you were anyone we'd want to take work from, you probably already knew how to get hold of us.

Us? Wait, who the hell am I, you ask? Okay. Let's not put my real name out there. Most people just call me Professor. It started as an insult; I know a lot of things and have a tendency toward long lectures and pedantic nitpicking. Both traits annoy people even when it's professionally necessary. A drill sergeant hung it on me as a nickname when I came back in for a second hitch and after that it kinda stuck.

Trying to decipher our murky history was a subject I had been ordered to stay out of. Personally, I believed Athenaeum, patterned after a law firm with the partners in charge, had probably started out on way more of a semi-official basis with Uncle Sam than it was now. It clearly had been going on for decades. Neoclassical names like that had been out of fashion for a long time. "Hey Hey! Ho Ho! Western Civ Has Got to Go!" went back to the early Nineties, after all. It was only recently that a fad for Greco-Roman myth was spurred by dot-com billionaires with pretensions of culture.

Carrying on the law firm analogy, the partners were the board of directors, the CEO plus six more. I was seventh in line and by far the youngest. I was only a few months shy of age fifty, while the five surviving old timers were mostly my dad's age or even older. None would admit to having been there at the beginning, whenever that had been. Admittedly as the new kid, I didn't get told shit most of the time. But the law firm style of organization just screamed WWII-era Office of Strategic Services stuff to me, either directly or through conscious imitation. 'Wild Bill' Donovan and the Dulles brothers had all been upscale New York City attorneys before they became America's spymasters.

The good side of government contracting was we got to know maybe 97 percent of what Uncle Sam knew. Satellite imagery, UAV coverage, signals intelligence, all the good shit you can get piggybacking off most of a century's worth of a major nation-state's intelligence spending and resources. It was a scary and addictive pile of data for an information junkie to play in. It made being awake at three in the morning with thirty Wikipedia tabs open look like kindergarten.

The bad side of government contracting was that it paid what Uncle Sam decided it paid, not a penny more, then the checks cleared whenever Uncle Sam bothered to write them. On some contracts, we lived on crumbs from the table and barely made a profit on paper. You don't like it? Fuck you. Uncle Sam will pay his buddies at SAIC, LockMart, or some other big corporate intel services shop instead. And send your quarterly payments in to the IRS on time, or again, fuck you.

Me, I barely get my laundry done on time. Ever since I was a kid, I can be kind of drifty and I don't track boring things like that well. I do better when there's a last minute emergency to get a little adrenaline going. I find it sharpens the mind. So we now had a fucking *corporate tax lawyer* on retainer. He wasn't privy to what we really did, of course. It wasn't so much that he knew not to ask questions, he just didn't give a shit. Then again most of his other clients were Nashville music industry shops. They needed reminding that having handwritten receipts for cocaine did not make it a legal business deduction.

Then on the other hand, we had the other company. Keeping something resembling a theme, we called it an archival research firm. It had four employees on paper. Two of those alleged people were paper aliases who didn't really exist. Archival Associates, LLC had no government ties except a state small business license, and on paper it shared no assets, personnel, or premises with Athenaeum. Legally, it was run out of a rented mailbox in a FedEx store over by the Nashville airport. That box had been rented years ago by one of the people who didn't exist. We hid a lot of stuff in 'Double A,' including the fact that it now owned both that FedEx store franchise and the strip mall it sat in through an intermediary. And Archival Associates was where, metaphorically speaking, the phone rarely stopped ringing. It was mostly encrypted email.

For the most part, both companies were a reference library on most anything for most anyone who either paid or would owe us a sufficiently large favor. As mentioned, Athenaeum provided this service to the US government and certain other contracted clients on a secure and legal basis. Archival Associates, eh... different clientele and different rules. Not the 'you can answer it with Google-fu' sort of things. We live in a smartphone age. Look those up yourself, though we are ruthless enough to sell you open source answers at full sticker price. We mostly made our money on the esoteric. Want to know where a certain Russian oligarch has his yacht parked and how many shooters it has on board to watch over the party guests and hookers? We know. Want to know which subset of which Mexican cartel controls which dirt airfield, and then what nights the half-ton loads of cocaine or industrially cooked meth fly or truck in? Sure, we can figure that out. Which Congressman or Senator has an extracurricular girlfriend or boyfriend stashed in an apartment somewhere nearby? There's some guessing there, at least a dozen, but we know a few of them socially from the right kind of parties.

The only things people regularly ask us that we really can't tell you are where the Air Force keeps its UFO crash site retrievals (I am working on it out of personal interest, not much luck) and some stuff about the Kennedy assassination. We have a guy on retainer we forward those calls to. It's his thing, not mine, since boredom set in on the subject some years ago. But yes, my inner child remains convinced the secret government warehouse from the end of *Raiders of the Lost Ark* is real and it's out there somewhere.

You the reader may be wondering something like 'Hey, Professor, how do you gather all this information?' Well, it's complicated. You'll hear that a lot in this story. Sorry, but it's true. Athenaeum's unusual contractor status gave us some extremely high-level access into most important agency-proprietary databases and the major joint ones. Not all of them, but enough. The goal was to then not get caught looking at more than we could justify in the event of an audit.

Then on the data-backup contract, we found a way into a multinational data farm based in another English-speaking country and whose code name changed frequently. Other systems were simply hacked, in a couple cases by the same guys who used to legally work on them.

What surprised most people was that some of the commercial systems were better spies than the governmental. Archival Associates was very good at that. For one example, your grocery store customer card knows a whole hell of a lot about you in exchange for the fuel points. Sure, I play that game too, but with a fake name and address. And never mind what your phone will tell your cell carrier or Google about you. Online shopping was a gold mine of information. We had found one of the aforementioned Senatorial boyfriends by the Senator's Ikea account. "Where are you sending all that brand new furniture?" is a question that prominent people setting up a clandestine love nest don't want to hear. Sometimes they will do you a favor or three just so you don't ask it again.

See, not everything worth knowing is electronic data, and people are easier to hack than computers. 'Social Engineering' is a term that predates Facebook. Way too many people will tell things to an alleged government employee on the phone without thinking. Then we also had friends that knew things. We had a deep, deep Rolodex (funny how that brand name has survived the effective death of the actual product) of contacts on both sides of the street, mostly because the older partners had personal ties going back decades with all sorts of fun people in and out of government. Through them, we could often rely on broad networks of personal favors. Maybe that was one reason Athenaeum's contractor privileges always seemed to exceed the written terms of the contract. Then sometimes we just flat-out fucking lied, cheated, and stole. I wasn't an Academy grad, and so the honor code didn't apply to me.

What kinds of lies? OK, this is a good one. I once hired a really hot blonde college journalism major who also had a thriving career in Internet porn. I handed her a bogus set of business cards from Fox News, loaned her three correctly equipped guys who could reasonably impersonate a network camera team, then she walked in and out of a major crime scene in Houston for me. Cost me twelve grand for her four hours' work. That included a nice cash tip to keep her mouth shut and she also billed me for her hair, makeup, clothes, and airfare, but it got me what I needed at the time and a couple days before any of my other sources could have done so. It worked brilliantly, really. Those cops were just so sure they knew her from 'somewhere' that they never asked much and she was hot enough they just talked and talked....

What people who freak out about hackers forget is that computers are just tools. It's really mostly about people. What they knew, who had been told what, where they left the notes and about who had listened. To find who had listened, the more ears the better. The companies were a two-headed monster that could do things no American law enforcement agency could legally do, and that most intelligence agencies this side of the Israelis wouldn't bother with. We sent pizzas to guys working in hospital morgues and police evidence rooms, paid off car loans for news bloggers, wrote apartment rental checks for grad students in library sciences departments, sent a squadron sergeant major from the Brits' 22nd Special Air Service Regiment and his kids to Disney World... whatever it took to make friends, keep friends, and get questions answered fast and accurately. But to reiterate, we were an intelligence service. We didn't do shooter gigs as a company. Personally, I had nearly gotten my ass killed twice in twelve hours in Dallas a few years ago while freelancing. An Army buddy needed fast help on a job he had taken. You may have seen the resulting high-profile goatfuck on CNN.

Now we did not sell sources or methods, either Uncle Sam's or our own. We did not sell information on nation states to other nation states. Not our game. We did very, very little to jeopardize our position with the US government and in general took the national security of the United States more seriously than some actual government employees did. I knew of times in the firm's history where actions had been taken in the absence of government action. Perhaps we had been the government's deniable action? I was too new and too junior to know for sure, but I could always wildly speculate. Now we did anonymously donate some finished product to various NGOs we felt were doing good against human trafficking here and overseas, anti-poaching in Africa and elsewhere; yeah, the wiretaps and the satellite infrared imaging were just sitting there, so why not?

My work cell phone rang as I drove more of the country miles out to the office. "Roland the Headless Thompson Gunner," by Warren Zevon. It was Eric's ringtone. Eric was not the senior of the surviving partners, but he sure as shit was the scariest. I'd met the old man on a rifle range one Saturday and followed him down several interesting rabbit holes over the years since. He lived a few hours north across the Ohio River, in his family's century-and-a-half-old farmhouse on the prairie of southern Illinois. Their gun laws? Their notorious taxes? He didn't give a shit. The man was a ghost and immune to either. I wasn't even sure he was entirely human. He was one of the last of the old school Vietnam War gunfighters who by some freak of genetics was still in physical shape to go throw down occasionally, going on short contract gigs overseas to smell the smoke one more time.

And believe me, the old man had smelled a lot of smoke. VII Corps LRRP Company in Germany, learning the recon trade before Vietnam heated up. Then it was on to 5th Special Forces Group. Two tours with them, then a break teaching at Bragg. He volunteered for two more years in

Vietnam, this time with MACV-SOG's Command and Control North. After Vietnam he spent some more time teaching at the Florida Ranger camp before heading back to Germany and 10th SFG, way back when it was still at Bad Tölz. After working plainclothes in Berlin then assisting Charlie Beckwith's guys on the ill-starred Tehran mission, Eric made a final move back to Fort Bragg. He retired with thirty years of service right after Somalia went bad, though he wasn't there for that one. Some business down in Colombia with the hunt for Pablo Escobar, I think. Then after a gap he was conspicuously quiet about, he went into Afghanistan early after 9/11 with 'another government agency.' He was still the mentor and spiritual adviser to a few really lucky warrior souls. He had spent enough time sitting on the barracks floors with the Nungs and Montagnard between '66 and '71 to have turned into some kind of shaman. I really needed that wisdom on bad days. I'll be honest. I have a lot of bad days.

"Are we good?" He was asking if my crypto was on. My work phone was a... semi-classified product from, um, a *VERY MAJOR AEROSPACE AND DEFENSE COMPANY ONCE KNOWN ONLY AS A BOMBER MAKER* made out of black titanium that had been further modified in-house. Of course my crypto was on. So was his, since he had an identical phone. He just hadn't decorated the back of his with various pinup girl stickers.

"On this line, always."

"Ah, far out. Look, I am not going to make it off this mountain for the meeting, brother. Big John is dead and not going anywhere. Current ops will continue. Yeah, you guys meet, I trust you to handle what needs handling. We all check out of the net eventually. We don't all get out of state elk tags in the Wyoming draw, you dig?" He chuckled, dry as dust.

I would have felt better if he was there, even by phone. "Okay, so I have your proxy?"

He kept the laughing tone in his voice. "Doubt there will be much of a vote, man. Just relax, take it one day at a time. I'm going to lose signal in a bit once I get further up this ridge. Be gone a day or three. Catch you when I get back. Just be cool, man." The line beeped dead.

Eric never did care much for the admin side of the business. It was all about fun, games, and interesting personalities to him. He was more fascinated by a chance at getting a good elk than anything that would happen in that meeting today. I don't think he really cared if he did get one. It was just another step on the journey; definitely the introspective book Rambo versus the movie version. Maybe his refusal to stress out over anything was one reason he had lived so long and was in such good health for a guy with five Purple Hearts and some other off the books damage. At a fraction of his age, I had three bad discs in my back, two wrecked knees, didn't sleep for shit, and was probably nursing an ulcer again. I always tell myself I'll finally go to the doc when I have time.

The company's primary piece of real estate was pretty indicative of having had heavy official patronage once and raised a mystery all its own. We were north of Nashville, Tennessee, keep going, keep going, a bit more, but stop before you hit the Kentucky state line. That is as close as I will tell you. We owned just over 400 empty acres in a weirdly shaped not-quite-rectangular plot between the road and a ridge. Even with the last ten years of local growth, most of it was way too hilly and rocky to be worth anything to commercially farm or develop. Occasionally we would sell a couple good hardwood trees to a local sawmill to keep our agricultural zoning intact. The deed file at the county courthouse showed it had been bought by the US government in 1942, sold to the original American Telephone and Telegraph Company in 1961, then 'Ma Bell' sold it in 1978 to a series of private owners I supposed were other government contractors. It was resold to our current 'agricultural, logging and mining' LLC in 1989. No, the word 'Athenaeum' did not appear on the land deed.

I turned off the two lane blacktop to the driveway gate, stuck my card in the box, punched my PIN into the keypad (two factor authentication, kids), waved at the camera (three factors is even better), and it slid open. The driveway wound back almost half a mile back into the woods, a long, twisting stretch of heavy-duty concrete shaded by tall oaks, hickories, and cedars. I pulled around the last corner to a small parking lot. That stopped at forty feet of near-vertical limestone bluff, an exposed scar on a much larger hillside. On top of that hill was an old radio tower now draped in an assortment of cell phone and Wi-Fi antennas. We made a bit of money from renting that out. The bluff was faced nearly halfway up with reinforced concrete, with both an antiquated sliding steel garage door and a smaller personnel door.

I turned off my Silverado and dismounted. While I adjusted my belt and holster a bit (modified Glock 19, IWB at 4 o'clock in an old Raven Phantom holster), I eyeballed the parking lot, noting who was here on duty by their cars. The cars were either upscale four wheel drives or mid-upper sedans. Nothing too flashy, nothing too expensive. See, we had a rule. Actually we had a lot of rules. But the relevant rule in this case was 'No drug dealer cars at the office'. Own whatever you like, but if it would attract attention, don't park it here.

See, between on the books and off the books money, most of us who had been at this enough years were hypothetically rich enough to drive most anything we wanted. At the same time, given our shadowy existence of tax evasion and patriotically motivated petty crime, we had no desire to field questions about anything from anyone at any time. We weren't far enough in the middle of nowhere to not have a permanent fear of curious news choppers or high school kids with camera drones. None of us wanted to be in some YouTube video of PARKING LOT OF FERRARIS

AND LAMBOS IN THE TENNESSEE HILLS. We had one exception that was sort of on the bubble, a last-generation Shelby Mustang in what I would call 'Hi, Officer!' Red, but she was also fanatical about keeping a cover on it so the Southern sun didn't dull the paint.

I grabbed my old Coleman cooler-lunchbox off the passenger seat. I had brought leftover Chinese takeout from the night before. We were pretty far in the sticks between towns, so there weren't many choices at which to stop on the way in for food except for a little redneck convenience store with gas pumps back a ways at a crossroads. While we had a nearly commercial-grade kitchen in the gazebo for picnics and a pretty fair home-grade kitchen in each of the break rooms, we also had a strict peer-pressure 'you use it, you clean it' rule and I wasn't going to dirty up a kitchen for just me. We didn't have a full time janitorial staff for both economy and security reasons. Everybody was well paid enough and had enough free time to grab a mop or run a vacuum cleaner for thirty minutes a week. Even I made time to take my turns, that 'lead by example' shit you learn in the Army and spend the rest of your life unable to shake.

Overhead, the sky was starting to darken and the wind was picking up. Probably going to rain. Unfortunately the weather fit my mood, but it was time to go hide in my concrete pit.

I hit the doorbell for the 'buzz me in' button on the personnel door. The door remotely unlocked and I entered. I showed my ID to the three guys in the thickly built and ballistic-windowed guard shack inside the door. Obviously they knew who I was, and they'd known I was here since they saw me roll through the gate on camera, but procedure was held to. The fourth guy was probably on break. With a single-entrance facility like this, four guys on shift at a time allows roving patrols or bathroom breaks without compromising your front end.

Upon joining the company, I was the new guy, so office security was one of the first shitty jobs dumped on me. Since I can be kinda lazy, I merely recycled some of the procedures I picked up early in my Army days from working a high-level headquarters security assignment in Korea. With that in mind, we usually hired ex-infantrymen or cavalry scouts getting discharged up the road at Fort Campbell, then maybe an MP or two. This gave us reasonably experienced troops who were staying in the area and who needed off-hours employment. We paid well, with fat benefits. Their W-2s and insurance paperwork said neither Athenaeum nor Archive Associates on them. They technically belonged to yet another paper subsidiary. We also supplied the duty weapons, accessories, and range time. We had a private range out back for that. Yes, quality costs, but we could afford it. You can't pay your security guys pizza delivery kind of money without getting pizza delivery kind of people. Don't get me started on the false economy of buying them shit-tier guns thinking they won't have to use them much. If your security guys need to go loud, they need top-tier gear and extensive training since they're betting *your* life too. Merely mil-spec will *not* do.

But running the guards day to day was one of the first things I had convinced myself to delegate around here. I just didn't have the time to do it all no matter how much my control-freak nature sometimes insisted on trying. I had a former infantry squad leader named Jake, an Afghan vet out of the 173rd Airborne Brigade and a kid compared to the rest of us, who handled the two dozen or so of them for me. He dealt with the platoon sergeant issues of attendance and payroll, inspections and training. He was a bright one though. He'd grow into other roles as I had.

Inside that garage door, once you passed the shack, was a decent size work area of almost five thousand square feet with a high vaulted ceiling. Everything we needed for wood or metal working, basic electronics, and so on was arranged on benches or in rolling toolboxes. Many of us saved some money by doing our own auto repairs on site. The back wall was at least two feet of concrete, faced in six inches of what looked like Navy surplus armor plate, all painted glossy white to match the rest of the concrete walls. It concealed both the machinery rooms and an elevator lobby.

It was another badge and keypad drill for the heavy door into that lobby. Mounted on the inside of that wall, the last thing you would see as you went out into the work bay, was a nicely done navy blue-on-gold replica of the stadium tunnel sign at Notre Dame. There was one difference. Ours said KILL COMMIES LIKE A CHAMPION TODAY. Yeah, the Cold War wasn't over yet when Lou Holtz hung the original and obviously one of my nameless predecessors was a fan. Despite way more of our workload being Islamic terrorism, I had left it. I am one of the last children of the Cold War Army who put on the uniform before the hammer and sickle flag came down at the Kremlin in December 1991. The first American flag I'd sworn in under had flown at a Fulda Gap checkpoint with the 11th 'Blackhorse' Cav. Spiritually, I felt like I should still hold a grudge.

The elevator lobby was a two-part item. We had 'inside the blast door' and 'outside the blast door'. Yes, blast door. It was a forty ton antique built by the Mosler Safe Company, set in a concrete wall that made the two foot thick one look flimsy. Personally I hoped it was never seriously damaged. Replacing it would cost more than most people's houses. More, since Mosler was as dead as Oldsmobile, Packard, or Bethlehem Steel. It was one of those historical realities that sort of put shit into perspective.

Outside the blast door was mostly blank space, probably intended as shock absorption. Just big enough for the eight foot wide door to swing out, it was just more painted concrete walls with a rubber-tile floor. A broom was propped against the wall. That was it. Inside the blast door, we had the access door to the machinery rooms, the stairway door, the elevator, and a small backup guard shack where we would reestablish top-side security if we ever had to lock down for real. Until we hit that point, I really didn't want the guard force inside the lobby. It would raise questions in young minds that didn't need to be answered. None of them except Jake knew what was past the first locked door. We just told them it was a backup communications facility for a 'major government contractor' and left it at that. We paid well enough that they didn't poke too hard.

We merely called it 'the office', or sometimes 'The Hole' for a kindred facility under the old SAC headquarters at Offutt AFB in Nebraska. That one was still used by the successor commands. I'd been there. It wasn't as hardened as this one. The only real peer I could think of was the NORAD headquarters bunker at Cheyenne Mountain. It was certainly nicer than the Pentagon basement- I'd been there too.

The elevator and stairs went down eight stories. Each of those floors was eighty by a hundred twenty feet of usable space with some extra for plumbing and ductwork, all shock-stabilized, climate-controlled, and electromagnetically shielded. We had room for tens of thousands of gallons of drinking water in stainless steel tanks. Heavy duty electric cables and the Internet fiber-optics came down steel-pipe conduits through two hundred feet of limestone from the tower complex up top, wired directly from a TVA substation off the highway.

That power supply was backed up by four Fairbanks-Morse diesel engines in the machinery rooms. One primary, one surge, two spares, all 1940s production by the data plates. I seriously think they had been intended for or had come off of WWII diesel subs. They were set up to spin AC rather than DC as in their submarine days, being hooked to old GE-made 50 kilowatt generators that also looked like war surplus. Two of them actually worked correctly, and I was looking for somebody I could trust to mess with the other two. The diesel tanks for those could feed a tank battalion for several months. And unlike gasoline, you can store diesel for a whole lot of years.

In all, the place would shrug off a near miss from a good sized nuke, maybe a direct hit from a small one. It was immune to most anything less, even stuff they hadn't thought of in the 1950s. Maybe a really good penetrating bunker buster would crack it if it was lined up just right on the doors... yes, this is the kind of shit I constantly worry about because I may be nuts. On the other hand, I'm told if you can still question your sanity, you're probably still okay. Maybe.

Now as I mentioned, our business is information. I fancy myself an amateur historian, with some solid academic publishing and presentation credits. Some of those even have my real name on them. I know my way around archives. That said, after five years of trying, I still don't know what the fuck this place started out as or was intended to become. I hadn't found so much as a blueprint, budget line item, or concrete truck delivery receipt that matched its location in any military records I could access. This very expensive and extremely durable hole in the ground should not exist.

Yet, it did. With the land sale to the phone company, I had then looked elsewhere. I had consulted system maps for the AT&T Long Lines commercial phone system bunkers, then the secured networks that AT&T or Western Telegraph had managed for DOD. Nothing. I went on to every other Cold War communications project I could find, both completed and canceled. Everything from SAGE to GIANT VOICE. I found precisely dick. I'd thought of Mosler's old records, now archived. I thought I could track down the door to whoever ordered it. That was no help either. The maker's data plate was still there on the inside edge of the blast door. The serial number and date of manufacture had never been stamped on the plate. Just another mystery the builders left us.

Past that, it was an ongoing exercise in frustration where no remaining guess seemed unreasonable. The location is way too far outside the so-called 'Federal Arc' to have been a 'continuity of government' shelter for VIPs. Those were usually within a hundred miles of DC, allowing prompt evacuation by the small, slow helicopters of the early Cold War era. Whole books have been written on those so I'll spare you the lecture. A certain expensive hotel in West Virginia even advertises tours of their abandoned one.

Thinking locally was no real help either. By the narrow two-lane roads of the time, it was an hour outside the fence of Fort Campbell, so it wasn't part of the 1950s underground nuclear weapons storage facility on Old Clarksville Base. It was much too far from Fort Knox to be anything related to the gold vault. Radcliff was over two hours' drive away even after the Interstate was built years later.

Whatever it was once meant to be, it had clearly never been completed. There was a spot probably intended for a decent size cafeteria, but it was just pipe stubs and electrical boxes in the walls and floor down on the seventh level. The bathroom plumbing was working on the top four floors, though many of the original bathroom fixtures looked like set dressing for a 1950s high school movie. A civil engineer buddy of mine had calculated the enormous septic system was good for at least two hundred people for twenty years. But most of the space was like a warehouse that had never been filled. The air filtration was unfinished. The space marked 'Decontamination Area' in the garage bay now had my table saw and an arc welder sitting in it. Most of the light fixtures down on 6, 7 and 8 had never even been installed. American made back when everything still was, they were still in age-brittle cardboard boxes from Rust Belt companies sixty years a-gone, stacked next to piles of empty or never-assembled steel shelving. The electrical system took constant fiddling because it had been one-piece-at-a-time'd together. That's great when you're putting a ceiling fan in your kid's room. Try it when you're running a couple high voltage lines to feed a major server rack and you are probably gonna light the place on fire. That's a serious fucking problem in an airtight concrete box a couple hundred feet underground.

Before this line of work had become so Internet-focused, the whole place was probably borderline useless except as a place to hide file cabinets. The fourth floor and half of the fifth were full of those going back to the Fifties. There were hundreds of them lined up, all unmarked as to their origin, but the archives department spent their small slivers of free time exploring and organizing them. They occasionally found some of the damnedest things, like a 16mm surveillance movie of a couple that looked a lot like Robert F. Kennedy and Marilyn Monroe on a beach without their bathing suits. Still, the blast door and all that rock and concrete was reassuring. Not much says 'Fuck you and your search warrant' like lots of heavily reinforced concrete with a smallish mountain on top of it.

Just for fun, I took the stairs, since I was only going one level down to where most of our office space was. Passing the break room, I cracked a Mountain Dew from my stash in the fridge. I obnoxiously stuck to the vintage cane sugar formula even if that sometimes turned into long road trips or special ordering at a high markup. The break room was very nice, with a full kitchen and comfortably classy furniture, but it was sort of plain since Big John had wanted it kept that way. With him gone, I might have to mess with this one a bit. The technology geeks staffing our IT department on the second floor had half a dozen vintage arcade games in theirs and covered the walls in old movie posters. Intel had gone for antique maps and a wall of flatscreens down on the third floor. Later, I thought. Not important. Meanwhile... shit. Even before I got to my office, I thought of something.

I went back to the stairway and headed further down. I needed a fast snapshot on the numbers. With Big John, partnership had its limits when it came to being read in on finances. The guy had control issues right up until the end, and he distrusted other people over money more than any other subject. With the rest of the full partners maybe knowing even less than I did and with those questions being possible on the call, it was time to talk to the Accounting Department.

Chapter 2

"Hey little girl, you want it all, the furs, the diamonds, the painting on the wall..."
~*"Money Talks,"* AC/DC

Fortunately I had hired the current Accounting Department.

Her real name was Korean, but I mostly tried to forget it since she was in our private version of the Witness Protection Program. Regardless of what her fraudulently obtained documents said on them, she went by the nickname Cash. She had a lot of good points for a potential employer. She was the sort of ruthlessly overachieving *summa cum laude* Asian chick that gave the stereotype a bad name. She was a finance major out of Princeton with a MBA from *Haaahhvaaad* by age 23. Her IQ was high enough to give you a nosebleed and altitude sickness. No close family; she'd lost them in a car crash. She'd then hired on at a Wall Street investment bank and commenced slaving away up the career ladder.

As might be expected from all that, she had a classically jaw-clenched Northeastern accent that made her sound like William F. Buckley after he'd knocked back three martinis. Yes, I know Buckley was a Yale grad, but close enough. This was even funnier coming from someone barely five feet tall who looked like the sex-doll lead singer of an all-girl Korean pop band.

Why was she hiding with us? Yeah. She also had a few bad points. At the top of that list, she had zero moral reservations about making a few erroneous keystrokes if she didn't like you and, to be honest, she really didn't like a whole lot of people. See, after doing a bit of nosing around at that large multinational investment bank and finding a unique opportunity, she patiently skimmed just over seventeen million in drug money out of someone else's carefully crafted half-billion dollar laundering scheme and hid it in various foreign banks and in her bedroom closet by her 27th birthday. Unfortunately since she was new at major theft, she hadn't been quite as clever as she thought at covering her tracks. Eventually people caught on, other people caught on to their catching on, so she sequentially popped up on the radar of several groups of people on both sides of the street. One of those groups was us.

Never mind, story time.

Detour 1

"A Learjet SWAT team, on a midnight run, got a CAR-15 and an Ingram gun..."
~ *"Jungle Work," Warren Zevon*

We, meaning Archive Associates since it wasn't legal, had been doing some intel work on the domestic money laundering of drug profits. Illegal wiretapping, email hacking, that sort of thing. We weren't really concerned with investigating the crime itself. We aren't cops. Almost nothing either company creates would ever be legally admissible as evidence in a courtroom since the prosecution would have to then explain to the defense in the discovery phase who we were and where we got it. What we were actually doing was electronically looking over the FBI's shoulders looking for dropped nickels. Occasionally we found some.

Let me pull an example out of my ass. If the FBI recovers ten million in an asset seizure and in the aftermath, the drug ring is missing twelve million, they assume the Feds have the other two and just couldn't count, or that the Feds then used that discrepancy to deniably fund something else. After a while, neither side asks questions where the missing two are, it's dismissed as the price of doing business. Those are the sort of 'mistakes' that either gets one of the agents on site a new fishing boat when they retire or buys us new computers for the office. So anyway, we were reading the emails of the agents involved. Don't ask how, it's a trade secret. That's when they started talking about a junior investment banker in New York City who was stealing dirty money. She had been just a little too aggressive at it, gotten noticed, and was now being surveilled.

Reading their several discussions about her were somewhat thought-provoking. There was room for that sort of cutthroat initiative and 'hoist the black flag' attitude in the firm. Financial crime was a big thing globally and we didn't have a single MBA on the permanent staff. We were all military-political intelligence types as a matter of previous experience. To be honest, it was becoming a weakness in our game, so I got even more curious. I detailed a couple of the hackers to get everything they could on her. New York State DMV, cell phone company, Consolidated Edison electric bill, condo rental company, her grades from Princeton and Harvard, etc. I was impressed. Even Big John was impressed. This went on for a few weeks of spectator sport. Finally in a Friday afternoon email, one FBI agent on the case suggested to his boss that they get a material witness warrant over the weekend, kick her door in on Monday morning, and haul her off for questioning.

Unfortunately, we were a smaller group then and also had some other irons in the fire, including sudden rumors of a loose nuke out of a Pakistani Navy depot. We didn't see that email until Sunday afternoon. We didn't have much time. Really, we had even less time since one of the DEA agents CC'd on the email was known by us to be as dirty as my cats' litter box. And since, as I have mentioned, we were into the cell phone carriers' customer records and billing computers, we knew he was warning his 'other employers' and they were trying to beat the FBI there to grab her. Meanwhile the supervisory special agent at the FBI hadn't answered the email or called back. Believe me, we were watching that too.

So, long story short, I consulted Big John. Never mind, this calls for some of the long story, since the rest of this volume occurs in the aftermath of his loss.

Maybe a year after I met him out on a rifle range one weekend and six months before the Dallas gunfight, Eric had told me he had a full time job for me where the guaranteed money was worth the change in career path. It was nearly triple what I was making just to start. I needed the extra coin, as things were tight at home after... never mind. Some of my painful memories are just for me. Anyway, he essentially sold me to Big John, who then worked me like a hired hand in an antebellum cotton field both in and out of the office.

Big John was not a huge guy, but he had both overwhelming charisma and a bit of a mean streak, rather like Burt Lancaster's villain in *Seven Days in May*. That was fitting, since like that mutinous general, he was also an Air Force officer. He'd started out flying fighters, but things went bad on his second tour coming "feet wet" out of North Vietnam. He'd been hunting SAM sites all day, got hit, then broke a leg badly ejecting out of a burning F-105G Wild Weasel. After flunking his next flight physical as a result, it was either go start over in civilian life or take that firsthand knowledge of cracking air defense systems he'd acquired the hard way and go down a new track into military intelligence. He chose Door Number Two.

He took his career change seriously and had a laser focus on his work, even in this later version of his career. I barely knew of his family. The only hobby he ever mentioned was in an offhand comment when he told me, "I used to shoot pistols a lot until my eyes got worse." He'd spent so much time out of sight behind vault doors with DIA or the even more secretive National Reconnaissance Office that he never made general, but as bird colonels go, he had apparently carried a lot of clout. The contracts we had spoke to that. Plus there was a shocking number of intelligence community VIPs he could call in the middle of the night at home and call by not just their first name but by old weird nicknames. Now John was not happy I took those few days off to go to Dallas, and even less happy I got near-missed a few times, but I went right back to work afterward so he eventually shut up about it.

A year and a half later, we got the phone call that one of his old cronies had died. Turns out that buddy had been one of the seven partners of the firm. He looked across his desk, sighed, then told me since I had worked out okay so far and there was no one else available, I was about to make full partner in Athenaeum and start seeing real money. He wasn't lying. My income went way up again and the IRS never saw much of it. Of course the workload went up too, but a lot of the pay and bonuses from the Archive Associates side was paid out in straight cash. *Dolla dolla bills, y'all*. Then six months later, he got the bad news from his oncologist and spent the next year and a half making it all the way to the scene of the crash where we now found ourselves.

During his treatment, I'd gone from being his briefcase carrier to usually being our senior man on site. I'd occasionally fought him to hire more help, or spend some money to improve the office. I'd usually won. Getting the money to establish the IT department had been a real battle. John didn't like IT or IT kind of people since he distrusted electronic gadgetry in all forms. But so long as he still lived, the potential to lock horns with both the FBI and a drug cartel in the same night was not my call to make. This was not a 'Forgiveness is better than permission' moment. John wasn't big on forgiveness. We had too many acres in which I could go permanently missing.

Since he wasn't in the office while he recovered from another serious cycle of chemo, I drove down to his house and presented my argument. I ventured that her academic background and proven skills made her worth recruiting. First, she had a skill set we could use in exchange for granting her safe harbor. We badly needed an accountant and portfolio manager. Secondly, we were weak on financial crime and international money issues. Putting her to work for us was preferable to letting the FBI snatching her to be a grand jury witness or, far more likely, just a future felon. Either was still preferable to what the angry South American fellows would do to her over that missing seventeen million. I was persuasive enough that he agreed. He gave me the go-ahead to go pick her up *if* I could do so without confronting the Feds.

If is a really big word, as the Spartans once proved to Philip of Macedon....

Yes, we are equipped to impersonate real Feds to civilians and have done so. We have done so often enough I will not incriminate myself with too many specifics. Impersonating Feds to other Feds without doing some serious preparatory work is a whole lot harder. And yes, we've successfully done that too.

But all this put us under a bit of a time crunch. I did have a contact in New York City. He was also ex-military, uh, just not *our* military. Still, he was not a guy I would ask to handle something this heavy and with this sort of risky legal exposure. Asking him to go stake out a no-notice target, not knowing if he would be up to his ass in Feds and/or cartel guys, was borrowing trouble it wasn't my place to give him. I would just leave him out of it and not say shit. I'd buy him a nice dinner the next time I was in town and just not tell him why.

The first issue was getting there fast enough. Flying commercial was right out at that time of night, since nothing was leaving Nashville before morning. Fortunately, money solves some problems and skill solves others. If you can throw them both around well, you can accomplish a lot quickly. To quote Dennis Rodman's slightly eccentric performance on the 1990s action show *Soldier of Fortune, Inc.,* "America does have a king. His name is Benjamin Franklin."

For those of you who do not get the joke, look up a picture of a hundred dollar bill and think about it for a minute. We'll wait while you get caught up.

Now the firm does not go to the aggravation of owning and maintaining its own airplane. I still don't think the more affordable 'compact' sort of business jets are worth it. You couldn't even stand up in most of them. I am a large mammal. Some of our employees are even bigger mammals. Having four foot nine of ceiling for hours and basically crawling to the refrigerator or the uncomfortably compact lavatory was like riding in a hamster tube. My back couldn't handle it. You want bigger, you're paying more. Eventually you're paying so much more that we never bothered. Like I said, John really hated spending money if he didn't have to.

Since we didn't fall under government lowest-bidder travel regulations and didn't give a shit about paying for first class upgrades, we then had another company rule: we only bothered chartering if we had more than three people going the same place, we couldn't get there commercially (Pig Knuckle, Arkansas or similar), or if we were flying stuff we didn't want to go through airport security. Guns, blades, body armor, bags of cash. Shit like that.

Some people can get away with that stuff commercially. I knew a SEAL officer once who had flown back into McGuire AFB in New Jersey from Somalia with his guys, then had been dumped with government-purchased commercial tickets at Newark. There they were; four really smelly guys in dirty, bloodstained uniforms with still-loaded automatic weapons that the airline had to crate and haul for them. They then went via Chicago O'Hare to John Wayne Airport in Orange County, California, trying to get home to their base in Coronado with their crate of war toys, ammo, and explosives, sucking down complimentary cocktails the whole way. Hell of a story, to hear him tell it at parties. That sort of thing actually worked if you had the right magic words in your travel orders to make it US Government Officially Legal. We were out in the shadows somewhere between contracting and crime, so we had no such ability. Complicating things, we were four for four on 'guns, blades, body armor, and cash' on this run.

But through the glory of capitalism, there were ways. If you don't own, rent. There was a broker of jet charters in Nashville who was hooked into a computer network of available birds. His primary clientele was either the music industry or the really rich folks down in Williamson County, not people like us. He didn't know what we did for a living and didn't need to. All he knew was that we never quibbled over a bill and always paid on time. Now we occasionally paid by going to his office over off Music Row and giving him literal envelopes of cash, but we still paid on time. That diligence had purchased some good will and paid off in the long run since he always found us a ride and had taught us a good bit about charter aviation in the bargain.

The first lesson. At a certain level, a private airplane is a badge of social status. Many of the newly wealthy who travel a lot decide they want a plane, buy it, but eventually decide the regulatory and mechanical hassles of owning anything with wings sucks too hard for them to deal with for long. Then they usually sell it at a loss. So, relevant to our needs, a certain country singer you have heard of had bought a Lear 60XR a few years ago. No, not Taylor Swift, she owns a pair of Dassault Falcons, a 50 and a much larger 900. She also hasn't actually *lived* in Nashville in years.

Anyway, while the 60XR is a nice midsize jet that seats seven including a half-assed excuse for a couch, the guy decided very quickly that it was too small and cramped for the entourage to keep it as the sort of flying tour bus they dreamed of. But instead of selling it at a loss like so many other owners, instead it was now available for charter out of the greater Nashville area whenever they didn't need it for themselves. It seats four just fine if you put your rifle cases or any other oversized luggage on the half-assed couch. It cost us right around five thousand an hour for flight time, including the fuel, the pilot, and all the maintenance. It even covered the complimentary food and drinks in the passenger compartment's cabinet and mini-fridge. With a little advance warning, the pilot even took requests. He'd hit a grocery store or something on the way to the hangar rather than make us pay the marked-up prices at the airport caterer.

Now who to take with me.... I was lucky. Two extremely skilled buddies of mine, Dave and Jimmy, more on them later, both used to live in the New York metro area. That experience helped in this matter. They were also conveniently near the office when this popped up. While I was trying to get the jet broker to answer his phone on a Sunday night, Dave picked Jake as our fourth, mostly because he lived barely thirty minutes from the office and kept a go-to-war bag packed like the good paranoid two-tour Afghanistan vet that he was.

I finally got the broker on the phone around 2100. I told him we needed to break ground by 0100 at the dead latest. He didn't need to know why, but I wanted us on the ground in New York with a couple hours of darkness left. Otherwise we were running the risks of higher literal visibility and the FBI actually being out of bed and moving by then. To kick the deal, I told him I would pay double. Somehow, some way, he made it work. Probably because he was pocketing the overage.

We had the same pilot most every time we used that Lear. He worked for the singer and it was 'his' plane. Matt was retired Air Force, and he'd finished his twenty commanding a fighter squadron in Korea. Like every other pilot who ever strapped on an F-16, he was short and stocky, blond going gray in his case. It was like he'd been sent over by Central Casting as the career stereotype. He wore his big Breitling aviator watch constantly and his A-2 leather jacket whenever the Tennessee weather allowed. We liked Matt. Not only was he pleasant enough, but Matt never asked questions. There was never a "Why are we going?" or "What's in the duffel bag?", and especially not a "Whose blood is that, anyway?" He was getting paid to fly, which was all he really wanted out of life besides getting laid, and we always tipped well in cash his ex-wife wouldn't know about when it came time to renegotiate her alimony checks. That helped ensure he continued to not ask questions, which went double this time around. Not knowing what we were in for, we had a few things in the luggage that were technically illegal in New

York and New Jersey and a couple more that were in most places. You know, just in case shit went really sideways.

We launched at ten minutes before midnight. In just under two hours and losing another hour for the time zone change, Matt took the Lear into NYC's primary business jet terminal across the Hudson River in Teterboro, New Jersey at nearly full throttle. We actually went *over* a thunderstorm in Ohio just to pick up the tailwind. Meanwhile, not giving a shit about FAA rules, we had been working the cell phones as we flew. This is where the City's reputation as a town that never sleeps helped. NYC caters to weird people willing to shell out lots of money to get what they want, day or night.

As we came in on final approach at Teterboro, we turned off our cell phones. We then threw them in copper-cloth bags that acted as Faraday cages, blocking radio frequencies and other electromagnetic waves in or out. It was a trick I had picked up from the protesters at the Republican National Convention a couple years back. The risks of our phones pinging a tower and then being traced to her apartment's area later were high enough it wasn't worth having them on.

Electronic footprints matter. Depending how much they decided that they cared about this, the FBI would get a list of every phone that had been in the area and be sorting for ones that didn't belong to residents. Given enough time, they could even track a prepaid burner back to at least to the point of sale. That nice, safe, investigative desk-work shit was what they did best. Rumors abounded online that they could even remotely ping ones that were seemingly turned off. We had some reason to believe that was true. But in the plan, we had an hour to get there, get her, and be moving. Otherwise, so as far as the office was concerned, no news was good news until we were safely homeward bound, maybe somewhere in New Jersey or Pennsylvania.

Piling off the Lear, we jogged to the nearby chopper pad. There, we paid out the nose for the charter helicopter we'd reserved that would get us to the Downtown Manhattan

Heliport at Pier 6 on the Lower East Side. The web site and the girl on the phone had told us two grand. Yeah. That was *per passenger*. Rather than haggle back down, we just shut up and paid, including a 'we gotta go right now' tip. That said, true to their web site advertising, it took eleven minutes. It was now just after three in the morning. Unloading and looking around, it was less than a mile straight-line distance to our objective. We could literally see the top of the building we needed to get to. This is where we had had the first hurdle on the ground. There were a very limited number of options to get across the East River. Technically it isn't even a river; it's actually a narrow tidal gap between Long Island Sound and New York Harbor. People forget that Brooklyn and Queens are actually on the west end of Long Island.

We knew about this problem before we even broke ground, but we had figured we'd use some tactical flexibility and solve it when we got here. The water taxis didn't start running until 0630 and we didn't want to wait that long. Why waste three and a half hours? In planning, we had actually debated just swimming the fifteen hundred feet or so. When one of your guys, Jimmy to be exact, had been a chief petty officer in the SEALs, it's a sure thing for at least one planned course of action to involve a swim in or out. The three to four knot current and the pollution levels made that the last choice, but we still had four pairs of fins and some float gear in one of the bags if we had to make it an emergency move coming or going.

Skipping the water and staying on some form of land, going the long way around by either footpath or taxi using the Brooklyn Bridge was still most of three miles since the bridge's on-and-off ramps took us way the hell out of the way at both ends. It was an extra mile over to City Hall Park in Lower Manhattan to get on the footpath, then a mile and a half across to the pedestrian stairs at Brooklyn's Prospect Street. Trying to do it on foot quickly? Eh... as I have mentioned, I am more than a bit crippled up from various service connected damage. I could do the distance, but I just couldn't run it like the others still could. Why not get some wheels? Cabbies or rideshare operators were obvious witnesses and our phones were turned off. We didn't want witnesses and the clock was ticking. We were still trying to steal a march on the Feds.

As we walked north thinking about the problem, we found who we needed. In *Dungeons and Dragons* terms, the DM rolled on the Random Encounter Table and we got lucky. A guy was out in a smallish boat fishing the river in the predawn dark. Yes, people fish the East River, though if they eat the catch regularly they are braver than I am. I wouldn't trust the water that much. But he had an anchor in just north of the Pier 11 water taxis by the dog park, maybe fifty feet out off the seawall. It was a nice boat, a nineteen foot Boston Whaler center console with a big Evinrude outboard.

Me, I love fishing, even if I don't have the free time to do it much anymore, so I spoke the language. I asked him if he was catching anything, we talked about striped bass season, good bait, best lures, and all that good shit. Then I asked him if he wanted to make a fast three hundred bucks. Spoiler alert; of course he did. Three guys who look like ex-soldiers walking around with surplus green gear bags at that time of the morning might not be drug related, but he probably figured our money was good as anyone else's. He edged into the seawall, we jumped aboard, and he ran us across to the pier in Brooklyn Bridge Park in less than two minutes. I wished him good luck, handed over a small roll of large bills, and he went back to his rods and reels with a grin. He probably thought he fleeced some desperate tourists out of money he could use for boat gas and his marina fee. He was right, but it was still cheap at the price. From there, we walked three blocks inland, heading easterly up Old Fulton Street and then made a right on Hicks to enter Brooklyn Heights.

Meanwhile, Dave had gone the opposite way to the Heliport main entrance and grabbed a taxi uptown to the rental place on East 43rd to pick up the getaway car. He'd booked a full-sized Cadillac Escalade SUV. It wasn't exactly subtle, but there were going to be five of us plus luggage. It was also the only car rental place in the Five Boroughs open before 0630 that wasn't out at one of the primary airports. You make do with what you can get in the middle of the night. The only other late night rental option in town had cars with strange proprietary paint jobs. That made both those options suck. Avoiding the surveillance cameras, cops, and delays at the big airports was one of the reasons why we did Teterboro and the helicopter in the first place, and proprietary paint was too easily traceable on a camera afterward.

I had several backup plans for the rental company fucking us over, but they were mostly just high risk and terrible. Keeping rental Cadillacs in mind, I had even looked up an on-call hearse service further out in Brooklyn's Red Hook neighborhood. I'd gotten that idea from an old rerun of *The A-Team*. Past a couple other really dodgy ideas like that, Plan E for wheels was just stealing something. With the number of traffic cameras between us and home, we didn't like that option much either.

Still, we had to get there first. Our target leased a little one bedroom apartment three blocks inland and two blocks south of the Bridge in the Heights. It was basically Brooklyn's original gentrified neighborhood. It was also close enough to Grimaldi's Pizza to smell it if the wind was right. I knew this because Jimmy was loudly wishing it was open. As we got close to her building, Jimmy drew the suppressed .22 we had brought and popped three streetlights with no more noise than snapped fingers. As befitted a guy who'd made his bones with the SEALs, he was an artist with a pistol. The camera above the lobby door died the same way. After pulling our gloves on so as not to fingerprint up the place, we then slowly went up two flights of stairs with our hands on our guns.

Jake was our primary breacher on this. He was good with lockpicks and brought the electric lock gun I'd bought him last Christmas to make the entry. If that didn't work, his duffel bag also had a compact eight-ton hydraulic car jack, two pieces of 4x4 timber, a short sledgehammer, and a Halligan tool. Basically most of what you would need to break a frame and open a door the non-subtle way. Instead, Jake's toy did its job inside of four seconds. I breathed a deep sigh. The goddamn door lock was the first thing since the helicopter touched ground that went strictly according to plan.

The place was cramped by my standards. The entire sparsely decorated apartment would have mostly fit in my kitchen back home. Despite that, a search engine had told me it still cost almost five times as much a month as my mortgage in Tennessee. NYC real estate may have location going for it according to some people, but in my rather biased opinion it sucks in the 'what you get for your money' category. I'd stayed in a friend's place by Times Square once and I think that one was actually even smaller.

Jimmy went back downstairs to the lobby door as a lookout, with an exquisitely counterfeited set of US Marshal's Service creds in his pocket. The phone number on them would, after some misdirection, ring on a desk back in our intel section rather than in Washington, DC if anyone tried confirming who he claimed to be. That might slow down any FBI or NYPD types enough for us to get out the back door. We'd then try to figure out how to get him away cleanly. If it was cartel types, he was to fall back past us and let Jake and I deal with it. Meanwhile, Jake had unfolded a suppressed AR-style 'pistol' out of his backpack, a home-built Sig Rattler knockoff in .300 Blackout, and was pulling security back toward the front door.

I didn't bother knocking on the bedroom door. Hell, I was still surprised there *was* a separate bedroom. Most things in this building were one room studios according to the leasing company's web site. The bedroom, tiny as it was, was barren too, just the bed she was in. She was out cold, right on the edge of quietly snoring. At least she was both alone and clothed. Good. This was going to be awkward enough as it was. Still, the direct approach was best since time was ticking.

My very bright Surefire flashlight came out of my pocket, and I clicked it on. I shined it down at the floor to illuminate the room with indirect spillage that was easier on everyone's eyes. I was not going to use the one bolted onto my Glock. I then tapped her on the calf lightly. That kept me out of punching distance if she woke up mad. She didn't even twitch. Fine. I really didn't have time to keep trying the delicate approach, so I grabbed her by the shoulder and shook her a bit. That sort of woke her up. Her eyes went wide, but she didn't scream.

Using the 'quietly commanding' tone of voice that I perfected in the Army, I calmly said, "Excuse me, miss. I'm from the Federal government and we *really* need to talk to you about seventeen million dollars or so."

That really woke her up in a hurry. "Oh... fuck. Don't you need a warrant?" I could tell she wasn't the sort to swear regularly just from her visible reluctance to drop an F-bomb. That made it really funny, but I stifled my urge to laugh. Gotta stay in character at a time like that.

"We aren't those kinds of Feds. Those kinds of Feds will be along in a couple hours at most. We are the 'here to offer you a cool new job commensurate with your abundance of skills and corresponding lack of morals' kind of Feds. We're way more fun to hang out with. There's flexible scheduling and great office parties."

She just stared at me, looking really unimpressed. Maybe I wasn't as amusing as I thought I was, or maybe it was just too early in the morning for jokes. "I don't suppose you have any ID?"

"Not that would convince you of this shit, no. Listen up, Ivy League. Here's the deal. We want to be out of here with you inside of ten minutes and you are literally going to drop off the visible face of the Earth. You will still be working in investment banking and portfolio management. But we really do need to get out of here fast.

"Should we not accomplish this before The Other Feds show up, we can probably get ourselves out of this mess. You, on the other hand, are fucked. You will get hauled off by the FBI and you are looking at 15 to 20 in a nice women's minimum security joint somewhere for a whole bunch of wire fraud. Once there, you will probably still get stabbed to death in the cafeteria line because you stole from people who don't like being stolen from and who hold grudges. On the other hand, those guys you stole from are trying to beat the FBI here, because they are trying to deliver the 'gang rape then cut up with a machete' combo platter their boss ordered for you. So really, Door Number Three where you leave with us in nine minutes is your best deal."

I could tell from her academic records she was a straight-line linear thinker. This was a hell of a curve and she still didn't look convinced. "You're really serious."

"Well, the humor is to soften all this a bit, but yeah. I am dead serious. You have about eight minutes now. Less would be better. Otherwise the Feds are going to nail your pretty little ass to the wall, assuming those drug cartel types don't carve you up like a Thanksgiving turkey."

She took a deep breath. Her brain was calculating, but I saw the switch finally flip to 'acceptance.' "Door Number Three it is, then." She jumped out of bed and pulled a hooded black and orange Princeton sweatshirt on over the sports bra and yoga pants combo.

I picked her phone up off the nightstand. "Anything on your phone you can't live without?"

"Uh, a whole bunch of pictures..." I turned it off and threw it in another copper cloth bag. Really, the smartest thing to do with her phone would have been to smash it with the breach kit's Halligan tool and throw the pieces in the East River, but I was trying to stay on her good side. We apparently had a decent rapport so far, so smashing her two thousand dollar iPhone XXVI-WTF-BBQ would probably just piss her off.

I figured six minutes to get her loaded then two minutes to get out and down the stairs. I cranked the dive bezel around on my watch to count it down. I was watching her pack, keeping my right hand calm but near my gun. Why relax? "You don't have a car to worry about, do you?" We hadn't found one registered in her name, but that didn't mean one didn't exist.

"I sold it when I finished my MBA and took this job. Do you know what it costs to park a car per month in this town? I'll tell you. Almost as much as the condo rents for."

"Cool, one less thing to worry about."

She was rapidly throwing sentimental T-shirts, her framed diplomas, her laptop case, and a surprising amount of what I guessed was her stolen drug cartel cash out of her closet into a very large suitcase. And then a purple velvet bag that clinked. Then more clothes went in on top of the clinking bag. A violin case, then another clinking bag. She closed the suitcase and slid it toward me on its wheels. She went back into the closet and came back out with a no-shit vintage Halliburton Zero aluminum briefcase, the choice of Eighties action villains. I hadn't seen one outside an old movie in ten years. She opened it. It was full of banded bundles of hundreds. She re-latched it before throwing it on the bed.

"Jesus, girl, how much of what you stole is actually here?"

She looked at me uneasily. "You pinky swear you really aren't those kind of Feds?"

"Not that kind. So yes, I pinky swear." I extended my little finger theatrically for emphasis.

"Two and a half exactly out of the seventeen point three, not counting some gold coins and other savings."

Goddamn. I sighed. This was a complete rookie move."Why the fuck would you put two point five million dollars in your closet?"

She was getting annoyed with me. I have two ex-wives and half a busload of ex-girlfriends. I am a world-class expert on annoyed females. "Because it wouldn't fit in the fu-, um, refrigerator? I couldn't wire transfer all of it; I was running out of places to hide it. Some of it I cashed out here in town through a couple dummy accounts and here it is."

I sighed again. "No, that wasn't suspicious at all. That was probably how they caught wind of you. Goddamn, girl, you may know money but you don't know crime. They don't teach it at Harvard Business School."

"But you obviously need me, or you wouldn't be here. Besides, walking down the street with a million dollars' cash in a nice briefcase had been a dream of mine since I was a little girl and I finally got to do it." She then pulled a large orange tabby cat from under the bed. He yowled in loud discontent. "Let's go, Rock."

"Rock?"

"Short for John D. Rockefeller. I found him stray on campus at Harvard when he was a kitten." There was some more of his deep growling and then a hiss in my direction. I didn't care if she named him for Dwayne Johnson. That cat was not happy to be there.

Jake looked in through the bedroom door at me. "We're really bringing the cat, boss?"

I looked at her. Fuck it, I was as devoted a pet owner as any. I wouldn't leave mine behind in her shoes. Plus she had to be way more scared than she let on and maybe the cat would help. "Yeah, Jake, we're bringing the cat." I looked back over at her. "I don't suppose you have a carrier?"

"It broke."

Of course it fucking did. Two point five million in the fucking closet and she didn't bother going to PetSmart to spend a lousy thirty bucks for a new one. *Sigh.* I looked at my watch. 45 seconds left of my six minute goal. Time to step. "Carry him and the briefcase. I got the suitcase. Jake, you're on security."

Rock balanced on top of the briefcase as she picked it up with her left hand, then he jumped to her shoulder. She walked out to the refrigerator, which was barren but for a few condiments and a lone bottle of expensive-looking organic iced tea. She pulled it out, cracked it open one-handed with her right in what had to be a well-practiced move, then sarcastically toasted us. "One for the road, right?" She took a last look around, shrugged, and walked out of her old life. We got out the door onto the landing, re-locked it behind us and waited for all of thirty seconds. Jimmy then whistled up from the lobby, loud enough to hail a cab in traffic. It must be a New Yorker thing.

As we headed downstairs, I stuck close to her, speaking quietly. "When we get to the car, which is supposed to be an Escalade, you're going in through the back hatch. The suitcase too."

"Why do I have to go in the back?"

I felt I owed her the full explanation. "Because once the Feds are here and find out you aren't, every networked surveillance camera in the Five Boroughs is going to have your face plugged into the facial recognition software and they are going to be looking for you. So first, pull your hood up. Second, the back is where the blackout glass is. So you need to be out of sight and we need to get you across the Hudson fast."

We moved out the door, with Jimmy and Jake discreetly pulling security up and down the street. Surprising me, it actually was the promised Escalade. Making things even easier, it was the long wheelbase version with the extra row of seats. I let myself relax one notch as Dave popped the back hatch. We put the suitcase and our gear bags in the back. She went into the back row where she cradled the cat and sipped her tea with a scowl. The rest of us climbed in and we rolled quickly. It wasn't even quite 0400 yet. We were actually running ahead of the plan.

The Brooklyn Bridge was right there, feeding due west into Lower Manhattan. That was why we didn't take it. Instead we took the nearby Manhattan Bridge which angled us northwest into the Bowery. From there we skirted around Little Italy and across Midtown. In twenty minutes we were to the start of I-78 West, moving through the Holland Tunnel into New Jersey. There were no tolls on the outbound route, so there was no electronic EZ Pass record or any photographing of our license plates to mail us a toll bill. The toll records were why Jimmy had previously ruled out exfiltrating via southern Brooklyn across the Verrazano Narrows Bridge to Staten Island then the Goethals Bridge into New Jersey. Without an RFID pass, itself traceable, our plates would have been photographed and a bill forwarded when we crossed the Verrazano. Technology was a bitch. The last time I had driven myself across the bridges into NYC, Bill Clinton was still President and you still threw quarters into the toll booth's mechanical basket while an actual human waved at you.

Running opposite the start of the morning rush hour, we got past the exit ramps for Newark Airport in 47 minutes, about what I predicted. It was still nicely dark. Looking in the back, she was out like the proverbial light, with Rockefeller making little snoring kitty noises in her lap. We debated amongst ourselves about stopping somewhere, but snacks could wait. Personally, I was too stressed to even piss yet as we headed across and eventually out of New Jersey.

First, there was the matter of the Caddy itself. "Dave, what did you tell the rental company?"

"I booked for three days, with free unlimited mileage."

Okay, cool. "Yeah, but did you tell them we were returning it somewhere else?"

Dave scoffed. "No. Figured that was an operational security issue."

"Dave, you know more about on the ground black bag shit than I do. How do we get the car back now?"

"Drop it off at another location, it doesn't matter which, let them overcharge the shit out of us, and we tip the counter person. That counter person is going to be a twenty-something junior management trainee who doesn't care, and then we get the hell out of there. The credit card is a company burner and the license is a DOD fake I kept when I retired. Short of them calling the cops and the cops dusting the car for prints then running them, they won't find shit. And they won't bother calling the cops because they got the car back two days early and got paid even more. Sure, they have the car out of position compared to their inventory projection, but again, they don't give a shit. And their inventory management is not our problem anyway." *Well, fuck.* I guess I got taken to school on that one. And that was exactly what I told him. We all had a decent chuckle at that.

"Listen, Professor, some of us have also learned a thing or two over the years and you don't have to do it all yourself." Yeah. That was the hard part. Knowing when to let go and let other people play their parts.

We had told Matt to have the Lear at Lehigh Valley Airport outside Allentown, Pennsylvania no later than 0700. I'm pretty sure he had just dropped us off at Teterboro, immediately flown straight down there, and then gone to sleep onboard the plane. He'd done it that way before. Why park, shut down, and pay a ramp fee just to wake up, preflight, then go back up in a few hours? It was only 99 miles from our start point in Brooklyn and was less for him from Teterboro. In the air, it would take him about twenty minutes at best speed. We did it in about an hour and a half, stopping only at an all-night WalMart next to the Interstate somewhere in Pennsylvania. We sent Jake in for a nice new cat carrier and a big can of tuna fish. I had no idea how Rockefeller would behave on an airplane and didn't want to find out the hard way. Better to contain him but bribe him.

As we were leaving WalMart and headed back toward the Interstate to the airport, she woke up and announced she was hungry. Shit, with the adrenaline crash, we all were. I looked around and spotted those familiar golden arches, known from Klamath Falls to Kuwait City.

"Will McDonald's do for breakfast? We don't have time to go in and sit down anywhere."

"Normally I don't eat processed garbage like fast food, but sure, I'll call it a cheat day." We pulled into the drive through and she pulled out a couple of twenties she had tucked away. "I'm buying."

Dave took the twenties as we pulled into the drive-through line. He looked back over his shoulder at her for a minute. "Thanks... we need to get you a new name. A nickname or call sign at least. You're going into hiding, so you don't need to be you for a good long while."

She smirked. "Good? Bad? I'm the girl with the cash." It was an excellent *Army of Darkness* reference and by popular acclaim, the nickname stuck.

We got to the airport, pulling up to Lehigh's dinky little terminal. Dave returned the Cadillac as easily as he said it would go, then we walked right out the side door and down the pedestrian ramp to the waiting Lear. Our pilot was sucking on his thermos of coffee, still getting it together. Yeah, I was right; Matt had spent the night there. Since he was already preflighted, we were airborne for home within twenty minutes of pulling in. Jake rode up front, musing about flight lessons, so Cash was in his seat. We spent the ride back explaining more about the firm's dual structure and what we hoped she could accomplish for our mutual benefit.

And of course the goddamn cat yowled, growled, farted, and threw up the whole two hours going back to Nashville.

Chapter 3

"I collect individuals...I create possibilities."
~ *Malcador the Sigilite, Regent of Terra... via Chris Wraight of Games Workshop*

I banged down the steel stairway to 5. By her own choice, Cash was down below IT (2), Intel (3), and the floor full of file cabinets (4). We'd offered her space on 1, but she turned us down. 5 had been deserted except for more file cabinets until she set up shop, just more of the mysterious empty space the unknown builders had left us. Naturally all of the lights were off except for the one coming from her office doorway. Some form of strip club techno was pouring out of it, loud enough there was no point in knocking.

The good news was that the Feds took almost three hours after we left to get to her apartment. We were nearly home by then. The angry South Americans showed up half an hour after that and tried picking a fight with the now-grumpy Feds. They lost, two killed and one wounded.

The better news was in the confusion, the dirty DEA guy killed the cartel guy he was reporting to. Dude actually got a medal for the confirmed kill that saved his own ass. Of course later on we made sure he knew that we knew all that, and he'd been a reliable source for us since. He was in Miami now. Nice guy in some respects, but just made really bad decisions. I certainly wouldn't buy a used car from him either.

The bad news was she still had a couple Federal warrants out for her under her original name and that group of angry South Americans still wanted her dead. With that in mind, Big John had the connections through one of the intel agencies to get an absolutely ironclad new identity cooked up, without the usual records kept. New Social Security number, birth certificate, driver's license, you name it, all of it probably from the CIA's legendary document shop at Langley.

In return, she dived headfirst into our finances, aggressively untangling the books. There was at least one internal audit, and then she set up stock portfolios under three separate 'private equity firms' she created. She explained that an 'equity firm' was different from a 'hedge fund,' though really I didn't care too much. In general, she was enjoying herself doing what we had hoped she would. She was having so much fun it was almost a month before she noticed she was working for free. That stopped everything *real* quick. A generous salary plus an additional commission structure was quickly negotiated. This was made harder because she had us bent way over; we needed her even more now to understand the work she'd already done. In all, it was a quite substantial amount, all of it payable in cash under the table because of her circumstances. Still, after some initial grumbling at the price, even Big John finally conceded that she was still worth it.

We did find her an apartment down in Nashville, over by Vanderbilt University. It was a trendy little upper-class neighborhood, about forty minutes each way not counting traffic jams, but she rarely used it. She stayed downstairs in the Hole for a week or two at a time for 'security reasons.' It was a polite way of saying she was either busy working or she was too scared to go outside. Flip a coin which it was at any given time.

With a lot of help, she actually had built a, not a full apartment, but I suppose '*en suite* bedroom' was the correct term, for those nights she stayed over. It was down the hall back past her office, with Rockefeller the cat as her roommate. I liked cats. I still had several myself. I had even been bribing Rockefeller with chicken nuggets and cheeseburger scraps to not hate me after that Learjet flight because, yes, I have a bit of the crazy cat lady gene. Still, not everyone in the company liked cats. I think a kid in IT was actually allergic. Did Cash care? Not a fucking bit, though she did pay for his antihistamines out of politeness for a while until other people joined in on Bring Kitty to Work Day.

But it went on from there. Since Big John was barely in the office three times a week even before he got sick again that last time, most of dealing with her fell on me while she wasn't allowed, per John's orders, to tell me everything. I didn't even know what I didn't know.

First, there was the sign on her door promising to shoot anyone who called her office 'Wu Tang Financial' after the old *Chappelle's Show* skit. I wasn't too worried about that. I was fairly sure she didn't have a gun in there at the time. Later was a different story. I knew that because I gave them, plural, to her.

Then the music started. Sometimes she was playing her violin at two in the morning when she couldn't sleep, sometimes it was loud techno. Since she was down there by herself, usually nobody else noticed or cared. A couple of the IT and intel guys actually liked Mozart string solos echoing up the stairs. I wondered if I should dig in the waiting-list resumes and find her a cello player to play backup, but it never quite worked out.

But after a couple months of settling in, she really started her journey of... reinvention.

Wall Street types are sort of like soldiers in that there's enormous internal and external pressure to perform, whether you're really up to it that day or not. The cocaine and hookers, greed-is-good hedonism of the financial community has been the stuff of legend, after all. She kept her doubts and problems to herself at first, but as time went on and we developed more of a rapport, she finally opened up a little. She'd admitted that who she referred to as 'the old her' had lifelong anxiety and depression problems she'd never wanted to seek help for. Showing weakness was frowned upon in her work culture. Her parents had been no help even before they died. Since her dad was also a Harvard MBA and stockbroker, she'd been raised as ruthlessly as people breed and train racehorses.

Since I have extensive personal problems of my own that I regularly conceal since my work culture frowned on it too, I was of course sympathetic and I asked if I could help. She said it was merely enough to know she was safe and 'being a good girl.' There were definite undertones there I could have pushed into if I were more of a predatory asshole, but... I left it alone.

I confess. In hindsight, I didn't watch her as closely as I should have. See, Big John had made it *abundantly* clear in the first two weeks of her employment that she didn't work for me. I hadn't been bitched at like that in front of a commander's desk since pretty early in my Army days. *He* was the Chairman of the fucking Board. Since *she* handled *his* money, supervising *her* was not on *my* to-do list whether *he* was around or not. Meanwhile, he kept me pretty damn busy elsewhere. I don't mean to hide behind that excuse, but some things happened for a reason and a lot of those reasons happened because there was an absence of command supervision.

At some point, and in my fuzzy ADHD way I'm not really sure when, she began calling me 'sir.' It was maybe military in inspiration. There were a lot of our military roots around both versions of the company and she was doing her nervous and socially awkward best to fit in. She told me she loved both *Band of Brothers* and *Battlestar Galactica*, not just because she found both Damian Lewis and Jamie Bamber hot, but I still wasn't comfortable prying too much. I did get her an autographed 8x10 of Bamber for Christmas since I'd met him at DragonCon a few times. He's a genuinely nice guy. Always comes out from behind the table for the late night fandom parties. On the other hand, I've never met Lewis.

See, it started small. Trying to look like someone else in her circumstances, she started buying new clothes off the Internet. She started with the 'U.S. Paratroopers, Camp Toccoa, Ga.' hoodie but her taste veered rapidly, going from Establishment Bookish or Wall Street Tasteful to Alternative Hot. Since she applied her workaholic nature to this as well, there wasn't a lot of restraint. If Cash had a personal motto, it would be 'Anything Worth Doing Is Worth Overdoing.' Before long, her revised wardrobe could often be best described as 'Goth Hooker.' Think Hot Topic at the mall back when they were still good. There was lots of tight shiny black. Plaid Miniskirt Monday was a thing. Chrome-stud trim and high heels were a given. There had been occasional anime-colored wigs and one slightly disastrous attempt at a DIY dye job. That had been funny. Well, at least I thought it was funny. Even when it isn't a fashion crisis, she doesn't have much of a visible sense of humor.

It wasn't like we had an office dress code, so it wasn't my place to tell her no.

Then she saw a Shelby Mustang on the Barrett-Jackson auction when it aired on late night TV and when, once again, she couldn't sleep. She decided it was appropriate for the 'new her.' She found this one in a collectors' dealership in Florida then bought it over the Internet. It was shipped in by truck for an additional fee. We actually met the delivery guy in a parking lot out by one of the malls, then she would drag race on our entrance road at night to improve her shifting.

Finally there were the not-even-subtle breast implants. She had insisted I drive her to her appointments for those. "They are for security. Who will look at my face with new tits like these?" She had a point. They were very effective tactical distraction devices. But I suspect the plastic surgeon thought I was either her sugar daddy or her 'manager'.

"Cash, I need something done", I had to partly yell. She looked back over her shoulder at me and clicked her mouse, stopping the music. She then swiveled around in her chair, theatrically crossing her legs, making sure the black leather miniskirt slid up to reveal way too much high quality thigh. Yeah, she'd become something of a tease, which she definitely hadn't been before.

"Mmmm, anything for you, sir." She "innocently" stretched, arching her back and shoving her upgrades outward against the tight Halestorm concert t-shirt. *Goddamn...Bs to Ds? DDs? What the fuck did she end up spending on those? I never did see the bill… not my fucking problem.*

After the detour, my brain came back to reality. "We have a substantial issue. Big John is dead."

The tease ended and she snapped back to being a walking financial computer. "This is my surprised face", she deadpanned. "We knew he didn't have long." Her surprised face wasn't very surprised.

"Yeah, well, he decided to hasten the exit. A whole bunch of fentanyl and some really good Scotch. I got the call last night. Figured there was no point in bothering you."

She shrugged eloquently. "I was here anyway."

I had to ask. "Do you even go home most nights anymore?"

"No, sir. It's dead silent except for my ceiling fan, so I sleep way better down here. You just hear too much at that apartment with other people above or below, doors opening and closing. I keep imagining SWAT teams or cartel *sicarios* creeping up the stairs. Down here? The armor plate, the yards of concrete, the armed guards out front, really fast Internet... I like being the Queen Under The Mountain. Well, maybe the princess."

"Go for Baroness and I'll buy you the costume." Yes, *GI Joe* costuming is a thing at sci-fi conventions. Or at home if you find the right girl. Don't judge me, hater.

She got the reference. "All that tight black leather fits my aesthetic and I can work the glasses, but you know I will never bother reading all of the back issues. I guess I better start looking for the boots though. These aren't quite right." She kicked them up onto her desk, reclining back in her chair and sliding her hemline northward again.

"Shit, you might as well stop pretending you live somewhere else and close out the apartment. Not like we will take this one out of your paycheck."

"Ha, like you could. I'm the Accounting Department, remember?"

Sigh. "Anyway, back to the important part. We're going to have a conference call in about thirty minutes among the partners to discuss the death, vacancies, state of the firm, etc. I assume the books are tight and if I need to call down here for a number, you have it?"

She grinned wickedly and gave me a 'fuck me' voice. "Sir, *everything* of mine is tight, and is available *whenever* you call."

I twitched a bit. She was punching me in several fetishes repeatedly. She knew it. She liked it. She was positively reveling in it. But I had been professionally raised that subordinates were off limits. "You know, you were this nice, shy, all-business professional when we picked you up."

"True. But I'm not really her anymore, am I, sir?"

"No, you really aren't."

"We made a new me for security reasons. Being the new me is a lot more entertaining. I like being Cash way more than I liked being J-"

I cut her off. "Yeah, you do. That's what worries me a little."

She grinned again. "This guy comes into my life, saves my life, and then gives me a literal mountain fortress with a big pile of money. And there are only two real rules. Keep real close track of it, and grow it without losing it. This is a financial manager's wet dream. I am a sick bitch. I know it. No SEC reports since we're deliberately under minimum numbers to file, no shareholder conferences or disclosure books, I am my own independent operation. This isn't investment banking, it's fucking piracy. I. Love. It. The boiler room con artists and the penny-stock day-traders can all lick the sweat out of my ass. Fuck Wall Street; you made me the wolf of the fucking planet."

I looked at her, her eyes smoldering with barely leashed madness, and was trying really hard not to let my nerves show. I think it was the most words she had ever said in a row the entire time I had known her, from that morning Jake had breached her door in Brooklyn. To be honest, it kind of creeped me the fuck out. Was she brilliant? Yes. Sane? No fucking way. And I don't have a lot of room to question anyone else's sanity.

She continued. "Short version, we are well off, so much so we could be cut off entirely for at least a year, more likely two, and get through it just fine on savings and investment income. Depending on the decrease in operational expenses versus reduced income, possibly longer with some layoffs. We are cash and hard asset heavy with several backup stock portfolios in three separate funds, all spread at a good rate of return. I will send you the numbers on the intranet. It's a fairly large Excel workbook, but if it confuses you, you know where I am."

I took a deep breath and started easy so I could understand it. "Obvious question first. How much do we have laying around in ready cash, say that we could spend on war toys for a contingency job without hurting anything else?"

She pursed her lips in a very suggestive manner. "Off the top of my head, eleven point five mil, plus or minus, some of that being actual cash or gold holdings in the vault. Though I would prefer those toys that earn some revenue back rather than merely sit."

I would have guessed a tenth of that. "I obviously need to start paying way more attention to numbers now that John is gone and I'm allowed. That is more than I would have guessed. And wait... gold holdings?"

"Do you remember in November of last year when I told you I was buying a used, disassembled bank vault at basically a scrap metal price and the IT and Intel section guys helped me get it down to the eighth floor and set back up?"

I just stared at her, blinking. Last year was blurry. Who was I kidding? Last month was blurry.

She sighed. "Okay, we will take that as a no. To recap; I have been using up some of that inconvenient physical cash we can't account for on the books as legitimate business income and buying bullion and numismatics with it since gold stores better than paper currency. Coin shows, estate sales, swap meets, pawn shops, whatever. I plan on getting to about two million in bulk gold here in the basement without being obvious about it, not counting collector value on some of the older coins. We have just under half a million now. There is more elsewhere. John didn't tell me everything either, but we will figure it out.

"Then I want to keep about five million in non-sequential used bills around just for convenience. We have a good bit more than that now; we have nearly fifteen in actual cash. That doesn't include mine, of course. Most of the two point five I flew with is in there. The clothes, the car, renovating in here, the new breasts... it added up. Then some more of it is my back pay. Still, that's too much on hand, I think. Five million is a good number, not counting my personal stash. That way we have a chunk on hand for gun shows, the grocery shopping for the company picnics, payoffs, whatever. Then we keep the rest in gold or earning in the market. Look, sir, you worry about the contracting and the hoodrat shit and keeping us all out of prison or the cemetery, I will make sure the books balance and the investment accounts keep doing what I want them to."

I had to laugh and it called for a movie quote. " *'Stay evil, dollface.'* But you'll be here a while? It *is* Friday afternoon and you gotta take a break sometime."

"I'll be here or doing pole workouts in my room."

Oh, no. "Pole workouts?"

"Yeah. Way more fun than regular yoga so I change it up every few days. That tall blonde in Intel got me started on it a few months ago." Things started to make a bit more sense.

I shrugged. "I somehow missed that."

"You've been busy and I have been learning. See, I was thinking. Who are some of the only people left in the country that regularly handle a few grand in cash a night? It's completely normal for them and no one gets suspicious? VIP bartenders or strippers! I can totally walk into a bank in Vegas or Atlanta, maybe New Orleans, with a bunch of cash, play the role of a dumb bimbo who cleaned out a high roller on lap dances, and they won't think about anything except wonder what I look like naked. They won't think 'investment banker and money laundress.' I am about ready for an audience though. You know where to go, sir. Right up the hall."

I sighed. "All right, in the interest of keeping this professional, I am going to go choke down some lunch, see if Mikey shows, then we have the conference call."

She smirked, knowing she had her hooks in. "Have fun, sir. I'll be here." I retreated, giving my knees a break and taking the elevator back up to 1, draining that first Mountain Dew as I went. Goddamn. Some men avoid temptation. Others let her live in the basement.

I went back to my office, firing up the work computer that was only connected to our internal network. I looked at the intranet message and file attachment from Cash regarding our finances. *Motherfucker, that is a lot of zeros and commas in a whole lot of accounts.* I hadn't been read in on much of this, so naturally Cash hadn't told me. Of course she hadn't. Until last night, Cash technically worked for Big John, not me. But damn. Who the fuck did we rip off and me not notice? Were we this well off the whole time? I resolved to go back down and talk to Cash later to see if she had any insight that I didn't.

I went back into the break room, unpacking and prepping the tub of leftovers, then cracking open a Coke as the microwave hummed and spun. The acid bite of the Coke was better with some foods than the orange juice sweetness, particularly the cane sugar 'throwback' Dew I stuck to.

I heard Mikey five seconds after the elevator doors dinged open, bellowing like an old elephant. "Goddamn it, who the fuck has been microwaving Chink food in here again? You can smell the red pepper oil and the onions all the way in the fucking elevator."

And this was why I brought Chinese food. "You know it was me." I called back, grinning. Mikey limped into the office on his favorite walking stick, rows of silver German hiking club badges pinned to it from his younger days. He had dressed to come in for this call like he was the undertaker at a funeral home viewing, in an old black suit, white shirt, and black tie. If he'd had the hat and the sunglasses, he would look like one of the Blues Brothers. I was sure his old Colt Combat Commander that the late Armand Swenson customized for him in the 1960s was under his suit jacket in a shoulder holster older than I was.

I just looked at him over my glasses, forking down fried rice mixed with the dregs of last night's Szechuan beef. He just glared at me. "Stinking up the whole office with that shit..."

His utter lack of charm aside, Mikey was the sort of fossil nobody had the heart to tell to retire. Even being past ninety, mentally he was still sharp as a good knife. He was a Brooklyn native who reminded me a whole lot of my long-dead grandfather. Drafted in '47 and already knowing the language from growing up in the right neighborhood, he'd been a PFC in the Counter-Intelligence Corps in Germany after WWII. Making sergeant in a year or two, he made it to Korea about ten minutes before the shooting stopped, just long enough to get an Eighth Army combat patch and a couple 'I Was There' campaign ribbons for sitting in a radio trailer eavesdropping on the Russian military advisors behind the North Korean lines. Then newly appointed as a warrant officer, it was back to Germany. By now his Russian was fluent, as was his Hungarian and Romanian. He said his Czech was only ever mediocre.

For the next four decades, he only came back to the States for Army schools or the occasional vacation until he retired the second time as a GS-13 civilian at US Army Europe's intel section. If the Cold War hadn't ended and he still had convenient Army hospitals and PXs across Germany to sponge off of, his ass probably wouldn't have come back to the States even then. He was still over there a hundred days a year, burning up Lufthansa frequent flier miles to see the seven kids and dozen-plus grandkids he had accumulated with his four German ex-wives, or to shake down his 'nieces and nephews' around the continent for information. Despite having a desk here, God knew he didn't come to the office much anymore.

"I brought enough for you too, old timer."

He nearly spat. "Fuck that. Only reason I was glad I never set foot in Vietnam was that I hate the fuckin' food over there. Not much on the menu east of Kiev or Volgograd is fit for civilized people. That bit of Korea was enough for me. And with the *Gerst Haus* gone, there is no decent German food in this town anymore. That place at the Nashville mall is terrible. With the force cutbacks, not enough German-born Army wives come back to Campbell anymore to get it up there either. Schnitzel at the old Rod and Gun Club is awful these days. Goddamn Southern fried pork chops is all that is, even with the *Jaeger* sauce."

"You Cold War Europe kids. It must suck to have worked yourself out of a job across a whole theater of war so thoroughly that all you have left to do is bitch about the food." I wasn't going to remind him that the restaurant out by the Fort Campbell riding stables hadn't been called the Rod and Gun Club since Reagan was President. He did have a point about the wives though. With barely a division worth of troops in US Army Europe, way down from two full heavy-mechanized corps and a full field army's worth of support units in the late Eighties, not many guys were getting hitched and bringing home *Frauleinen* anymore.

He half grinned. "Least we won. Or thought we did."

"Fair point."

"Still, this beats retiring. A man needs a good hobby."

"There's always chasing strippers. Find some cute little blonde thing with granddaddy issues and go find Wife Number Four. Or is it five?" I knew damn well it would be five.

"You goddamn kids today, all it is with you is sex, sex, sex."

"And money. You need that to get by too."

"And it was all harder to get back then. Girls saved it for marriage and-," he pointed at my can for emphasis, "Cokes cost a nickel. Being a millionaire back then meant something."

I took a long drag at my drink. "World ain't what it was, that's for sure. That's always been my problem. I kinda bridge the generations. Too young to be one, don't fit with the other." Having spent my childhood around Grandpa's WWII buddies then being professionally raised by the last of the Vietnam guys can do that to you. I got old early, but in other ways never grew up.

Mikey nodded thoughtfully. "We are gonna need that going forward. I didn't quite trust John making you the junior partner as fast as he did, but you have done well these last few years. Made good money for us all. Now it would have sucked for us if you had gotten killed in Dallas. That's why we don't do shooter work. Eric would love it if we did, he loves that throat-cutting killer commando shit and always has, but he gets his thrills elsewhere for it. He's also too long in the tooth for it, not that I have room to throw rocks at anybody just for being old."

I waved dismissively. "You know how favors with friends go. Sometimes it's a duty thing."

"Speaking of duty, get them last few bites of your Chink bullshit down and let's get on the phone with the others. It's almost time. Wish Eric wasn't off hunting."

I picked a bit of rice out of my teeth. "He gave me his proxy if it comes to a vote."

"He told me. Also told me I was supposed to kick you under the table if you were going to do anything dumb with it, and to aim for your bad knee."

"They're both shit, especially in this weather. We using my office or yours?" I asked as I chewed.

"Yours. Don't want the smell of that food in mine."

Leave me an opening, why don't ya. "You don't use yours but once every six months."

"Fuck you, kid."

Ha.

I kept music going in my office 24/7 even when I wasn't there. There was a junky old Dell laptop with ninety gigs of music on it, mostly classic rock, sitting on a side table, with the .mp3 player set on Random. It made the otherwise silent space feel less like King Tut's Tomb when the lights were off. I hit Pause on it in the middle of ELO's "Do Ya, Do Ya?"

I rolled a nice antique leather judge's chair into position for him facing my desk. I had gotten a deal on it and the matching oversized, overstuffed couch at a very upscale used furniture place near Music Row. One of the guys in Intel joked it had been the Nashville casting couch that started Shania Twain's career. Whether it was or wasn't, it was damn near the size of a twin bed and occasionally I pulled a poncho liner out of my desk drawer and slept on it during overnight projects.

While he got settled, I cranked back in my own Herman Miller Aeron. We had picked up a few dozen of the 'dot-com throne' chairs cheap when a local tech startup had folded. My back was in shitty enough shape from years of hauling heavy rucksacks cross-country that I usually liked having the range of adjustment the antique didn't have.

Our conference call system was a heavily encrypted voice-over-Internet chat room. No actual telephone calls or phone lines were involved. Presumably the NSA at Fort Meade could find a way in if they really tried, since it was a small tweak of their own proprietary system, but fuck it, nothing was perfect unless we all met face to face out in the woods somewhere. I slid my desk phone to the center, and hit the key sequence for the partners' conference. Lights came on next to Lines 2 and 7, and we waited for the others to beep in. We were still as secure as we could be, given some of these other dickheads could be phoning it in from a golf course with fuck knows who listening in. Well, they probably wouldn't. I was just being an asshole out of anxiety.

The phone beeped and the red light next to Line 5 came on.

"Hey, all." Little John's nasal Maine accent came through as clearly as if he had been in the same room. He was no relation to the John who died, we just had two Johns and he was the shorter of the two. A US Navy intelligence officer, primarily Asian affairs, he'd retired as a rear admiral (upper half). These days he lived down in south Florida for the fishing and to be close to a cardiologist he trusted for the heart problems that shortened his career. With that trouble in mind, he had a rule. He was not in charge of anything. He was just there to consult. I know having vacancies between him and command were going to make him nervous. At the same time, I had to question how much direction a former attack submarine commander who'd then been chief of intelligence for the Pacific Fleet would be willing to take from an ex-sergeant with zero time in command of anything bigger than an infantry platoon's weapons squad.

"Hey, John. Catch anything good lately?"

"82 and sunny, light seas, so I went out this morning with the grandkids. We caught a seven foot white marlin I let go and some really good *mahi* for dinner."

I had to laugh at that. I was kinda jealous. "Sounds great. We have a typical mid-October cold front here. Not even sixty and it's about to rain."

He laughed too. "Sounds shitty. That's why I'm glad I'm phoning this in."

Another beep. Line 4. "James here, how goes it with you fine gentlemen?" James's phone voice had a touch of *Haaahvaad* to it as well. He was a retired senior officer in the CIA, I knew that much. He lived in the northern Virginia suburbs off US 29, out in the classy horse country between the Brandy Station battlefield and the old NSA site out at Vint Hill Farms. I wasn't sure how high he had been in the Agency, but I was also pretty sure Mikey knew and hadn't told me. Again, I hadn't been a partner long enough to know all the backstory and dirt on these guys. It left me at a disadvantage sometimes, but that came with being the junior partner. At least I had the seat. If anyone was going to buck for being the new Number 1, it would be James.

"Better than it is for Big John," I replied.

"Amen," Mikey chimed in.

"What are they doing for a funeral?" Little John wondered.

I didn't know for sure, but I knew a little. "His daughter is handling all of it. Might just be ashes going in a niche at Arlington. I know his wife is already interned there."

Beep. Line 6. "Greg's on." I wasn't too worried about him. Former deputy director at the National Geospatial Intelligence Agency. A complete desk guy, he probably hadn't been in a fight since elementary school. Greg's primary lane was business development on the government side and he left it totally in other hands how we made money in other ways. The contract lawyers who handled the paperwork for our white-side legal government income worked directly for him out of a firm in Virginia. Now that didn't stop him from taking the cash from the dark side of the company, but he would always defer to others because he really didn't want to know. He and Little John were always racing to be last in line. Big John never cared about that because Big John loved being in charge. Me, I would probably need a lot more motivation and initiative out of those two no matter who ended up in the command chair.

My cue again. "Roger that and Eric won't be joining us because he said he wasn't skipping out on having an out of state Wyoming elk ticket. He's up in the mountains somewhere and doesn't have a signal. I have his proxy if we need to call a vote, Mikey can verify."

Some grumbling. I couldn't tell who.

"Little John here. That was what he told me as well. Said he trusted your judgment."

I had to chuckle. "Well, that makes one of us. Gentlemen, I hate being the youngest one at the table, but I have been more involved in day to day operations as Big John's assistant. Anyone object if I start this?"

More grumbling. Mikey looked at me from across the desk. "Mikey here. Let the kid take point. He knows more about what's really going on than we do."

I nodded back at him in silent gratitude. "Okay, gentlemen. We had known Big John was in physical decline for some time, which does leave a seat at this table and a void for all of us. The guy had forgotten more than many men ever learn. But that gave us enough time here to prepare as best we could. We took the time to make really good notes. We have all his personal business files secured. Still fucking with the passwords on some of them and are looking for keys for one of the lockboxes, but they are secured. As you guys know, he occasionally had problems with sharing things, even at the end."

"Greg here. Ain't that the fucking truth." Across the desk from me, Mikey nodded in agreement.

"In terms of day to day operations, we will be okay. Accounting has a good snapshot of where we are at on the money side. I have the numbers if anyone wants them. We are plenty well off for the moment and we will get by.

"Little John here. Yeah, that Ivy League girl you found has done great things with the numbers. I had her take a look at my retirement accounts too. She took care of me."

I grinned. I'd have to tell her that. "We kinda got lucky finding her, and she's a low density asset we have to take good care of. Now comes the secondary issue, and I am going to throw this out first before we get into any other business. While we have taken one hit, of the six of us left, what shape are we in? Anyone else have any medically bad news, personal troubles, or other reason you might not be here six months from now? Little John, we know your heart trouble and we know your role. Nobody is looking to put anything else on you. But we are looking for previous unknowns."

To my surprise, Mikey spoke up first. "Gentlemen, at my age, I don't even buy green bananas anymore and I probably shouldn't be driving the hour each way as much as I do. Now I want a little more time with the grandkids and great grandkids, maybe, but I want to stay on the roster. Gives me something to do with whatever time I have left and, especially since Big John is gone, I am the only other partner close enough to the site to keep an eye on Junior here. I'm not cashing out my chips yet, but I probably ought to take a bigger step back. So whoever we vote in to be the new seventh, better have another name ready for my replacement. I may not have long."

It had been five years now and that was the first time I ever heard Mikey admit he wasn't going to live forever. It kinda stung.

Greg and Little John murmured their acknowledgement.

"James here. I have been thinking about it. I'm out."

There were a few muttered "What the fucks?" at that. One was from me.

James continued. "No, I'm quite serious. I made enough money with the firm. At risk of being immodest, I didn't need what I made. I rarely put in much work these last few years and, unless I pick up an odd project, I feel I am not carrying my share of the load. The worst part is I cannot muster enough 'give a shit' to really get back in the game enough to truly matter. I have made the cardinal mistake of thinking too much about my life."

He continued his Ivy League oration. "I have two ex-wives, three children that mostly hate me, one more at Langley trying to be just like me, and there are several grandchildren I only see in pictures online. I feel like it has all passed me by, so I just want to retire for real and get out of the house... get out of basement offices and lunch meetings. Maybe concentrate on my golf. I haven't played a full round in five years, and that was the first in the five years before that. Perhaps I'll take a fishing trip with Little John sometime. If I can help, call me, and I do mean day or night, but I'm not going to tie up a partnership slot at the table any longer merely to cash checks other men made for me. My day has... simply passed."

I stepped back in, recovering quickly. I was not expecting that. "Okay, so Big John is still dead at 1, Mikey is stepping back from 2 and James is out at 4."

"Little John here. Not it." We all grinned at that.

Mikey snorted. "Eric ain't here. Let's fuck him over and make him do it."

That was even funnier.

"Greg here. I just want to concentrate on managing the government contracts for Athenaeum. That is the legit income, let's not fuck with it. Keep me out of the shady shit with the archives side so I don't have to lie to our principals. I wasn't a HUMINT guy and my poker face sucks."

Mikey looked across the table at me. "Call the question, Junior." He was smiling too much. That wasn't like him at all.

So, I threw the matter out there. "Who succeeds Big John as CEO and Chairman?" Mikey grinned even wider. I saw quickly I was being sandbagged.

They answered with nearly one voice. "You do." Mikey winked at me.

Oh, fuck. Fuck me to tears. The bastards set me up. My inner voices screamed that I wasn't ready for this and the rest of me was willing to agree with them. "All right, so that leaves us two and a half vacancies out of seven. Any recommendations?"

"Little John here. Everyone we know is too old, sick, or tired at this point. Maybe they were too honest to ever get into this shit to begin with. Ain't one of us below seventy except you. It's a younger man's game, which is what Big John told us when we voted you up to full partner two years ago."

The back of my head started running names. We were going to run out of candidates fast. Most anyone I had working for me was too young. Problem was anyone I knew in my age bracket who genuinely had the experience and skill set to handle the workload could be better enough than me that I might be squeezed out. Never mind, that was stupid. There was gonna be more work than we all could handle. Still, some of the people I could use? No fucking way they would sign on, or they would bring peculiar disruptions to a company that was supposed to be a simple machine. The Texas connections had their own goats to fuck. So did the DC area ones. This… this was my goat.

"All right, pending a thorough examination of the options for the two partnership vacancies, I propose to continue with five for now." There was a general assent to that.

"Longer term, I want to talk to Dave who's been in day to day command of the intel section and see if he may be interested in a seat at the table. To be honest, he is a better me than me."

"Nah, don't sell yourself short, kid." That from Little John. "Big John might have grumbled at you constantly, but you did a good job for him and did things the way he wanted them done. Otherwise you never would have made full partner when old Pete went down."

Mikey grinned as he clicked in. "I agree with Little John. I've watched you work. You're no Bill Casey, kid, but you do okay. Give yourself some credit."

"James here. If your David seems a good fit and you trust him, talk to him about the position and feel him out on the subject. Over time, the board of directors is going to have to bear your stamp and not that of Big John or his several predecessors. Eventually, you will have to pick some of your own people. On a long enough timeline, all of us go away and you'll probably be the last of us to go."

Sigh. "Okay, good point. Now keep going. What else needs doing right now?" I asked.

James continued. "It's simple enough in concept, old man. Sit down with Michael. Go over the books with that brilliant little Korean doxy you hired. Get into Big John's notes, and then develop a list of questions based on what you can't find the answers to. We don't know everything either, of course, since you know how John could be, but we know a lot. We have time for an orderly handover." Mikey nodded.

Mikey grinned at me as he took over again. "We do have a lot to hand over, but you have a good head on your shoulders and we will get you set up right on all this. It will all work out, kid."

I wasn't reassured. Not one goddamn bit.

Mikey then asked the group, "I got a poker game tonight at the Legion. Anyone else got anything?" No one did and after some perfunctory 'See ya later's,' the lines beeped dead and the lights on the phone went out.

I looked over at Mikey. "You guys kinda set me up."

He shrugged, looking unapologetic. "We discussed it amongst ourselves last night when we got the word and again this morning. You were the best choice we had. Not ideal, but the best we had. If any of us old fucks took it, we'd be picking a new CEO again in a year after the next one of us died off. Me? Yeah, I'm senior, but I could be dead in a week. I'm just too damn old. It'd kill Little John in a month if he tried. First, he'd have to come up here, and then his heart gives him real trouble when he overdoes it. James would never move down here and he doesn't have the right command ethic. Though him retiring like that was a shock. He hadn't mentioned that last night or earlier. Eric doesn't have the attention span. He just wants to wander his path and occasionally shoot somebody. Greg's not the right material either. Staff guy, not a commander. Plus he's way too honest. He's needed where he is. Now with you, there is a lot of retainability while we are still around to help develop you in the role. Big John had years to grow, since he was Chairman for over twenty years after he already spent years being a big deal at DIA. He'd taken over and held on."

My nerves aside, it made a coldblooded sort of sense. I think some of what was scaring me was I have never been truly self-employed in my life. Pizza delivery, bouncing bars in college, the Army, contracting, my brief time in the civil service, I had always had a boss or a commander somewhere. I may have ignored them, or had them give me intentionally loose guidance in exchange for them having some plausible deniability when I handled business, but I had never been no shit, totally on my own, The Man, ever. Let alone having this many people dependent on me, which made it worse. It was going to be hard to adapt, I think. Maybe? I really had no idea.

Mikey and I shook hands in the hall. I declined his offer to go play poker at the Legion. They all loved playing Texas Hold 'Em and I was just not a fan of that version of the game. Besides the fact I had dinner plans already, I now had even more things to do before I went home.

First things first. I went into the break room, opened up the refrigerator, then took a couple long hard drags off the gallon of milk I habitually kept on the door. I could kill a gallon a day without trying hard. I like the taste, it's good for you, and more practically, it soothed that constant stressful burning in my guts that told me I was probably going to have a shiny new ulcer within a year. The first few swallows didn't quite do it. I looked at the last three inches worth in the jug and walked off with the whole thing. I'd pick up another two or three on the way home, knowing they'd be empty by Monday.

I wandered down to the third floor and into Intel. It was the heart, soul, and guts of the firm since again, we are primarily information brokers. We didn't run four or more separate-but-unequal staff sections like a true military unit would and had no separate command center. The Intel office was manned 24/7 and supervised by one of our several senior personnel at all times. Even I sometimes took a rotation as the senior officer. See, the world didn't sleep, so neither could we. While the big round-the-clock watch centers at NORAD, the Pentagon, or the CIA did the heavy lifting with their near-limitless resources, we had to at least sleep with one eye open if we were to keep making our parasite's living off of them. We also had to be constantly available to the private sector clients where we made even more of the money.

One of those senior personnel on the supervisory rotation was sitting in another one of our second-hand Herman Miller chairs. Her headphones were on, clicking away on a large desktop computer rig. Kara was Intel's #2, maybe #1.5. I knew her from the East Coast sci-fi convention and Renaissance Faire scenes. A tall blonde, her office nickname came from her distressing resemblance to a particular mid-2000s sci-fi actress. That blonde, famed as a gunslinging space-fighter pilot, had told her, "Shit, you look more like me than I do!" in the autograph line. When Kara finally hit a point of seriously health-jeopardizing burnout in US government employment, I was in a position to give a skilled buddy a soft landing. A large black cat was asleep on the desk. That was more of Cash's influence.

I grabbed a chair and slid in across from her. "Anything big going on aside from our own problems?" She already knew about John, as she'd been the watch officer last night as well.

She looked at the milk jug in my hand as I took another pull off it. She sighed. "I see those problems have driven you to drinking heavily in the office again?" Her and her acerbic humor.

I had to be honest. "Eh, so long as it keeps the acid level down to a point where I don't vomit all over the floor, I'll be happy. The boss nervously puking in front of everyone would be bad for unit morale, you know."

She merely sighed at me before snarking back. "They make pills for that."

Uncharacteristically, I went for two honest answers in a row. "Going to the doctor and getting pills for it would be tantamount to admitting I have a problem and that the accumulated stress is getting to me."

She just stared at me. "Denial ain't just a river in Egypt. Just saying, buddy."

I sighed again. I do that a lot, I guess. "Yeah, but it's three decades of habit at this point. I'll get around to it one of these days." *Christ, three honest answers in a row. What do I win for that?* I changed the subject. "Now, what else is going on out there?"

Thankfully, she accepted the opportunity to get back to work stuff. "We have some really interesting SIGINT from the Pakistani border. I don't think the initial analysis at Meade really thought hard enough about the nature of code names and cultural contexts when they wrote it off as nothing. People aren't getting on satellite phones at one in the morning to discuss their laundry."

No, no they are not.

"This a formal red-teaming analysis or are you just digging in the discard pile for fun?"

She nodded. "Actual formal red-teaming. Which is good, since we can bill hours on that."

I had to laugh. "See and that practical outlook is why I hired you."

She rolled her eyes at me. "You hired me because we're old buddies, I speak five-five Pashto and therefore reasonable Farsi, some Arabic, quite decent Korean, and also had a current clearance."

"Meh, all that too. Anyway, small job for you since you're the senior watch officer."

She scratched her nose with her raised middle finger. "How much am I going to hate it?"

"Text everyone in Intel and IT who's not going to be on mandatory downtime that we're meeting at 1300 Monday in the first floor conference room." One of our IT departments' clever innovations was coming up with a way to mass-text cell phones from the desktop computers downstairs without having to run through any Silicon Valley third party applications. "Just between you and me, it's going to be about Big John's death and aftermath of, but no sense emotionally ruining everyone's weekend by telling them that."

She shrugged, "Makes sense, I guess. Besides, to most everyone, Big John was some remote figure we barely ever saw, even in here. It's not going to be a personal tragedy for anyone except maybe you."

I snorted. "Professional, yes. Personal, not so much. He was not an easy fellow to like."

She let that pass. Why speak ill of the dead? "How did the conference call go?"

"At risk of shitting on the big surprise for Monday, if you can keep it to yourself," she nodded, "the board of directors has made the worst decision in its recorded history. They voted me in as Chairman since none of the old guys want the job."

She merely shrugged again, an island of calm. She really was one of the more stable personalities here. "With John going downhill this last year, you basically have been. Just do what you do."

I sighed. A bunch of people seemed to have way more faith in me than I did in me. "I really don't know if I have it in me to pull this off." I dramatically took another hard pull on the milk jug.

Kara smiled, leaning over to affectionately punch me in the shoulder. "Come on, you can do this. And it ain't like you are doing it alone, since you have your handpicked crew of geniuses like me to push it all along and help you look good. You don't have to internalize the stress or die of a milk overdose."

"Fucking awesome. Wanna be on the Board? We have vacancies."

That got another laugh out of her. "Oh, *hell* no. Suck my metaphorical nuts if you think you are fucking me over with that level of responsibility. I just do intel analysis, I don't like doing real management or admin shit."

"Well, you do some of it anyway. Hell, if you take over as chair, we can claim to be a woman owned company for contract awards."

"Yeah, but then we lose disabled veteran and I think that scores higher at contract award time."

I chuckled. "Eh, good dodge. But you do some of the admin as it is."

"Subjectively, not objectively, speaking, the little I do takes ten percent of my time and is basically natural overhead. It's in the same category as us taking turns vacuuming the floors. It becoming my primary thing? Hell no. I don't care how much more money you throw at me."

I shrugged. She would probably be surprised how many more dollars I was willing to tack on to keep the key personnel I liked and trusted around, particularly right now when I was not overloaded with faith in myself. "Fair. In that case, you may have to either recruit yourself an admin flunky from somewhere to do it for you, or slowly overcome your resistance. Because the old guys we work for are dying off and in a few years I can see it being just our generation doing this."

She scoffed. "What's this 'our' generation shit, Gen-X Boy?" I was eleven years older than her and she rarely let me forget it.

"That's all the more reason for me to have a designated line of succession for when I finally go down. Think that one through, and speculate where the deputy chief of our primary department would fall in that line."

Kara winced and leaned back in her chair. "Fuck, you might have me nailed there."

I forced a grim smile. "Gets ugly in a hurry, doesn't it? Now you know why I drink."

"Milk doesn't count as a drinking problem no matter how much you want to pretend it does. Still." She shook her head in thought. "Goddamn it, how did you talk me into this again?"

"As I recall, it took about ten seconds to talk you into this after I told you two hundred a year, half of it tax free under the table, with full medical. Then I told you to bring your asshole of a cat to work so he didn't trash your house when you were gone all day." I'd hired her about five minutes after Cash moved in and her cats were second in the door. This one, a shaggy black monster, kept ignoring us. Kara normally named her cats for characters from her favorite sci-fi and fantasy fandoms. This one was Duncan Idaho from *Dune*.

She muttered a particularly vile Arabic obscenity and pointed finger-guns at the ceiling. "I hate having obvious weaknesses like that."

I grinned a bit. "We all have them, so don't feel too bad."

That pulled a short chuckle out of her. "All right, boss, now piss off and let me get some work done trying to read Pashtun minds. You're fucking up my concentration with this mundane and trivial shit."

I looked around. Four other analysts were head down in their computers too. "Quiet otherwise?"

She turned. "Yeah, the phone hasn't rung with anything weird, so we're digging through the inboxes and contract jobs trying to clear some backlog."

"Sounds good. You handle it as you need."

She smiled and nodded as she pulled her headphones back on. I was effectively dismissed.

I went back upstairs into my office and sat down, letting thoughts stir as the music cycled. I decided I was keeping my office. I was too lazy to move everything next door into what had been Big John's space. The rooms were the same size anyway. I would pull a few things in here and leave John's vacant once we cleaned it out. If I ever found a decent adjutant, that would become theirs.

The one thing I was definitely going to steal out of John's office was the plaque. It was at least fifty years old by the woodwork, and I don't know if it had come from DIA, NRO, or somewhere else in the Air Force intel community. I'd asked him about it once and true to form, he'd merely told me to shut the fuck up and mind my own business. A standard USAF heraldic shield design, it was two feet high and hung on the front panel of his desk. The upper slice was sky blue with the compass rose and sword design of Army military intelligence in gold, which seemed weird on an Air Force patch. The bottom slice was blood red with an upraised Fairbairn commando dagger in black. The bottom scroll read 'Cognitio Generat Actionem,' or "Thought Generates

Action." It was very retro-cool and allowed me to keep something of that grumpy old son of a bitch around as a luck piece.

The 1950s industrial feel of the room had been softened somewhat with my modifications. The walls were a medium tan from the original stark white and the linoleum tile vanished under a pretty nice dark green carpet. I also had the leather couch, a vintage walnut desk from another Nashville antique dealer, a wall-length and ceiling-high bookshelf I had built myself out of some good oak from one of our own trees, and a few tastefully framed World War II and Civil War prints. James Dietz and Mort Künstler, mostly. I did resolve to put a nice gun cabinet in here, and maybe a sword rack with a few things from my excess at the house. That way I would have a few conversation pieces for the few guests I ever did have.

The bookshelf was the same. It was also overflow from home. One part work texts, one part cool antiques for show. Did I really need the 1944 hardcover set of the British *Naval Intelligence Division Geographical Handbook Series,* all fifty-eight volumes of it? Fuck no. I didn't need that 1910 *Encyclopaedia Britannica* I had at home either. Book collecting is sort of like heroin addiction. Once you get going, it's really, really hard to find a convenient stopping point. I had several hobbies like that, which opens up questions about my personality I'd rather continue to ignore.

The biggest question was the nature of the business and where it was going to go. My opinion had differed from Big John's, which in his opinion meant I was automatically wrong. It was becoming a real sore spot between us before his final illness and death. See, it was pretty clear to me that as the firm's personal ties to the intel community retired or died off, we weren't going to be able to primarily get by on the government contracting. Legally, contracting sometimes paid less than shit on paper. As their old-timer buddies around DC went away, the suitcases of cash paid as 'consulting fees' would go too. That business would end up with the big players in the game, the corporations who employed retired generals and who bought hundred dollar lunches for congressional staffers and Pentagon gofers at the Old Ebbitt Grill or Morton's. Ongoing service to the nation was all well and good, but we had mouths to feed and bills to pay. Money isn't everything in life, but poverty fucking sucks. I tried it once or twice, and I found it didn't agree with me.

Worse, if we couldn't pay our people and they went elsewhere, our secrets went elsewhere with them. Since we did so much borderline illegal private-sector shit, constituting well over half my time and an unknown percentage of total revenues since I hadn't been allowed into the books, the last thing I needed was one of our people who knew that business going to work for another government contractor, or worse, going back to working for The Man directly. Someone in that position growing a conscience and diming us out was about the Worst Case Scenario.

Now I generally trusted the folks inside our metaphorical perimeter, since they wouldn't be here if I didn't. But if it came down to loyalty to a potentially dying company or the ability to make their house payments, I preferred I not have to find out *how far* I could trust a few of them. Though most of us were some form of veteran, this wasn't the active duty military. *Esprit de corps* only goes so far when the electric bill is due or the kids need dental work. I had been through something like that once with my first contract gig after the Army. I learned the hard way that you don't want to be the last rat off a sinking ship.

Out of milk, I walked back down to the break room. I threw the empty in the recycling bin and grabbed another Mountain Dew from the fridge. I then went back down the hall into my office and threw a legal pad on my desk. The music kept churning as Aerosmith went on to Queen. But Freddie singing *"Just waiting for the hammer to fall"* was too much of a bad omen for my current mood to handle. Okay, time to really think. I clicked another playlist. Nightwish's bagpipe and fiddle-intensive "Last of the Wilds" led off a really weird mix of symphonic metal, various Celtic-themed bands, and war movie soundtracks as I started inking in an assortment of boxes, lines and names.

I sketched it as a military MTOE, Modified Table of Organization and Equipment. Stick to what you know, right? We had the headquarters, the board and myself, then what I thought of as the 'line companies' even if some were only squad-sized.

The 'intelligence company' was eighteen or nineteen officially cleared personnel on the books, depending how I counted Dave. In addition to being the titular intel head, he was the closest thing to an XO we had right now. That was Athenaeum; the legit contractor side of the shop. Another twelve were ghosts behind them. That was as the private sector intel section that leeched off the legit side. Those troops were the ones who worked all those ugly commercial penetrations we didn't like to talk about. They all fell under Archival Associates. We really tried to not overtly mix the two. I didn't even like carrying business cards for both companies at once, even when they didn't have my real name on them.

The Information Technology Department, the nice civilian term for our 'signal company,' were the keepers of our key infrastructure. Sixteen were on the contract books as legally cleared employees supporting official government contracts for Athenaeum, then eleven more 'archivists' that weren't on the official books. That didn't count all our piecework hackers and hired online thugs who existed way off the books and usually way off-site.

Then there was the security 'company,' even if it was only the size of a small platoon. I think we currently had 27 on the payroll there, the guys in the guard shack and looking over the grounds. None of those guys knew shit about the real business going on downstairs except Jake and dear God, I hoped it stayed that way. And as mentioned, they worked for a wholly different LLC.

We also could generate an understrength troop-sized element.... Wait, not a cavalry troop, which is what the cavalry calls its company-sized elements the way artillery comes in batteries. Certain units cross-trained with then copied the British SAS. Those blokes use a cavalry-inspired troop and squadron naming system even if the numbers are different from actual cavalry. Anyway, I digress again. Google it if you care that much.

The point was that I could lay hold of maybe twelve to fifteen guys, maybe twenty at best, who were too good, and thereby too expensive, to be wasted in the guard shack rotation but who would still be available to roll dirty for the right mission and/or enough money. They were various alumni of the 75th Ranger Regiment, including their Regimental Recon Company, various 18-series MOSs from a couple SF groups, a couple guys retired from the Army's now-deactivated Asymmetric Warfare Group, and so on. We also had a couple Navy SEALs including Jimmy, a few loose Marine Raiders and Force Recon guys, then various small-niche Air Force ground guys like pararescue jumpers or combat controllers.... But again, we didn't do shooter gigs. We're intelligence brokers, not professional gunfighters, regardless of any past experience or additional skills in that field. That on-call element was our desperation option, not a routine cash cow. Over time it would age out like the rest of the firm. Not one of those dudes was much under forty at best. A couple of them were even older than me.

And both last and least, five guys for roads and grounds maintenance outside the Hole that didn't know shit either. I had another old Army buddy running that. He was willing to take my money and not ask shit. Some jobs he had to hire out and those guys knew even less.

All right, this is what I had on hand. What did I need?

First, I was going to need to have a long, long talk with my 'closest female partner.' Girlfriend was not quite the word, failing to cover all the complexities. Angel was a 5'3 Taiwanese-American, 38DD ("Chinese complexion, white girl booty because I actually eat and work out!") who didn't give too much of a shit about politics or current events. She had started out as my massage therapist for my ongoing service-connected back problems and had very little idea what I actually did for a living. While that was going to change, she was not going to be taking care of too much business stuff. Fuck, I was going to need her help taking care of *me*. And yes, it was another case where I really needed that level of personal trust and dedication. This would be easier than in some conventional dating relationships. Suffice it to say, without me unpacking our mutual kinks, she took orders really well. She *loved* taking orders in some circumstances. And what the hell, she loved guns and knives. So if I couldn't trust her with a few ugly professional secrets after most of a decade together....

Second, pretty soon I was going to need a professional assistant, someone to play the regimental adjutant or executive officer role; someone to be to me what I had been to Big John. That was going to take some thought. Maybe promote Dave then bump Kara up, assuming she wanted the chance of psychological stress that went with the raise. Based on our last conversation, I was going to call that a probable no unless I eased her really slowly. Or Dave could wear two hats.

Third, I needed a firm grasp on how much of our income came in from the private sector versus the governmental. That was going to require time with Cash now that she was allowed to tell me things. I knew I didn't know enough there. Orienting on where the money was dictated our next moves. So I was going to have to get deep into all the books and get a solid handle on our income and our reserves, both the clean and the dirty. I wasn't going to keep a super solid handle on it, and I knew it, but that was what good help was for. Fortunately Cash was working on that and I figured I could count on her enthusiastic support. The problem there was with the way she was headed, I was probably going to have to sleep with her to keep her enthusiastic. Note to self, consult Angel on that problem. Fully aware that was the sort of difficulty that rarely occurred outside of semi-pornographic fiction, it was also the sort of unreality that kept me from stressing the fuck out. It was just too weird to make me panic.

After we get the money figured out, then get a handle on the 'stuff.' What did we own, where was it hidden, and what did we need? I probably needed a good logistics type for that in good time. Fortunately I knew a guy, another of my sci-fi convention buddies. A bit inflexible, but with some supervision he would do. West Pointer by background, and due to get out soon since not enough quartermaster captains made major every year. His main hobby in life was a crippling obsession with Games Workshop's *Warhammer 40,000* novels, and anybody committed enough to his gaming faction to have a fairly elaborate Legio XIII tattoo was weird enough to work here. I had contemplated getting the wolf's head of the Sixth done myself. Other members of the company had ink including everything from all four Hogwarts houses and assorted Pokémon to former Army assignments and the fictional Arashikage ninja clan. But he also had very serious personal and professional ethics and I didn't know if we could afford those. Remember what I said about the honor codes not applying to us?

Then, thinking about my talk with Kara, we probably needed a couple full time personnel administration types. Right now department heads handled time sheets and leave days. Intel managed all the security clearances in addition to the paying work. As much as we had grown in the last couple years, that needed to get off the department heads' plates. Adding personnel and eventually logistical functions nearly gave us all four primary staff sections, the S-1, 2, 3, 4 system the US military had picked up from the French in 1917 while ramping up for the 'Great War,' but I wasn't going to go there as we reorganized. One, this wasn't really the Army and two, a retired colonel I knew had convinced me the German staff system is better organized even if I couldn't always instinctively think in it.

Shit, it was after well after four. I could do more thinking in the truck heading home. But first, I had to go share some news. I went back down the stairs to Cash's office. She was still blasting music while typing away; I think it was Korean pop. Seeing me, she turned the volume down to a reasonable level. "What the hell are you doing, anyway?" I asked.

"Since the markets closed back East, writing triple-X *Star Wars* fan fiction."

I was not expecting that. "Really?"

She laughed charmingly. "No, sir. I'm just plotting out some before-hours day trading for early Monday local time when Tokyo and Shanghai open."

I shook my head in amusement. "You really need to get a hobby."

Surprisingly, that got another burst of laughter out of her. "Coming from you? If that isn't the pot and the kettle..."

I sighed. "OK, you have a point. Still, do you want the good news or the bad news?

She shrugged, which did *amazing* things for the front of her shirt. "Bad news first, sir."

"Okay, the board voted. We have a retirement and a half to go with the death of Big John."

Her look was unusually quizzical. "So we are going to roll with a board of four and a half for now?"

Really, I didn't know how long it would stay that way. "Yep."

"How the hell do you half-retire, anyway? Never mind. So what's the good news, sir?"

I sighed deeply, collapsing into her other chair. "I don't know if I am done with the bad news yet. They voted on a new CEO. Unfortunately for all of us, it's me."

Her eyebrows shot up, then came an especially charming full-body shiver. "No, that is actually very good news, sir."

"Maybe it is for you. Me, I dunno if I am willing to handle this degree of responsibility and stress. By nature, I tend to be kind of a slacker unless I have a crisis to make the adrenaline kick in."

She just smiled. "The number one concern of any business is the money. If you're selling cars or cat treats, it all comes back to money and you have a secret weapon. Me. I'm telling you to relax, we are in good shape. We have generous and productive investments, a heavy cash and hard asset mix with constant income both overt and covert that nicely exceeds expenses for our two sides. I am starting to dig in John's stuff and I'm finding he didn't tell me everything either. Even if things did temporarily go upside down, that is what the cash reserves are for. We could survive that. You can go hide out at a nice all-inclusive resort in north Thailand for a year. Cool mountain air, massages for your bad spine, and a good buffet table."

Interesting idea. "Not sure if that would be my first pick."

She sighed. "It's an example. Hide in Argentina with the grandchildren of the ex-Nazis. Buy a game preserve in Africa. Whatever. It doesn't matter terribly much. Enough untraceable money gives you options."

I nodded. "Fair point. But if we had to scatter, I would miss having a nuclear war bunker."

She smiled. She could be cold and mechanical often enough that it was actually nice to see her happy. "Exactly. And I like hiding in it, so we need to keep it. Though FYI, of that original drug money she stole, I really do have a little over three million of it in Argentina. The lake district around Bariloche reminded us of the nice part of Vermont but with fewer meth labs, so we hired a local lawyer down there and set up a blind real estate trust, their local equivalent of an LLC. With some of the money, she then bought a couple nice lakefront villas and two small apartment buildings there they rent out for me. I bank the money down there."

Not for the first time, I noticed she was having real trouble keeping her pronouns and tenses consistent as she tried to internally cope with which one of her was her right now. I decided to try making her laugh a bit instead. "Funny, you don't look German. What was that about hiding out with the Nazis?"

It didn't help. "I will get the hat to match the boots if you don't stop making jokes, sir."

"Joke's on you, I'm into that shit. Now, any plans for the weekend?"

She thought about it for a minute. "I will probably go up above the surface long enough to go out to dinner for once and then get back downstairs. Friday rush hour is a reasonable hiding spot."

I conceded some ground. "I ought to talk to my girlfriend and see about us going out together." Outside the office and without work as a crutch, I'd probably feel less socially awkward around Cash if I had Angel to hide behind.

She grinned wickedly. "You really should, sir. You told me just enough about her for her to be interesting. I think we would get along quite well. I definitely would ignore my full-blown case of agoraphobia and come out of the Hole for that."

God, I hoped they got along. Being the CEO was going to have Cash in my hip pocket, to stretch a metaphor. If her necessary presence was then going to cause me a shitload of drama at home should Angel decide to get bitchy and territorial for once, that thought was not a happy-making one. "Well, we will figure out a time."

If anything, her grin was even more predatory. "Drink plenty of water and stretch out first, sir, especially if it's going to be two of us at once."

This was past what could be called flirting and was just blatantly offering. My kinks were at war with my ethics again. I sighed. "Cash, you are an eight-figure sexual harassment lawsuit waiting to happen."

She pouted. "Sir, if I were just after the money, I could steal eight figures from you in a weekend. And you, being you, would never notice until it was far too late. You probably wouldn't notice until after people's paychecks started bouncing. You're awful with numbers, which is why you hired me in the first place, and for the administrative side of the business you have the attention span of a hamster. Besides, how is someone legally missing for over a year, with an active Federal arrest warrant, and who is living on fake IDs in your basement then going to get you in a courtroom to sue you?"

"I have no idea and would prefer not to find out. I already know you are much smarter than I am." I was still twitching at the 'steal eight figures and me not notice' part. I think she had a point there. That was more unnerving than anything else.

Pulling her boots off the desktop, she leaned forward in her chair and stood, then sauntered up really closely. I stood up, but she neatly cut off my retreat to the door. Even with the six inch heels, she wasn't even up to my nose. She looked up at me with a sudden air of grave seriousness. "It's okay. At some point, you will realize you can really trust me, sir."

For once, I was struggling with the correct way to phrase something without bruising anyone's feelings. "I really trust you now. Sometimes I just try not to cross certain lines."

"But at least you want to cross them, sir, which is good enough for now. Because that's how I know I'm being your good girl. For some reason, the voices in my head say that's very important."

Voices in her head. She's taking orders from voices in her fucking head. Fucking wonderful.

Then my internal monologue kicked in. *Like you have room to talk, asshole.*

Chapter 4

"Home's where the guns are"
~ *"Double Zero," by Flotsam and Jetsam*

Retreating from downstairs, I then shut down my office and went home, driving to the strains of Randy Edelman's soundtrack from *Gettysburg*. It was good thinking music. And damn, did I have thinking to do. I thought I had woman problems thirty years ago when most of them were merely content to hate me.

I had what was, to my thinking, a pretty nice house back in the woods about an hour away from the office, just south of Fort Campbell on the Tennessee side of the state line. It was the same place I'd lived in since my last year in the Army. I liked to split the difference between having enough land to shoot rifles in my yard and taking less than an hour to get to a grocery store. The little roadside market where I stopped for two gallons of milk and forty bucks worth of gas didn't quite count. Yeah, I could have lived closer to the office, but even with the ongoing Middle Tennessee real estate boom where McMansions grew atop former corn fields and cow pastures, there wasn't much in between except more woods and a lot of remaining farmland. Plus I was just too goddamn lazy to move. I have a lot of stuff and packing is such an inconvenience.

Living here had already outlasted two marriages just out of inertia. I liked the peace and quiet. I liked having a crime rate around zero. I liked not having to live in a built up area with my head on a permanent swivel while keeping a hand near my carry gun. Shit, I didn't even like going into Clarksville if I could help it, much less the much larger Nashville. But between shopping and restaurants, sometimes I couldn't help it. You can't stay out in the woods forever.

I let the dog out, turned the oven on to preheat and went over to the refrigerator. I pulled two steaks out to let them begin gently coming up from the chill, then took a long hot shower. Throwing on an old pair of gym shorts and a Metallica t-shirt, I made it out to the kitchen in time to be working on dinner when Angel got home. She'd finally moved in last year.

Forgive my slight detour into foodie-land. I subscribe to Food Network host Alton Brown's theory that the broiler is the most underused implement in the American kitchen. When doing two steaks quickly for a quiet couples' dinner at home, it is much less trouble than firing up a grill. It gets to temperature faster than charcoal or wood and there's no propane aftertaste on the meat as with a gas grill. A cast iron skillet is another good option, but most people can't handle or clean cast iron cookware properly and I won't go that far off topic right now.

For the broiler method, all you need is the broiler pan and a long corded meat thermometer to help while you're learning. Get two good ribeyes at least an inch thick, inch and a half if you can. If neither of you are that hungry, split a thick one rather than go for two thin ones. Thin steaks have no room to get your done-ness right so they get tough quickly. Assuming an electric oven, get it going on the broiler's high setting, as hot as you can get it, with the top rack of the oven as high as it will go without the meat touching the coils. Season the upper surface of the meat with Lowry's seasoned salt and coarse black pepper, put the meat on the pan, then the pan onto oven rack under that nice hot broiler coil. Give it about six minutes. Pull it, flip it, season the other side, give it about four minutes, pull it, should be about 125 degrees with a decent crust on it and serve immediately. Tonight it was served with a Caesar salad and microwaved wild rice.

The whole meal was complete with less than thirty minutes of prep. With a bit of practice to learn your oven's peculiarities, you really can do a better steak dinner at home than most lower-end chain places will sell you. And yes, you can do New York strip, porterhouse, whatever. I prefer ribeye for the marbling and texture, plus good scraps for the pets. Tenderloin/ filet mignon works too, but it's very lean so it turns chewy if you aren't careful about your timing.

As a secondary note, when you transfer onto a plate, don't use a hot one. Some places broil on the plate and the plate's residual heat keeps cooking the meat at the table. This turns a nice medium rare to a medium well before you finish your meal. Looking at you, Ruth's Chris. End of lesson.

In all my relationships after my college-years fiancée, a physics major who was a part-time professional chef at an upscale Italian place, I have done ninety percent of the cooking. Angel was content to sit and look cute while I got everything done and on plates. She was perched on one of my counter stools, in a tight black Harley Quinn t-shirt from the Hot Topic clearance rack and a pair of camouflage shorts. While we ate, I hit the subject slowly. "Angel, I may have a small problem with a girl at work."

She found that so funny she laughed with her mouth full. "You have girls at your job, sir? I thought it was all tattooed combat vets with beards and big pickup trucks."

That was a gross exaggeration. We did not look like the stereotypical collection of Iraq and Afghan vet-bros you see selling high-end gun parts or military-themed coffee on Instagram. "We have a couple. Hell, you know a couple of them."

"Yeah, but the only one I saw, you treat her like your sister. It's adorable."

I *think* she was talking about Kara, since several of us had carpooled to the Renaissance Festival together last year. Regardless, probably better than my sister. My family difficulties were legion. Not least of them was that my sister, a lawyer for the EPA, couldn't be told what I really did for a living after I left actual government work to join the firm. She thought my well-paid, cash-heavy lifestyle after years of genteel near-poverty and all the questions I wouldn't answer to her liking meant I was doing illegal shit for either the Pentagon or a drug cartel. I was waiting for the day she called the Feds on me, not realizing I myself kinda was one. "You haven't met this one. She's complicated."

"Important question first, is she hot?" Well, leave it to her to have her priorities in order.

I was honest. "Extremely. Making this more difficult, appears to be deliberately molding herself to my tastes. Our tastes, even."

"Ooooh, nice." Yeah. I am pretty damn straight. Angel is... not.

"Yeah, she dresses like a Goth stripper and has started calling me 'sir' a lot."

I think Angel was drooling. "Is she actually kinky or just dressing the style? Can I play too?"

I sighed. "Damn, dear, whose side are you on?"

"The side that hasn't had a good threesome in a minute. What's she look like?"

"Korean, a little shorter than you, narrower ass, but she bought her boobs."

She sighed happily. "Goddamn, gift wrap her for my birthday, please and thank you, sir."

I just do not understand my own life some days. "Okay, the morals of sleeping with an employee aside, it may be a terrible idea."

She laughed again. "That's easy. I can always sleep with her first."

That shot my eyebrows up. "Not quite the answer I was expecting."

She laughed. "After all these years? Come on, sir...you know me well enough. I've slept with more other girls in that time than you have."

"True." She really had. My personal life was a wreck much of the time and I just didn't randomly pick up new partners well. I could be described as hard to get along with. Of course I'd also spent nearly seven of those years married the second time, and not to Angel. "Anyway, change of subject, on to the next problem. I am going to need a good bit more help around here way more often since work is about to get way more challenging. My boss died last night. I told you he'd been sick for a while. I found out a few hours ago that I have been promoted."

Her face went a bit blank. "Wow, that is shitty and really awesome at the same time, so I really don't know how to feel about that. Sorry for him and thrilled for you? Was there a raise? Need me to take over the laundry? Do we need to hire a cleaning service?"

"Laundry, definitely. More likely, we're gonna need a whole-house maid service. Shit, I probably ought to hire you at the company. I am going to have to get a professional assistant, but you are damn near my personal assistant as it is. No point in you having another job to commute to. You make good money at the spa, but I can beat it easily."

She slowly nodded. "If you say so. I don't even really know what your company does. Some Defense Department computer thing, right?"

"It gets way more complicated than that." I didn't normally talk about work stuff around Angel, but she and I went back to when I was getting divorced the first time and was still broke. I walked her through the parts of the firm I was willing to discuss above ground. We decided she'd take Monday off, come in with me, and then drop her notice at the spa while part-timing with me at the firm. A decent little transition period, I suppose, long enough to bring one of her assistant managers up to 'lead assistant manager' to the owner.

I then pulled a spare Black phone out of the bottom of my gun safe, plugged it into start charging, and logged into *That Bomber Maker*'s secure web site to begin the initialization and setup. If Angel was gonna be on the team, she needed the hardware. Her pistol was next. With my tutelage, she had become a decent shot over the years and a few of the guns in the safes were hers, but carrying to work every day where most everybody was also armed was a good excuse for her to upgrade. I left her with the safe open to figure out what she liked while I kept setting the damned phone up. We'd try whatever she picked on my backyard range tomorrow. Probably another .45 since she loved 1911s. I guessed Monday would be a big day.

Chapter 5

"You know what the chain of command is? It's the chain I go get and beat you with 'til you understand who's in ruttin' command here...."
~Jayne Cobb, the Hero of Canton

I was up before my alarm clock, Angel still softly snoring. I am an expert on not-good mornings, and it was not a good morning. My heart was racing near 200, the burned-acid taste of an anxiety nightmare I couldn't remember was in my throat, and the insulated steel tumbler of ice water I habitually kept on the nightstand was only so-so at washing it out. My back felt like shit and I knew I'd need Angel to pop a couple discs back in when she woke up. I could feel a faint trail of fire down into my right leg. Yeah, the sciatic nerve was pinched. Standing up was more of a chore than usual.

I stumbled down the hall, my dog close at my heels with a look of concern on his face. Probably worried I'd fall on him. I let Odin out, then stumbled to the refrigerator and started taking long rips off the milk jug. Drink, breathe, drink more, breathe, and then drink more. My heart rate slowly edged back down and I felt a wave of weakness as the adrenaline finally faded. I leaned hard on the counter. Jesus, I wanted to puke. Fuck knows I'd done it before.

I let Odin back in and we went back toward the bedroom. Maybe Angel could sort my back out before we had to start getting ready.

***

Driving in on Monday with Angel was pretty simple. She could get ready very fast by female standards and my office was still closer to the house than the gentrified corner of East Nashville where she had been working. She'd gone for a tastefully professional look, with a nice skirt and blouse combo. The rather rakish black heels were her main concession to her usual self, that and a particular steel necklace that didn't come off.

She'd put in more effort than I had. Since we had visitors about never, we didn't have an office dress code. It was mostly a jeans and T-shirts kind of place. For me, it was usually jeans from Bass Pro Shops, an UnderArmour polo shirt since this was a meeting day (olive drab, I only ever bought one of three colors), and old Sperry boat shoes. Cowboy boots start aching on concrete after too long. Usually it's the heels that do it. And most hiking boots are a bit much for sitting behind a desk.

Signing her out a visitor badge at the shack until she got one of her own made, I took Angel down to my office. Her eyes were wide at the parade of unusual sights. The work bay wasn't too bad, but she lost her mind at the sight of the massive old vault door. And she definitely wasn't used to elevators that started at the top and went down.

"Holy fuck, sir. *this* is where you work?"

Watching her freak out a bit was entertaining. "First, where *we* work. And yeah. And as of about two o'clock Friday afternoon, I am technically in charge of the whole thing. Who actually owns it is a legal mess by deliberate design." It was true. Neither Athenaeum nor Archival Associates owned the place; the separate agricultural LLC owned the Hole and its 400 acres.

"Why a deliberate mess?"

I went for honesty. "It wasn't my idea, but I think in addition to making our home base harder to find, it's legal firewalling. If one of the three parts of the company get busted, the other parts have some wiggle room in court to salvage part of the operation and stay in the fight."

She thought about that, nodded, then flopped out on the leather couch in my office, posing a bit for fun. "I really like this couch. We should play on it."

I shook my head. "Maybe later. Too much to do, especially on Mondays." I then proceeded to outline all the parts of the job I didn't want to discuss above ground over the weekend. It took a while, me lecturing and quizzing her while skimming the intelligence summaries and admin notes in my intranet email box. At some point she was going to have to learn her way around the system.

***

The first floor conference room wasn't all that big and really, packing almost fifty people into it was a problem. Most people were standing. But I wasn't going to have to say much and this wouldn't take long. "All right, pack it in. I know it's cramped, but it just gives you less opportunity to fall asleep on me. Intel and Archives over here, IT over here." I looked over at my department heads. "We good?" They nodded. All hands present or accounted for. Great.

It was rare to have most of the troops in one room. At times like this, the split between the firm's legal halves disappeared. Since we'd mostly drawn from intelligence and signal veterans, we had more females than you'd guess, maybe one out of three. Some were right off their first enlistment, while others were grandparents who'd retired the first time before I had ever joined. Active duty dress and fitness standards were a dim memory for some. I had fat nerds and rail-thin workout freaks, a few guys in kilts, one girl in a dinosaur onesie, and more assorted geek and fandom T-shirts than the DragonCon dealer hall. But they were my command, such as it was, and I'd handpicked about half. Others had been handpicked by people I'd handpicked. The rest were the old guard upon whom I still relied. And now I was really in charge.

A few heads turned as Cash slid in through the door with a *Sorry I'm late* wave and nod. A few of those eyes stayed on her. We had our fair share of thirsty bachelors even if she regularly ignored everyone. She was still the most overtly hot female in the company even if this hadn't been a Plaid

Miniskirt Monday. She'd actually dressed down somewhat, in a gray New York Yankees hoodie from one of their World Series wins, black leggings and low-heeled ankle boots. Angel was definitely drawing attention too. Shiny and New, right?

I shook off the thinking and began.

"Big shit up front. Big John, who most of you may recall was our CEO, has finally lost his battle with cancer. Some of you may have heard this from pulling duty this weekend. Regardless, he passed very painlessly late Thursday night, but there was no reason to fuck up everyone else's weekend with the news." There was some murmuring. A couple people closed their eyes or bowed heads, while a couple of the Catholics crossed themselves.

"Second issue. The board of directors, partly by virtue of all being old men but mostly by wanting no part of the workload, has voted me in as the new CEO." There were some surprised faces at that. "Okay, not to put anyone on the spot, but putting you on the spot. Who is drastically upset by this?" Dave raised his hand with a grin. I looked at him with a sigh and he put it back down with a self-amused cackle. *Thanks, dick.*

"All right. Seriously, all of you have some experience working for me already and in some cases have known me a couple decades. We are not going to have too many drastic changes around here. It's like always. We do the job and we get paid." I could tell by their faces that most recognized the vague *Firefly* reference. There was a certain amount of Malcolm Reynolds to running this crew anyway. "Okay, so keep doing what you are doing. No immediate changes. Intel and IT, we may have some long term moves we need to make. Dave, Kara, Petey, Morgan, I need you either this afternoon or tomorrow for a sit-down, so get a time that works for all of you then let me know.

"Now onto the little shit. First, we are collecting again this fall for the Nashville Humane Society, so get with Kara if you want in on that." We gave a lot anonymously to various charities; for just one example, one of our guys had dropped five thousand dollars out of a dead child pornographer's wallet into a Salvation Army kettle last Christmas. It was a morally acceptable way to dispose of dirty money. Some cash was so tainted that even we wouldn't keep it.

"Second, mark your calendars now. The Veterans' Day picnic will be in the gazebo the Thursday prior, with the grills lighting up at 1000 hours. Guests and such we somewhat trust are welcome, no shop talk with the uncleared, same as always, etc, etc, you know the drill. Volunteering to help in the kitchen or on cleanup is officially encouraged, also as always. Anything for me?"

"New CEO buys the beer, right?" This from the new kid in IT, one of Petcy's stray children he'd dragged out of Atlanta. Skinny blond kid, hipster beard. Couldn't think of his name. Michael something.

"Yes and it will be good beer, no bullshit IPAs or anything with fruit in it."

See, the standard deal for our parties was that the firm just paid for everything except hard liquor out of the petty cash so everyone ate and drank for free. We could afford it. We'd have maybe two kinds of beer on draft and some other interesting odds and ends in bottles or cans on ice, but to simplify logistics and accommodate everyone's wide range of tastes, you had to bring your own bottle for the hard stuff. Anyone too drunk to drive didn't make it out of the gate until they slept it off in their cars. The guard shift on duty handled that. They got to eat too, just not drink. They had enough non-drinkers that Jake could, and did, handle scheduling that internally.

"Third. I now have an admin assistant by the characteristically unethical expedient of hiring my girlfriend. Some of you who have known me a while have met Angel socially over the years, but this is her-" She stood up and waved at everyone. "Anyway, don't panic, she's from the allegedly on our side Nationalist Chinese, not the Godless devil-worshiping mainland Commie Chinese."

Angel laughed. "Don't listen to his bullshit, I'm a DC suburbs kid originally and I understand almost none of this. I'm just here to help him out."

I continued. "We'll work on getting her formally cleared so she can get billed on the books for a couple of the overt government projects since we can always use another Chinese linguist, but her main job is making sure I don't lose my car keys again and I make it to meetings sort of on time."

Kara snorted derisively. "If you can get him to meetings on time, you're already a fucking miracle worker."

Dave piped up, "Just keep him supplied with Mountain Dew."

"And remind him what day it is!" Petey threw in.

Kara cut back in. "Oh, and make him go to the doctor one of these days before he accidentally dies of something preventable out of his usual self-neglect."

Everyone's a fucking comedian. "If anyone else has significant others who can actually fill staffing holes on either side of the company, if only as subcontractors, do not be afraid to speak up. Past a point, *arrrr, this be a scurvy pirate crew that care naught for the rules of regular men...*" I got more sighs and eyerolls than chuckles. "All right, if you aren't even going to pretend to laugh at my jokes, fuck all y'all and we're done. Anything else?" Nope. Nothing. "Dismissed, back to work everyone." Sure. They all smiled at that. Cash did an immediate fade out the door, beating the rush.

Petey caught me near the door. "1400 good?" I nodded.

I grabbed Angel. "Dear, go on down to Accounting on the fifth floor and keep Cash busy. I am having a meeting in half an hour in my office I know she will disagree with, so I need her distracted until...threeish."

Angel smirked. "That was her?" I nodded. "Oh, *nice.* I'll go start keeping her busy now then."

"Wish I had time to socially introduce you, but bigger shit going on."

She rolled her eyes at me. "Babe, when do I need help starting conversations with girls?"

I smacked her on the butt as she stepped off. I'm pretty sure you're still allowed to do that if she was already your girlfriend before you hired her. "Good point, dear. But get going."

I went back up the hall into my office and checked my Friday afternoon notes where I had begun sketching out my questions. IT was going to be just a lot of little itty-bitty shit issues, mainly equipment related. That I could handle. They mostly just wanted approval to spend money. Big John was not a computer guy and he hated spending on electronic gadgetry. Fuck, we didn't even have a full time IT department in the Hole when John had hired me. Now it had become substantial, so they figured I would open up the funding faucet. It usually ended up being money well spent, so to be quite honest, I didn't care. Intel was another story. I had two motherfucking huge questions for Intel, Making that more stressful, I really didn't think easy answers existed for those questions. Fuck. I hate those kind. I mostly drew and doodled, playing with music on the junk laptop, until it was time for the meet. The four of them filed in pretty close to hit time.

In some ways, this was easy. The leadership of our two primary departments were my people even before we lost Big John. As noted, Petey ran IT, with the unofficial title of 'signal officer.' He was a tall, rail-thin Georgia kid who never really had the drawl and was blonde-haired and blue eyed enough he would have made the *Leibstandarte Adolf Hitler* recruiters happy. He and I had done two Iraq tours together, me in a rifle company and him in the battalion signal platoon, before he had gotten out and chased a couple of computer science degrees. He had made a fair pile of money in the industry before I lured him back to the dark side of life. Boredom was his weakness.

Don't tell anyone, but he had been my second choice to run the whole thing. My first choice, another Army buddy of mine, had surprised herself, if not me, by staying on active duty. A Dartmouth ROTC grad, ruthless and hyper-competent, she had just gotten picked up 'below the zone' for major, working in a Pentagon basement doing interesting things that she wouldn't tell me about. In an interesting coincidence, she could also pass for Cash's cousin, right down to the yoga habit. I think there is a lab somewhere doing God's work turning them out in small batches.

Morgan was the #2 in IT. He also did a shitload of our welding, but then he was a multiskilled guy. We thrived on multiskilled guys. He was an obscure subset of Apache by blood despite being from Indianapolis. Apparently his parents had moved for work, so he wasn't born or raised around the tribe. He was also the best guy we had for the electronic intercept side of hacking places. I had seen him walk in and out of high-end restricted buildings in a UPS uniform he bought for ten bucks at Goodwill, pushing a hand truck full of (empty) boxes with an old Palm Treo in his hand and a homemade wi-fi scanning rig in his back pocket. Electronically speaking, he had done more backdoor jobs than the porn industry. He also ran our 'dark side' IT department, handling the various off-site hackers and subcontractors who did much of our dirty work. I didn't usually know the details; delegating that was what I had him for. But for that reason, his Christmas bonuses were always generous and we made sure his "Boss, uh, I fucked up, and I gotta run to a non-extradition country" escape and evasion package was both airtight and well-funded.

Kara was the number two in Intel, as you readers already know. She was paler than usual. Weeks of night shifts had taken a toll, even if she said she preferred them. This was in the middle of the night to her daily pattern. She was holding onto her *Battlestar Galactica* coffee mug for dear life and trying not to yawn at me.

Dave was in charge of the Intel section. He was to me what Obi-Wan was to Qui-Gonn, a former student who now far exceeded me. Friends since the first night on Benning and platooned together through infantry school, we'd then been roommates at jump school. He'd never lost his thick New Jersey accent and his extensive tattoos were quite distinctive. But books, covers, etc. He'd had a long and brilliant career in SOCOM, either a shooter who thought like an intel guy or an intel guy who thought like a shooter. Doing what we do, we needed that flexibility. When he finally hung up the uniform at just past twenty years, his career not having been injury-shortened like mine, I then waved a lot of money under his nose to stay in the fight. The fact I promised him way less bullshit than the big contractors helped. Dave had nearly as many authority issues as I did.

"As is our tradition, big shit up front. Dave and Kara. Structural question for Intel. What the fuck do we need to do to preserve a profitable intel gathering and analysis capability in the event that all the government contract shit, both overt and covert, went away?"

They silently stared at me.

"No, I haven't lost my mind any more than usual and I am not saying we break up the government arrangements. But, assume the worst case scenario. We get edged out, lose a bid, the personal connections go away as old age severs our insider hookups. How do we avoid being blinded and how do we then turn a profit? Second, and an even bigger question in my book, can we supply the commercial clients to a level that justifies the billing without using the things we have from the government contracting side?"

Kara took the lead. "To be honest, half of our income comes in from the... commercial clients."

"But one, can we survive long term on half of our income? Cash says yes, at least for a couple years. Cash also believes very strongly in the power of investment portfolios, insider trading, and her voodoo to make this work. That assumes the stock market keeps going the way the world wants. That's a very big assumption as we saw during the last virus scare when it dropped forty percent in two weeks. That's also why she isn't in here to argue against me, and then hurt her feelings by doubting her. But Big John also believed the good times with Uncle Sam would never end and refused to let me ask the question. Big John is gone, so now I'm asking."

Kara took off her glasses and rubbed the bridge of her nose. "Most of what goes out on the commercial side comes from commercial penetrations. Through the subcontractors and cutouts, we are into everything from the credit cards and a few big banks to the God View admin tool on the rideshare companies. You know how careful we are with anything classified off the Fed side."

"Understood, geese, golden eggs, trips to Leavenworth..."

"Exactly."

I continued. "So can we satisfy the commercial demand with merely commercial assets?"

Petey didn't care and sat happily. He was the mechanic who made the systems work. He didn't much concern himself with their use. The three who did? Dave leaned way back in his chair and looked at the ceiling. Kara was contemplating the tabletop. Morgan just looked pensive. It was Kara who finally spoke. "Maybe."

I thrive on chaos and uncertainty, partly because my life is usually a disaster zone where well-laid plans usually collapse spectacularly into varying levels of tragedy. I learned to improvise really well as a result. That doesn't mean I actually like having to do it, so this was one time I wanted a better answer than *maybe*. "Guys, we are betting our future house payments on our ability to keep customers happy enough to keep paying us. You know as well as I do that what Uncle Sam pays us overtly on legit contracts to Athenaeum is barely enough to keep the lights on."

Kara gave me That Look. We had known each other long enough that she had the privilege. "It is not that bad. The overt pay for nineteen analysts and the associated IT support is quite fair. They cover all the security clearance expenses and they eat all the secure communications infrastructure expenses, which is partly IT's lane, not Intel's, but it's still not cheap and it's also not coming out of our pockets. That's the whole core of the company; it's Athenaeum in a taco shell."

Petey looked at her funny. "Taco shell? Nutshell? That's mixing metaphors."

She just looked back at him. "Fuck off. I haven't eaten yet, and tacos sound good."

I cut her off before we spun off the rails. "Well fuck, does that mean they own all the communications shit and we have to give it back if they ever cut us off?"

Petey cut in since it was now in back in his lane. "Boss, you're freaking out over nothing. I promise. If they ever do cut us off, everything they would take or mandate secure destruction of is going to be so fucking obsolete it isn't even worth keeping, so we'd just replace it anyway."

"Which costs how much?"

He shrugged. "Assuming we're just buying new laptops and hard drives and they don't scrape us all the way to bare walls, taking the racks and cables and shit, under three or four million. Computer shit gets cheaper ever year. We could get started back with thirty or forty good laptops at under a grand each then go from there. We wouldn't need to spend another three to four million rebuilding the disk drive farm since nobody would be paying us to use it. Even then, I could rebuild that for under three if you didn't want it pretty. Pretty always costs more."

That actually made me feel a lot better now that I knew what the books looked like. We could rebuild out of on-hand cash if we had to. I wasn't going to tell Petey that. He would want to have Cash sell off some stocks or empty a savings account to install a major supercomputer system to play with down here. He liked his big stupid toys as much as I do.

I went on from there. "Okay, additional tasking. Have a 'rebuild everything' shopping list premade, updated as appropriate and stored somewhere safely. That way if we ever do have to rebuild from a cold start, or at a backup location, you have an idea already put together. Second additional tasking. Back up the hard drives way the hell off site."

Petey said, "We do have a data recovery plan, but I see where you're going. Got it."

Morgan raised his hand. "Dude, we live in a fucking nuclear war bunker that's older than we are and probably can't replace at any price anyway. What are we going to do that we need a backup location from this?"

I looked at him. "I have no fucking idea. And I pray to God we never have to find out."

He shrugged. Any disapproval in my voice rolled off him like water off a duck's back. "Fair enough, man."

***

Sometimes you just need to get out of sight for an hour and take a deep breath, even when you're in charge. I had a hiding spot for that, one very few people knew about.

Some previous member of the operation had decided that the deserted sixth floor was the place to put the arms room. It was behind a false wall with a recessed vault door. Keyed lock, not combination. I had gotten the keys away from Big John two years ago and the first thing I did was get a set of spares cut that eventually went to Dave. There was another set of spares inside the fake potted plant in my office.

For a firm that did not do shooter gigs, somebody had invested heavily in the equipment to do so. Unfortunately they had done so about fifteen minutes after the Vietnam War ended. Now I absolutely loved old guns, but this shit was all two or three generations out of date. It was a time capsule, not a working armory. Complicating that, there was exactly zero paperwork on two-thirds of the fully automatic stuff. That made it a room full of Federal felony indictments if the wrong people ever looked down here. Still, I had worked here a year before even I managed to find the damn thing, so I supposed it was safe enough for now. It was just my place to putter around in peace and quiet sometimes. The smells of old forged ordnance steel, manganese phosphate Parkerizing, and CLP oil soothed my fraying nerves sometimes when the answers were unclear and my sudden responsibilities seemed more a prison than a fortress.

Now the first thing I had done after discovering the room was get the several dozen cases of grenades, Claymore mines, and actual demolitions material like det cord and blasting caps out of it. With some effort, a few of us quickly put in a decent-sized root cellar-style ammo bunker on the far side of the property where it would take real effort to even accidentally find it. Some people's explosives storage practices give me fucking heartburn, no matter how long the shit had been there.

Much of the room was old US Property-marked hardware. A hundred scuffed-up old M16A1s sat in GI armory racks of ten each. Virgin M60 machine guns and M79 grenade launchers, a dozen each in their old fashioned 'straight out of depot rebuild' foil wrap and cardboard boxes were stacked next to a dozen each M1A1 Thompson submachine guns and old Winchester trench shotguns with the long Enfield bayonets. One of the Tommy guns was unwrapped. I'd been using it on the range out back before I finally bought a legally registered one from a dealer I knew in Pennsylvania. I even had a pair of heavy water-cooled

Browning .30 caliber machine guns that had been considered obsolete since the Korean War, but someone later rebarreled to 7.62mm NATO.

A circular Army surplus floor rack stood off to one side with eighty, yes, eighty GI M1911A1 pistols in it. None were the most valuable, the five hundred made before Pearl Harbor by the Singer Sewing Machine Company. Believe me, I had already looked. There was one incredibly rare WWII OSS-style sound-suppressed M3A1 'Grease Gun' that might as well have had PROPERTY OF ERIC engraved on it. MACV-SOG had used them and the old man had most likely smuggled it out of Vietnam at the end. Boxes of magazines and .45 holsters were piled under the work table. They'd taken a while to sort out and inventory, and I was still making up the shortages.

Then we had the non-USGI stuff. For AKs, we had thirty Chinese-made ones, beaten-up Type 56s with the red plastic furniture and the folding spike bayonets. No paperwork. They just screamed *these came home illegally in a crate from a war zone somewhere.* Then there was the pre-May '86 stuff, most of it legally papered to another LLC with a Nashville address. Two dozen suppressed Ingram submachine guns in .45ACP, original Powder Springs, Georgia guns as opposed to the later numerous knockoffs. Their suppressors were from Mitch WerBell's infamous Sionics company. There were Uzis, Sterlings and Swedish Ks, both suppressed and not, all in 9mm. If you wanted 7.62 NATO, we had a couple dozen FALs. Israeli, British, Belgian and a few where the markings had been ground away and suspiciously original Rhodesian camouflage paint jobs remained. I also had six Ciener-suppressed Ruger .22 target pistols, one of which had been Jimmy's 'streetlight special' in Brooklyn that night. Maybe Ciener's legendarily bad attitude and shitty customer service hadn't been quite so awful in 1983.

Hanging on the wall over the workbench was the one personal rifle I didn't keep in my large safe at home, my Ohio Ordnance Works HCAR. It was five thousand dollars worth of modernized Browning Automatic Rifle in .30-'06. I'd originally bought it because I am a barely restrained WWII nut and I had come into the money for it after I first joined the firm. Then, thinking I would need the ability to punch people out of cover behind cars on that security gig and also thinking my buddy Bam Bam would think it was really cool, I had hauled it and 400 rounds of WWII surplus armor piercing ammo to Dallas for what was supposed to be a 24 hour security job. Fast money in cash, government contract, all the soft-sell bullshit.

After a whole lot of carnage we hadn't planned on, a whole lot of bodies got swept under the metaphorical rug in the name of political expediency. Still, just in case the tides of power shifted and somebody ever wanted to prosecute murder cases on account of all those dead cartel shooters, I then didn't want a rifle I had killed upward of forty people with stored at the address on my driver's license where a casual search warrant would find it. At the same time, we now had history together and so I loved it too much to throw it in a lake. I had replaced the old AAC suppressor that had been destroyed that day with a Surefire SOCOM can and the Trijicon mini-ACOG ruined at the same time had been upgraded to a 1-10x Swampfox Warhorse in a Larue mount. Because I knew a guy, I'd gotten a better deal with Swampfox than with Vortex or on a Nightforce ATACR. It's all imported anyway.

The ammo was stacked deep against one wall. The American stuff was all in US Army crates, none of it newer than 1978. All the 5.56mm was Vietnam-style 55 grain. It was antiquated for modern guns, but fine for the A1's 1:12 slow-twist barrels. About half of the .45 ammo was Evansville Ordnance Plant stuff sealed in spam-type cans, dated 1943 through 1945. It was steel case stuff from later in the war that was actually better for submachine guns than pistols. It was hard on a 1911 extractor. If I was ever desperate enough to open it, I don't think I'd care. The 7.62 and the nine mil were a wide variety of NATO surplus, stacked a thousand rounds at a time. The 7.62x39 was all Chinese commercial steel-cored stuff from the mid-1990s in yellow cardboard boxes that you couldn't legally get into the country anymore. It was like looking at the gun shows of my college years all over again.

I went back to my ongoing project of getting the frames and slides and barrels as well matched as I could. I generally did three to five guns at a sitting. Colt barrel back to Colt frame and slide, etc. Playing music off my cell phone with an alarm set for ninety minutes, it was mindless entertainment. Making the pistols closer to factory original despite the ravages of time and various rebuild stamps was soothing. I checked oil stained Xeroxes from the late Charles Clawson's *Collector's Guide to Colt .45 Service Pistols: Models of 1911 and 1911A1* occasionally to identify the small bits, a Remington Rand thumb safety from an Ithaca, or a Colt mainspring housing from a Union Switch. When I had left active duty over a decade earlier, I really had just wanted to fix guns at a war museum for a living. Peaceful, quiet tinkering. Instead, I was now the director of a private CIA. That lack of solitude would eat at me, no matter how much better this paid.

I hadn't locked the door, but I was still sort of surprised when it was pulled open and Dave walked in. "When I couldn't find you upstairs, I had a feeling you were hiding down here."

I sighed. "Needed to take a break."

Dave wisecracked, "That's what your new secretary is for."

"Yeah, yeah, whatever."

He continued. "She's hanging out in Accounting, by the way."

"That was actually where I sent her. But since you bothered me down here, I got a job for you since I ain't got time to do it myself. We need to go on a discreet shopping binge." I finished reassembling the now-all Ithaca .45 in front of me and racked it.

That got a groan out of him. "Sure, not like I don't have an intel section to run."

"No matter how much she complains, Kara is perfectly capable of running it, otherwise she wouldn't be your deputy."

Dave merely shrugged in agreement. "Good point."

I went on. "Then you are the one guy actually here on a regular basis that I trust to do it right, not to mention one of very few guys I am willing to hand that much cash to. As much as I want to fuck off and play around doing it myself, that's a poor use of my time since I already suck at delegating to other people. Get Jake to help you out."

He gave in. "Fine, fine, flattery will get you everywhere with me and you know it."

Finally, on to the point. "All right, prepare to copy and use your imagination on some of it," he snatched one of my pieces of scratch paper and a pencil, "and basing this on a sixteen man troop equivalent. We need an armorer toolbox newer than 1981 since we're going to rebuild some of the 16A1s," I gestured toward the racks of them, "because this isn't Vietnam anymore. Some form of M4A1 Block II upper, quality free floated kinda shit for a zero to 600 meter world. Knight's, Compass Lake, Geissele, whatever. Spare bolt carrier groups. Spare triggers. New stocks. Lasers, lights. An Aimpoint and a variable optic per gun, which means quality swappable mounts, probably Larue. New slings and a shitload of PMags. About a pallet of ammo, I assume Barnes 70 grain for an operational load. We didn't sign the Hague Convention." The all-copper TSX hunting bullets were extremely lethal but not Law of Land Warfare compliant. Even the few SOF units that had been allowed to buy them could only legally use them in certain applications. He nodded. "Then a pallet or two of cheap blasting ammo."

Dave knew the answer. "The 55 grain we have is good enough for shoothouse workups and CQM, even out of modern barrels, and we have a lot of it."

I nodded. I think I remembered that once it was too late. "Still, get more. We can afford it. Then we need new pistols. I love GI 1911A1s, as you can tell, but for work, we will want something modern. Suppressor capable, red dot capable, lights, holsters. Tricked-out Glock 19s?"

"Roland Specials are a fucking meme gun by now, but a meme for a reason since Chuck is a smart guy." Yeah, Dave and I knew a lot of the same people.

"Those we can do, but then .45s suppress better since it's a heavy subsonic. Some of each."

He nodded. "Cool. I like the power of 'and.' Plus, like you said, we can afford it."

"Don't feel limited to one pistol per guy. Now, we need long guns. Two M110s or equivalent. Call our buddy at Knight's and see if we got the hookup on good-guy pricing. Refurbished is okay. Then NODs, armor, etc. We will have at least a dozen ready to go sets of stuff, so we'll put gear lockers in down here on the sixth floor. Eventually go-bags and everything."

Dave kept nodding along. "Cool. This is fun. I like it. But why?"

"Because John isn't here to tell me no anymore, Past that, I have a feeling a storm is coming."

Dave looked at the floor, shaking his head as his mood shifted. "What a buzzkill. I should have told you to shove this job up your ass when you called me."

I threw my empty can in the recycling box of empties. "Dude, who else would pay you what you make here with the minimal oversight and lack of bullshit that we have going on? That outfit in Fairfax was nothing but rules. You were only there a year and hated it."

"Which I can't live to spend if we then use all these cool new war toys to then get stuck in balls-deep playing the Second Battle of Ramadi in the streets somewhere over some illegal secret squirrel shit." Leave it to him to be the rational one.

"Dave, we aren't going to start trouble, I just want to be a bit more prepared for it."

He laughed at me. "That's what you said before you got drunk and hit that Air Force dude with a chair in that bar in Osan." He picked up one of the antique Winchester trench shotguns and racked the action.

I had to laugh too. "You weren't even there for that! You were literally on the other side of the planet! How the fuck did you know?"

With a grin, he dry-fired at the lights. "Yeah, Rob told me. It's a great story."

This was almost embarrassing. "Shit, unbelievable."

Sha-shak. He racked the Winchester's action again. "Don't care. Still funny. Occasional dumb shit like that reminds the rest of us you are still human no matter how much you stress out and try to deny it."

I sighed. "All right, while we are onto my failings as a human being and leader, I have another issue that I need your counsel on both as an old friend and as a better professional than I am."

He rolled his eyes, grabbing another one of my Mountain Dews out of the dorm-style mini fridge I'd put in under the arms room workbench. He passed me another one as well. "What have you gotten yourself into this time?"

"Nothing yet. And it might be *who* I get myself into."

Dave snorted. "Man, if you think anyone really cares about the ethics of you hiring your girlfriend to work here, you're even more nuts than I thought. Literally no one gives a single shit except you."

I shook my head. "Worse. I have Accounting hitting on me."

He laughed again. "You finally noticed?"

Wait, what? "Huh?"

He laughed harder as he went on. "Dude, she's been staring at you for months like you were on the menu. Maybe after she started dressing like Jenna Jameson in the office, but definitely before she made you give her a ride to her boob job. That was when, back in May? It's only lately she's gotten blatant enough your possibly slightly autistic self is actually noticing. I think IT's got a betting pool going on when she finally bags and tags you. Check their desk calendars."

Morgan would do something like that, the asshole. "Great. Just fucking great. So the professional ethics of this are?"

He shrugged. "This ain't the Pentagon, it ain't XVIII Corps HQ. We don't have enough people for it to seem like blatant favoritism over her peers since, well, we only have the one accountant and she's it. She's got what she sees a great job but can't fuck you to get a better one, since again, we only have the one accountant and she's it. She's not going to fuck you to get off the charge of quarters roster or avoid hazardous duty, since we don't do any of that. Though, I suppose with some train-up we could add her to the watch officers' roster since she is almost always downstairs anyway and she is our economic intel subject matter expert. Hm. I might ask her about that to save you the trouble."

I think I saw where he was going with this. "So?"

"I ain't the fucking chaplain, nor the JAG, not that we have either anyway-"

Wait a sec, that reminds me of something... "Hang on, note to self, we need a JAG."

Dave nodded. "Well we have the tax lawyer and contracting is-."

I really was completely distracted. It happens. "That doesn't count. John wouldn't let us get a legal staff because he hated lawyers and yelled at me every time I mentioned the idea, but if we ever need one, like if we get disavowed and busted, we don't have time to check the Yellow Pages and find one, especially in criminal defen-"

Dave ran out of patience fast. "Dude, curb your ADHD for a minute and let me finish this. Anyway, we need her to keep the money flowing smoothly and this party going on. So with that critical requirement in mind, if she's got to get dicked down to stay happy and continue keeping all of us well paid, I vote you go for it. Shit, the way those two were looking at each other when I was trying to find you, your girlfriend might be looking to get in there first."

I shrugged. "That wouldn't shock me, really."

He shook his head in disbelief. "Why the fuck do nerds always have more and weirder sex than regular people?"

Sigh. "It's complicated."

"I hate complicated. Forget I asked." He racked the Winchester one more time and dry-fired it at the *Art of J.R.R. Tolkien* wall calendar. "Though if you're going to go through with it, lemme know when, so's I can put down a hundred bucks on the date and split the pot with you after."

I rolled my eyes at him. "Yeah, having ethics is a bitch sometimes."

"Fuck ethics. Winning isn't everything, but it's only second to breathing."

I'm good at quotations. "George Steinbrenner."

He grinned. "That's why I like the accountant. She's also a Yankees fan."

Chapter 6

"Just trying to make a livin', workin' nine to five..."
~Dolly Parton

Tuesday. My first real day in charge. I'd dropped like a rock at nine o'clock the night before and then woke up around one in the morning, twitchy and anxious. I'd barely gotten two more hours of sleep before the alarm went off at six. I spent most of the time between that in the kitchen drinking milk and trying not to wake up Angel. Two bad nights in a row. Yay. That sleep deficit would send me running for more Mountain Dew to get through the afternoon, and then the extra caffeine intake would probably get me a third bad night.

See, you may have gathered I don't sleep well. I haven't in years, if some years aren't as bad as others. It's not a combat PTSD thing. I'd slept like a kitten after my only *real* combat tour, and calling it "post" would imply the stress ever stopped. The stresses had changed several times, the traumas added up, but they never ended. Depression, anxiety, and so on made an always-changing combo plate. Sometimes it's just a sucking void, a sense that things will get uncontrollably worse and then just... end. Not anything I can blame the Army for, it just is. So in the middle of the night, sometimes I end up staring at the ceiling or shitposting on the Internet.

One time back, way back before all this, when I was buying PowerBall tickets, someone cautioned me, "Money won't solve your problems." They recommended religion instead.

My answer was succinct. "Fuck you. Enough money will solve every single problem I have right now. It may give me new ones, but I will happily trade those for what I have." Sure, I didn't win. Too bad, the variety would have been nice. Still, with all this, I had still hit what certainly qualified as big money by the standards of my middle-class suburban upbringing. But there were enough responsibilities to go with it that the bundle of them would choke a goddamn cow.

I did what I always did. I got up, stumbled into the office and faked it as best I could. It was good enough to get through the day. Eat, sleep, repeat.

The weeks began to blur together as the firm continued its operational pattern. On the government side, we tracked Salvadoran gang members by cell phone traffic, cracked a Mexican human trafficking operation in Boston then data-mined an interesting procurement fraud case for the Navy. Civilian side? We brokered a contract on a software piracy case to one of our subcontractors then did some research on Chinese crop yields so a North Carolina company could calculate their soybean export market for the next few seasons. Mostly boring, grinding stuff that paid the bills. It's not about being James Bond or Jack Ryan, it's about finding somebody to pay you to generate analytics from available information in profitable quantities and then making sure you actually get paid for the work.

But one afternoon it dawned on me I hadn't seen Angel in hours. Yes, she'd been downstairs in Accounting a lot with Cash while I did other things, but I didn't remember sending her down there either. The last time I remembered her being down there, she'd been closemouthed about what had been going on. She said some things had to stay between girls, so I just shut up about it. I had too much work to do to think about it much. But Angel was also supposed to be in here with me learning how to do some of this shit so I didn't have to do it all alone.

Finally, she walked back in, giggling as she entered. "Yeah, I beat you to her. Well worth it."

I looked down over my glasses at her. "It wasn't quite a competition, you were volunteering to go in first as the reconnaissance effort, remember?"

She smiled and slumped down in her chair. "And believe me, totally worth volunteering. Glad I did it. Yay me!"

"Yay you. And I've been up here sorting intel reports since Dave's in Warsaw and Kara's on night shifts. I'm supposed to be teaching you how to do some of this."

She looked appropriately contrite. "I'm sorry, sir. But if it makes you feel better, the Accounting Department is a very good girl and you don't need to worry about her."

I sighed. "Great. Now I need a hand trying to get all this shit into folders since it's coming upstairs faster than I can file it, let alone look at it too closely before it goes out."

***

We were way past closing time on a Friday when I came upstairs out of IT. I'd been arguing with Morgan over his bribe money budget. I intended to grab Angel and head for dinner down in Nashville before we looped back home, but she wasn't in my office. Really, there was only one other place to look for her.

Checking down on the fifth floor, she wasn't in Cash's office. The music was thundering out of Cash's room up the hall instead, classic strip club techno stuff from the Lords of Acid that was older than they were. I went up the hall with some degree of trepidation. Cash had retained a few of the original bunker-type architectural features, so I banged on the heavy steel door with the butt end of my Emerson pocket knife. She probably couldn't hear it. I imagined this was what having teenagers was like. I banged on it again. Nothing. So with a deep breath, I opened the door.

Cash's room was impressive now that it was done. For several reasons, I had never been in there since it was built. I had helped out with the framing and some of the electrical, but I hate doing drywall and really hate painting. It used most all of the twelve foot ceiling. The sheetrocked walls were a dark wine red and much of the room was thickly carpeted in a rich cream color. The remainder of the room was hardwood-floored, a red-brown shade of mahogany that matched the two high dressers and a king size bed. But the hardwood-floored area was where she had mounted the stripper pole, with an overstuffed couch that sort of matched the walls. She was nine feet in the air in mid spin, naked except for some over the knee black leather boots with long stiletto heels. She spun with the pounding music and slid down, landing on her feet and dropping further into a split. Seeing me, she grinned and beckoned. Giving in, I sat down on the couch, unwilling to offend her by doing the sensible thing and getting the fuck out of there. I wondered where Angel was.

She delicately crawled over, kneeling before me. She reached into the couch cushions and pulled the remote for the stereo, dropping the volume to a more reasonable level. She leaned into my lap, me acutely aware of those augmented breasts pressing between us.

"You hadn't been down to see me in several days, not even for work stuff. Are you mad at me because I fucked your girlfriend, sir?"

"Not at all. I was very busy but rather hoped you two would have fun."

"Well, you got your wish. We have had a lot of fun this last week."

And then Angel walked in out of Cash's bathroom, also naked except for a nice pair of heels and her usual necklace collar. She came in behind Cash, putting a possessive hand on the back of her neck. "Don't worry, sir. Cash and I have had a lot of nice talks just between us and I think we have an excellent plan on how to do the best possible job for the company's needs and, even more importantly, for yours. You are the company now, after all, and all of us are going to be dependent on your leadership. So we have to help you take care of yourself, because you always put yourself last. That's not healthy."

She walked over to the steel door, throwing the locking lever over. Angel walked back over, sliding into my lap and straddling my right leg. At a glance from her, Cash moved up and straddled my left leg. This was already one part 'Shit you normally need to drop at least a hundred bucks in the back room of a strip club for' and one part 'I still should feel somewhat bad about this since Cash is an employee.'

Cash hugged me tight. "I'll be a good girl for you, sir. Always. We'll talk more after."

I had a feeling where this was going. "After what?"

Angel picked up the stereo remote and hit a button. The music got loud again. They both started grinding into me and to each other. "Since it's after closing time, after we are done making you relax for once. Now shut up and enjoy it, sir."

This was mutiny, goddamn it. Mutiny.

***

I woke up with a curious sense of disorientation. It was too quiet. The fan sounded wrong. The mattress didn't feel right. It smelled weird. *It wasn't my room.* I looked around... oh, fuck. The memories of the night before and the early morning all came back. Oh, fuck. Cash and Angel were both still out cold, but then by the end they had been doing most of the work. Everything hurt, like I'd pulled every muscle from the back of my neck to the arches of my feet. Damn. *Pants. I needed pants.* My primary Mountain Dew stash was in the first floor fridge. That was up four floors and I was not going up there pantsless. Down a floor to the arms room fridge maybe? But I needed my sugary green caffeinated fluid to wake up enough to process this.

I slid out from under arms and legs and breasts and stumbled into Cash's bathroom to piss. *Jesus, she had a four seat hot tub in here. Huh.* With that taken care of, I then crept back out into the bedroom. Angel was wordlessly waving toward the small fridge in the corner, her eyes still shut. Sure enough, three retro green cans of Mountain Dew Throwback were in there with Cash's organic fruit smoothies and tea bottles. The ladies had planned that far ahead, bless their wicked little hearts. I drained the can, looked at them, and went back to bed. What the hell, it was only 4:33 on a Saturday morning and whatever damage was done had been. I did have to get home though. I hadn't laid on a dog sitter for Odin. He might eventually eat the couch or something.

***

Angel and I usually had our best talks in the truck. Not about work stuff, since vehicles are pathetically easy to bug and sweeping isn't foolproof, but about other things. "So you and Cash have obviously clicked."

Angel giggled. "Oh, she is a filthy little girl. I love her already."

"Yeah, but I still think of her as the, um, girl she was when I found her." Angel knew the story by now and why a word of it couldn't ever be breathed outside the Hole. Life was complicated enough without grudge-holding cartel shooters being on the hunt for our one-woman accounting department. Let alone the Feds.

"She can never be that person again. More importantly, she didn't like being that person all that much. She felt very constrained, trapped in a life that made her unhappy. You knocked a door open and are giving her a chance to live her dreams. She's basically got immunity from Federal law to a certain point, she's got better physical security than the President, and she can go to work in her pajamas if she feels like it. Since you gave her all that, why wouldn't someone with her inclinations fall in love with you in the process?"

"Seems like I took away some of her choices. You know how I am on consent. You really have to want to give in before I want you giving in."

"I know, sir. But the erotic implications of Stockholm Syndrome aside, better to keep a happy employee. Plus, face it, she's hot as fuck. Saying no to that is not natural. Her technique needs work, since I don't think she has had a lot of practice and you can only get so much from watching porn no matter how good it is, but that's okay. I can work very closely with her."

"I need you to. And not just in that aspect either." Yes, Angel was giggling. "She's got a unique skill set when it comes to the finance end and the absolute lifeblood of the firm is the money. Her loyalty and reliability are more important than anything unless we find a qualified backup, and people with her brains and education still walking around with pirate souls do not grow on trees where we can get at them."

"Let alone with boob jobs like hers. Dear God, those were fun to play with."

"Again, for emphasis. She is really important. We gotta take care of her and at the same time make sure she doesn't screw us. No, I don't mean like that." Angel giggled again. "That's why I feel bad about this. I don't want her to think we fucked her just to buy her loyalty."

Angel looked thoughtful. "No, sir, the loyalty was pretty freely given."

***

We got home, let a very annoyed Odin out in the yard, cleaned the puddle he'd left on the back door mat, then I gave him extra ear rubs and treats to let him know he hadn't been completely abandoned. Soon he was asleep on the couch with his paws in the air. After some food, Angel and I staggered back to bed for a nap. Before I fell asleep, I texted Dave to get with Cash and throw some money in IT's pot with an effective date of tomorrow. His reply was a series of emojis. I don't speak emoji. Fucking kids.

Chapter 7

"Behind every great fortune, there is a crime."
~Honore de Balzac

It was a relatively warm and sunny afternoon for early November. Tennessee could be like that. A year ago we'd had snow flurries. The company Veterans' Day party was winding down a bit when I finally cornered Mikey. Normally, I would not have pressed the old guy. I would let him sip his beer in peace and let the day pass. Unfortunately I was in one of my moods, and I sensed time slipping away from me in a way I normally didn't. I refilled my cup at the keg tap and sat down across from him. Because of the pending holiday, the toast was simple. "Absent companions."

He looked up at me and raised his glass. An actual glass-glass. I think he'd brought it with him. We were pouring in plastic cups for the sake of easy cleanup. "Too many." We both drank.

I looked at his glass. "'You need a refill?"

"Nah, one big one an hour is my limit if I am gonna drive home after all this. Spent eighty years building my tolerance up."

"Fair." I drank deep. Like I said, we had good beer for this. We bought the kegs from a Nashville microbrewery I'd gotten a fondness for at the Renaissance Festival's beer pavilion back before the buyout when that still existed. Looking around, we were in a quiet corner and I could get some things off my chest without being overheard. "Mikey, I have to ask. How far back do you go with the company? There were a shitload of questions I was basically ordered not to ask with Big John in charge, or didn't know about, like where the fuck did all that money come from, but now that I am CEO, I don't want to be the keeper of a lost tradition I don't fully understand. There is a lot I don't know about how we got here. It's the shit you don't know that bites you in the ass."

Mikey sighed, looking into his beer. "Not supposed to be drinking this stuff anymore, but there comes a time in a man's life where listening to the doctors is more trouble than it's fucking worth." He took another long pull. "Not bad stuff, for American. Anyway. Full story, my piece of it. As you know, I retired with my thirty years back in '77. Campbell Barracks, Heidelberg, mostly, though we moved around some as they shuffled headquarters buildings or rotated people. A couple years I was at SACEUR in Belgium, or over in the Farben building in Frankfurt. Me, I went from one desk in USAREUR G-2 to another desk twenty feet away as a civil service employee. There was no six month layoff rule back then for retirees. I didn't even take terminal leave. Went home Friday in uniform after my retirement luncheon, came back Monday in civvies.

"That was the same year Carter made his old asshole buddy Stansfield Turner the director of the CIA. Cut eight hundred or so career Clandestine Service officers that October, which was a big piece of the Directorate of Operations. They called it Carter's Halloween Massacre later. Lost a shitload of No Official Cover assets too, informants, contract guys, you name it. Broke up networks going back to the OSS days, including some guys who had been around that long. Now the CIA's problems kinda weren't my problem, but one team, one fight, all that shit." He took another drink, visibly collecting his thoughts. I did the same, listening intently.

He finally went on. "So I get a call from a guy I knew who'd finished his twenty-plus and retired out of SF after Vietnam. One of Eric's SOG recon buddies, it turned out. I didn't know Eric that well back then. But I knew this guy from when he'd been down at Bad Tölz with the 10th Group, then he worked off the books for Ted Shackley when Shackley was at Langley. Wants to meet, so he flies over. For what international long distance phone calls cost back then, flying over was cheaper than calling, particularly if you are thumbing a ride with the Air Force for free."

Ted Shackley had been the CIA station chief in Miami during the peak of anti-Castro operations, then had worked the 'secret war' in northern Laos before going on to the Saigon station chief job at the height of Vietnam. He probably knew as much about 'modern' covert and clandestine irregular warfare as any one man in American history. His name popping up in this really got my attention. He had stayed busy through the 1980s when he finally died. His book is totally worth it, too.

"So we meet up in this little *Gasthaus* fifty klicks outside Heidelberg. Nice private lunch where we aren't going to run into anyone we know. He says there is some close-hold compartmented Agency stuff that was going to get lost with the Massacre. Everyone read in on it had then gotten canned because Turner's guys who came over from the Navy were being dicks. There was some HUMINT networking going into East Germany and the USSR, a ratline to smuggle things in and out through Hungary, and so on. He also had the grid coordinates for some really good caches that the SF guys were going to need in wartime for stay-behind operations in West Germany. A few of the caches were on the other side of the Iron Curtain and dated back to just after the war; maybe Gehlen's guys had been involved. Then there were sterile bank accounts, safe houses, you name it."

Finally I had a chance to comment without sounding like an idiot. "That's a lot of stuff to keep track of and even worse to lose. How did you do it?"

Mikey shook his head. "Officially we couldn't do it. That was the problem. Legally DOD couldn't be involved in any of this kind of shit when it was peacetime, but now the CIA didn't want to have to do the work anymore because it was all going to be SIGINT and satellites. No more messy and politically ugly HUMINT jobs, and just because Turner had promised Carter they were washing their hands of all of it. Jimmy was a good Georgia Christian who didn't like all that shit, even if he was also an Annapolis grad who learned to be a micromanaging asshole when he was working for Hyman Rickover in the nuke reactors office. But if we didn't grab the accounts and keep them active, the German banks would get suspicious, or the fucking Swiss would just keep it all the way they ripped off the Holocaust survivors and their next of kin for decades.

"Anyway, a guy he knew, I never caught his real name, was putting together a small little 'board of directors' to keep all this stuff together so nothing got lost or embezzled in the cutbacks and firings, and he wants me to be Their Guy In Heidelberg. Why not? I figured I would be in Germany 'til I retired again or died anyway, so I kept all the notes for him. I don't remember if they were calling it Athenaeum yet or not. SOCEUR didn't exist yet because this was ten years before SOCOM was formed, but there was a deputy G-3 who would handle special operations. Problem with serving officers though, those guys came and went every couple years as they moved around punching their tickets trying to make full bird or general. When the balloon went up, I figured I could pass it to whoever was in the right chair then, or to the 10th Group guys. Back then we thought it was gonna go hot in a year or two. Always in a year or two." He chuckled and drained his glass. "Like you said, we worked our way out of a job instead."

I set my beer down. "So the firm started as an off the books holding company and reference library of other people's go to war stashes. Wow. That is..."

Mikey nodded slowly. "Yeah, sorta. Pieces of it are way older though. Investment bankers and lawyers with proprietary clients was what they called it. And it's old money by our standards. You ever hear the conspiracy theory about how the OSS stole a bunch of Nazi and Japanese gold after War Twice was over and then used it to fund the Cold

War? Sold some of the gold to the Arabs for cash they didn't have to officially account for?"

It was an old story, though I'd never seen solid proof. "Yeah."

"Ain't a theory. Arabs definitely bought a bunch of stolen gold from the Germans during the war, since the Arabs were heavy on US dollars and British pounds from wartime oil sales. There was neutral flag shipping going in and out of Odessa and later Trieste heading for Suez and the Red Sea the whole time. And we sold a bunch after. Look, Arabs are traditional. They trust gold more than they trust somebody else's paper, no matter how much pretty ink is on it. Pretty sure we still have a slice of it too. Look for a line item in John's books about a gold holding account in Switzerland."

Okay, at this point I was mentally over my head in deep water. "You are fucking kidding me. Real Nazi gold, not History Channel bullshit?"

"You know the Army found plenty after V-E Day and every unit was collecting what they could find for 'safekeeping.' There was a Seventh Army headquarters stash, the Third Army headquarters stash... there are fine lines between legend, rumor, and 'no shit, it really happened.' A lot of the brass got a couple of small bars home in their luggage from some of the piles.

"But that's the stuff we're on record as finding. That's all pretty well documented."

"Then there's what didn't get found officially. Grow up, kid, you know damn well most official records are fabricated at a time like that. You're sitting in the wrong goddamn desk chair to be that trusting. Anyway, the German Foreign Ministry lost a few tons that no one ever found, or at least 'fessed up to finding. There is probably still some buried around Garmisch that people have missed, maybe in some of the lakes, or over in Poland if the Soviets didn't find it.... what the Soviets found and did with what they found are a whole other story nobody knows the ending to.

"Now of what the big units didn't get, OSS and CIC were looking for, then were fighting over it. That got worse as the OSS got shut down and merged into the Army's CIC. Then the CIC, the Counter-Intel Corps, which I was in, was fighting with the CID, the Criminal Investigation Division, because the CID wanted it for war crimes evidence while half the CIC was trying to keep it either for themselves or for funding off the books intelligence projects post-war as the peacetime budget cuts kicked in. The Israelis got a taste of the CIC's piece, too. The Zionist groups in Europe had a lot of good sources in the Soviet zone that us or Gehlen's guys needed the take from and they weren't giving the information away. All the good Jewish kids in the CIC worked those connections hard. And the Zionist groups were filling the piggy bank because they knew they had their own war coming over in British Palestine in '48 to fund."

"Web Griffin stole a bunch of those stories to make novels later."

"Kid, remember, Griffin was in the CIC at the time under his real name. We weren't in the same detachment, but I drank with him a bunch of times at the reunions. As for the stuff that came up missing, look up a story about Singleton's missing cubic yard of gold bars that got lost between Munich and Frankfurt. Guy officially logged finding it, was sending it to the collection point, and it vanished en route. You know how much a cubic yard of gold weighs? Fourteen thousand kilos, or thirty-two point five thousand pounds. You don't just put that in your pocket or your duffel bag and walk away with it."

I knew gold weighed a lot. Getting all that gold into one stolen German Army truck was considered one of the Hollywood bloopers in *Kelly's Heroes* for example. But never having had to deal with moving that amount of the metal, the math just never stuck in my head. I had way too much other shit on my mind on a regular basis. "Damn, sixteen tons of metal in a cubic yard."

"Six deuce and a half loads, well, maybe three or four loads on pavement. But you gotta work to lose six trucks' worth. And do the math on what it would be worth today."

"You got me curious." I whipped out my phone, looked up a number and did a little multiplication. "Just shy of nine hundred million, if you could find it."

"Oh, it's gone and spent at least three times over by now. It could be in my granddaughter's earrings. Plus we, meaning Army Intelligence, not our company, recovered a lot of gold coins that had gone into France or Norway or the Balkans to fund the wartime resistance groups. We bought the coins back cheap in the 1950s and 60s for greenback dollars, and it all ended up in old fifty cal' ammo cans stacked in one of the munitions bunkers at Hohenfels. There was more stored in England. Even half full they still were heavy as shit, so there was no sense sending it all back to the States if we'd need it all again in theater in a hurry. The Army was still setting wartime caches with it up through the early Eighties for possible resistance ops in case of the next war, working with the Brits and the Germans by sector. Guns too. Lots of buried guns out there still. So if you find some old gold coins, usually $20 St. Gaudens double eagles or some pre-1945 British gold sovereigns, that was leftover from that. I have a few of the double eagles and a couple sovereigns in my sock drawer. Gave a few to the grandkids, but there might still be a can or two in the arms room."

"I was gonna ask about that too. Why the arms room? It's a fucking museum. Hadn't been touched in years before I went in there. Same with the file cabinets on the fourth and fifth floors."

Mikey looked into his empty glass as if contemplating another beer. Wordlessly, I took his glass, walked to the keg tap, and refilled it before handing it back. After a sip, he continued. "First, I don't know about those damn file cabinets. I'm still blaming James or one of his Langley bosses, though he denies it. I don't think anyone's ever been through even half of them. My pet theory is there's CIA shit in there that Helms didn't want the Church Committee investigation finding in the 'Family Jewels.' You know that Congress subpoenaed and allegedly got all the DCI's personal files that had been handed down from director to director back to Donovan's wartime records. Helms claimed he gave it all up to Congress, but no fucking way."

Fuck, I hadn't thought of that. "You think?"

He shrugged. "Hiding off the books files in an even further off the books spot for his boss in exchange for a career fast track is something an ambitious prick like James would do. But... I really don't know and past a point I am too old to care. Just another problem you inherited, kid."

"And the arms room?"

Sipping, he waved dismissively. "Eh, you know how Eric likes his guns and some of the Vietnam shit was available from an Agency supply warehouse at the 'Midwest Depot' down in Texas at the time as systems changed over. I dunno if he bribed somebody or if he had the clearance to get in there and then just stole it. He spent more time sheep-dipped to the Agency than he likes to admit. Regardless, he told me he drove back here in the middle of the night around '87 with a big U-haul full and squirreled it all away downstairs."

That was a surprise. "Kinda shocked he got away with that."

Mikey took another pull at his beer. "Who knows how he did it. The guy can keep a secret, even from us. Besides, ever since the Fifties, everyone was still obsessed with nuclear war and fighting it out in the ruins. If you had a bunker like that, wouldn't you stock the shit out of it?"

There were a lot of holes in the stockpile then. "No medical, no bunks, no food, no toilet paper..." The toilet paper was no joke, especially after the scare during the COVID-19 thing. I had been working on that much.

He waved off my objection. "Going to WalMart for Chef Boyardee and shit paper ain't as much fun as scrounging guns, and we were always busy with something else. We only had a couple part time caretakers working on the Hole back then. We all lived somewhere else, so we kinda half-assed it. You have the time, so stock the place and do it right. It gives you something to do now. You have money, you have minions."

"With what money? So far, I have a list of accounts, many offshore, that may belong to the company and are ex-CIA, ex-Nazi, whatever, that we are holding in trust. Shouldn't mess with those. We have the company operating accounts we need to make payroll and keep the lights on. Can't fuck with those. We have bags of cash coming in on an irregular basis for the archive business. That goes to operations. Shit, some of it goes right back out as bags of cash. We have the contract money for the US government side we have to not do anything squirrely with-"

He shook his head. "Kid, some of that old WWII money might as well be company money now. Whoever it belonged to is dead and most anyone who knew we had it is dead. The only ones still living who really knew what was going on with most of it were me, Big John, and to a much lesser extent James. Now Big John's gone, I don't have much time left, and James quit. Eric knows some, but he gives even less of a shit about money than you do. I don't know if you have looked at all of it to let it sink in how well off we really are, relatively speaking. You have a lot of zeros and a couple commas to play with. Some of it is in John's paper notebooks because he didn't trust computers too far. Think of it as a trust fund. The important thing is that most of the money gets preserved and grown for good causes. I personally liked it when Big John started letting intel go to the African anti-poaching effort. I personally have no desire to go to Africa, but elephants look cute on TV."

I just shook my head as I kept sipping my beer. "Un-fucking believable."

Mikey shrugged. "It was the last wreckage of the post-WWII pirate days. When all this got set up, you had Jack Singlaub running around the world for another ten years after Carter had him relieved of command over Korea policy. He claimed he was working for the World Anti-Communist League that Chiang Kai-Shek founded out of Taiwan, but it was probably Agency shit too. Remember, he was OSS as a lieutenant in WWII then went into SF in the Fifties and years later he was the MACV-SOG chief in Vietnam. Of course that meant he had Agency ties all over Asia. He turns up in a lot of the 'Yamashita's Gold' stories out of the Philippines too."

General Singlaub was one of my serious personal heroes. I missed that old man.

"Then you had Mitch WerBell from the OSS down outside Atlanta making suppressors for Ingram's submachine guns while running a COIN school back in the woods. His old OSS boss Helliwell was running a bank in the Bahamas for the CIA and setting up shell companies in damn near every major city. Their OSS buddy Lucien Conein was claiming he was retired from the Agency, but he was still living in Saigon 'til the end which to my mind is suspicious as shit. Then you had BCCI, which was the Bank of Crooks and Criminals International and that was all dirty money, intel community money, or both. But all that goes away after Iran-Contra when everything ends up on CNN and all the WWII vet middle-management boys finally got too old to play the game anymore. Our books look like where a chunk of it got buried."

I nodded. It kinda made sense. "They had an unfair advantage, stacking three major wars like that close enough together that it made for a good career progression. Good looting, too."

"Goddamn WWII generation was better people, but also the unwritten rules allowed for off the books stuff back then without recriminations. That generation coming out of

Vietnam, most of them didn't last long. Shackley did good work, but finally quit. God, I knew Shackley when he was a lieutenant. Camper tried being the next WerBell down in Alabama, but he didn't last. Too many TV cameras on him and most of his students were flaky. Bo Gritz turned into a joke-"

Memories clicked. "Yeah, I heard that one from some old-time SF guys. He blew his one chance to maybe find any of the supposed MIAs in Laos. Spent two weeks drunk and whoring in Thailand before the mission while talking to every reporter in sight. Worst part was, um, another unit was planning something in Laos using Gritz and his bullshit as a distraction and he drew so much heat he blew their operation too." There were some old timers who had to be talked out of killing Gritz after that. It's a great story, if anyone ever tells all of it. Not my place to though, as I was in third grade when it went down. Sadly, I figure most of the guys who knew enough about what happened to actually write it are dead now.

Mikey sighed. "The Seventies were a bad time. We fucked over the Taiwanese over the permanent China seat on the UN Security Council and used that to get leverage with the ChiComs against the Soviets, and then the Shah of Iran went down. What we should have done is what the British did to the first Shah and replaced him with his son. Instead we got Khomeni because Carter assumed the Iranians wanted a democracy, but we didn't get that either. That set up Wilson and Secord, who were spending the start of the Eighties running guns and C-4 to Libya, trading for intel on the Iranians, while their buddy Terpil was doubling with the Cubans. Then we were selling weapons and weapons parts for stuff they already had from before the Revolution to the Iranians then using the money to fund the Contras in Nicaragua when the Democrats in Congress did Moscow a favor and cut the money, but then the Contras were trying to self-fund with cocaine sales at the same time."

Yes, for those of you who didn't know, that part of the story is completely true. The only question is how high up the American government involvement went.

Mikey continued. "And don't get me started on us and the British fucking over Rhodesia because they were suddenly all about supporting some Commies as long as they were black. Rather cheer for actual Communists than be called racist, I guess. Then with Iran, Charlie Beckwith retired after Eagle Claw aborted and then he died, Marcinko from the SEALs went to jail over some bullshit when they didn't need him for the second try at the Tehran Embassy..."

Damn. Heir to a tradition was right. Between late-night war stories and old issues of *Soldier of Fortune*, I knew every name. Had even met a few. "Yeah, now we have the third pirate era with the Middle East wars that haven't ended giving us a whole new crop of vets and crazies who grew up in it and can't stop riding the wave."

He nodded. "And what is the problem? Sorting the real players from the pretenders and the whackos. Who's connected, who's just bullshitting. Telling good opportunities from some asshole's delusions. Same problem we had then. It's way worse now with any jackass who ever drove a resupply truck for KBR claiming to be 'an in-country contractor' when it used to be you kinda had to earn a rep for being a mercenary, goddamn it. World sure as hell ain't what it used to be."

He had a point. I had gotten some weird late-night phone calls from guys over the years, everything from *I wanna get back in and finish my twenty years for the medical benefits* to *The CIA parked a UFO on the lawn and had the Grey Aliens put things in my butt*. Dudes seeming completely lucid but spinning complete schizo bullshit. They wanted to knock over foreign banks, or go kidnap some terrorist scumbag in a foreign country and ransom him to the CIA for the reward money. Guys with solid reputations who should have fucking known better had turned up arrested or dead from Haiti and

Venezuela all the way to Syria, Ukraine, or New Guinea. Varying combinations of psych meds, sleep meds, stupidity, and delusion. "Damn. So that's how you finally got from G-2 to here?"

"Well, I'd retired again in Germany, gotten divorced again too. This was '95 and even the grandkids were too old to be any fun by then, so I was waiting on some great-grands to play with. Then my favorite commissary was shut down in the base cuts and the hospital I was using for my various old man problems went too. Bill had died and Big John had taken over as chairman by then. Told him I was going to come back to the States for a while, so he said he needed me and my European connections here near the office. We already owned The Hole, but there wasn't as much to it. You have done more with it in five years than we did in twenty."

I was proud of that. "It's too cool a building to waste. And I like the privacy and thick walls."

He scoffed. "You're just a paranoid loon, junior division. No wonder Eric likes you so much. He always has though. Be happy about that. He's not easy to get along with sometimes either. He fools people with that smiling 'Nam hippie shit and his New Age shaman stuff. Man's a razor blade."

I was proud of that too and that shaded my next answer. "'Paranoia is simply knowing the truth.' It's a good line. I stole it from one of Larry Hama's *GI Joe* comic books when I was a kid, but it's a really good line. But lemme hit you with another stolen line. 'Fixed fortifications are a monument to the stupidity of man,' George Patton. The Hole is a really awesome facility by 1950s or 60s standards, but its main security is that almost nobody knows it's there. It can shrug off a casual air raid, or a near-miss nuke, but a determined heavy combat engineer unit with the right technical breach skills could crack it. Or a big enough bunker buster aimed the right way. If we piss Uncle Sam off to the point he wants in, it becomes a siege and it isn't manned or equipped for that. I may work on that part though."

"Why?"

I continued. "Because like you said, I am a paranoid loon, but that doesn't mean I'm wrong. Not counting Uncle Sam, some of the people we occasionally fuck around with are more than capable of eventually figuring out where we live. Extrapolate from that, better to have as much of a fortress as it can be."

Mikey nodded thoughtfully. "Fair. I may not live to see it, but it makes sense, I guess."

"Cool. I have another job for you too, if you don't mind."

He chuckled. "Depends what. I am not mopping this floor and I don't do dishes anymore."

Oh, I had nothing so easy planned. "Get with Accounting and start trying to help Cash figure what came from where. She's working off what we have of John's books, but after what you said I am pretty sure stuff is missing or redacted. I'm afraid some of the knowledge died with him."

Mikey nodded slowly. "Probably. God rest Big John's soul, he was a go-getter, but the man had very serious trust issues and was hard to get along with. Even for the rest of us."

I laughed a bit. "But the good news about that is you get to sit next to Cash a lot. If she decides she likes you, she might wear something low-cut and you'll at least get a free floor show out of the deal."

He chuckled. "Heh. The dick's too old to be good for more than drainage these days, but I ain't so far gone that I won't at least appreciate the view."

***

Before I forgot about my idea, I set up a rotation where one of the sections would send a minion to one of the many Costco or Sam's Club stores around Nashville once a week.

We never sent the same person in a row, and never hit the same store twice in a row. Toilet paper, canned food, feminine hygiene, fifty pound bags of rice or bulk pasta, you name it. Getting a batch of volunteers, we assembled the old steel shelving on the seventh floor in segments and started stocking and inventorying. We started refilling the water tanks, too. Once we filled 7, we'd go to 6 and then upward to the three quarters of the fifth floor that Cash wasn't using. Eight was staying empty, though we'd eventually have to set that up for emergency billeting which meant finding a few good plumbers we could trust. Yeah, the pipes were roughed in, but there wasn't even a working toilet down there.

So since the stuff took a while to go bad on the shelf, I figured we'd then use our employees as the rotation mechanism. If you worked for us, you could eat off the shelves at a discount, and then we'd use that income to stock fresh material. I even debated putting in some freezers down there. We certainly had the electric capability. Finally I found one of Kara's kids in Intel who liked to binge-watch reruns of *Doomsday Preppers* and got him to run it. I just didn't have the fucking time.

Chapter 8

" Money was never a big motivation for me, except as a way to keep score. The real excitement is playing the game. "
~Donald Trump, New York real estate guy. Heard he did other things later.

Over the next few weeks, Mikey would drive out to the Hole once or twice a week and sit with Cash. Lining up the location and size of the various accounts with its historical origin involved a certain amount of guesswork, but we had also gotten further into John's private records, a lot of which had been several someone elses' private records before him. That was just going by different handwriting and typewriter work, since we got back before the personal computer era by 1987. Some of this stuff was from the late 1940s.

For the next month or so, they would point at notebooks and computer screens and then argue, sometimes sharing lunch. Like I told Mikey, this indulged both my historical curiosity as to where the various accounts had come from and also gave me some idea of who the hell may come a-calling one day wanting what we were holding for them. Conversely, it let me know what was safe for us to use elsewhere. Except for occasionally dropping by at lunch, sometimes bringing Angel, I just left them to it while making sure the rest of the operation ran. There was just so much to fuckin' do.

But eventually, after one of his departures, I asked her how it was going. I'd had the barest idea they found a lot, but figured I better get some details.

She looked almost overwhelmed. "Holy shit. You know dirty money is kind of my kink, sir-"

"Well, one of them." I had found some others. A lot of others. Not that kind of story.

It was good to know she could still blush and she did, nearly purring. "Mmm, I concede the point, sir. But this is even hard for me to acknowledge. We have eight hundred kilos of what is probably Nazi gold in a bullion brokerage account in Switzerland, right about thirty-four mil at morning spot price. More cash banked with the same firm, just under ten million, then three other Swiss accounts in three other banks totaling nearly forty-five...so about ninety mil in Switzerland."

"Compared to some of the stolen fortunes parked there, we are pikers."

"It is still nice, when you figure Cokes cost a nickel when those accounts were set up."

"You *have* been hanging out with Mikey a lot," I chuckled.

She uncharacteristically smiled. "I like that old man. We know some of the same restaurants and such from the old neighborhood."

I rolled my eyes at that. "You didn't even live there two years and spent most of your waking hours across the river in a Lower Manhattan cubicle farm."

She hit me with a bit of a stare. "First, *sir*, I'm from the City, even if it was out in Queens. I lived there before I went to Princeton." Huh, I had forgotten that and probably shouldn't have. "Second, I rarely wax nostalgic for her old life before this, sir. Indulge me a bit. I miss the food some days. Neither she nor I will ever casually walk across the street into Grimaldi's Pizza again, or take a working lunch at Fraunces' Tavern or Luke's Lobster-"

Lobster did sound good, or some really good Italian. You could get decent Italian in Nashville with the various transplants, but some believe New York City has better Italian food than Italy. "Fine, we'll go on a culinary vacation for a week sometime. But finish this point you are trying to make first."

She clicked to another page of the spreadsheet. "Next, the big offshore accounts that might as well be Martian for all we can figure out. We have the account information, all in bullshit company names like Universal Exports which even I know is a James Bond joke, and the amounts, but no indication of where it came from originally. London, about five, split into several sub-accounts. British Channel Islands, Jersey to be exact, there's another five. Those I knew about. The rest is kind of a shock. Riyadh, Saudi Arabia, just under *fifteen* million. Kuwait City, twelve million. Panama City, there's *twenty* million. Twenty! All in respectable national-tier banks, nothing sleazy. Then there are at least seventy misplaced CIA-ish operational accounts from the 1960s and 1970s-"

Okay, she had my attention. "How do we know it was CIA?"

"Crappier banks, ones apparently known for crooked spy stuff. Handwritten notes in the margin say that Bahamas money, about ten million, went from Castle Bank and Trust, which Mikey says was CIA, to some outfit called Nugan Hand Bank, which is a stupid name, also in the Bahamas, which was supposedly also CIA, but that then went fast to Credit Suisse's branch in the Bahamas. Which is good, because Nugan Hand went under and some Internet research tells me Nugan ended up shot in the head."

"Oh, jeeez, I remember that story. Nugan was an Aussie, and allegedly shot himself in his car with a rifle that didn't have his fingerprints on it. Hand, who was American and an ex-Special Forces guy with Vietnam experience, then dropped out of sight, legally changed his name, whatever. Turned up in Idaho twenty years later running a knife company. It was a mess. You're right. I'd like to think the CIA had better banks than that." I'd also bought two of Hand's knives before I knew the story. It's a *real* small world sometimes.

She nodded. "They did, sir. One of my professors at Harvard swore Riggs in DC was their go-to and the Cold War cutbacks were the reason Riggs finally went under."

"Yeah, that and they finally got outed for the money laundering they did all those years for Augusto Pinochet in

Chile and some of the Iran-Contra stuff, so the Feds went after them hardcore when Clinton was President and the political winds shifted..." I looked past her at the updated spreadsheet, "which might be why we still have fifty grand left in PNC, who bought Riggs. Huh."

She scrolled further down. "But we also had money in the Australian and Singapore branches of Nugan Hand, which then got pulled and moved to another Swiss bank's Singapore branch... About five million more total there. So we have cash in Singapore. There is also a really old account at their Post Office Savings Bank too, that I had to look up. A quarter million."

I shrugged. "As fucked up as Singapore was after the war, that was real money back then. Maybe there was more and it got spent."

She shook her head. "Oh, there is more than that in Singapore. There is five hundred kilos of gold there that is either British stolen by the Japanese then reclaimed when Singapore was retaken, or Japanese that was stolen from somebody else. It's about twenty million worth. It's in a no-shit commercial depository vault and we get a storage bill."

"How can you tell it was Japanese?"

She looked back at me with almost loving disdain. "Where the hell else do people like us find five hundred kilos of gold in a former war zone?"

She had me there. "Good point. But as for the Swiss. The Swiss are assholes lately trying to clean up their act. The question is are the Singaporean and other overseas branches of Swiss banks going to be as unfriendly to people like us as their Swiss motherships are?"

She looked thoughtfully at the ceiling. "Good question. I haven't had an issue yet with our existing accounts in Switzerland itself so long as I keep the transactions small, maybe since those accounts are pretty old numbered accounts and their compliance folks aren't watching them the way they would a newer customer. But they still send me a bitchy email every quarter about their cooperation with 'international tax authorities' and would probably refuse to open more."

That surprised me. "They have your email address?"

"They have a burner e-mail address that John set up when they demanded customer contact information back in 2009. Now it forwards through a couple layers before I see it in my work box. Pretty sure they don't know who we really are."

Well, Big John was no fool either. "Huh. Okay."

She went on. "But these other European accounts that look like old CIA stuff are nickel and dime by comparison. Fifty of them. They are all scattered across Europe in small locally owned banks. Copenhagen. Stockholm. Mostly in western Germany though. Hamburg. Frankfurt. Fulda. Heidelberg. Bonn and a couple dozen more, lots of places ending in 'ich' or 'ach'. Munich, Ansbach, Weissach, whatever. All with number passwords in addition to account names. And the names are just stupid. They weren't even trying. Dwight Eisenhower? Werner von Braun? Charles Lindbergh?" She scrolled a dark red fingernail down the screen, then pulled up a dusty stenographer's notebook that had obviously had the original data and started flipping pages. "I don't recognize some of these others."

"I do. Albert Wedemeyer, one of the great unsung American heroes of WWII even if his biggest contribution was staff work before Pearl Harbor. Walter Schellenberg, *SS-Sicherheitdienst* intel officer. Otto Skorzeny, *Waffen SS* special ops guy. Kinda overrated, but still memorable. Kurt Steiner, fictional German paratrooper officer from a Jack Higgins novel. Ritter Neumann, Steiner's second in command from the same book. Larry Thorne, absolute SF legend. Guy was a Finnish officer who then fought on the German side before joining ours. Killed in Vietnam. He hated Communists that much. Wendell Fertig... he was the guy who ran the biggest behind the lines resistance operation in the Philippines." I thought about it for about half a second.

The pranksters had made it obvious with the names. "Those were meant to be seed accounts for resistance cells and stay-behind operations in case WWIII happened and the Soviets came west. This is what Mikey was talking about. Some of those are the reason the firm exists in the first place."

"What's a stay-behind operation?" Finally something she didn't know.

Fortunately I did. "You put a small group of specialists who speak the local language in civilian clothes and leave them behind as your main army retreats and the area gets overrun. Weapons guys, demolition specialists, communications and intel guys. NATO had several units that trained for that mission from '52 until the Berlin Wall came down in '89."

"I barely remember 9/11. The Cold War is something from another century."

I laughed. "It *was* another century, dear. I remember sitting in the dorm lobby with two dozen other ROTC kids watching the red flag come down at the Kremlin, drinking and crying."

"Because we won?"

That earned a derisive snort. "Fuck no, we were watching our career paths die live on CNN."

"Good Lord, and I thought I was amorally ambitious."

I shrugged. "At least we didn't have any more mushroom clouds. Even keeping them out of Germany could have gone nuclear-bad fast."

She looked at me in disbelief. "Doesn't that blow up the country you're trying to save?"

I shrugged. "Yeah, but a lot of the policy at the time was kind of nuts by our modern standards. That's one reason everyone was afraid the Russians would pull out tactical nukes in Ukraine when their steamroller ran out of steam. Anyway, before I get distracted again. The guys you leave, they have secure communications back to you, plus hidden stashes of supplies, weapons, and explosives. They have

---

access to operational funds like these bank accounts. They can buy food and pay bribes. Then you tell them wait a week, wait two weeks, wait for where they are hunkered down to become a secure rear area for the other team, then they start sending intel reports via radio and begin training resistance fighters. A month or two later? The twelve guys you left each trained a dozen, those guys trained guys, pretty soon you have a lot of guys behind enemy lines causing problems. Even if you lose half of them, you keep making more. Makes it easier when you finally send your real army back in. But since we never fought that war, the bank accounts are still sitting there."

She slowly nodded. "What do you want to do with those then?"

"How much is there?"

She flipped a couple pages, shaking her head. "I can't really tell from the notebooks. This isn't John's handwriting. Initial deposits look like fifty thousand per account, but depending on what they had for an interest rate, you leave that alone for forty or fifty years, you could have real money there."

Dismissing fifty grand as "not real money" did not come easily to me. There were plenty of years I'd made substantially less than that. Once I mentally moved on, I thought about it for a second. The individual accounts were hard to get at, relative to what else we were holding and their location was an insurance policy for the region's inevitable problems. Like she said, leave them alone and let the interest roll. Maybe at some point, I could send somebody with better German than mine to go check them in person. Somewhere in the files we probably had the grid coordinates to the weapons stashes too. *Hmmm. Money and guns.* You can accomplish a lot with that. *But leave it where it is until it's needed.* "You know, someday Europe will blow up again. Let's leave them right where they are until history turns a page."

She shrugged. "Your call, sir. And they are loose change compared to this next batch."

"What now? How do we top that?"

"This is like every 'the CIA sold cocaine' conspiracy theory ever came true, but there are a bunch of accounts in the Cayman Islands, the British Virgin Islands, St. Eut-something, that's Dutch, St. Barth's and a few other yacht towns. It could be stolen Colombian drug lord cash from the Pablo Escobar days, or missing Contra aid money, since Mikey says a lot of that was embezzled and never found, or they never found all of Manuel Noriega's cut from what drug money he stole, or..."

"The answer is he doesn't know for sure, so we're spitballing. How much?"

After a deep breath, she answered grimly. "Twenty accounts totalling over two hundred and seventy million."

At some point a real level of unreality had set in. "Well, at least we know we have the money to pay the electric bill."

"No kidding, except getting it here would raise every red flag there is in the system. All of this offshore money would. Now there's other weird things on the list. You explained the account at PNC, I guess, but some of these other accounts make no sense at all. Like why do we have a quarter million in the First National Bank of Wichita, Kansas? I barely know where Kansas is. It is one of those big square states out that way where nothing interesting ever happens and you can't get quality sushi. I can't find Wichita without a map."

This sparks joy. "Oooooh, leave that there."

She looked at me with disbelief. "What's 'ooooh' about a flat state full of wheat fields?"

"Wheat fields and airplane factories, dear. There are numerous builders, rebuilders and dealers of airplanes in Wichita. And if I ever get sick of paying that guitar player with the cowboy hat and the cocaine problem the marked-up hourly rental rate for that Lear of his, I might just go buy myself something for Christmas and use that for the down payment."

"Renting an airplane is cheaper over the long term than buying one, sir. We have had this discussion several times and the numbers don't price out at all."

"Until that plane is somewhere else when we need it, or we need something bigger, or...fuck it, we can let that one go for now. So what are we looking at?"

"It fluctuates based on gold, but we are well past four hundred million counting all the Caribbean accounts. Maybe more depending on what's really in those little numbered accounts in Europe. But... sir, we could probably just split it, go legit and retire...."

I shrugged. "And do what? Feds would steal way over half for taxes, assuming they didn't steal it all and claim it was criminal revenue. Particularly the Caribbean stuff."

She laughed. "Keep it offshore. Live a life of mindless hedonism in expensive hotels. Drink on beaches, watch sunsets over mountains. Watch the world burn."

I merely looked at her over the tops of my glasses, a disapproving expression I had stolen from my high school German teacher before Cash was even born.

"Yeah, yeah. I know, sir, in a year we'd all be broke, bored, and back doing the same stuff."

I thought of something else. "Now how have these accounts all stayed active all these years? I know eventually they are considered abandoned and some places the bank actually keeps the money."

"This was the clever bit. The accounts are clustered. Not in the same bank, that would be too obvious, but in cells or clusters of five accounts at five different banks. And I had nothing to do with this, by the way. This was going before I was born. Maybe before you were. The newest account of these was 1993 and John never said a word."

"Typical. And with... some of these accounts being 1940s or 50s, the idea predates any of us, or even him."

"Yeah. But whoever did it, it was genius. You have a string of accounts making unequally sized automatic payments to other accounts in their cell. A sends 2000 to B, which sends a thousand to C and D the next month, they each send a thousand to E the month after, which kicks back to A. Anyway, that and accruing interest kept the accounts technically active. And because there is a valid account holder to be contacted, none of it escheats to the bank or the government."

I derisively snorted. "Fuck the government, let them rob somebody else. Anyway, good work. Keep it up and make sure we don't lose anything."

She smiled wickedly. "Oh, you got it, sir. I can misuse some of this beautifully. I might even buy a little bank somewhere..."

Now that was an interesting idea... probably a lot of state and Federal regulatory paperwork we didn't want to fuck with though. "So are you guys close to done on this?"

She shrugged. "Probably. He said he was popping over to Germany for a couple weeks, some Army anniversary ceremony he wanted to attend while he still could."

I thought about it for a second, but there was no point in asking Cash more about it. "Okay, when he gets back we can have a nice lunch and compile a final list, maybe." On to the next project.

Chapter 9

"Death smiles at us all. All a man can do is smile back."
~Marcus Aurelius, Roman emperor

With my habitual sleep problems, I try to get as much rest as I can. Usually I prefer an extra half hour of trying to sleep instead of getting up in time for making and eating a decent breakfast. That's also the reason I can be the king of being five to ten minutes late in the morning. Sometimes I am just not moving well. I was just getting dressed and Angel was trying to hand me my customary microwave breakfast burrito. But then my work phone buzzed in my pocket, the guitar riff from Danny Elfman's "The Little Things" telling me without looking it was the main office line.

"Yeah?"

"Boss, it's Morgan. Just got it off the 911 scanners. Mikey dropped dead at the check-in desk at Nashville Airport. Heart attack."

Goddamn it. Not Mikey. Not yet. "Well, fuck. He wasn't getting any younger, but he looked okay."

"I am going to miss that old man."

"Won't we all, mostly. All right, get word to the rest of the wise men. I was already on the way in. Thanks" and thumbed the disconnect. No sense letting even an encrypted work call go on too long with idle chatter. Damn, this stung.

When we got to the office, I found Morgan and the first thing I told him to do was locate Mikey's work phone and his laptop. For an old guy, he was unusually adroit with electronic gadgetry and the last thing we wanted was any of his stuff in the wrong hands. Securing the data on it was incredibly important.

Angel and I went downstairs to Cash's office to give her the news, but she had already heard. Cash was usually a breed apart from the rest of the company, but she had spent possibly more one on one time with Mikey than anyone else except me or Kara, not counting Angel. She was sentimentally attached in her own way and therefore not taking it well. I'd never seen her cry like this, but then there'd never been a reason. I gave her a hug and told her I'd be back in a minute. Angel just stayed there and hugged her as I went back upstairs.

I retrieved a bottle of Edradour single malt Scotch (the smallest distillery in the Highlands, maybe all of Scotland!) and a couple glasses from a cabinet in my office. I was not normally a fan of hard alcohol in the office during duty hours, especially not at this hour of the morning, but sometimes it's medically necessary. Walking back into her office, I poured her a finger's worth, cut hers generously with some good bottled water from the fridge and slid the glass to her. I am not a fan of ice in Scotch. Getting it *too* cold ruins the flavors, I think.

She stared into it for a minute. "I knew he didn't have long, but I am going to miss him. He was too old to flirt with safely, well, safely for him, but he knew an awful lot about dirty money." That called for a toast, so we clinked glasses and sipped. She coughed and snatched the tea off her desk to chase it.

"Yeah, it takes some getting used to sometimes." I was pouring myself one as well. I spent a minute thinking about Bill, my dearly departed Dallas Arms Collectors' buddy who'd given me my first bottle of the stuff. I drank to his memory too as Cash still spluttered.

"Fucking hell, for a medicinal sip or two it's one thing, but how anyone can make a habit of that is beyond me."

"Eh, it's an acquired taste, sort of like your hibiscus martinis."

"Those are awesome. This is..." she sipped more delicately "okay, maybe not that bad. Still not something I'd actually order regularly."

I shrugged. "Sometimes it's just to knock the demons unconscious for a bit."

"At least you didn't try feeding me straight Jack Daniel's or something."

Hey, I like Jack. We were buddies for a long time. I think he sponsored my second senior year of college. Before I poured a second round, Morgan stuck his head in to let me know the 'electronics retrieval crew' was out the door and southbound.

***

The conference call was quick and somber since there wasn't much to say. I'd cut myself off after two Scotches, but was still slightly feeling them. We agreed to table the vacancy Mikey left for thirty days while we all thought about who could fill the slot.

While we talked, I had Dave sitting in with me. He was hanging out on the couch in silence and I also kept looking across my desk at that old judge's chair sitting empty. Damn, I missed the old guy. I would miss his wisdom as this went forward. The list of people I could turn to for counsel was getting shorter and shorter. When the call ended, I looked over at Dave. "You know I'm nominating you for the board when it comes up again in thirty days, right?"

He groaned in simulated agony. "Shit, do I really want that annoyance?"

I gestured with incoherent frustration. "If not you, then who? Kara would stab me in the neck if I tried drafting her to fill the space and no one else except maybe Jimmy really has the operational background. And we're already way too shorthanded on the Board. It's down to Eric, Little John, Joe, and me. That's not good enough. The Board is going to want somebody else with voting power around here to keep an eye on me. You had a very respectable military career, probably worthy of the word 'distinguished,' and have done well here. They'll trust you to stop me from fucking up."

He sighed. "Yeah, I reckon you have a point."

Chapter 10

"When I die, I hope my family doesn't sell my guns for what I told my wife I paid for them."
~Very old joke

It was finally Friday. I had just been home from The Hole for twenty minutes.. Cash had ridden back to the house with us. I told her she needed a night above ground and that Angel missed her. Well, considering as the two of them had gone downstairs for a nice break Wednesday, they were seeing more of each other than I was. I had been stuck in a Homeland Security conference call regarding a certain Iranian-backed Palestinian political party/ terrorist group that was trying to carefully infiltrate the cocaine and heroin business in the southern United States.

No, I am not joking. Ever been to a nice, independent convenience store and gas station run by a small squad of smiling, fit, military-aged Arab males, but way out in the country somewhere where *there are no other* Arabs? The merchandise always seems to include water pipes, cheap Chinese-made digital scales, and phantom-brand energy drinks with illegal drug imagery? You look on the counter, there are at least two varieties of 'smokeable incense,' 'bath salts,' or 'relaxation brownies?' Double points if they asked to buy your car for actual cash because a 'cousin' wanted one like it. You probably just saw a piece of what the DEA once investigated. They called it 'Operation Cassandra' before the case was shut down. It's a fascinating story if you look it up. Much like King Priam's daughter before the sack of Troy, no one listened to them. Anyway, what needed to be done at our end was done. It was up to the Federal government to fuck it up again.

I was hoping to start a weekend where nothing weird happened and nobody else died. A long soak in the hot tub while the girls lost their bikini tops sounded good. That would not count as weird to me, though your mileage may vary. But I didn't even have my boots off when my personal cell phone rang. The caller ID screen read that it was a Marburg, Germany number. Shit. Mikey's eldest daughter had flown over to handle arrangements. Mikey was going to be cremated, ashes divided between Brooklyn and Germany. I knew that much and that fit. I think the old man's soul was forever divided too. But I had met her once and she didn't like me at all. She was pushing seventy herself and had the typical lack of humor that usually affects Germans after a certain age. Time to exploit that again. Why? Because I am an asshole, that's why. I answered in the old German style. *"Ja, hier ist Professor...-"*

She cut that off fast. "You are not funny. None of *Vati's* associates ever were. Keeping an old man working well after he should have been long retired-"

"Uschi, you didn't want him over there full time and the old guy was happy to do what he did. He didn't play golf anymore and he didn't care for fishing. Now to what do I owe the pleasure?"

"First, I have half his ashes for you. As the one remaining American friend of his I know, I need you to take the ashes to Brooklyn for me. I must leave for home in the morning."

I was almost surprised at that. "It will be done. Next?"

"Second, there is a box of his things here at his apartment that you would be the best keeper for. Some books, military things..."

I checked my watch. "I can be there in an hour and a half."

"Excellent." She hung up without another word. I looked over at Angel and Cash. They were... entangled on the couch and already missing clothes. "I hate to interrupt. Feel like dinner out tonight, girls?"

***

Mikey had lived one floor up in an upscale condo off Charlotte Pike in Nashville. He had sold his house some years ago. He'd said he couldn't get the local kids to cut his grass for a reasonable price anymore and finally the overheated local real estate market made it worth way too much to keep. I left Angel and Cash in the car to play on their phones while I went in to deal with Uschi. It was liable to get unpleasant and Angel wasn't above playing 'See a bitch, smack a bitch' if she thought somebody had it coming.

I knocked and she let me in. Uschi was a pale blonde, with visible traces of having been hot forty years ago. She didn't look a thing like Mikey, so I figure she had taken after her long-gone mom. I wasn't even sure which one of Mikey's several exes had been her mother. The guy's personal life had made even mine look reasonable.

I will say this. The old guy had only been dead four days, but the place had been sterilized with the stereotypical Teutonic efficiency. Absolutely everything was gone and the carpeting had been steam cleaned already. I pointed toward the corner where Mikey had his TV and chair. "What happened to the big chair?"

"*Goot-vill* came for everything yesterday morning."

"Shit, I would have bought it from you. That was a nice chair." It really had been, the sort of big soft leather chair you normally only find in cigar bars anymore. I might have to call Goodwill and look for it if I remembered, but leather furniture and cats didn't mix well. Too bad. Maybe for the office, though. She shrugged wordlessly and walked into the kitchen. It was cleaned and polished to the point you could probably do heart surgery on the counter, the whole room just stinking with bleach fumes. There sat a medium-sized cardboard box, the sort printer paper came in.

"One of your men already came for his work phone and his laptop. As for this? I would have trashed all of it, but he left a note in his drawer that the big envelope, those dozen books and that fucking shiny pistol of his went to you. I hate that gun. Everywhere with it all those years. It should be thrown into the ocean or melted for scrap." That made me wonder. Desk pukes in intel were not and are not normally authorized 24/7 carry of sidearms, even in the Cold War days, and a hard-chromed full-house custom Colt was not exactly subtle. And how had he gotten away with it as a civilian in Germany? Well, it was just one more secret the old man had taken with him.

"Uschi, I know you don't like me or anyone else your father worked with. Just know that we loved that old man in our own way as much as you did-"

"Spare me your bullshit. You and your spy games and private wars for seventy years. You all love it. No peace or normal lives for you, no. You even made your secret boys' club so you could keep playing your silly games for yourselves and not your political masters."

There is not much leftism on the planet like German leftism. The aggressive children of the Third Reich they are not, not by a long shot, yet they have retained the rudeness and sense of superiority. It's disconcerting.

I lifted the lid and looked in the box. The holstered Swenson Colt, the urn of ashes, some old hardcover military history books and a fat manila envelope. Not much to show for ninety plus years. "You didn't trash his old *Wanderstock* walking stick, did you?"

She snorted. "Of course not, that is for my brother. He is still an avid hiker with his sons."

"Good. Nice to know something of his here is going to the family over there. He loved that damn stick even more than he did the pistol." There wasn't anything else to say, so I wished her a safe flight, she grumbled at me, and I got the hell out of there. There was a good family-owned Italian place up the street that I really liked and I didn't get into Nashville that often anymore during normal dinner hours.

Coming back downstairs toward my truck, there was a rather skeevy looking example of the Southern American

Meth Addict edging up on the passenger side door. I sighed and pulled my Glock out, hitting the switch for the Surefire light bolted on the frame. I'd spent the money for the latest "Turbo" version of the X300U pistol light, and the sudden burst of portable daylight sent him scurrying across the parking lot for the underbrush by the railroad tracks. No visible weapons, so no reason to shoot. We couldn't shoot the retreating unarmed in what was allegedly a real war, so you certainly can't in civilian life. Still, I just hate coming into town sometimes.

Angel snickered as I opened my door and sat down, tucking her .45 away in her purse. "Babe, I had the situation well in hand."

"Of course you did, dear." Damn, I love her.

I had Angel put Mikey's Colt in her purse. Its squared off trigger guard, a Swenson hallmark, didn't work with the holster I was wearing and I wasn't dressed to wear a shoulder holster discreetly. His wouldn't have fit me anyway, as I was twice his size. But I certainly wasn't going to leave my new heirloom pistol in the truck by itself as we went in to dinner.

Discretion was important. Nashville was less gunslinger than the rest of the state. Over the last twenty years its downtown had become to Tennessee what Austin was to Texas, attracting Democrat-leaning hipster transplants looking for music careers, tech startups, or just slumming around the Vanderbilt or Belmont campuses for the parties and girls. As we forked down their best-in-town chicken parmesan in the dimly lit dining room, we talked about things other than work, work people, or world events. Angel was trying to talk Cash into some nightclubbing sometime, while Cash was preoccupied feeling up Angel under the table. And yes, I was in on the fun too.

We eventually went back to my house for the night. Saturday we just said the hell with it and went out to enjoy ourselves like normal people for a change. You can't live 365 days a year like the world is ending tomorrow. That corrodes the soul after a while, even for a weirdo like me. It was a nice day, so we set Odin up with a little campsite on the back deck. After a morning flying kites at Centennial Park and an afternoon at the zoo, we stumbled home from our favorite small, quiet club around three in the morning, then all slept till nearly eleven.

It was only after I'd woken up and cooked everyone a nice Southern big brunch where four basic food groups (grease, carbohydrates, salt, and caffeine) were all involved and the dishes were handled that I finally opened Mikey's envelope. Angel looked over my shoulder while sharing the leftover bacon with Odin.

There were a couple unit crests I recognized as the long gone VII Corps headquarters, another pair each from Seventh Army HQ and SACEUR, a full set of his ribbons still clipped together, a couple unit presentation coins, and a loose Class A jacket button. It was the sort of thing any longtime soldier ends up with. After a while you don't need it but you never want to trash it. In the back of one of my closets, I still had my meticulously organized fishing tackle box of spare dress uniform parts. Why? No idea. I'd been off active duty well over a decade. Unless I felt the urge to pull one out for another funeral, the next time I would probably wear a correct uniform would be when they buried me in one of them instead.

There was a regular white envelope, taped shut and with my real name written on it. I popped my knife and slit it open. Yeah. It was a farewell note, dated back in October, right after Big John had died.

"Hey, kid.

Like I said, I'll probably be the next to go at my age, so I just wanted to leave a couple final words on my way out. No big rah-rah motivational shit. You don't need that. You know what you're doing and you have a good, solid crew of your own generation you're leading into battle now. And yeah, it's battle. I hope I have time to explain it all to you before I go. If I don't and I kick off unexpectedly; shit, who am I kidding; it's never unexpected at my age. Still, if I go without telling you everything, you're a smart guy with smart people. You'll be okay. Sometimes the dead have to keep their secrets to themselves.

Raise a glass,
Your old pal Mikey

Fucking great. Thanks, Mikey. Now I get to freak out over the idea you didn't tell me everything and something is going to sneak up behind me and whack me over the head. Paranoia is a real bitch to live with sometimes. I'd had a lot of practice but sometimes still didn't have the hang of it.

I found an empty spot on one of my curio cabinet shelves in the hallway and made a space next to my long-dead great-uncle's pilot wings. I then emailed Tucker Gun Leather out in Texas where I got most of my dress holsters. I told him I needed modified inside and outside the waistband holsters that would accommodate the boxy squared trigger guard of Mikey's old Swenson Colt. I figured I could wear it as a Friday gun occasionally. As a general rule I tried to avoid carrying anything unique or sentimental that I then might have to shoot somebody with. I didn't want to throw anything irreplaceable in a deep lake or have it end up in a police evidence locker, but sometimes you have to dress to impress and wear something nice.

***

Sometimes lightning strikes twice.

John's daughter called a week after that, asking me if I could stop by his old place. I had been there a few times despite our general lack of closeness or sometimes even civility. He had a nice little house in a well-shaded neighborhood over by Sylvan Park. Nice little Craftsman-style bungalows on tiny lots. You fart too loud, the neighbors will hear it. Worse, most of his neighbors were wealthy white liberals who taught at Vanderbilt and voted Democrat. Never could figure out why the hell he lived there, since he could afford way nicer and the people weren't his type, but I never bothered to ask. Knowing Big John, he would have just told me to shut the fuck up and not ask pointless questions.

John's daughter was typical for the neighborhood, what Angel would call a Basic White Bitch Soccer Mom. Tries to look ten years younger, a 'Can I speak to your manager?' haircut, an expensive SUV to haul the kids around to soccer or swim practice, and a Starbucks habit. Her name really was Karen, which made it funnier. That aside, I really didn't know her well and so didn't have the great history of personal turbulence I had with Uschi. Even at the end, John had always kept a lot of things to himself despite the long work hours together.

Angel was more spun up on the workload by now, so I left her in my office playing adjutant and just drove down myself after lunch. I figured it wouldn't take long. She could keep an eye on things while I was gone, while Dave was slowly moving out of his alcove in Intel and into John's vacant office next door.

Entering, the house hadn't been sterilized with the ruthlessness Uschi had applied to Mikey's place despite John having been dead much longer. I was half-tempted to cause trouble by suggesting Uschi help, but I doubted she'd ever leave Germany for the States again. Still, the house was slowly emptying out. Half the furniture was gone and that "comfortably lived-in" feeling had faded. Now it just felt abandoned as she led me into the living room. There was a rifle case on the coffee table, the old brown plastic sort Sears or Montgomery Ward once had in the sporting goods department with a molded scene of ducks and deer on the side. She pointed at it like it was a snake. "If I could ask you the favor of getting rid of that for me, I would appreciate it."

"Well, let's see what we have."

"The last of his collection. He sold all the legitimate sporting guns a few years ago. He only kept the pistols, which annoyed me. Handguns are more dangerous according to the statistics."

It seemed a poor time to tell her I had bought two of the hunting rifles, a pre-WWII Griffin and Howe sporter built on a Rock Island-made '03 Springfield action in .30-'06 and a British surplus Pattern '14 Enfield turned into an express-sighted dangerous game rifle in .375 Holland and Holland. Fuck me if I knew why I bought the H&H, I had no plans to go hunt Africa with it. Now that I had the money, I didn't have the time. I couldn't imagine John ever taking enough time off to have done so either. The workmanship was exquisite though and the price was right for both. 'Sure, boss, keep half my paycheck next month...'

But as for pistols, I knew when he bothered at all, the grumpy SOB carried an old custom Colt Commander he never let me get a good look at. He'd mentioned a bullseye competition habit years ago, so I wondered what else was filling up the rifle case. I clicked the latches, opened the lid and... not going to lie, nearly beshat myself as I looked down a row of various vintage 1911s.

The first was his carry piece, still laying atop its holster. Now that I could see it, I recognized it as a polished blue pre-Series 70 Colt Commander. It had the crown-logo stamp of the old King's Gun Works in Los Angeles. Possibly old enough to have been done by 'Al' Capone himself. Every bit of two grand. Maybe three.

A stainless steel Detonics Combat Master subcompact .45. Even smaller than the Colt Officer's Model, it was the classic Eighties backup gun for those with a certain amount of taste and a willingness to spend the money. Thousand bucks, easy, assuming it was one of the ones that actually went bang when it was supposed to. Some of them were cranky.

A somewhat plain Colt with what looked like real ivory grips and their old style mirror-polished dark bluing... yeah, a prewar .38 Super. There's five grand right there. Maybe eight if that isn't a refinish and the ivory is genuine.

A full size Colt-made .45 heavy slide, long slide bullseye gun from Clark Custom. It was an old one, with the hand-engraved Shreveport, Louisiana address and their characteristic 'tiger tooth' stippling. Hadn't seen one in a while. Two grand at least. Clark still had a waiting list for them, even though bullseye was an old man's game.

A well-used 1960s US Air Force National Match pistol on a GI Ithaca frame, what their pistol team gunsmiths out of Lackland AFB called their Premium Grade. It did have AFPG stamps in several spots. Goddamn. At least another three to five depending who bit on it at auction. And I'd sell it over my dead body. John owed me this one for all the ruined weekends and the verbal abuse.

A Colt Series 70, worked over into a 'Pachmayr Combat Special' back when Southern California was still the custom gunsmithing capital of America. They'd given us King's, Swenson, Mac's .45 Shop, Pachmayr, and the Big Bear Leatherslap Matches with Cooper, Reed, and Weaver where the "modern technique of the pistol" was born. Damn. Holy shit, it was a pretty one with the first pattern slide markings. Hadn't seen one outside Volume 2 of *The Vickers Guide To...* in thirty years. Another three to five easy. It was a rarity that would have Boomers or GenXers running up their credit cards at an auction.

Finally, a funky stainless steel... a Charlie Kelsey-made Devel Gammon in .38 Super. Oh my God. A Grail gun for me. Wayne Novak kept buying up every Devel that hit the market, so it was hard to price them. Didn't care. I'd wanted one since high school.

I was kinda speechless. This was probably close to thirty thousand dollars worth of vintage pistols, easy. I took a deep breath as my morals woke up and kicked in. "Some of these guns ought to stay with the family. I see some fairly valuable things here I know he had for years." Actually I didn't know that for sure, but it was a pretty reasonable inference.

She looked at the floor. "No, none of us are shooters and I don't feel comfortable having the handguns around. I don't want money, I just want them gone. I just know Daddy was deep into things I don't approve of and I want to get my children out from under that sort of legacy."

Holy shit, what was it with these guys having leftist daughters? I have been into the concept of inherited heirloom weaponry since I saw the original *Star Wars* in the theater when I was four years old. 'Your father's lightsaber' kind of moments are embedded in the DNA of the human race's hereditary warrior class. This was fucking bullshit, Karen. I made a mental promise that if her kids came looking for one of Grandpa's .45s one day, they would get one.

Not the Devel though. Fuck me, that was a forty year bucket list gun for me.

"I will make sure they are safely taken care of."

She nodded. "It's going to be a long waiting list to put him in Arlington with Mom and my brother, but when we get a date for it, I will let you know."

I bit back my surprise. I didn't know she'd had a brother, let alone had buried one. More things Big John had kept to himself. "Thank you. He wasn't always easy to work for, but he got me off to a great start."

"I still don't approve of a lot of it. I am sure too much of it is illegal war crimes."

Like there is such a thing as a legal war crime. Damn, girl, lay off the *Jacobin* or the *Mother Jones*. "We are actually supporting anti-poaching efforts in Africa and fighting human traffickers in Eastern Europe. It isn't what you think."

"Yeah, yeah. Daddy used to say that he was making the world a better place, then I found out he did targeting reports for nuclear missiles."

"Before my time. I was in grade school during the late Seventies."

"Don't waste your life like he did."

Shit. The time I wasn't spending working was wasted. The map of the world was a big stovetop with a dozen pots boiling over at any given moment. You scrape away the cover stories and propaganda that most people get by on for their own happiness, then get into the layers of buried realities and the world is a truly terrifying place.

Around '04, after Operation Iraqi Freedom, the first one, you know, before we started having to number them, I thought I was finally salty. I told Mom, "If you knew the things I knew, you wouldn't sleep well either." The joke was on me. Compared to now, I knew very little at that point. Every day, I learn several more things that I wish I didn't. If ignorance is bliss, I am one of the unhappiest people on the planet. With that cheerful thought in mind, I closed the case, said my goodbyes and headed back to the office.

That evening, Angel announced she was cooking. While she started in the kitchen, I carried the case of pistols into my 'war room' library. I set it down and opened the safe. I realized there was another layer of pistols below the foam. Huh, I thought it had been heavy.

An Alton Dinan .45 hardball gun, made out of a GI surplus frame, an actual Colt by the markings, and a postwar Colt hardened match slide. The front sight blade had his characteristic two holes drilled through it and his stamp was on the left side of the frame.

A rather rare, "United States Property" marked Smith and Wesson 41 target pistol, the .22 that murdered the Colt Woodsman in match competition so badly that Colt stopped making them. Turning it over, it also had a DINAN stamp on the frame.

Two more Clark Custom 1911s, both 5 inchers, one each in .45 and .38 Super. The .45 was a newer one than the .38; it was marked Keithville, Louisiana so it was made after their move from Shreveport. The post 1990s guns were Princeton, Louisiana. Well, the old guy had been at Barksdale Air Force Base a couple times, so he did have his Louisiana connections.

And last but not least, in the One Of These Things Is Not Like The Others file, there was a worn and battered USAF marked Smith and Wesson Model 15 'Combat Masterpiece' revolver in .38 Special still in its shoulder holster. It was a rather unremarkable standard issue piece from the 1950s and some Air Force units still used them through Desert Storm. Nothing fancy, but it would still look great shelved next to my rather similar Smith 'Victory Model' with the WWII Navy markings. I was sure there was a story behind it. Unfortunately Big John had taken that story to the grave with him the way he'd taken so much else. *The dead do keep their secrets.*

Angel walked in while they were laid out and I was writing down serial numbers. She picked up the Detonics Combat Master, dropped the mag, expertly locked the slide to the rear to clear it and then shivered a little as she fondled it and dry-fired it. "Oh, baby, I love it. Thank you!"

I thought about it for a second. The chopped grip length wasn't a problem for her the way it was for me with my gorilla-sized hands. "We'll take it out back and make sure it's one of the ones that actually works properly before I trust it with you, but if you like it, it's definitely your style. Want another full-size to go with it?" I pointed at the Dinan and the Clarks.

She pursed her lips, thinking about it. "Maybe for special occasions, sir. I don't want to have to completely re-dress around concealing a five inch 1911, and I don't need another big purse gun since I already have one in there. This is just my size, really. Besides, we share the safe and just about everything in it anyway." I shrugged, locked the safe and followed her back into the kitchen to see if I could help out with dinner. Sometimes you just have to try to have something resembling a normal home life if you want to stay sane. Sometimes all you can do is fake it.

Chapter 11

"You can call me, any, any time, call me..."
~Debbie Harry of Blondie

Time for another history lesson.

A 'hello number' was a piece of tradecraft from well before the cell phone era. An unlisted phone number would take messages from anybody for anybody, no questions asked. Then, anybody could call to check their messages. Snitches, spies, homicide detectives, cheating husbands. It wasn't a one way intel collection asset so much as a two way tool for HUMINT folks. Sometimes the phone's operator knew to forward some messages. That tends to be the intel agency versions. The DNI still had the term in the book if you Google it:

Tradecraft jargon for a cutout telephone where the speaker does not identify himself or his/her location. This procedure is used by proprietaries, devised facilities or cover offices of clandestine intelligence agencies for certain types of contacts with agents or affiliated personnel, usually in an emergency and only information given by the caller over the phone is a codeword or danger signal to be relayed to the appropriate case officer for immediate call-back or other pre-arranged action.

~ Office of the Director of National Intelligence, National Counterintelligence and Security Center Glossary

Otherwise, it was just a place for Fred to call and ask if he had a message. The phone host didn't know who Fred was, or who Wilma who left the message had been. Nowadays with Caller ID and burner cell phones, it is obsolete tech. But some professionals on either side of the law are enlightened enough to know walking around with even a dumb-type cell phone was volunteering to carry a combination wiretap, surveillance microphone and tracking device, so with that in mind there were still a few out there. Baltimore PD Homicide Division had one I used to freeload off of in college when I didn't want one of several out-of-town girlfriends calling Mom and Dad's house looking for me, but they either changed the number or got rid of it. NYPD still had theirs, the tradition-minded bastards that they were. Chicago's DEA office had one and various intelligence agencies had a few both national and international.

So did we.

Hang on. Let me back this up. Every one of our numbers, and we had a couple dozen of varying types, were answered with "Hello?" except for the one listed in the Nashville phone book for Archive Associates, LLC. There was some method to this madness. If it was the government calling Athenaeum about contract work, they fucking know who they called. Answering with the last four in the nature of military numbers that didn't like admitting who they were (call the charge of quarters desk at a Ranger battalion barracks sometime) was telling a wrong number or a telemarketer we were somebody alive and interesting. We got too many computerized spam calls as it was on the conventional landlines. No, I don't want an extended car warranty or to refinance the student loan debt I never had. Answering by name? Fuck. No.

Now all that said, we did have one phone that rang in the intel shop with a sign over it that said "HELLO LINE, TAKE A MESSAGE." Sometimes we forwarded messages, sometimes for a fee. Sometimes we just wanted to see who used it. It tended to ring at odd hours, so the second shift intel staff got some late night entertainment out of it. We'd also spread it around with bail bondsmen, bartenders, bookies, tame detectives, strippers and so on, just to chum the waters and see what floated up.

Lately we had been getting a lot of Hispanic-accented calls. "Is Pedro there?" "Is Miguel there?" But no one wanted to leave a message when it was offered. Still, when Intel let me know this, I was curious. Since we had call-tracing abilities equal to No Such Agency... well, actually we were using their call tracing abilities and just not telling them. Yeah, it's a long story, but we were getting hits to cell phones down in Tamaulipas, Mexico, specifically around Ciudad Victoria. That was a nice, hot cartel war zone a few hours south of Brownsville, Texas and a bit inland. That was interesting. I had one really, really good Spanish speaker who could pass for a native of three different regions of Mexico, and I idly wondered how best to get him in a position to answer. And we also put computerized taps in on every one of those South of the Border cell phones, just to see what happened.

***

A couple months passed in those post-Christmas doldrums. The winter season seemed to drag onward, so much as you ever get a solid, lasting winter in Tennessee. You want snow on the ground for seven months straight? Move to Vermont or Minnesota or someplace. Down here, between November and April, if you don't like the weather, just wait a day or three. It'll probably change by thirty degrees up or down and possibly rain a lot. That corrodes the spirit.

The problem for me is that seasonal cold and damp gets into my bruised bones and bad joints. It doesn't help my Iraq cough either. Every passing year makes it worse, which of course fuels my not so secret anxieties that the profession took years off my life and I am going to die young-ish with a lot of unfinished projects. I was spending a lot of my home time in the hot tub and Angel had moved her portable massage table into the first floor storage room near my office. Frequently, she had to work on me in there just to get me through the day. Sometimes I was so bad off that I had to use Cash's hot tub.

Still, some things got done. In a conference call, Dave was formally voted onto the board. Athenaeum then picked up a three year renewal on the 'red team' contract for one of the intel agencies, which was guaranteed and legitimate income. Work just kept going.

Other things were somewhere between legitimate housekeeping and just me fucking off. I called Superior Safes out in Utah and got a third one of theirs, this one for my office. I drilled into the concrete and expoxyed bolt studs into the holes to secure it to the floor. I then half-stocked it with interesting goodies from the sixth floor arms room and my two safes at home for decoration and conversation pieces. I started with one Thompson, a Winchester trench gun and a couple of the more original GI 1911s from downstairs. I then brought in a few of the custom and match .45s from both John's estate and my existing collection, the .375 H&H Griffin and Howe Enfield, then one of my several Garands, my M24 sniper rifle, a really nice Persian-marked Mauser... you know, that sort of thing. Also half a dozen swords, one reproduction Norse axe, one tomahawk, two spears... okay, okay, I may have a small hoarding problem when it comes to weapons. Then once I did it, Dave ordered his own safe for his office next door. His wife frowned on some of his collection's excesses and so he needed a safe place outside the house to hide shit.

We were into late February when one of the baited hooks hit. I was coming out of the first floor latrine when Morgan grabbed me in the hallway. He was IT, not Intel, but fuck it, you know by now that shit overlaps, particularly with the number of our subcontractors (read that as 'paid snitches and insane minions') he handled. "Boss, we may have a live target. SIGINT is giving rumors of a major drug and cash exchange and collection point in rural Mississippi."

You already know that I consider it like finding a bag of free cash somewhere. This was just going to take a bit more work. Wheels were spinning in my head already. Be an interesting planning exercise even if it didn't work out. Even those have organizational training value for the staff.

"You, me, my office, now." Since Morgan wasn't on Athenaeum's books with a security clearance, not with his criminal record, legally we couldn't use the third floor intel conference room since that was "officially cleared" space per the regulations. Too many innocent and law-abiding ears on the third floor anyway.

Dave wasn't next door, so I buzzed down to Intel and told them to kick his ass upstairs. Having Kara would have been nice too, but it was a day off for her. Dave was in my office two minutes later, followed by Angel. She'd been up the hall in the break room working on lunch. We quickly recapped everything for those two. Strictly speaking, was it Angel's lane to know this yet? No. But odds are I would vent about it in her direction anyway. Better to bring her in now.

First question was for Morgan. "So what kind of SIGINT?"

"You remember those calls the hello number was getting from C-Victoria?"

"Yeah. Still wondering how they got our number."

"Dude, the entire Internet probably has that number. It gets at least two fucked up calls a night from the 4chan kids. Somebody thought it was a Gamestop and was asking for *Battletoads*. You know how old that meme is."

Bless me, Father, for I have sinned.... "I should have known. So the taps we put on..."

"Those phones are talking to Texas phones that are talking to Mississippi phones. Or, more accurately, to Texas phones that are pinging on various towers along the Interstates in central Mississippi."

Dave looked slightly bemused. "Why the fuck in Mississippi?"

I took this part. "Any of you been to Mississippi?" They shook their heads. "Remember, I used to live there. Way too much of that state is fuck-all nothing square miles of pinewoods or soybean fields. Cotton's not that big anymore since the American textile industry died out. Egypt and India do it cheaper. Pinewood is a cash crop for lumber and there's a huge export market for soybeans, so farmers grow what sells. There's several major Interstate junctions, plus it's on a cultural boundary. Black gangs from Chicago or Detroit still have family there-"

"Wait, what?" Everyone was looking at me funny.

"Okay, think back to high school or college, specifically US History 102, more specifically the Great Migration. After the Civil War and Emancipation, then when the boll weevil destroyed the cotton economy and then again during the Great Depression going into the WWII industrial boom, Southern blacks moved north and west looking for work. Southern whites as well, but for WWII a lot of them were going in the military since this was before the 1948 desegregation. Blacks were more available in the Stateside labor pool. Before World War II, LA was more Mexican than it was black. Wartime employment requirements changed that and it's only swinging back the other way now as Mexican gangs are ethnically cleansing some neighborhoods and blacks are heading out to the suburbs or back to cheaper states."

I was in full blown historical lecture mode. This had been a couple weeks' worth in History 305 long ago in Mississippi. "Anyway, the point is, younger and mobile black men and women were moving out of the South. Many of them stayed gone, but family is important. So after those industries re-segregated after the war, collapsed, offshored, whatever, and the younger males of the families couldn't find paying work and went into freelance pharmaceutical distribution by the 1970s and 80s, they still had family ties. A cousin gets in trouble, he skips town and then hides with

Grandma or Great Aunt Whoever back down south. It works in reverse too. Half the guys I had warrants for when I was working bail bonds fled north up I-55 to get lost in St. Louis or Chicago with their cousins. The bonds were too small to be worth the gas and time of going to try getting them back. Losing that money when they ran was the price of doing business."

Okay, I'd rattled on long enough. "All right, I digressed again. The point is, it's familiar ground for them. There's a lot of quiet little rural counties with more trees than people. The Interstates running through means a lot of traffic passes, but very little stops and looks around outside of the few developed spots around the off-ramps. It's also not too far north for the Mexican cartels, who are smart enough to travel incognito and blend in with the Mexican migrant farm labor. All that deserted real estate and small town truck stop infrastructure means no one bats an eye if a trailer gets dropped, sits a day and gets picked up again. They drive down from St. Louis or Chicago to see the cousins and sometimes the cousins are on the payroll receiving and storing shipments from further south. The same goes for meth labs, weed growing operations, or anything else needing privacy. Unless you attract attention, you won't get any attention."

Morgan shrugged. "All the big meth labs are down in Mexico anyway. That industrial process shit, not cooking Sudafed in trailer parks a few grams at a time. Those dudes are making by the ton and transporting it like they do coke."

"Yeah, I remember reading something about that. Buying their precursor chemicals from the Chinese and bringing them in on the Pacific coast-"

Dave pretty much cut to the chase before we instead got bogged down in the mechanics of Mexican meth production. "Okay, so we are interested in digging further on this?"

"Fuck yes. That is a top tier collection target. Don't lose focus on any of the critical shit, I don't want to lose a nuke somewhere because we were preoccupied eyeballing this, but find out everything you can on it. Whose it is, how much is there. And be really fucking careful not to get *caught* eyeballing this. Don't want to spook them."

Morgan merely nodded. "Can do."

Angel looked at me with her *'I'm going to take care of you whether you want it or not'* look. She never took no for an answer. "Lunch will be ready in about ten minutes, sir."

I laughed inwardly at the tone on the 'sir'. Smartass. "Thanks, dear. Will be down in a couple minutes."

Dave wandered past the break room with me. Angel had done a quick batch of Nathan's hot dogs. You know, eat like a New Yorker without being one. Cash had come upstairs to eat as well. *Woman does not live on fruit smoothies and veggie chips alone.* She was glued to something going on her laptop though; she barely blew a kiss at me when I said hello. I had ADHD, she had hyperfocus. *Maybe if we had kids they'd have a happy balance and not be miserably insane like we both were.*

Jesus Christ, where did that thought come from?

Anyway, it might have just been nerves, but I ate about twice as much as I intended. Four hot dogs with horseradish mustard and the potato salad was pretty good for store-bought. Was it the healthiest lunch? No, but sometimes you need some quick carbs and fat to get you through the day. Dave grabbed a plate too. I hugged Angel to thank her, hugged Cash too, but then I had to get back to working. My brain was moving at five hundred miles an hour.

"Dave, I need your counsel, brother. Come take a walk." We went down to the sixth floor, opened up the arms room and sat there with the smells of steel and oil in our nostrils. At first, we didn't say much as we poked at the guns. Dave took ten minutes reminiscing about dirtying up piles of Q-tips and torn-up T-shirts trying to get our old M16A2s clean enough for arms room turn-in so we would actually be allowed to eat that night. Damn, Fort Benning had been most of a lifetime ago. Finally I got to the point. "That could be one big damn pile of dirty money sitting down there. The civilized thing to do is not let them have it."

"So what do we do about it? We gonna tip off the DEA? Maybe the Mississippi cops?"

I leaned back and looked at the ceiling. "There's always Door Number Three. We have more than sufficient skills and resources to grab it ourselves."

Dave, one of the oldest friends I had left that was still willing to talk to me, gave me a *'Motherfucker, you're back on your bullshit'* look. "Armed robbery of drug dealers? Why?"

The idea was emerging out of the fog, so I shared. "Because someday, maybe soon, the government contracts are going to end, the overt income will stop and all this goes away slowly if we have to live on the under the table commercial income alone. In addition to liking what we do and wanting it to continue, we as a group have mouths to feed and kids to send to college and I would rather do that than let El Chapo get another solid gold toilet or let the Feds grab it."

Dave sighed. "I think the gold toilet was Saddam Hussein. And Chapo Guzman is busy doing multiple life sentences without parole in the Colorado supermax."

I sighed. "I know that, it was rhetorical. I just mean whoever the fuck replaced him as the biggest coke lord south of the Rio Grande. I don't know that name off the top of my head. But you get the point. Grabbing the money not only denies it to our nation's enemies, but that kind of money, if properly hidden and cared for, jacks up our available resources for what could go on as a very long war, a war that in time we may be fighting alone. If this works, this won't be the last shipment we hit, either. "

Dave was staring at the ceiling too. "Fuck, man. All I wanted to do was finish grad school and lecture on the Russian Army."

I shrugged. "Versus getting a Stateside rifle kill and putting a couple mil in the bank." I pulled another Dew out of the mini fridge and wordlessly offered Dave one. He shook his head, pointing towards the bottles of Dortmunder Lager. Yeah, I guess it was a beer moment. I put the Dew back and grabbed a beer for each of us. I passed him his and he deftly opened it on the workbench edge.

Dave was like me, or like any of the GWOT generation of trigger pullers who had grown up on Michael Mann movies like *Heat*. *The action is the juice.* "I gotta admit, I always was kinda jealous of that Dallas fight." He pointed at the HCAR over on the wall. "Giving somebody the bad news with one of those has got to be a rare thing."

Thinking about it darkened the mood. "Sad but true. We buried several good men doing it."

Dave took a long drink of his beer. "How'd you get sucked into that, anyway? That's not your usual niche in life."

"You know a cat name of Jeb Shaw? Short, stocky Texan? He was in V Corps LRS out of Germany when I was in the 101. Radio call sign was Bam Bam after Barney Rubble's kid on *The Flintstones* because he benched about five hundred and deadlifted more before he broke his back on a jump later. Anyway, this was when you were just getting to Brigade Recon in Vincenza, so we were all in on the invasion together, just in different places." Us and forty thousand of our closest friends. I don't know if I really missed it or I just missed not having turned thirty yet.

Dave shook his head. "I got there from 3rd Batt at Benning about ten minutes before we loaded up for the invasion- I barely knew the guys in my unit."

"Eh, was worth asking. I didn't know him back then either. I met him later when he'd gone contractor in Baghdad. Anyway, Jeb needed guys for a short notice job in Dallas. He was on contract for DHS to keep some shithead alive who had cartel shooters, Chinese spies, and probably the fucking space aliens mad enough at him that he wasn't supposed to see the inside of a courtroom alive."

Dave groaned. "Oh, no. And when your buddy asked, you didn't have it in you to say no."

"Nope. See, I'm like the anti-shit magnet. Patrols I was on never seemed to get hit, I missed the big fight in Karbala Gap having been sent to lead a slice element elsewhere, so I'm remarkably unblooded. You know that."

Dave was sick of me being moody on the subject ever since he'd gotten back from his first combat jump on Objective Rhino. "And I keep telling you to get the fuck over it. Fate gave you a different thread."

"But I was trying to help out a buddy and maybe spare him some trouble he didn't need."

"Didn't work out so well, though I guess you can tell yourself it might have been worse had you not been there." Dave had seen the results on the news. As I said earlier, it had been exceptionally bloody.

I continued. "It also convinced me that a whole new dark age is coming. Somali-looking technicals on American streets, a foreign fucking army by another name coming up from down south? People on our side of the border working for various foreign powers? Let alone what the last couple Presidential elections did to us. Fuck, you've talked to Alen and what he went through over there. We could be five years from having live-fire Yugoslav Civil War reenactments here."

He shook his head. "Nah. Ours will be worse. More small arms, more multipolar grudges, and too many concentrated urban populations you can kill in three weeks flat by sealing the perimeter then cutting the water and power. Yugoslavia had nothing like New York, LA, or Chicago. A big city is a very fragile organism."

Grim, but he was right. "Yeah and to that point, taking a container of cash out of one enemy's war chest has got to count as a worthwhile goal."

Dave had an intellectual streak of his own. "Philosophically speaking, the drug cartels aren't so much the problem as your ex-Commie globalist types. Starving people in the ruins aren't buying product. The cartels want to make money off the slow decline of civilization, not crash it so they can rebuild on ideological lines. A really good parasite never kills its host."

I hadn't thought about it that way in a while, but if Dave wasn't at least as smart as I was, we wouldn't have been such close friends for over twenty years. I definitely wouldn't have promoted him to be the spare me. "Fair. But it's still a great big pile of money we can use. I have an interest in grabbing it for the long term good of both the firm and of our various causes and I cannot do this without you."

He thought about it for a minute, then finally nodded. "Yeah, on one fucking condition." I looked over at him as he took another pull off his beer. "That you don't get any closer to this shit than a UAV feed." I might have been glaring at him a bit. Dave didn't care. That guy had more years in combat than Achilles and Hector put together at this point. He continued, "You are too old, way too fucking beat up, and far too valuable to catch a stray bullet on this. We don't have another you."

"Meh. You could do my job. And I'm only four years older than you."

He shook his head. "First, I'm still way healthier, thank God, and between the two of us I was always the better athlete. Having lost both Big John and Mikey, I couldn't do your job without a long learning curve we don't have time for. You have five years' experience on me in this off-books shit. Everything I did had military backing and automatic Get Out Of Jail Free cards. Plus, if you want me to be the backup for you, all the more reason we stay the fuck away from each other when lead is flying. We both get tagged out and then it's a bad day for the home team."

I sighed. "Baseball metaphors are not your thing, dude."

Again, he didn't care and his face showed it. "My point stands, however."

I slumped back in my desk chair, conceding. "Fine, then you are officially the ground force commander. You know who we have close and available for this, you know who we think we can trust. My suggestion is fifty thousand each for them, rehearsals and performance together, then a hundred thousand kicker for you as the ground force planner and commander past what you are already making. Dry hole? Sure. We let it go at that. Otherwise we calculate internal bonuses based on the size of the take. This is a fundraiser for the organization, so most of it stays with the organization. If it goes well, everyone involved, including the hired help, gets a decent bite, but not so much as to bring serious heat."

He nodded his assent. "Sounds good to me."

Chapter 12

"Plan: A list of shit that isn't going to happen."
~Ryan "Mister Parker" Philippe, in 'The Way Of The Gun.'
A truly great film.

I was awake an hour before my alarm clock again, and I'd already woken up twice in the night. My back felt like shit, as usual. There was no hope of getting more rest, since my mind was spinning up to daytime RPMs pretty quickly. I was already thinking about that money as I limped to the kitchen, fire trailing down my leg from that same damn pinched sciatic nerve. Odin padded along beside me toward the back door, watching me carefully in case my leg decided to fold up and me go on my face. I let him out and stumbled into the hall bathroom.

I thought about it while I pissed. Intellectually, part of me realized this was a shitty idea. We probably had enough money in the bank for the firm to sustain itself. If we could get our hands on any of the foreign accounts without getting our asses nailed to the wall by the normie Feds, we'd be doing really well. Just the Panama City account would do nicely for now, or London. But we just needed to avoid attention. Stealth was our defense. Like the catch phrase of the WWII Pacific Fleet submarine force, we ran silent and ran deep. We were not a company configured to play war in the streets with a bunch of cartel shooters after we knocked over their cookie jar.

At the same time, this was the sort of opportunity that did not come along every day. Once in a lifetime and that's if you are lucky. Wars take money and there is no such thing as too much of it. We worked both sides of the street and there was way more loose money on the other side. We had bought and sold a lot of information, but we exploited relatively little of it for ourselves.

That done, I then stumbled to the refrigerator. I poured two inches of orange juice and shot it down to cut the stomach acid taste with a better acid taste, then grabbed the milk jug and started pouring about a quart worth of it down my neck. It tasted so good that it almost took my mind off how bad my back felt. I put the cap back on the milk, let Odin back in, and stumbled back down the hall to see if Angel could get that nerve unpinched again.

I collapsed into bed. Angel was still sleeping the sleep of the untroubled. Good for her. I kissed her gently and she sort of purred. I waited for the alarm to go off before I asked her to reset my spine. It hurt enough I let my mind wander while she worked on me.

First, how to actually do it. Misdirection and stealth would be the key here. When you are ripping off drug dealers at two o'clock in the morning, let them see what they expect to see. Guys in black SWAT gear or fashionable Multicam kit with masks, bright lights in their faces, and so on. Of course then they wake up somewhere handcuffed rather than getting booked at the local jail and they start wondering which of their rivals did them wrong. Or they don't wake up at all and never get to wonder about shit. Depending on the level of scumbaggery involved, I was personally okay with either. Later, when the real cops find a few bodies with extensive rap sheets laying dead in the countryside, maybe they get distracted by the bodies and never wonder what else may be missing.

And once we had it, I had an idea for what to go with it. The getaway was going to be the stuff of the old sagas. Too bad we couldn't ever tell the tale. Then lightning shot from my right toe all the way up into my neck as the disc reset. I may have even blacked out a minute.

***

Just because planning is sometimes flawed and doesn't quite work out doesn't mean it is a waste of time and therefore something you can deliberately skimp on. With that in mind, it was time to start planning the raid. It was also time to bring in some outside intellectual guns. Adam was a helicopter pilot retired from "America's premier rotary wing special operations aviation unit" who had copious Iraq and Afghanistan experience. He wasn't the best guy in the world on covert air movement, but he lived locally and was the most trustworthy acquaintance with the right skills I could get on 24 hours' notice.

Backstopping him was a freshly retired Air Force intel colonel named Chris. I had known him for years, him being another sci-fi convention scene pal who also packed a solid resume. He was willing to drive up from his retirement house in the Florida panhandle for the per diem.

I then pulled in Dave and Jimmy for raid expertise, Cash for financial genius, Morgan for his criminal instincts and underworld knowledge, and finally Kara for extra intelligence analysis and her truckload of common sense. For an extra margin of privacy, I scheduled the meeting for Friday evening when the building would be emptier and told Angel to spend some time distracting anyone else who was still on site working but not invited into the room. That way no one walked in on the conversation. I kissed her on the forehead and told her I'd fill her in later. She grinned a bit and told me Cash would be upstairs in a few minutes. She was slightly smirking but I had no idea why.

We were generally assembling in the closest thing the first floor had to a lobby and I was explaining a bit of what we knew about the place's history to Adam. It wasn't Chris's first visit and so he'd heard some of it before. Then the elevator began ascending from downstairs. The door dinged and slid open. Cash sauntered in with everything but entrance music.

At some level, she knew this was an important occasion with guests, so she decided dressing up was critical. At another level in her rather fragmented psyche, 'chief financial officer' got badly crosswired with 'trophy girlfriend.' Her hair was puffed in an early 90s cheerleader look and her makeup was dialed up to about 9 out of 10. I saw Angel's professional touch in the eyeshadow blending. She'd then chosen a *really* short Black Watch tartan miniskirt that barely concealed her assets, white thigh-highs, tall black platform stripper heels and a navy blue cardigan sweater thrown on over a white dress shirt and, uh, I think that was *my* Black Watch regimental necktie.

I couldn't even be surprised, this was simply who she had made herself into.

As she no doubt desired, all eyes went to her and stayed there. Chris and his wife did enough sci-fi conventions that he could handle the visual spectacle. He'd missed Cash on his last visit, but he at least kinda knew who she was. Adam? Nah. Target lock. The poor guy was staring and his jaw was hanging even if the drool hadn't started yet. To make this slightly worse, I knew Adam was single again and I figured I'd be lucky to have eighty percent of his attention. Since he was part of the decision tree on air operations, I kinda needed his brain on that instead of being focused on the front of her abundantly filled shirt.

She slid next to me, her arm around my waist, while I tried to hold her closely without mussing her hair. "Gentlemen, meet Cash. Cash, you at least know Chris here by reputation and Adam is our guest air movement expert."

She smiled like a supernova, offering her hand. "Gentlemen, I know you both by your envelopes of consulting fees. In addition to various other tasks, you may know I run the Accounting Department."

Chris grinned at us both. "Nice, nice, obvious teamwork."

Adam merely blushed and stammered. This was more than he was mentally set up for today. But it was time, so I waved everyone into the meeting room and closed the door. With the principals assembled, I explained what Morgan had told me and then gave them the decision Dave and I had made, that we were going to begin the planning cycle to snatch it. I asked for objections. At first there were none, but then Cash raised her hand. "Look, I am all for the ruthless acquisition of capital. It's kinda my thing, I'll concede. But... why the hell are we going to Mississippi to steal it?"

I shrugged. "It's like Mallory said about Mount Everest. Because it's there. The cell phone intercept says it is literally a twenty foot shipping container full of cash."

Cash snorted, "This is not what private banking generally means."

Chris looked at me, thoughtful. "And didn't Mallory die up on Everest, man?"

I shrugged, "Yeah, his third time wasn't the charm. But the quote still works."

Jimmy raised his hand, ignoring our historical detour and focused on Cash's comment. "Hard currency guarded by reliable people is safer than using a real bank, assuming your money is ill-gotten and you have to be discreet."

"There's zero rate of return," she sneered. You know that rate of return is Cash's religion.

"But it's harder to find and can't be seized by mere computer keystrokes," Kara threw in. Since this was not DragonCon, Kara had not bothered dressing up for this. She was in jeans and a *Mandalorian* parody shirt where a furious Baby Yoda was clutching an Uzi submachine gun.

Cash scowled as she thought about it. "Hmmm, you may have me there."

I nodded. "Yeah, and we're the ones with a bank vault in the basement. We don't get to criticize anyone else's financial arrangements."

Kara aggressively scratched at her head. She'd razored the sides again and that always brings out the itches. Of course she'd also dyed the rest bright green and it wasn't even St. Patrick's Day yet. "How much cash fits in a shipping container anyway?"

Dave propped one boot up on the table, stretching his leg. "I'm thinking of it this way; if you can get a million dollars in a briefcase, how many briefcases fit in a twenty foot container?" Dave had done more unit load-outs than I had. Leave it to him to hit the good question.

Uhhhh..."Hang on, let me think. Now that we're all caught up to the same start point, take a thirty minute break. Everyone eat and drink something before we get too far into the tall grass."

Really, if I had thought more than two days ahead on this, I would have gotten a catering package going so we didn't have to stop and cook. Maybe good barbecue, but then the horde of other people working here would have followed their noses to it and started asking questions that I didn't want to answer yet. But before I attended to the food, I wanted some numbers to come back to. A twenty foot container full of hundreds. But how full? What weight? Numbers from the Unit Movement Officers' course at Fort Campbell and memories from all the JRTC and Iraq load-outs started popping back into my head from a long time ago while I looked up some others.

Paper was 76 pounds to the cubic foot. Huh. I would have guessed a bit less. Okay. Standard twenty-foot container was 1360 cubic feet. Calculator on my phone tells me that filled completely with paper was 103,360 pounds which is nearly twice the maximum load capacity of the container at 55,000 pounds. So they are going to run out of weight capacity before they run out of space. They can't fill it and if they load it crooked it won't lift well. Floor area was 150 square feet... they could cover that nearly five feet deep before they maxed out on weight, a little more math, say four feet for 650 cubic feet.... 22.5 cubic yards of paper. Multiplies out to 46,000 pounds. Over 62 million dollars to the cubic yard, since a guy on a classic car forum did the math on a cubic yard of cash and the Internet found his work for me. So best case scenario, we were looking at 1.4 to 1.5 *billion*, with a fucking *B*, dollars. I doubted it was going to be that much. I closed the calculator app on my phone and laid down my pen. I was as hungry as anyone.

I joined the others in the break room. The oven was preheating and the air fryer on the counter was going. Bags of pizza rolls and cheese sticks were coming out of the freezer and some people had brought food from home. Communal meals actually mean a lot to soldiers and ex-soldiers and the hangers-on. We also weren't somewhere where you could just pick up a phone for delivery. Sometimes the remoteness of the facility was not exactly a good point, but that was just one more reason why we had a full kitchen in here.

We got our hot, greasy goodness onto plates, pulled fresh cold drinks from the fridge, and then headed back into the conference room. Skillful use of aluminum foil minimized the cleanup. Rules are rules and even now we tried to stick to them. Once we were all seated again, I walked everyone through my math and invited them to check it. They got the same results.

Dave, waving a mozzarella stick like a field marshal's baton, was the first one to say it out loud. "Okay, so we are stealing a billion to a billion and a half dollars."

I chimed in, "Maybe three billion if it's a forty foot container."

Jimmy nodded. "Sure looks that way. Guess the juice is worth some squeezing."

This was too much cash to deal with domestically. I had a plan sprouting in the back of my mind, but I wanted to hang back for a minute and see what other people had for ideas.

I looked at Cash. "If we get it, we gotta hide it."

She shook her head. "Nowhere in the legal banking system. You know what we have for accounts both here and overseas. Absolutely none of them, not all of them together, can absorb this without setting off red flags everywhere from the Atlanta branch of the Fed to the gnomes in Zurich. Interpol, State Department, and Treasury all have people who do nothing but look for this sort of thing and so do the banks themselves."

Jimmy threw up his hand, "Hey, how would the cartel have laundered it?"

Cash kept the lead on this one, delicately sipping on one of her organic tea bottles. "Bought a lot of export goods through their longtime shell companies with their dirty dollars, legally shipped them to Mexico and resold them for clean pesos there on their side of the border. Farm products, manufactured goods, you name it."

"We could do that, then resell for some foreign currency somewhere else, then reconvert."

Now that we were actually getting into criminal shit, Morgan cut in. "No. Too much effort, and too much time. Totally not worth it. We'd have to change our full time business into just laundering that billion without getting caught and everything else would wither and die meanwhile."

Dave and Jimmy looked at each other. "Man, just leave it in US dollars and then throw it in the basement. We have the room and we could run a long time on that money."

Cash shook her head. "The fuck we could. It's hard enough running the shadow books on our unreported funds as it is. Those of you who get paid under the table, you know what I mean. If we start running cash-only with no visible income or company tax filings, then the IRS would be fisting us like a particularly foul sort of German porno film." There were some snickers and grins at that. Inwardly, I had to wince. *You know, I think I am a bad influence on that girl.*

She continued, "Even with our legal covers and cutouts, there is no way to hide that kind of income. We'd have to keep the mice from getting into that much paper. Treasury would probably redesign the bills twice before we got around to spending the last of it. And God help us all if we ever got caught with it. Assume at least some of the serial numbers are recorded somewhere."

I looked around the room. Time to set them against each other to frame my own plan. "All right, everyone else, you were hired for your brains and diverse skill sets. Your ideas?"

Kara shrugged. "We could take it to Pakistan, bribe an admiral we know of, and buy three or four decent Chinese-designed tactical nukes out of their navy's weapons depot for that kind of money so long as we extracted him as well. Other than that, this is totally not my lane of expertise."

And what the fuck would I do with three nukes? One more thing to gather dust around here.

"Morgan? You keep saying you know crime better than the rest of us."

"Fuck, man, I was a nickel and dime hoodlum. This much money is Starfleet Command kind of shit compared to what I'm used to. We'd argue about it when we were high, what would we do with a billion other than spending it all on cars, hookers, and more drugs. Now the old Sicilian mafia guys would have put it in commercial real estate. Used car lots, coin-op laundries, vending machines, trucking companies, self-storage places, bars and restaurants, but it all takes time. That's all predicated on washing steady dirty income over a long haul, not hiding one huge score. You saw *Goodfellas* and what happened after the Lufthansa robbery at JFK. As for regular washing? The Feds got wise to most of the tricks thirty years ago shutting down the Five Families in New York. All the Midwest used to launder in Vegas, but that died with the Eighties when Vegas became Wall Street territory and the Chicago Outfit old-timers mostly went to the slam. You saw the movie."

I continued to look around the room while everyone sort of looked at each other. Angel picked that moment to finally creep in and join us, locking the door behind her.

"Okay, I thought about this. One, most of the money laundering in this country is run for the benefit of drug dealers, human traffickers, corrupt politicians, and the other trash of this world that we as a company generally are pledged to fight. So if we launder with them, we're subsidizing our own opponents somehow. Ladies and gentlemen, not to sound like Ed Harris in *Apollo 13*, but that is unacceptable. Not on my watch." There were several quiet nods at that, so I drove onward.

"Two, the people we are ripping off know more about money laundering than we do. If we try washing it like they do or buying our way in to wash it in the same places they do, they're going to notice it. That means they figure out we're the ones who robbed them, they find us, and then we're playing World War II in the streets, with wives and kids in the crossfire. This is also unacceptable.

"Three, that means we have to make it physically vanish. No ripples in the pond, no sudden increases in the bank accounts. We have to get it somewhere out of the purview of the Latin American cartels or anyone they bought off, which means out of the Americas. That means we got ourselves a covert cargo job to do. That's why I brought Adam in. He knows air movement and he can keep a secret. So, we have two questions. How do we move twenty to thirty tons of cargo and then what do we do to hide a billion dollars in literal cash?"

Adam looked across at me. "Twenty tons is easy. We move container loads in and out of frontier war zones all the time. You obviously have the starter funds to rent or buy a used cargo plane. I'm mainly a rotary wing guy, but I could at least co-pilot and work radios for another driver."

Morgan interjected. "We gotta find it first. We know it's somewhere in twenty to thirty percent of a big rectangular state that takes three hours to drive across the narrow way." He had a point. Some states are a hell of a lot bigger than they look on the map, even at Interstate speeds.

Dave shrugged. "So obviously we have a third task that's the new #1, and that is to narrow down the target. We can't snatch it if we don't know where the fuck it is."

Morgan waved at him. "Hello, this ain't my first score, man, we're working on it. That's my lane. You run the Son Tay Raid doorkicker lane and then the hot chick who scares me can handle the money end."

Cash smirked and blew him a kiss. "Awww, Morgan, you're such a charmer, baby. I bet you get all the girls with a pitching game like that." And yeah, he sometimes did.

I cut back in. "Yeah, so what's now the third task breaks down into movement then secure storage somewhere far, far away from here. Somewhere where a pissed off Mexican cartel doesn't have the connections or muscle to look for it."

Jimmy looked over at me. "Dude, if you are warming up to suggest burying it in a hole somewhere on an island like pirate treasure, I am going to jump across this table and smack you like Ike Turner smacked Tina."

"Sorry, not being a Rosicrucian, member of the Illuminati, or a space alien, we are not going to have an Oak Island reenactment. Besides, that's a lot of work to dig a hole that big and you know how notoriously lazy I can be."

Jimmy sat back with a grin. "Good. So no pirate shit."

"No, a little bit of pirate shit. What do all the late-night TV commercials tell nervous Boomers to do with their paper dollars?"

Dave groaned. "Oh, no. I see where you're going with this."

I nodded, then looked over at Cash. "Gold holdings?"

She nodded. "Agreed, sir. Gold holdings, as much as we can, at least. Trickle some of it into the market through the offshore accounts, but do too much too fast and, I reiterate, the Federal Reserve and the multinational banks have people who do nothing but look for things like this. Getting caught would be bad."

I tried for a Johnny Depp voice. "Ever been to Singapore?"

Cash was slightly aghast. "You're fucking kidding me, right, sir? I hadn't been west of the Pennsylvania state line before that day you and your goons popped the front door open."

Jimmy glared at her, but with a trace of humor. "Call me 'goon' one more time, hooker." She just sighed and rolled her eyes at him.

Chris shrugged. "Of all of us, I have been to Singapore. Lots of cops, lots of TV cameras. It's a very expensive, very well-policed theme park of a city that covers most of the island."

I threw the follow-on question out. "Any other suggestions for where to buy a fuck-ton of gold bullion, have it stored, and do so with no notifications to Uncle Sam? Or where we could put that much cash? We already have more in the basement than we should."

Cash retained the lead on this. "When it comes to us being American and that amount of cash being *de facto* evidence of money laundering and/or tax evasion to them, you absolutely cannot trust the Swiss anymore. You know they are bitchy about the accounts we already have. Since we're American, even the Liechtensteiners get twitchy and they are where the Swiss traditionally go. We have nothing there and can't start now."

Chris slumped in his chair, really thinking. "Could we do the Hollywood thing where we pretend to be foreign? I still look Italian, I speak the language, and I can work on the accent. On the other hand, I also speak pretty good Russian and Dave's Russian is perfect."

Dave laughed. "*Cyka blyat!*"

"Chris, not a bad idea. I still remember when you had to try convincing the Moscow subway cops you were American that time because they wanted to roust you for something." I won't get into where Dave perfected his. It's a long story and it's quite classified.

Cash shook her head. "No. If we were stealing Euros or something, maybe. Showing up with pallets of US dollars while claiming not to be American isn't going to work. Not with the Liechtensteiners or the Swiss, at least. They are not trusting people. And I don't know where we could buy a billion dollars' worth of Swiss francs in cash to then deposit instead. That would raise only slightly fewer red flags anyway."

Dave sighed. "Oh, well. Not my lane of expertise. So they really are concerned about more than appearances?"

"Yeah. They don't want the big hammer of Uncle Sam coming down with sanctions and they know he's watching. The IRS wants their cut even if it's clean money. We can put maybe 15 or 25 mil away slowly, like a few years slowly. All we have to do is charter a plane to the British Virgin Islands then bounce it from there to the Cayman accounts, then do the same trick from Cayman back to the BVI. Uncle Sam ignores the little nickel and dime shit like that looking for bigger fish. But the rest? If we want it hidden fast, it has to be gold and for gold, the Caribbean is useless.

Cash continued. "Now South Africa has gold. We'd be buying about fourteen percent of their yearly production, so a bulk discount would be possible at risk of being conspicuous as shit. But with their current government and ongoing domestic crime rate, they would fuck us over on the deal in a heartbeat. They'd be just as likely to meet us at the dock with a tank or something and steal it all at gunpoint. Russia produces twenty times that, but they keep their production for themselves, especially with the Ukraine war and their economic fallout from that. So it's got to be Asia and for gold... Singapore. They handle much of the Australian production and the Australians produce even more than the Russians. More importantly, Singapore still deals in discretion. They do for rich Chinese what the Swiss used to do for rich Europeans." She took a real deep breath and sighed. "Angel and I have the right looks and right languages to make this work. We can do it."

I had an idea. "What about the gold markets in the Gulf?" Again, as Mikey once said, Arabs love gold more than they do dollars. I already had a feeling I knew the answer but had to ask.

Kara shook her head and cut in. "There's no gold mining there. All their gold in the markets comes out of several different places in Africa, same as conflict diamonds, plus some South African export. It's already changed hands enough times that you're now buying at a retail markup. And the entire Gulf area is so wired for counterterrorist surveillance on the financial side that we couldn't show up with even a percentage of that much money. To the locals, we'd look like the worst CIA sting operation ever. If we don't look properly American, instead we would have the Agency up our ass in five minutes. Then anybody connected enough to have the weight we need would kick a fat percentage to fund the *jihad*. Saudi, maybe not so much anymore, especially after MBS cleaned house and buried some of his inconveniently extreme relatives in unmarked graves. The Emirates, especially Dubai and then Qatar? Absolutely guaranteed it would have ties to our radical Islamist friends. Cutting a slice off gold and oil transactions is how they fund their side of the war."

Cash grinned. "Looks like it's back to me."

I turned and looked at her with a slight degree of doubt. "How the fuck are you going to go? Pretty sure you still have warrants out on you."

"American passports don't have fingerprint data on the chip and past that? Everyone knows all Asian girls look alike. I've got a passport that matches the driver's license. Big John and some buddy of his handled that last year. He thought I might have to make a bank run to London for him once." I made a note to get with our guy at Homeland

Security to make sure none of our passports were flagged in the system. "The hardest part is going to be getting the cash to Singapore. A suitcase is one thing. Bank drafts are another. This is..." She trailed off and shrugged.

"Yeah, A twenty foot shipping container full of used hundreds. Hopefully mostly hundreds. It would be a bitch to go through all this work for just fives and tens. But regardless, it's at least twenty tons of dead weight to move halfway around the world."

Dave shrugged. "Containers come and go all the time and not more than a tiny fraction ever get checked. Shouldn't be too hard to get it out by sea, right?"

Morgan shook his head. "You really want to take a chance putting a stolen container full of our money on some Third World-registered rustbucket freighter as deck cargo, with a dummy bill of lading as "machine parts" or "printed goods" and hope it gets to where we need it? We can't insure it for what it's worth, so what if it gets stolen or even just falls off the boat?

Now while Morgan's choice of method was off, Dave did have a point. Doing this by sea was probably the way to go. How? Well, the Gulf of Mexico was right there and while the Gulf was essentially an American lake, it was still a fairly straight shot out to open ocean. We just needed the right boat. That gave me an idea. I popped open one of the dozen messenger apps on my personal phone. Last active three hours ago, thinking on the time differences. I texted the girl I was thinking of in this case. *"Debi, you up?"*

The answer was fast, so obviously she was. *"Just leaving client. Why are you awake? You need your sleep."* Bless her, she never changed. She had a tendency to fuss over me, never mind the fact it was still mid-evening here.

Debi was Lithuanian by birth, New York City by upbringing, and generally the sort of girl who existed only in the fevered imagination of erotica writers. She was a slender five foot seven, with a perfect ass and long slim legs. The cartoonishly spherical breast implants came later. Think Jessica Rabbit but blonde. You ever hear wild stories about five thousand an hour call girls? She was one. She did have a slight discount off that hourly rate for a full twenty four hour minimum, but it was still the sticker price on a new Corvette. She worked worldwide and stayed gone over one hundred and eighty days a year for tax reasons. I think she was in Rome at the moment.

For all our other strange ties, Debi was the one who got me Tommy, my other former SEAL. He liked following her around Europe on business playing bodyguard, but was missing his kids in Ohio. That having come up in conversation, she then traded him to me in exchange for an introduction to a just-divorced British NCO who was taking his discharge from Her Majesty's service (Elizabeth II still being alive at the time) in 2 Para who needed civilian work with his old skills. Anyway, Debi knew a lot of guys who parked large yachts in St. Barth's, Monaco, or other glamour ports where her and her professional peers did their thing, and some of these guys were willing to do side charters. As in 'we can move a few tons of discreet cargo for you in exchange for a cut of the proceeds' kind of charters.

It was better for me to get to the point quickly, either before she got distracted or she got me distracted. *"Is your friend in the Caymans interested in a paying trip soon?"*

The little *typing* squiggle squiggled. *"Will relay. I am not available though, baby. Booked solid next month."*

"That's fine. I miss you though." It was like missing a dear cousin, though, or a really good stepsister. I never had slept with her, neither for love nor money. I couldn't afford the 'for money' part anyway, not even now.

"Kisses. Tell China Doll hi." She did have a bit of a crush on Angel since she admitted she had a fetish for Asian girls. God only knows what she would think of Cash. Debi hadn't heard that story yet, even a sanitized version.

"I will."

The squiggle squiggled. *"Good. NOW GO TO BED!"*

Well, I got fucking told. I then shared my thoughts with the group. If a big yacht will hold twenty or thirty tons of passengers, luggage, booze and so on, why not charter one and stuff it full of twenty tons of our freshly stolen money?

Jimmy was chewing on a pen. "Boss, speaking as our senior former naval type present for duty, I think we are fucking up just a little on that."

"How so?" He had me curious.

"Okay, assume this hit really is 1.5 billion in literal tons of paper. We are all in agreement that is the absolute best case scenario, right?" He looked around the table for general assent and got it. "So we are going to offer to pay this guy ten percent of that, or 150 million, as a haulage fee. We assume that's a going rate for underworld transit. Maybe. We don't know. Gotta research it. So that's four weeks at least. Those big yachts rent for two hundred grand or more a week. Maybe he takes that out of haulage, maybe he doesn't. Plus fuel."

"Four weeks," I replied, "and that makes an extra point eight million in expenses on top of 150 million we are already paying him, plus fuel. Do we fuckin' care if we pay 151 versus 150? That's a loose dime at this point."

Jimmy cut me off. "Lemme finish. Once he sees the pile, we're lucky if he doesn't get greedy and try to fuck us for twenty percent or more. Do we then pay twenty? What do we do if he wants half? Fuck, if this dude is sleazy enough, we're lucky if we don't get into a gunfight over the cargo and have to kill all of them to feed the sharks. Meanwhile it's going to take..." he was into a navigation program on one of the red-tagged secure laptops, "twenty-five days minimum via the Med and Suez to get to Singapore. That's if we can hold twenty knots with three or four refuel stops en route, in a now-stolen yacht, with a dead crew, which we might not be able to man by ourselves."

Kara piped up. "Let's assume it doesn't go that badly. Even then, this asshole, whoever he is, knows you picked up 1.5 billion off the Gulf Coast and where it went, since he knows what his cut was and where his boat took the rest. The people we are taking this hypothetical 1.5 billion from are going to be shaking the trees looking for it. Do we trust him or his crew not to talk when there will be prices on our heads and their possible capture and subsequent torture involved?"

Hmmm. Gods of war, thank you for the right sort of friends at times like this. "All right, good points, both of you. I will put you in for a Coca-Cola with Oak Leaf Cluster." It was a very old joke from a deployment I did once that I had injected into company culture. I'll explain it another time. "So are there any easy alternatives? Do we go by air instead?"

Adam scratched his head. He had done more cross-border air insertions than some guys had pieces of ass. "Air movement going out of the country is gonna be tricky. Anything with intercontinental range for twenty-plus tons of cargo is gonna light up air traffic control transponders and Customs computers the second we break ground and at least a computer will track us, leaving a trail for later. Even if we truck somewhere else, load up and fly, questions are eventually gonna be asked somewhere. There's a whole flight-spotter culture online using the transponder squawks even before we deal with official government tracking. This ain't forty years ago with Barry Seal running planeloads of cocaine at low altitude across the Gulf and on up into Arkansas. Any airport big enough to land the load where we're going is going to have customs inspectors somewhere along the line."

Jimmy smirked a bit. "Easy fix for that. We buy our own boat. We get a nice big used yacht for thirty or forty million bucks, maybe sixty tops, and get it outfitted for long range hauls. I find a few ex-surface warfare and special boat unit types to crew it. Once we're ready, we take a month, get it to

Singapore and the banker here," he gestured at Cash, "meets us in Singapore by air. She does the deal, and then we flip the boat for sale there."

I admit, going by water had been my original idea since I got out of bed this morning, but this creative leap in how to accomplish that rendered me nearly speechless.

"Or we keep it, dock it, or maybe even put it out on charter through a brokerage until we need it again for some other spook shit. Because with us, there will always be more spook shit and as they tell us in the Navy, seventy percent of the planet is water."

I reclined the chair back and stared at the ceiling for a minute. Cash was pounding away at her laptop next to me. She piped up. "Found the boat, I think." She clicked and it came up on the big screen. She grinned, "I even like the name."

I just stared at it. For sale, currently in the British Virgin Islands, the 171-foot aluminum-hulled, diesel-powered yacht *Ecstasy* laid at anchor. She was American-built in 2014 on the Great Lakes in Wisconsin by Monaco-based Palmer Johnson. *How's that for a global economy?* The white hull was long and rakish. There was a swimming pool on the foredeck, which smoothly blended into a swept-back superstructure that looked like a highway on-ramp with radar domes atop it. It was more ostentatious than George Patton's polo ponies or Craig Lowell's airplane. Ten points if you get *that* reference. I was aghast. "Fuck, couldn't we get something a little more pedestrian? A small freighter, an old Coast Guard cutter, you know, something that looks less like a drug lord's floating pimp shack?"

Kara shook her head. "No. You have to present a certain image of class. You get below that and then you look like the floating equivalent of the local weed dealer in his shitty old van. That will attract more customs or police attention, since the upper class always has a particular immunity from casual harassment. The yachts the Arab princes, Russian crime lords, or dot-com billionaires buy are twice the size, so we are actually showing restraint here."

I was still kinda staring. "Twenty-one point nine million Euros; how much is that in real money?"

Cash closed her eyes in a long, slow blink as she thought. "Twenty-two three plus loose change, US." *God, my pretty little walking calculator.*

Jimmy was already flipping through pictures and charts in the broker's online sales brochure. "Oooh, she's fast. Will cruise at 24 knots, range isn't ideal for our purposes but I can throw at least a pair of diesel blivets in that forward swimming pool since we won't be using it underway. Chris, how big do you make that pool out to be?"

Despite being retired, Chris was a school-trained and very well-experienced intelligence officer who had several interesting party tricks. Imagery analysis was one of them. He put his reading glasses on and eyeballed the screen. "Overall length 171, so that pool is about 30 feet long, about a third of the beam, beam is 28, so call it nine, nine by thirty is 270, looks about five feet deep... 1350 cubic feet which is..."

Jimmy was still clicking on the sales brochure and a calculator. "About seven and a half gallons to the cubic foot, so that gives me an extra 11,000 gallons in diesel. Maybe more, we don't need to be only flush to the deck, we can come up a foot or two with the bags. Main tank is only 14,500... sixteen thousand gallons with their bonus tank, then we add ten or eleven to that, anything past that is reserve, sixteen thousand times seven pounds per gallon, divided by two thousand, 56 tons usable plus our add-ons. That 11,000 gallons ups our fuel capacity by... 38.5 tons, for 94 tons total. Yeah, I can do this with about seven or eight guys. Dibs on not sleeping in the pink bedroom."

I looked over at him. "How many stages?"

"Gulf Coast around Florida to North Carolina, then tank there along the Outer Banks. Maybe top off in Bermuda if I have to, but prefer not to. Across to Gibraltar where the fuel is cheap. Across the Med, maybe top off at Malta or the Greek islands, then through Suez down to Sharm el Sheik or one of the other Red Sea boat party towns, Down the Red, maybe top off in Djibouti and then across to the Indian east coast. That's still easier than the leg across the Atlantic. There we find some small local shithole to gas up, then around the tip of India and across into Singapore. You guys fly in and meet us there. Five or six fuel stops, trying never to be more than half empty, but it's going to be expensive as hell to fill her up. After everything shot up over the last couple years, marine diesel is running close to 900 bucks a ton and like I said, the boat will take most of a hundred tons with our add-on tankage. That's why people normally put them on flatbed float ships to get them around in a hurry."

Dave shrugged. "We're stealing a billion dollars. Do we give a shit about paying ninety thousand dollars for a fill-up?"

I supposed not. I looked back at Jimmy. "Don't be afraid to slow it down rather than run it out of gas." Jimmy just silently replied with the *go fuck yourself, boss* glare endemic to Navy chief petty officers. Eh, I had it coming. Then something else popped into my head. "Customs issues in Bermuda if you gotta go in there. They aren't as Wild West as the rest of the Caribbean, so do we have any early ideas to keep them from not noticing ten to fifteen pallets of cash in the main salon?"

We stopped, and then we all did some Internet searching. Finally, he answered. "We could e-mail for the transit permit on the way in, get in after midnight, pay more for fuel off a tender, and then split before Customs opens at 0800. Might need to avoid the place for a while after, but I think we can pull it off."

Angel started looking up "inbound boat customs clearances Bermuda" in more detail and then started frowning.

Meanwhile, I continued. "Also, look into Eilat in Israel versus Sharm, I think we have friends of friends in Israel we can lean on versus taking our chances with Egyptian customs. Yeah, it's back up that east fork of the Red Sea-"

"The Gulf of Aqaba," Kara supplied helpfully.

"Two points for the intel section. Anyway, as I was saying, if we can make a solid contact with one of our Israeli friends of friends, I think that would be safer than trusting the Egyptians or Saudis to not rob us. And that Indian coast stage seems a little dodgy. A lot dodgy. Scares me even worse. You're going to be way low on fuel by the time you get out there."

Adam still preferred moving by air and was grumbly about it. "There's no money in yachts. What the hell do we want a yacht for?"

Jimmy threw a wadded up page of scratch paper at him. "And you win the obscure *Kelly's Heroes* reference of the day, asshole."

Dave shrugged and chortled. "See if the fuel guys will cut you a cash discount."

We all laughed at that and then I shrugged. "Okay, Jimmy, it's your goat to fuck, man. Like you said, you are the Navy expert here. Who do you want from us with you on the float?"

"Not it!" Kara piped up. "Being out in bright sunshine plays hell with my migraines, never mind the bouncing around."

I looked over at her. "Oh, don't worry, I wasn't thinking of sending you along on this insanity. You have way too much paying work to do here." She actually looked relieved.

Jimmy shrugged. "It ain't hard. I will find about six or seven guys for engineering and bridge crew, including an actual captain. Plenty of ex-destroyer kids out there that are available to hire. Past that, I'll take Dave for his ability to look and sound Russian and take Tommy for a spare dive or small boat guy. That should do the job well enough."

Angel had been quiet, but she finally spoke up. "First, according to their web site, Bermuda doesn't work that way and they want you to quarantine until you clear customs. Will a commercial fuel tender refuel a boat in customs quarantine?"

Nobody knew. We resolved to dig into that. Did they even have fuel tenders?

Angel continued, "Second, it's not really my primary knowledge base, but a yacht that size with no women aboard is going to look suspicious, right? Aren't bikini-clad stripper-looking chicks sort of standard equipment?"

Jimmy shook his head. "When the boss is aboard, yes. When it's just a transit crew for a boat that just got sold or is being moved from one party hotspot to the next one while the boss and his girls fly? Not so much."

I turned and looked at her, sighing deeply. "No, dear, you are not taking a free month-plus boat ride. I don't get to go and I need you here. Cash, that goes double for you." She pouted in a non-sexy manner. "One, Jimmy's right. Two, we can't have the finance chief out of pocket way offshore for a month. And while I could probably get some of Debi's associates from the ranks of the discreet and well-paid Professionally Hot, then they hear or see something we wish they hadn't. For example, there is a 100 percent chance of some Russian hooker, ex-NFL cheerleader, or 'aspiring actress' then seeing all that fucking stolen money. Depending who they are, we then have the same problem we did with the charter idea. We don't want to have to trust too many people."

Cash was still pouting. "But I have never had a cruise before!"

Jimmy looked at her like the salty old chief petty officer he had been. "It's not a cruise. This is going to be a long and bumpy haul done on minimal manning. There's not going to be much sleep, there's going to be much more work to do and more risks to take than you would think, and so the whole thing has to get done in sort of a traditional Navy manner."

She smiled back at him wickedly. "Don't talk to me about naval tradition. It's nothing but rum, sodomy, and the lash."

Angel slightly shuddered. "Fuck, I could go for some of that this weekend." She looked my way with a crooked grin, then back at Cash who nodded.

Jimmy and I both rolled our eyes while everyone else contemplated the ceiling. I sighed.

"Dear, Churchill did deny saying that." Like many quotes attributed to him, when asked later, Churchill replied, "*No, I hadn't said it, but I wish I had.*"

Cash smirked. "Yeah, but it's still a great line. You know I know next to nothing about naval history and even I've heard it."

Kara snarked a bit. "That's just because you're into whips."

Before we got to flip a coin on whether Cash would take that as an insult or not and whether we'd be breaking up a girl fight, I tried to get everyone back on track. And not just because I sadly had to predict that the nearly six foot tall Kara would mop the floor with Cash.

I continued. "Okay, everybody get back to the point of all this. Jimmy, with the cargo you're hauling, you aren't going to be able to stay anywhere long. Security is paramount. Everything comes second to making the destination with the cargo intact."

Jimmy ostentatiously made a note on the pad in front of him, then started cracking jokes. "Okay, terabyte hard drives of porn and no shore leave. Got it."

Dave snickered. "It's not gay if you're underway, right?"

"SEALs do it deeper, Ranger. And remember that you're coming too."

Dave cackled. "Unlikely. You don't even have me breathing hard yet."

Ugh. I thumped the table a bit. "Knock that silly shit off. Let's get onto the next problem." Though I knew somewhere in the frogmens' chain locker of Valhalla, Dick Marcinko and Roy Boehm were laughing at us all. Dick had used that joke in his first or second book. I missed him too.

All right, so now that we had a greasy, slippery handle on how to get the money to Singapore, now how did we get the money from the raid site to the boat? The meeting broke down into two schools of thought. One was that it was easier to get the cash out of the container and move it. The other school of thought was that since it was already packed to move, why waste time fucking with it? I made a command decision. It was already packed once and getting off the objective fast was more important. Waiting around for either cops or enemy reinforcements was a bad thing.

Eventually we realized it was pushing midnight, so we cut it off for the day. As we walked out, Morgan was snickering at Dave. "That was something, man. When you dropped the B word, and I mean *billion,* I could have pulled my dick out and nobody would have noticed."

I sighed. "That's one thing I have always admired about you, Morgan, your overwhelming sense of tact and restraint."

Chapter 13

"You can go to Hell, and I shall go to Texas."
~Davy Crockett, Tennessee frontiersman and Congressman turned Texan martyr

I woke up the next morning with my brain already spinning. I figured we couldn't just pull into Singapore with a billion on board and merely roll down the street from gold dealer to gold dealer. We would need to know somebody, or at least have an introduction from somebody who knew somebody. And despite my Jack Sparrow half-quote, I had never been to Singapore either, while Chris had been there doing Air Force things. I needed to talk to someone who had done dirt there, or who had the right sort of family connections. And this is where another small tidbit of Asian history I had learned over the years worked in my favor.

When the Chinese Civil War finally ended in 1949 in a win for Mao Tse-Tung and the Filthy Godless Communist Scum, Chiang Kai-Shek's Nationalist Chinese (the Kuomintang) decamped for what is now Taiwan where they tried to maintain the continuity of the pre-1949 Republic of China. They were still rabidly anti-Communist after decades, which was nice. But not all the Kuomintang military went to Taiwan. Instead some of them took their military skills, portable loot, and *we got nothing left to lose* attitude everywhere from the heroin poppy fields of north Burma to the Chinese diaspora cities of Singapore, Vancouver, and Manila. And further, not all of the Republic of China's military officers had come out of their Whampoa Military Academy. Since the establishment of their modern army in 1912, Nationalist Chinese military families had sent their sons everywhere from Norwich to The Citadel to Texas A&M. That worked to my advantage in this case, since I think I knew a guy.

I had met 'Mad Jack' Chen at the Dallas Arms Collectors' gun show at Market Hall a few years back. We were both eyeballing a 1912 Navy contract .45 out of John Holbrook's well-known collection that tracked by serial number to the old USS *New York.* John always had a thing for an early Navy contract pistol, particularly authentic battleship guns. Mad Jack ended up plunking down a thousand above the price tag for the pistol because he wanted it that much more and could afford to, but to make sure there were no hard feelings, he dragged me out to dinner afterward.

I later found out he owned the restaurant. He also owned the strip club where we ended up. Somewhere between the 24-ounce ribeye steak, the Wild Turkey Rare Breed bourbon, and the lap dances, I got some of the story. His grandparents had skipped out of China in '49, his grandfather being one of Chiang's battalion commanders at the end. Taiwan looked like a bad idea in their opinion, so they ended up in Vancouver with a bunch of cousins. Since Grandpa had been an early 1930s Aggie, one Canadian winter was enough to get them moving south. Granddad found work with an Aggie classmate, then Jack's dad was an Aggie. As one might presume, Jack ended up being an Aggie too. He'd spent his four years as an armor officer in the Eighties, enjoying the Texas National Guard's Cold War glory days as the 49th "Lone Star" Armored Division. These days, Jack's younger kid was an Aggie. In a couple years, one of the grandsons would probably also follow along. He told me his daughter was the family rebel, so instead she'd been second in her class at Annapolis. Yeah. Nuclear engineering.

So the paranoia born of ex-Kuomintang officers and relatives thereof in worldwide Chinese "family business" meant, at least according to rumor, you needed either blood ties or a serious introduction to do business with them. I thought Mad Jack could be that introduction if I caught him in a good mood. But I was already thinking about what I would have to give up as a gift to get Jack talking and make the deal work. Walking into the war room, I opened up my large gun safe of pistols and thought about it as I pulled my personal phone and dialed.

I guess he had also kept my number in his phone and remembered me, because he answered with "Oh, shit, it's you."

"Hey, Jack, how have you been?"

"Not bad, not bad 't'tall." Man, that Texas accent could sound weird coming from him.

"Listen, I am going to be out your way for something and I need some friendly advice on a business matter."

I clearly heard his groan. "Oh, boy, this sounds like I better light the grill then oil up. I want a good dinner and plenty of lubrication before you try and screw me. What, you want the USS *New York* pistol I beat you to?"

I had to chuckle. "Wouldn't say no to it. I did get a raise at work and gotta blow it on something. But I am bringing you something else as a token of my goodwill. Smile, it's not that awful."

That didn't make him feel better, or he at least dialed the theatrics up to 11. "Oh, this is gonna be great. I can just tell. Better and better every minute. Beware of geeks bearing gifts. Especially what they claim are nice gifts." It was an old joke now, but he obviously wasn't above ripping off *The Iliad* in the name of being funny.

I had to push back a bit, though I grinned. "Well, I would offer to buy you dinner, but you would just take us to some restaurant you secretly owned and take my money that way."

He really laughed at that one. "Ah, come on, round eye, I can't fuck you over that blatantly. Neither the ancient laws of Chinese tradition or those of Texas hospitality would let me. When are you coming down? I can have a car meet you at DFW."

"We were gonna take a small bird into Addison, maybe tomorrow or day after if you have the time." Addison was a northern suburb of Dallas, with a small-ish airport. Actually it was a big enough airfield it had been the backup base for the CAF's ill-fated B-17 *Texas Raiders* for a while, and not just because it had a really first-class little air museum, the Cavenaugh.

He thought about it. "Day after is better. Just gimme a call when you break ground there. I will have somebody waiting for you if I can't get there in time to do it myself. You can stay out here at the house if you got the time to linger some."

"Cool. Thanks, man. See ya then." I hung up.

Now as for that token of my goodwill. After the bidding war that made us sort of pals, I knew what he liked. I went back into the safe, started pulling out a bunch of 1911s, and thought about it. I kept going back to the Jim Clark-done .38 Super; the nearly mint condition one from Big John's estate. It was the right combination of vintage-rare and *I am probably not going to shoot it much* that I was willing to sacrifice it to get Mad Jack talking. Easy come, easy go, I guess. I had five other .38 Supers now, including the two other of John's. One of them was a very similar Clark I'd found in Baton Rouge a few years back. Now that one looked like someone had plowed a field with it, but it still shot well. Better to part with the pretty one for maximum diplomacy points. Gift-wrapping things well was not my strength, but fortunately Angel was unusually skilled at it and was there to help me. Thinking about it, I also wrapped up the Pachmayr. There was somebody else I knew in Dallas who would really appreciate it instead of it gathering dust in my collection.

***

Angel and I caught our usual chartered Lear and we were off to Texas. With the amount of money we spent chartering small jets a year, usually this one, part of me still wondered if we were going to end up buying one of the damn things eventually. Probably a bigger one. Then I'd have to find some ex-Air Force guys to run it... maybe Chris knew somebody.

I was asleep before we finished the climb-out and jolted awake when we touched down at Addison. Angel merely smiled at me over her laptop's screen. She'd apparently spent the ride getting caught up on an anime series. I sat up and stumbled over to the cockpit door as we were taxiing over to the ramp. I never could fully stand up in the low-ceilinged cabin; it lacked about three inches of headroom. Another reason to buy bigger if I ever gave in to that temptation
. "Matt, I have no idea how this meeting is going to go. Either way, take the night off. Park the bird, relax, and enjoy some night life or something." I slid him an envelope of money.

He rolled his neck, stretching as he popped his seat belt. "Fair. She doesn't need any serious maintenance, but I'll get her turned around for tomorrow before I wander off. Any particular time?"

"No idea. Like I said, this will either be angry and over in fifteen minutes or could turn into a long, ugly bar crawl of two days. And if it's fifteen minutes, we'll still grab a hotel and stay over."

"So nothing before noon tomorrow?"

"Nah, aim for 1400 at the earliest. If anything changes, I will text you. And I trust you not to be too wretchedly hung over." He laughed.

Jack was there at the railing as we came down the stairs. We waved at each other and we rolled our bag over. Like I'd told Matt, we weren't even sure if we were going to spend the night, so we had shared one large rolling suitcase. Jack shook my hand and blatantly eyeballed Angel. "Well, you brought a date, so the strip club is out."

She laughed and preened a bit. "I packed my good leather and two pairs of heels just because I thought we were going!"

He looked back over at me with a grin. "You got a live one here, doncha?" He then turned back to her and started speaking some version of Chinese. Angel laughed, answering in Chinese as well. They both laughed. I didn't have a clue. I have a serious lack of talent for languages, which should be a disqualifying handicap for someone pretending to be an intelligence officer for a living. "All right, I brought something for ya in the truck, so let's go find something to eat and then you can tell me why you came all the way out here to fuck up my *feng shui*."

Jack had one of his younger minions driving his Yukon, a tall, pale kid with a classic Ranger haircut and the look of College Station to him. It was only slightly lifted and slightly stretched. He piled in the limo-style back with us and we got out onto Dallas Parkway heading south toward downtown. He hit the switch for the privacy divider, then handed me a nicely wrapped gift box. Angel turned and leaned over the back seat, giving us all a nice view of her tightly miniskirted butt while she retrieved his out of our suitcase.

I looked at him. "Who opens first?"

He tore the paper on his. "It ain't Christmas morning, so I ain't waiting. Let's see what you brought an old man..." He pulled out the Clark. Dropping the mag, he racked the slide then dry-fired it once. "Damn nice. Old enough work Jim Senior might have done it himself. I have a couple Clarks, but not a .38 Super. Damn. You done good, kid. Now I feel bad for not upstaging you. Open yours."

With the familiar weight of the package, I suspected where this was going. Unwrapping mine, sure as hell, it was that Colt from the *New York*. I looked at him. "I really do appreciate the gesture, but I know how happy you were to score this one. Now I actually do feel bad."

He laughed, pouring a glass from the crystal decanter on the sideboard. "Nah. About six months ago, I was up in Tulsa. I stopped by the big gun show there and found one from the same 1912 Navy contract that authenticated to the USS *Nevada* and had much better finish left on it." He pointed at the decanter. "Y'all want a sip?"

For politeness, I went with it. "Yeah, I will take two fingers worth. What is it, the Rare Breed still or are you on to something else?"

"Rare Breed is good car booze. Quality enough to really enjoy, not so rare, pardon the pun, that I will cry if some gets spilled. I wouldn't go putting Pappy van Winkle in here. Temperature would be terrible for it when the truck is parked." I sipped. Damn, this stuff was strong, 112 proof. And Jack was sipping his neat, so I couldn't be the wuss and throw some water in it. Great flavor, but at full strength it felt like it would eventually dissolve the enamel on my teeth. "Remembering your advice on how easy cars are to wire, where do you want to go for dinner?"

Gasping a bit from the cask-strength bourbon, I shrugged and told him, "Anywhere you are comfortable talking business."

Angel just squeaked, "I skipped lunch! Feed me!"

He laughed. "Not too much, girl, you did bring your dancing shoes. But since it's business..." He pulled out a drawer below the liquor sideboard and threw his cell phone in it. Ours quickly followed. "I couldn't get the right kind of copper mesh in a hurry. I had my guy use old lead sheeting from a dentist's X-ray room instead. We were knocking it down to put in a twelve-unit condo building, so I got the lead for free."

As I mentioned, Jack owned a pretty nice steakhouse in Dallas, the sort of place that snobby food writers consider below their annual top ten list but will still give a nice review. Not the YO Ranch or Sullivan's, but a competitor further out in the suburbs. He also owned a piece of fifteen or sixteen allegedly mom-and-pop Chinese carry-outs in various neighborhood strip malls, three strip clubs at different price points, and was a franchise holder for at least four national fast food and pizza chains with multiple locations of each. We had plenty of dinner options.

The kid pulled into one of the carry-outs, going around the side of the building. We walked through the back door into a hot, noisy kitchen. We eased past hissing woks, me noticing the staff was really pointedly ignoring us, when Jack took a sharp right turn. We now found ourselves in a very nicely appointed private dining room. It was pretty goddamn clever. Even with my knack for navigation, I'd been riding backwards in a limo for half an hour through suburbs that mostly looked alike. I don't think I could find the place again on a dare without cheating and dropping a pin in my phone's map app. And that would be rude, right? If our phones hadn't been out in the parking lot in that lead-lined drawer, I would have done it anyway. Business is business.

One of the women came for our order before we even sat down. He and I both went for Mongolian beef, while Angel had the sesame chicken. We agreed to split the green beans in black garlic sauce and a plate of egg rolls.

Jack pointed toward the soda dispenser and a lavishly outfitted bar. "What d'ya'll want? Odds are I've got it."

Angel got comfortable while Jack poured. I volunteered to help with the drinks just because I wanted to eyeball his bottles. I was happy but not surprised to find some Oak and Eden. That was often quite hard to get east of Texarkana and I'd missed it. I'd tried it once with some Texans at a convention. The cabernet infusion sounds weird but tastes much better than you'd think. Suitably fortified, we sat down and awaited the food. We clinked glasses as Jack grinned. "Not that I am trying to cheap out on dinner, but this is the one place I have checked for bugs twice a week. Last time was this morning."

"Thought you were a legitimate businessman?"

"Even paranoids have enemies and if the Feds want, they can nail anyone on anything, even my allegedly upstanding and law-abiding Aggie ass. All right, spoil my appetite. What brings you out this way bearing gifts?"

"Need some quiet business advice."

"Restaurant startups have the highest failure rate of any small business. Trying to manage strippers is worse than herding cats. My best line cooks do more coke than the strippers. What else do you want to know?" He giggled into his glass as he sipped, delighted with his own wit. You had to give the guy credit. Mad Jack was an easy dude to like.

Still grinning, I reminded myself we were on a timer, so I had to steer the conversation where I needed it to go. "Not that kind of business. Relying on your encyclopedic knowledge of the Nationalist Chinese military's diaspora in 1949-"

Jack scowled a bit. "Diaspora. Fancy way of saying a retreat, nay, a rout...."

"Did you actually say 'nay?' Rather Shakespearean of you."

"We do read books in College Station, Yankee scum." He laughed and said something to Angel in Chinese that had her giggling too.

I sighed. "You do remember I went to college in Mississippi, right?"

"That's north of here, ain't it?" Even I thought that was funny, even if the joke went back to around the time Grant took Vicksburg.

"Not by much. Anyway, no shit. We may be coming into a fair pile of offshore cash we need to park somewhere safe."

We paused for a moment when there was a knock at the door; the same older woman rolling our plates in on a cart. She then bowed and left without a word. Taking a few moments to pass the food around family-style and dish everyone up, Jack then kept going. "So, you're wanting to park cash offshore. Not Switzerland?"

I shook my head. "Nope. Not Switzerland."

He grinned. "Ah and entranced by the beauty of Asian thighs," he winked at Angel, "you're looking now to park your ill-gotten gains offshore with one of the members of my tribe as opposed to the expensive watches and complicated pocket knives tribe up in the mountains where everyone since the Nazis put theirs."

I laughed again. Damn, I did like this guy. "Back before the Nazis. You ever hear the story that the Swiss established the banks of Geneva and Zurich with some of the missing Templar treasure?"

He sipped at his bourbon. "Yeah, I saw that shit on the History Channel too. Was right before the Bigfoot hunters came on. I love those guys. A couple of drinks and they are banging logs on trees and howling in the dark. Shit's hilarious."

"It is funny, when I have the time. Problem is since the Feds got Weglin and UBS for money laundering and tax evasion some years back, most of the Swiss won't touch new American clients with a ten foot pole outside their US branches, though I don't blame them much."

Jack grinned. "Ah, and this is why you need a new and better plan. And obviously you won't use the Caribbean for anything really big because it's full of fucking Feds, no matter what their legal disclaimers say."

I nodded in agreement. "Yeah. Five or ten mil is one thing. This is bigger. A much better plan is needed and with people who have more of a cultural commitment to secrecy. And correct me if I am wrong, but Nationalist officers, hell, fully intact units, went everywhere from the Golden Triangle heroin fields to various Chinatowns around the Pacific Rim. And they still control a certain amount of the money laundering and covert banking around the entire region on top of the heroin."

He leaned back in his chair and thought a minute. "No, you are right there, but what you run into with those Whampoa grads and their kids and grandkids is that way too much of the pre-'49 Nationalist officer corps were gangsters in uniform, from Chiang on down. He came out of the old Green Gang in Shanghai even before he joined the Army. Corruption was their thing, not actually winning the goddamn war. If they won the war, there was less to steal, particularly with all that American Lend-Lease money from '42 to '45. They just stopped wearing their uniforms in '49 after they spent four years getting their asses kicked out to Taiwan, then most of them stayed crooks after. And yes, I can tell your lovely date is also Taiwanese. The accent is a giveaway. No offense meant by any of this, darlin'."

She smiled back and fluttered her eyelashes at him. "None taken. It's not like I was born there either."

He grinned at her. "Good for you. Anyway," turning back to me, he continued. "So rather than dealing in the Nationalist Army Alumni Association, you are safer dealing with old-timers who have been set up somewhere pre-1949, the further back the better. They're still criminals; they're just a better class of criminals. You buy them and they're honorable enough to stay bought. And they also don't generally deal with you round-eyes at all. Now just between us old pals, what are you trying to move? You don't strike me as the drugs type. You're too softhearted to be running working girls and there ain't enough money in that to be worth hauling overseas. Guns, maybe?"

I held up a hand while I chewed. This was really good Mongolian beef. Maybe they tried extra hard since it was dinner for the boss. I then answered delicately. "Just trying to put a literal pallet or three of US cash offshore somewhere safe. Gold bullion, probably. I start shoving too much physical cash into actual bank accounts, red flags are going to pop somewhere no matter where in the world banking system I put it." There was a brief hot flash as my tongue found a bit of red pepper stuck in my teeth.

He slumped in his chair a bit. "Bud, I wish I had some great ideas, but shit, you probably know more about Asia than I do. Me, I am Texas born and raised. I haven't even been to Vancouver to see the cousins in a while. They find me embarrassingly redneck and start talking shit again after the first two days. Then I have a couple drinks, I want to fight somebody in the front yard, it ends up happening, and then I don't get invited back to the family Christmas party again for a couple more years. Mom hates it when that happens. She nags the hell out of me, too. And not many people can nag your ass like a Chinese mom."

Angel nodded in sympathy. "You got that shit right."

I frowned. I somehow expected Jack to have a magic wand to fix this. "Well, shit."

"Don't let it spoil your appetite, man. I will reach out to a couple of my less uppity cousins for advice and let you know. One of those crooked fucks has got to know something."

"Well, I appreciate it." The conversation then rolled onto what we were wearing for carry guns and onto the upcoming college football season as we finished off the food and had another round of drinks.

Angel said, "Thank you for dinner. Now should I get changed for a night out here or there?"

***

It had been a great night at the club. I think Angel bought more lap dances than I did and seemed to get a few free. I slightly regretted not bringing Cash as well, but I would make it up to her. We'd lost Jack around ten, when he claimed it was his bedtime. He left us his Yukon and driver. That was nice of him, and not just because it still had our luggage in it.

We finally left the club around one and caught a ride to the Omni. I had stayed there for the NRA convention a few years before and liked the beds. I gave Jack's kid two hundred bucks for beer money before dismissing him and I could tell he reflexively wanted to salute. We woke up late, missing the breakfast buffet downstairs. It had closed at ten and we were pushing eleven. I texted Matt and told him 1500ish. Emphasis on *ish.*

While Angel got ready, I'd texted Bam Bam to drop off his new pistol that he didn't know about, but there was no answer. He might have been out working, or out of the state on larger business, or merely on the couch and out of his mind. But I also didn't have time to rent a car or take a fucking Uber all the way out to Athens looking for his brother to drop it there. Might not have been a good idea anyway. His brother tended not to think too much of the rest of us who he was convinced kept Jeb on his road to ruin. While there were a few other spots I could have left it for him to pick up, better to just keep it safe until a better time came. Could only hope there was one. You have to do something nice for your brothers occasionally.

So, hungry again, we went off in search of good barbecue. You can get reasonable brisket in Nashville, but there is just something about it in Texas you never quite duplicate elsewhere. Maybe it's the selection of wood, I dunno. We caught a rideshare north and hit a very highly rated place just south of Addison Airport. That lunch meant our two hour stroll through the Cavenaugh was definitely a slow one while we digested. Maybe it was a bit of a waddle. But I do love old airplanes and since many of their collection flies regularly, the Cavenaugh is as much working hangar space with toolboxes and drip pans as it is a museum. We actually ran into Matt partway through the tour, admiring a B-26 Invader. He didn't look too worse for wear and said he'd had a good night. Once we were all done, we got in the Lear and flew home. There was still much to do.

Chapter 14

"Good help is hard to find."
~Apocryphal proverb

There was the question of who was going to watch my house and take care of the animals while we were going to be head-down working on this score and putting in weird hours at the office. Angel and Cash took care of that. Angel had suggested hiring a long term employee or two just to work the house even before this. We were just too far behind on our chores on the few days off we did have. So they scrounged around in our collective online social circles and pulled in an adorable little brunette from east Texas we had distantly known for a while. Jeanie had just finished her sophomore year of college and needed a solid summer job so she didn't have to go back home. Home wasn't good for her. So the change of scenery was for her own sake, never mind whatever Angel was paying her.

Of course the girls didn't tell me they had worked all this out. The first I found out about it was stumbling in pain into the kitchen at six in the morning with my glasses off to let Odin out the back door. Jeanie was already in there working on breakfast for everyone.

Yeah. That had made a hell of a first impression on the new hire. I was naked and squinting, so I barely saw her at first. Odin, being the ferocious guard animal that he is, proceeds to slobber on her and get ear scritches. He then flops on his back with all four paws in the air so she could get his tummy. Apparently they had met already. Me, I was thoroughly confused. "Who the hell are you?"

"Hello, it's Jeanie, remember me?"

I could barely see her to remember her and I was trusting Odin's judgment that I didn't need to go for the kitchen gun. Wait, what do you mean you don't have a kitchen gun? Poser. Regardless, without glasses on, my eyesight is 20/Go

Fuck Yourself. Past twelve inches, the world is one big multicolored blur. "Uh, yeah, but why are you here? When did you get here?"

She reached in the fridge and handed me a Mountain Dew. "Angel hired me to be the new house manager since you guys are going to be gone a lot for a while. No, I don't know why, I was told not to ask. I'm staying all summer. As for when, I got here... three days ago? I'm in the back guest room."

"Well, fuck, nice of her to solve that problem, really nice of her to tell me about it." I really should have noticed. I was slightly distracted with work though. I had barely been home in those three days. The world was being busy right now and we had to squeeze our little fundraising caper in between several other geopolitical crises that constituted paying work.

"Our job is to handle the little things so you don't need to think about them."

"Fair enough, but don't clean the rec room off the back hallway unless you want to see stuff you may be too young to see."

She laughed. "How do you think Miss Angel bribed me into coming out here?"

Shit. The only problem with this I could see was that I knew that Jeanie had a problem with liking to organize things. I was liable to come home and not be able to find so much as a pair of socks. I also made a mental note to detail off a couple quality shooters from the guard force to cover her and the house if we were gone too long.

"Oh, and I found you two dozen twelve-packs of your weird Mountain Dew at HEB. It's in the pantry closet."

Okay, so this maybe had its upside.

Chapter 15

"Eastbound and down, loaded up and truckin'..."
~Jerry Reed

We knew the container was going to be a truck job. So now I needed a good CDL-holding trucker with experience in the shady side of life, but at the same time somebody I could reasonably trust. That meant my buddy Steve. One does not normally hire your ex-wife's new husband for a job like this, but everything was very friendly and he did have the skill sets. He was another multi talented guy. Even Morgan liked him.

Steve was a tall, rail-thin dude with a bushy red beard, the sort of pureblood Scots-Irish border reiver you still found up some hollers and hilltops in the South. He was merely a fair hand with a pistol but could successfully do truly ridiculous things with wheeled vehicles. Now after a very checkered past, he had mostly gone legit, but I just figured I would pay him twenty grand in cash for two days' work during the raid itself and just not tell him everything. Truth be told, if we were going to be doing stuff like this more often, I might need him more often. So I called him up, and told him I needed him to consult on something. We met for lunch, and I gave him a rough idea on the physics of what we needed done. Then I told him I needed a preliminary plan in thirty-six hours and handed him two grand for his time.

The plan came fast, God bless the Internet. He had wanted to go with a "low boy" style heavy equipment trailer that came apart to load, but that was too slow for my taste. Some YouTubing on his part found us an Australian company selling a specialized moving rig for 20' containers, similar to a rollback tow truck. It was basically a specialized draw bar that worked with the tow winch. I told Steve to find us a US dealer for the Australian thing and get whatever the fuck it cost from Cash. Really, I was so happy I didn't care if we had to order the fucking thing from Australia ourselves. It was perfect for the second hardest part of the whole mission, which was picking the container up and moving it to where it met the boat. What kind of boat? This is where another Gulf Coast peculiarity worked in our favor.

Crew boats are all over the place on the Gulf of Mexico. As one might guess from the name, they exist to rotate crews on and off offshore oil rigs. About 150 to 200 feet long, they have a nearly airline style passenger compartment in a forward superstructure, with a large flat cargo deck on the rear perfect for vehicles and containers. With the right dock, and of course we could find one, you can even stern-load one by driving the truck and container right onto it. They have excellent offshore range and handling as an essential function of their mission and you can run one with just three guys. On the Gulf, they are easy to find, easy to rent, and no one really pays attention to them so long as you stay west of the Florida state line where offshore drilling stopped.

So the tentative plan was that the truck with the container would come down the dock, back right onto the crew boat's deck, drop the container, then pull off and depart. Then the crew boat starts moving, the deckhands get the container chained down before the boat clears harbor, and it's off to the rendezvous point with the *Ecstasy*, which was coming up from the south.

Jimmy had run down his list of Navy buddies and found three ex-Naval Special Boat Unit guys to run the crew boat. Seven more, well, a couple were frigate and destroyer types, would be needed to crew the *Ecstasy*. That was his lane to handle and his Christmas bonus would reflect that accordingly.

The next tricky bit was going to be getting the cash out of the container and onto the *Ecstasy*.

Some heavy research into the technicalities suggested that we did not want to bring the newly purchased yacht into an American port and clear Customs with it. It was foreign-flagged, which meant an inspection when we cleared Customs. If we changed that flag to American, there were heavy taxes and fees involved. Then there was the suspicious nature of an all male and visibly former US military crew on a foreign flagged vessel. It just was all just a bunch of issues we didn't need. Sailing too far into American waters without clearing Customs could be an issue as well, but we were researching that.

My thought was to do a Jean Lafitte. Pull up into Mobile Bay behind the Fort Morgan point at slack tide in the dark, ramp the pallets across using a barge or something as a fixed point, get the stuff onto the yacht, and the yacht leaves, never having touched American soil or done anything with American customs.

It was Chris and Dave who came back with the counter argument. "Dude, we're thinking like criminals. Why do it that way if we don't have to?" I just looked at them. They continued. "We don't fucking have to. We have all these lovely DOD and intel community-looking contract assets and such, we have tons of solid fake IDs, we just write the *Ecstasy* up as a US Navy contract asset under DIA or some shit, have some nice bogus paperwork with a spoofed verification, then we work at a real dock on Stennis or the Seabee base at Gulfport that night. No pitching and rolling offshore, so we are in and out in two hours."

"From a technical perspective, is it doable?"

Chris was enthusiastic enough. "Hell yes. It's the functional equivalent of all those Air Force special ops birds with dummy civilian registration numbers on them, or their civilian rental birds with dummy USAF serials."

Jimmy and Tommy were shaking their heads. "No fucking way are we getting that yacht up the Pearl River into Stennis. Not easily. Running a forty foot gunboat in and out of there is easy; we have both done riverine live fire exercises with the gunboat unit that's home-based there, but it looks way easier on the map than it is. The big NASA stuff that goes in and out by barge from the engine test stands use the same tug and towboat crews all the time. We are going to be using ex-destroyer crewmen or small craft guys who have only a couple weeks' experience with the yacht at best. And the Seabee base at Gulfport is in town, it isn't waterfront. There is a big-ass artificial harbor though. Mostly commercial leases. Navy uses it sometimes."

That gave me the first big question. "Can we get a crew boat backed up to it and tail load the container?"

They looked at each other and shrugged. "Probably."

"Gentlemen, I love you both like brothers, but probably ain't gonna cut it in this case. So your immediate tasking is to identify whoever is going to be the crew boat skipper, grab a car, a company rental will do, and get yourselves down to Gulfport to identify primary, alternate, contingency and emergency load points for the crew boat in the area. Maritime-related reconnaissance is a core SEAL thing and you two are the aquatic mammals present. Figure it out and give the joint task force commander, me, a solid plan."

Jimmy nodded. "You got it. And fuck you if you think I am saluting though." We all laughed at that.

"I wouldn't expect it if we were all still in. We're below decks, so even I know better."

Tommy shook his head. "Way below decks. This goddamn hole in the ground is like the bilges on a carrier, only it smells better." Tommy really didn't like the office all that much. Didn't hate it as much as doing combat swimmer operations off of submarines, but he still didn't like it much. He was a little claustrophobic by SEAL standards and preferred fresh air.

Now, how to make the *Ecstasy* look like a Navy contractor? I didn't know how, but I suspected someone else did. That was why I messaged Little John off the Black phone. Yes, we were deep underground but we had a very good cell phone repeater system that would allow authorized phones access to the system, all the way up to the antenna on the hilltop a few hundred feet above. *"Navy ? Call me when you have time."*

I was actually shocked by how fast he answered. *"Call secure in 20?"* Guess he wasn't out on his boat. I went back upstairs to my office while everyone else kept going. I grabbed another Mountain Dew out of the fridge as I passed the break room. I then called him on the desk phone's secure system.

"Hey, John."

He sounded happy. He usually did. "How are they hanging, man?"

"Lower than usual. Now serious naval type question for you and I am in a bit of a rush."

That got another chuckle out of him. "What else is new? Go for it."

"I need to get smart on naval auxiliary vessels and deniable maritime assets."

I could hear the wheels turning in his mind, metaphorically. "Huh. You need one?"

At least we weren't starting from scratch. "We have one lined up, I think, we're just thinking making it look official is a safer route than making it look criminal."

Another chuckle. "Backwards from your usual method."

He had a point. "Yeah, well, this time we are bringing a boat in and don't want any Customs or other bullshit hassles, we'd prefer them think it's an off the books clandestine SEAL thing than actual Colombian drug smugglers."

He made a vague grunt of approval. "Crew?"

"All recent ex-Navy, Jimmy has been handling that."

There was another grunt of approval at that. Admirals usually liked chiefs and Little John had grown quite fond of Jimmy these last few years, "The easiest thing is to set up a shell company like usual, but instead of setting it up as some corrupt offshore bullshit like you usually do, you set it up in the States, a Delaware PO box is traditional, or in a town that will send a message. Think Norfolk, Little Creek, Virginia Beach, or Coronado. Then you have some official Navy looking contract paperwork from the Navy to that shell, then subcontract to whatever foreign company owns the boat on paper."

Now for the important bit. "How do we mock up the paperwork?"

He thought a moment before answering. "Good question. I know there is a format for it; I just don't know exactly what it is. It was done below my level and I wasn't the one who signed off on it. That's more a logistical or legal issue than an intelligence matter."

Well, shit. "Okay, so the implied task for us is to find the guy who knows what that paper looks like and make a sample of it happen so we can run off of that."

I could almost hear him nodding in approval. "That would work. You don't have to fool anybody for long, right?"

We really didn't. "Nope. And it's got to be easier than doing it straight up criminal."

He laughed a bit. "Good thinking, for once. Way less risky. But the best tradecraft trick for that is make sure the phone number is wrong, or better yet, answered by somebody tame. That buys you your time to do what you gotta do. Then run like hell and change your transponder squawk settingon the boat before they figure it out."

Okay, I had a plan now. "Sounds good. Thanks, man."

He laughed a little more. I envied him his jolly nature, as I'd left much of my joy somewhere along the way. "Anytime. When you finish whatever this insane project is, and I am definitely not gonna ask because I don't want to know, come on down and fish. Spending a day drinking beer and waiting for a marlin to bite is good for the soul."

"Amen. And thanks." I cleared the line and took a good relaxing breath. I did miss fishing, but I was short on time lately. One of these years.

I went back to the conference room thinking about it. Since I didn't know, or know for sure who would know, I loudly addressed my question to the room. "Okay, for high dollar leases or purchases by military assets, is that an S-4 function because it's logistical or a JAG thing because it's contracting?"

Naturally Dave knew. "Depends on what. This kind of money, assume JAG. They are gonna want a lawyer looking at the lease at least, then the 4 and then maybe Comptroller looking at the money versus the budget."

I sat down and stared at the ceiling again. "All right, so we need a crooked ex-SOCOM JAG type to help set up something that looks like a DOD shell company, not a criminal shell company."

Jimmy shrugged. "What's the difference?"

"One kind will make the Customs guys walk the fuck away politely, the other will eventually have us all in handcuffs and the Feds wanting to steal our stolen boat."

Jimmy wasn't fully going along with this. "But we're buying the boat."

I sighed. "With money that was probably stolen somewhere, so it's kinda the same thing."

Dave scratched at his chin. "I don't know why I didn't think of that dickhead sooner, but anyone talk to Fast Eddie Netherton lately?"

I knew a lot of names. Not this one. "Who the fuck is Fast Eddie Netherton?"

"Eddie used be one of the assistants at Command Legal. Something like a dozen lawyers in the office and he was back of the line. I liked him because not only was he ex-173rd Airborne, but he was another asshole from New Jersey. We used to see each other at the gym. Anyway, he got volun-told for the gig because he was the only JAG captain in the Army with a scuba badge. He went while he was on the West Point swim team. Then he managed to go to freefall school while he was with the Command, so he had all the extra badges to fit in with the cool kids.

"Really, he is a scumbag ambulance chaser kind of lawyer, has the personality of a really crooked used car salesman. That made the serious JAGs not like him, so instead of doing operational law like the legalities of sniping somebody versus putting a Hellfire through their window with a UAV, he got stuck doing all the operational support law, the 'this is only legal because we're the US government and only legal for a military unit because it's under the counterterrorism statutes' cover documents like shell companies, dummy leases and shit."

I didn't know this dude, but I kinda liked him a little already. "So where is he now?"

Dave laughed. "Got a really shitty Officer Evaluation Report and resigned his commission. Heard he was out west trying to get into entertainment law in Vegas or something."

Jimmy got curious. "What did he get the bad OER for?"

Dave was really laughing now. "Payback for sleeping with the commanding general's daughter. Two hundred years ago it would have been dueling on the front lawn kinda shit."

That got my attention. "No fucking shit?" People always joked about stuff like that going on, but it verifiably happening was pretty rare.

"That was the rumor. With Fast Eddie, who the fuck knows. The West Pointers who knew him said he was kind of the class clown and he definitely had a serious problem with chasing pussy, so it's entirely possible. He had enough bad luck in his career that it spoiled his enthusiasm for taking orders well."

Decision made. I looked over at Angel. "Job for you, dear. Get with the backside of Intel. You find this guy, or find somebody who knows him and have them find him, tell him I will pay him ten thousand in cash just for having a nice dinner sit-down, then get him on the first thing smoking into

Nashville so we can talk. We may need this guy. No, we definitely need this guy."

Chapter 16

"Send lawyers, guns and money..."
~Warren Zevon

Jimmy and Tommy headed off south to meet whoever was commanding the crew boat and recon the coastal sites we'd need. Meanwhile Morgan put the "archives section" hackers to work and they found Eddie Netherton in the space of about three days. He was couch-surfing in the Vegas suburbs with friends he'd met at a strip club. From there, I supposed he was trying to make better friends he could then leverage to get a law practice going, but apparently it wasn't going well. When Angel cold-called him, he jumped on the offer to come talk to us. I arranged to meet him at the airport in a few days.

It was now the time of the month when Angel wasn't feeling well and she was distinctly antisocial as a result. At her suggestion, I then asked Cash if she wanted to go with me instead. I was shocked that Cash said yes. She then decided to look her best in case a little psychological torture was needed. "He thinks he's a pussy hound, sir? We can leverage that. I will make him suffer a bit for you until he falls into line." She rolled out as a symphony in black, wearing a quite low cut leather corset top with a nice summer-weight blazer thrown over it, a leather pencil skirt and knee high stiletto heeled boots. *Anything worth doing is worth overdoing.*

We snagged him off the sidewalk at the Nashville airport's main terminal, got him into the back seat of my truck and got moving before the airport cops had time to blow their whistles and yell at me for taking up time in the pickup zone. He was about five ten, with hair on the blond-brown boundary, somewhere around the color of overcooked French fries and it hadn't been cut in a while. He'd once been wiry, but now had that pasty "I have eaten nothing but cheap junk food and haven't seen the inside of a gym in a year" look that some guys get when they are readjusting to civilian life.

Look, I got over my personal dislike of West Pointers a very long time ago. I had some very good commanders come out of there and some of their graduates are friends and were damn near adopted family. Still, every now and then you meet one that gives the rest of the breed a bad name. My initial plan to like him was now on hold, since this motherfucker got the hair on the back of my neck standing up within thirty seconds. He just radiated "unreliable weasel" from the second I laid eyes on him, but we dragged him out to dinner anyway. He didn't seem to care whether I liked him or not. He couldn't keep his eyes off Cash's cleavage, her aftermarket upgrades enhanced even further by Miss Martha's Corset Shoppe. Fair enough. Cash's plan for psychological leverage was clearly working.

We pretty much rebuffed any attempt at serious conversation past 'How was your flight?' until we got to the restaurant, a quiet little barbecue joint back in Sylvan Park where 46th Street southbound hits the Murphy Road traffic circle. We took a seat out on their back patio. It was a nice night, but we had plenty of privacy. We were into late June by now. It was time for the NHL playoffs, with the Nashville Predators hockey team out on the road at Winnipeg. All eyes and ears were on the TVs, so you could barely ask for a better distraction. We flagged down a waitress for brisket sandwiches, two large draft beers, and an ice water. Cash was not a beer girl.

I laid an envelope in the middle of the table, fat with hundreds. He looked down at it then back up at me. I had a time where I would have taken the job to stab somebody for a fraction of what was in there. As a result, part of me felt a little bad about taking advantage of the guy's shitty situation, but that's life. I have done way worse when I've had to and no doubt will again. He looked back up at me, meeting me square in the eye for the first time. "Okay, seriously. Who the hell are you guys?" If Dave hadn't told me he was from *Noo Joisey*, him opening his mouth left no doubt. It had come out *youse guise.*

"People who need your skills."

He snorted. "Which ones? A near-death drowning in dive school, being the worst PL in the entire Herd according to my CO, getting shot in Afghanistan, losing the only woman I really loved while I was in law school, or being the expendable scumbag lawyer in an unnamed headquarters I signed an NDA on and can't talk about for twenty-five years?" He took a long, long pull on his beer. His weasel act was slipping and I was seeing the wounds he hid behind the act. Unfortunately he reminded me of me about twenty years ago when I was on a bad streak. It brought back bad memories. I hate having empathy.

Cash leaned forward, deliberately giving him a bit more of a view. "Show a little backbone, Edward. You're better than this."

"How sure are you of that?"

Under the table, I laid a hand on Cash's thigh. "Eddie, you're having a crisis of faith, both in yourself and in your future. I get that. Been there, had the nightmares and the drinking problem for a while to go with it."

He nodded. "Yeah, says you. I've gotten the 'cheer up, you aren't the only one who ever got fucked over' speech before. Usually thirty seconds before I get fucked over again."

"Then I'll skip the speech and just ask a question. What if I told you I needed an LLC formed to look like a legitimate DOD contractor, then a DOD contract written to that LLC that will pass external examination as valid?"

"Any specific service?"

"East Coast Naval Special Warfare. Whoever does clandestine small boat support."

Eddie nodded. "That's easier than you think because of the boat reorganization. Boats don't belong to the SEALs anymore anyway, except one case we won't mess with. So we do a fake contract from the boat group's HQ support section at Little Creek to your LLC. Then you fake a sent courtesy copy to one of the boat team XOs. I assume the East Coast one. So you need the LLC and a fake boat lease. So I'd tell you it was dirt-shit easy, and I could shake it loose in about six hours. Instead, I could probably do it in three by just changing dates and names on shit I already did for them and saved copies of illegally. You can e-file an LLC in a lot of states now. So, then I'd bill you for eight hours, work three, then pocket the difference because I need it and I don't know when my next paying work will be. I am actually debating selling the first class return ticket you paid for and going back coach. I can live off the difference for a week or so until something else comes up. Get an apartment with the money from this." He tapped the envelope.

I admired his planning and thrift. "You have any particular reason to get back to Vegas?"

He chuckled grimly. "Cheap booze, twenty four hour buffets, and the morally casual atmosphere. But since my truck got stolen last week and Vegas PD has a fifteen percent closure rate on car thefts, I won't see it again. And the stripper I was staying with for the last month firmly suggested that I find somewhere else to crash when I come back to town, so not really. Going back is more a force of habit. I grew up in the Army. Dad was in too and I don't really have a civilian hometown."

Cash delicately elbowed me, gave me a sideways glance, and then took the lead. "Home is where you make it if you don't have a place to go. My parents died my freshman year of college. I had nothing left in the world except work and ambition. Then after a few years of that, I had a sort of career misfortune so I needed a place to hide and start over. I was given that and have had a good opportunity since. I found both profit and love."

I knew her parents were gone. She knew I knew. She had never opened up about it and we had never spoken of it. Ever. The one time I mentioned it, she had quickly dismissed the topic with "They were her parents, not mine." Even I thought that was kind of ruthless. And weird, but... mostly ruthless.

I focused back on Eddie. "Your stuff still back there?"

He shrugged. "Meh. Nothing I care about. Anything important is in a storage locker in Fayetteville that's prepaid a year in advance. Now, do you guys do a lot of this? LLCs, blind trusts, dummy leases, shell companies?"

I shrugged. "More than I ever thought I would have to. Legal smokescreens to cover other actions are useful. You know that from your background. We may do some sketchy shit in the line of duty, but we aren't genuine criminals and are trying to stay off law enforcement's radar."

That got another nod out of him. "Yeah, that's one reason the FBI gets a seat at joint task force meetings, so they know what to keep their agents away from. Can't have the Feds trying to arrest other Feds and letting the bad guys get away in the confusion."

I snorted. *Yeah, that sounded like government efficiency.* "You get the concept then."

He looked at me thoughtfully before he finally spoke. "Yeah, but you ain't Agency. They have their own lawyers. You? The age, the vocabulary, and the unflattering lifer haircut all scream 'retired field grade officer' to me. You have that bulky cross-country heavy rucksack kind of build you still get in some of the SF old-timers. But unless your eyesight got real bad later, you were never on that side of the fence with glasses that thick. You'd never pass the physical. Still, you know who I am and what I used to do, so that tells me you at least work with guys who were read-in. And if you were willing to cough up ten grand and a plane ticket just to get me here for this meeting, you obviously have a fat pile of operational funds and about zero oversight on how you spend it. Under the circumstances, that makes you look more interesting than anything else I have going on."

I smiled a bit. "Maybe you aren't as fucking stupid as some people say you are. Were you really dumb enough to be fucking the CG's daughter?"

He smirked. "That the rumor?"

I nodded once. "That was the rumor." Cash merely snickered. She hadn't heard that part.

He took another long pull at his beer, mostly draining it. His head swiveled looking for a refill. "Well, the rumor is seventy five percent bullshit. His daughter is a no-shit 'Untouched by Man' gold star lesbian, like her going to fucking Oberlin wasn't a clue. When called out on it by her very Southern Baptist dad, she tried using me as a smokescreen for some time, before having a very messy coming out at their Thanksgiving dinner table with her girlfriend-slash-fiancée present. Her dad being her dad, he then assumed she rebounded to girls after I behaved in my allegedly characteristic manner. He blames me for the entire mess. So I end up out on my ass with the worst OER I ever even heard of, the daughter and the girlfriend moved to Seattle together, got married, then got divorced six months later. But the story grows with every retelling."

My eyebrows went up a bit at that ending to the tale. "Huh. The truth is less interesting yet still funnier at the same time."

"The truth often is. It will either set you free or get you doing ten to fifteen." Good joke, but I'd heard it before. Then again, much of my material is stolen too.

This was fun, and I was enjoying it, but it was past time to get to the point. "Anyway, here's the deal. We'll get you a nice little extended stay suite over by the airport so you aren't homeless but aren't tied down either. Some per diem to live on. Company rental car if you want it. Nothing fancy, not a shitbox either. We put you to work from there. Work will come and go by courier; nothing emailed. It's going to be a while before you see the home office. No offense meant, but we're kinda secretive. If this works out, we will bring you on more regularly. Think of this project as your first audition."

He sighed. "Well, it's way more my background than trying to become a talent agent for strippers." He looked back over at Cash, his eyes still tracking on her chest.

"Don't even think about it. I only play for fun." She laid her head down on my shoulder.

It was my turn to brag on her a bit. "She's actually the accounting department."

His eyes widened. "Damn. You don't look like any accountant I ever saw."

She arched an eyebrow at him. "That was my intention."

Chapter 17

"Boat; a hole in the water into which one throws money."
"BOAT: Bust Out Another Thousand."
~Bumper stickers seen at numerous marinas

Back from the reconnaissance of the Gulf coast, Jimmy then flew to the British Virgin Islands to meet the yacht broker. He had taken a Black phone with him so we'd have some communications security; he actually had Mikey's old one. For what they had cost and how few of the damn things we had, we couldn't be sentimental and retire them over a little thing like death. Big John's phone was next in line to get handed back out when needed.

Cash had fixed him up with everything he would need to pay in full for the *Ecstasy* out of the "local" bank accounts in the Caribbean, and with some operational funds besides, assuming he came away from the inspections with a good feeling. If not, there were plenty of other big boats out there and I was sure we'd find something somewhere. The LLC Netherton did for us would own the *Ecstasy*. In turn, they would then lease it on paper to the Navy for the move into US waters, even if the Navy didn't actually know it.

The Navy guys he had found had flown down and met him there. The senior of them was a retired commander (lieutenant colonel for us Army types) who'd formerly been the CO of an *Arleigh Burke*-class destroyer and had professionally acquired some yacht experience since. He would serve as ship's master while Jimmy concentrated on SEAL shit like intel and guns. Jimmy was a little bummed he was missing out on the raid, but I made the point that we had a lot of guys who could walk through woods and pull triggers. The only real Navy types who could handle the boat guys were him or Tommy, and since I'd known him a lot longer I trusted him more.

The first question Jimmy needed to answer was, "how wide is the main portside hatch where the gangplank ramp is?" We sure as hell didn't want to have to manhandle the bundles in one or two at a time and we had to know if we were limited to 36" pallets, 48" pallets, what weight, etc. It also affected how we pre-packed the provisioning and resupply container.

Twelve hours after he got there, he texted, "48 barely". I found out later he had borrowed a boat and gone out with a tape measure before the sales meeting. We took that as a cue to order twenty heavy-duty polyethylene pallets, 42" square, from a wholesaler. We already had the jacks to move them around on the deck and ramps. Then Jimmy had to find a maritime surveyor for the pre-sale inspection. He then had to get the Navy guys helping him examine the engines to make sure they could handle them correctly. All sorts of fun shit to do before the deal was completed.

While the legalities were working out, they were still trying to calculate the load plans for the cargo. The *Ecstasy* was not a freighter. Yes, working off her published numbers she would more than take the weight, particularly with zero passengers instead of ten, no luggage, less furniture, a smaller crew... but weight was still weight. Jimmy actually had the Navy boat guys working on it; it involved a lot of dynamic naval architecture kind of math. That was totally not my thing, but I made a note to create a bump plan, a 'this ain't going to all fit so some of it ain't going' contingency. Jimmy said the worst case scenario was buying a different boat instead. That would upset Cash though. She liked this one.

Past that, an additional duty for the gang on the *Ecstasy* was that they'd have to count the loot. Before they pulled into Singapore and before we went into the local bullion markets, we had to know what was there. Really, we would have no idea until then. And Dave, Jimmy, and Ben, who I had all known for over two decades each, were going to have to figure that out for me. Well, Tommy too. They had electric cash counters, currency bands, then lots of shrink wrap in the pallets of stuff that was going to go on the *Ecstasy*. Places in Vegas sell it, so we ordered it through another dummy account and picked it all up at the UPS warehouse. We even bought four heavy duty hydraulic pallet jacks. Four? Did we need six? What if one falls overboard? When in doubt, have spares. We could afford it.

But would we have stolen half a billion? A billion? A billion and a half? That was part of the annoyance. I was sending friends out to do battle without knowing exactly for sure what was up for grabs. There was a huge difference between half a billion and a billion and so on. And not just risk versus reward, the logistics of moving the haul were vastly different. Half a billion dollars was eight cubic yards of paper, or eight tons. One billion dollars, sixteen cubic yards, sixteen tons. Or more. And what kind of bills made a huge difference.

***

Jimmy texted me on the Black phone to let me know the yacht deal was finally good. I called him back. "How did it go?"

"Slick as shit. At the meeting, I think the guy thought I was an Asian gangster 'til I opened my mouth."

"Yeah, that *Noo Yawwk* accent of yours kinda spoils the Hong Kong *Replacement Killers* movie vibe." It was the truth. Jimmy was mixed; he looked Korean but he sounded like Joe Pesci.

"We haggled, we bitched, there was some yelling, but eventually there was a cash discount so we saved a million off the original ask. But she is all ours now. Paperwork is done and the registry has been swapped over to the LLC. We kept the BVI flag for tax purposes."

Neptune Spear LLC, PO Box Whatever, Virginia Beach, Virginia, was about as subtle as a kick to the balls, but it sent a message. Hopefully the Customs guys would get that message. Fuck it, let word leak to the military fanboy Internet that the SEALs bought a yacht for black ops shit. Let the rumors screen the truth, "a bodyguard of lies" as Churchill once said. I'd have Morgan put one of the hackers on it. "Fucking awesome. Availability for sea?"

"Maybe a week. Provisioning and such right now, at least enough for a short hop north. Better to work on her in Florida than pay island markups for parts and supplies. The crew's all here. I'm up to nine total. The captain is overqualified for this; besides commanding a destroyer, the last yacht he ran was almost twice the size. But he doesn't give a shit, since he seems to think we're Agency. No idea how he got that thought in his head." He chuckled. "The two machinist's mates I hired as engineers are solid; they were SWCC diesel guys used to running gunboats and whatnot. Five were deck division guys on cruisers or destroyers, lower petty officers like E-4s and 5s. Three bosun's mates, two quartermasters – regular black shoe Navy types. This is coming up in the world for them. Then I grabbed a cook too. Running a galley afloat is an art I don't have and I don't trust the kids to do it as a side job. They have enough else to do that they're actually rated for. And to cut the grocery bills and storage requirements a bit, the guy I hired can do sushi. We'll run a couple tuna lures behind us as we go so we can try to hook some dinner occasionally."

"No shit?"

"Yeah, I got a Japanese-American kid from Fresno who did a hitch cooking on the *Chancellorsville*. But his parents own a sushi place out there and he says he can do it well enough to feed Americans. Wouldn't last long in Tokyo though, I guess."

That was odd. "How'd you find him? That's pretty niche."

"He was in my *World of Warcraft* raid group and we got to talking offline."

You know, if I didn't have a flexible mind for handling weirdness, I would have ended up locked in a mental hospital a really long time ago, but even now some things were still in the 'nobody could make this weird-ass shit up' category.

Jimmy continued. "So when I found out he was available, I asked all the blackshoes if they'd eat it. Lucky for us it's in fashion. Wouldn't have been so lucky back in the Desert Storm days when it was something you only saw on TV. But you can get a lot of burgers and fries in a freezer too. Don't worry about us. We won't starve."

"Route home?"

"Here, Key West, Tampa Bay, do some serious shopping there, then the meetup."

I was curious. "Serious for what?"

"The four 3,000 gallon fuel blivets we are gonna cram in the pool once we drain it, a couple big chest freezers from Home Depot, Lowes, or whatever, then a pair of 10K diesel generators for a floating standby and then a backup for that. Two is one, one is none."

"You got the cargo plan worked out?"

"Yeah, it actually made things easier that only about half the furniture was included on the sale. This was a good thing. Freed up a lot of space and enough weight to matter. All the potted plants, chrome unicorns, couch pillows and extra bullshit from the sale flier pics were gone. They threw in the two jet skis, the dive gear and the Zodiac though. We're gonna add some more emergency gear; I emailed my list in. Tommy's putting in an order with a place in Louisiana that supplies the fishing industry and the oil field boats. We'll have it with the provisioning container on the crew boat. A few canned life rafts, more fire extinguishers, that kinda shit."

"You got a handle on the provisioning otherwise?"

Jimmy laughed. "The cook does. I delegate better than you do."

Sigh. Yeah. My control issues and micro managerial tendencies.

He went on. "Look, man. It ain't hard. It's thirty-five days at economy speeds with a cushion and it's not like there aren't seaport grocers and chandlers along the way. We basically need food for fourteen, which makes 56 meals a day for 35 days, plus mid-watch snacks and fuel, that's it. We will clean out a couple Costcos and Sam's Clubs on shit paper, trash bags, groceries, coffee, Cokes, a couple of air fryers, and so on. Relax, let the Navy guys do the Navy shit."

Even though I was in the room alone, I nodded. "Got it."

We kinda hit a pause. Not much else to say.

Jimmy broke the silence. "Unless you ride to the transfer, I won't see you til we get there."

I sighed. "And I probably won't. Gotta get everyone else put away after the job." I had to get the entire raid element and support sections out of Mississippi and back to base without getting caught.

"See ya there then, but we'll talk sooner." *Fucking well better.*

"Safe trip, man." I hung up.

***

It took a few days to get there, but the *Ecstasy* cleared US Customs without a hitch in Key West. Being at least partly a Navy town, we figured that might be the place CBP would ask the fewest questions of the slightly dodgy paperwork. Maybe the fact it was an all male crew, most of whom had only been off active duty for ten minutes and still looked Navy, helped Customs not ask questions. I was told they looked at the company name and instead guessed what we wanted them to guess. I could just imagine how it had gone.

"We only got paid to get her from there to somewhere. Another crew takes her from there. No idea. Nope."

Their eventual destination was Mobile Bay and they'd loiter around Point Clear or Bon Secour until it was time for them to load up and get moving. The problem would be getting something to them to then load up.

Planning for "surprise, speed and violence of action" was worthless unless we figured out where we were going to be fast and violent. Morgan's crew of hackers back behind the official IT section had been busy on that issue for months. Well, they weren't literally located behind IT. Most of them were scattered across thirty seven states and at least eleven foreign countries. Combining real estate transactions, shell companies, agricultural leases and cross-referencing some of those lawyers and law firms to criminal defense attorneys who had worked narcotics cases in the southeastern US, one name popped heavily and repeatedly as an intersection.

See, most law firms that do criminal defense stuff won't touch real estate deals and vice versa. But if you get one guy you really trust to handle everything and pay him to do it because you trust him, you just made a target of him. Every target can eventually be detected. We had to pay this guy a visit. Fortunately he had not been subtle in his choice of home address and was easy to find.

Chapter 18

"We're on the side of the demons...we're evil men in the gardens of paradise, sent by the forces of death to spread devastation and destruction wherever we go. I'm surprised you didn't know that."
~Colonel Saul Tigh, the Colonial Fleet (Battlestar Galactica)

Mount Paran Drive was in the northern edge of Atlanta, running up from north Buckhead across the city limit into Sandy Spring. It was a thickly wooded area of narrow, twisty side streets filled with large numbers of very large and expensive houses. It was where professional athletes, successful doctors, corporate presidents and a couple well-off rappers lived. Sometimes visiting actors rented there during filming at Pinewood Studios outside town. The point was that with that amount of money, it was understood you were buying some privacy. Even the neighborhood association web site said *This is not a social community.* The Atlanta PD or the DEA are a little less likely to blow in a door when the door itself cost thousands of dollars and the person behind it probably has a couple pet politicians.

Really, it wasn't the first time the rich side of town had been associated with doing dirt. The Black Mafia Family had a mansion up there in the late 1990s and early '00s where they ran their largest trap house; a place where they cut, repackaged and delivered bulk product and then hid cash before starting a record company with the profits. Nice to see some shit never changes.

The lawyer we were looking for lived on one of the side streets in a great big medieval-styled stone mansion that looked like it should be hosting a Renaissance Faire if the front yard was bigger. The pool was nice too. Really, if the damn thing was near me in Tennessee, I might have said the hell with it and bought it. Of course then I'd have to clean it, which means I'd need people around.

The advance recon of the place had been yet another Morgan job. His faithful thrift store UPS uniform and his pockets full of electronic voodoo had sniffed the burglar alarms (one wire, one cellular), the window and door sensors for the alarm, the wireless cameras, the wi-fi password and so on. Knowing Morgan, he probably also cruised past a couple bored housewives in the area on some down-low dating app while he was in the neighborhood. I didn't mind. He had already done what I needed done, so any other fun he had was a bonus for him I didn't have to pay for. At hit time, we would put a small quadcopter drone up to confirm when the Porsche SUV left hauling the kids off to soccer or whatever and that the target would be home alone. We just had to get the drone down before we unwrapped our surprise for the event.

The, well, uh, call it a 'Whitestone' was an early-war US Army effort to prevent some types of IEDs from going off by jamming the cell phone signal to the homemade detonator. Originally a US Secret Service system designed to secure the Presidential motorcade, it was already obsolete for that by 2004. That was probably why the Secret Service gave them to the Army in the first place. It took up the entire rear of a Humvee gun truck, including both back seats and the gunner position. It was not frequency-agile or sophisticated. Instead it took a brute force approach; it jammed damn near everything in a most of a kilometer radius. Cell phones, WiFi, broadcast TV and radio, commercial walkie talkies, and even our own drones and radios. The damn thing probably caused cancer with heavy use. This lack of elegance is why just two years later, the very few made were then gathering dust in the Baghdad motor pool after they'd been replaced by smarter systems. We literally never used the one we had. I just had to check it off on my serial number inventory every week.

But sometimes you need that complete cone of silence effect. While trying to scrounge something else a couple years ago, I found two of them sitting lost in an Indiana National Guard depot. They literally might have been the same ones I'd had years before- I didn't have my serial number list from 2006 to check. They weren't on the unit's property books since no one remembered what they really were, and so I arranged for them to disappear. I figured they'd be good for something someday. Since a Humvee gun truck is not subtle for domestic use, Petey's guys pulled out all the black boxes, installing them and the upgraded power systems into the back of a blacked-out Chevy Tahoe they then fitted with a set of police lights and two kinds of sirens. In between its infrequent test uses, it lived under a tarp in the work bay at the Hole for safekeeping.

As for the Humvees, I had both of them sitting in the barn behind my house. The other Whitestone was a spare and the cannibalized truck could just sit there until I could find the correct gun turret somewhere on the surplus market and make a real "eleven-fourteen" gun truck out of it again for my personal collection. By now, you the reader should understand something of my hobbies.

The initial entry element was Ben, me, then Tommy. The girls were the follow-on. Yes, bringing the girls on a raid was a calculated risk. But Angel could flip her psycho switch pretty fast if we needed to pull a hasty interrogation. People expect larger thuggish fellows like me to be threatening. With her, it's a sudden surprise. As a secondary matter, if we ran into a lot of financial paperwork, Cash was the only one with the background to make an on-the-spot assessment of what was worth hauling out of there quickly for detailed exploitation later.

Morgan would stay with the Tahoe. If the cops came despite our precautions, he would hit his handheld air horn ($2.99 on sale at West Marine!) to warn us then unass the area, leaving the Whitestone on for a while as he drove. Then as we got signal again, we would cue our diversionary element. They would pop a large smoke bomb, an Army surplus thirty-pounder originally designed to obscure combat engineer operations, in the parking lot of an (empty) church then call 911 themselves. That would buy us a few minutes to escape, either back down Mount Paran southwest to the Interstate or going northeast to the shopping centers across the I-285 Perimeter in Sandy Spring. If we were really desperate, I wondered if it was worth having an extraction chopper. *Hmm. We did have Adam.* Nah, that was a little too Hollywood since all of Atlanta's airspace was too well radar-controlled. Something to think about in the future, maybe.

***

Morgan parked the Whitestone at the curb, now dressed in a black suit, tie and sunglasses. Though there were no US Government tags on it and the Georgia plates on it were fakes, it did look terribly official with its blinking lights. He climbed out, reached in and flipped the switch. All our cell phones went to NO SIGNAL. I figure we had five minutes tops for him to either talk. Otherwise we would take him for a longer talk elsewhere.

With the burglar alarms remotely killed, we pulled our gloves on and literally walked in the front door. The easiest breach tool is a doorknob and this one wasn't even locked. A glance at the alarm panel showed it was disarmed anyway. God bless complacent and lazy targets. We did a slow sweep of the house and damn, it was nice. I kinda did want it.

Sure enough, Dudebro was upstairs in his office fiddling with his router. His back was to us. If this had been a kill mission, we could have put two in his brain stem and he never would have noticed a thing. But, alas, we needed what was in his head so I got to be a sarcastic asshole instead. "Hi, I'm here from Comcast and we're here to fix your wi-fi."

He was still poking at it. "Really? I hadn't even called-" He turned to find two nicely appointed ARs covering him. It was a work occasion, so I brought a Glock rather than one of my antique .45s. It was politely aimed down at the floor since I got to be the reasonable one today. "Oh."

"Dude, come on. You really think Comcast's customer service is that good? What fucking planet have you been on the last decade?"

"Uh, so what can I do for you guys?" He was taking this pretty well. Too well.

I rolled with that line of thought. "You know, the fact that three guys coming in here with a pair of automatic weapons doesn't bug you all that much should perhaps be good cause to reevaluate your life decisions, or at least get a better lock on your front door. Now hand me your cell phone, please."

Sheepishly, he did. I turned it off then left it on his desk. Not ideal, but close. It didn't have signal, nothing did right now, I just didn't want him hitting the useful voice recorder or camera functions to immortalize our little chat. "Well, you know enough of the wrong people, something like this is going to happen eventually. I kinda got used to living with the idea. Are you guys Feds?"

I sighed. "Did we bring a camera crew, use C-4 on the door, then shoot your dog?"

He didn't get the meme reference. "Uh, no. We don't even have a dog."

"Then no. We aren't Feds. At least not the sort you are thinking of."

He was getting more confused. "What sort are you?"

"The sort that aren't law enforcement, want answers to a couple questions, and aren't above hurting you very badly to get those answers. Listen, man. You have several ways out of this. Most of them are painful." I pointed toward the door. Cash and Angel were standing there in their Goth girl best, trying to look nonchalant. Angel was unwrapping a surgical scalpel and ostentatiously dropping the wrapper on the carpeted floor. I knew she would pocket it before we left. Cash was just staring at him, holding an Estwing framing hammer. Personally I don't think she had ever done much more with it than hang the picture frames in her room, but this guy didn't know that.

"You see the two sexy Asian girls? Yeah. They want to see your blood. All of it. Expect to spend several hours screaming before you finally die of shock and blood loss. And before that happens, you will give up everything. I have seen it happen before." They'd done no such thing, but he didn't know that. *Never give a sucker an even break*, as they say in pool halls. Also, never bet anyone who brought their own cue. Still, I didn't want this idiot thinking too much right now.

"Uh, hi, ladies-"

Angel cut him off. "Shut the fuck up. When I want you to talk to me, you'll know it." I suppressed a giggle. She never got to pull out her dominatrix streak at work, not unless she and Cash were taking a long lunch break together downstairs. She was loving this. Cash didn't say a word. She was just tapping her hammer against her shapely thigh, keeping her face impassive. Personal reinvention or no, this was a long fucking way from Harvard Yard.

"Um, what kind of questions? Like grand jury testimony?"

"No. And I don't mind having this discussion since your wireless cameras, wireless mikes, alarms and so on are all being remotely killed. You did a series of real estate transactions in Mississippi for some friends of yours from way down South. We are looking for one of those pieces of real estate. Since you seem to do a lot of business with those friends down South, including moving duffel bags of cash for them in and out of Atlanta, we think you know which one it is, or can at least narrow it down for us so we ain't wasting our valuable time."

He was smiling a lot less now. "Oh. Those guys. If I tell you anything, they will fuckin' kill me and my whole family."

"If you don't tell us, we might just well do the same. We are the ones standing here. Now, if we get what we want, we are gonna leave you out of it. We're just going to go talk to some people. You don't know shit and in return for you not knowing shit and continuing to not know shit, I don't let the pretty Asian girl there take her favorite hammer to your wrists so bad you can never do little things like wipe your ass correctly for the rest of your life. Never mind what that would do to your golf game, right? And maybe I can talk the other pretty one out of just carving you up like a biology class project until she gets bored. You gotta watch her though. Once she gets an idea in her head, she's pretty stubborn. But you got about ten seconds to think about it before we just taze your ass, put a bag over your head and haul you off somewhere to do the damage."

Angel grabbed him by the front of his tennis shorts and crushed down hard. Never underestimate massage therapists. Finger strength is a professional requirement. "Sir, should I just start carving on him now so he gets the point? He can talk without a testicle. Or two. Or a layer of skin off his dick."

I sighed theatrically. "No, dear, because that makes a messy crime scene. Don't cut on him til we get him to the next stop." I looked at Ben and nodded once. He let his AR drop on its sling as he pulled a Taser out of a thigh pocket.

That was all it took. "Okay, okay. It's the piece of land south of a truck stop on I-20, near the National Forest. Exit 96, I remember that much. I've been there two or three times. If you have the transaction list, which you probably do, it's easy to find." I looked over at Cash, who consulted a list saved on her phone. She nodded without a word.

"See, that was easy. Pleasure doing business with you. We may come back and visit sometime; love the pool." He flushed at that. Angel picked up her scalpel wrapper and we all calmly walked out.

As we got back in the car, Cash looked over at me. "I really like the kitchen and the upstairs suite was nice. Remind me to put in an address alert on this one for when it relists; I may buy it and lease it." The fucked up thing is I wasn't even surprised. If there is a kink in a woman weirder than compulsive real estate investment, I don't think I have found it yet. That neighborhood though... if I am paying that much for a big party-sized house, I want to be able to shoot a machine gun off my porch or have the girls in the pool lose their suits at their whim. Can't do that with three rich and bitchy neighbors within fifty yards.

We drove out, Morgan killed the Whitestone as we passed him and we headed for the Interstate. Time on target, five minutes and thirty-four seconds.

Chapter 19

"In the end, weapons don't mean jack. It's the quality of the troops who utilize the weapons that counts."
~First Sergeant Conrad "Duke" Hauser, via Larry Hama

Now that we knew where to go, we could begin the planning and rehearsing in earnest while we gathered intelligence on the target itself. August was a shitty time to do anything in Mississippi except for getting heat stroke, but it couldn't be helped. Meanwhile, it took a couple weeks, but Mad Jack was as good as his word. He sent me an old fashioned snailmail paper letter (less chance of casual, warrantless interception) with a handwritten list of businesses in Singapore and a few elsewhere like Hong Kong or Macau that the 'Honored Grandfather' in Vancouver said were solid choices to deal with. A couple of them in Singapore were circled in red with exclamation points and arrows. I wasn't sure if that was a good thing or bad thing. At some point I'd have to ask Jack what he meant. I gave the list to Cash and let her tear into any verifiable financials to see who she liked.

Dave worked the roster of candidates that he and Jimmy made well in advance and put a team together for the raid itself. All the candidates were asked was 'it's a Stateside direct action raid for X amount of money. Yes or no?' A few guys said no, enough said yes. Some of the nos were for the damnedest reasons. One guy asked me to wait a few months so he was done coaching high school football for the season. Sorry, man, time-sensitive target. We had to move before the container did.

Jimmy wasn't going to be there himself, of course. I needed his nautical experience elsewhere, which was why he was still down south with the yacht guys. If the yacht didn't get to the pickup point, we were kinda fucked. We still had Tommy from the SEALs, then Dave and our old friend Ben representing the Rangers. Jake represented both the 173rd and the JRTC's 509th Parachute Infantry opposing-force unit, since he was also a well-known commodity.

See, it wasn't just a matter of getting guys with the skills. That was easy. The Afghan and Iraq wars had mass-produced guys with SOCOM-style raid experience both in and out of the 75th and the SF groups for the last twenty-plus years. The Ranger Regiment had been fulfilling the Abrams Charter of 1974 and producing the tactics, techniques, procedures and leadership cadre for the rest of the infantry community since before the Grenada jump in '83. A couple good sharp Spec-4's out of the 10th Mountain could hold their weight on this job and the guns were definitely out there for hire in large quantities. But, and this is a very large but, guys we trusted and who could keep their mouths shut, who wouldn't go on conspicuous spending sprees with the cash and draw heat to the rest of us, now that we had to be real careful about. Not to repeat Morgan's reference, but you guys all saw *Goodfellas* and what happened after the Lufthansa robbery at JFK. *No new Cadillacs.*

I definitely didn't want to recruit from the guys who guarded the Hole. Nice guys, but they knew where we lived, metaphorically speaking. Below the leadership level, we wanted some separation between the job and us. So it was down to a couple more Rangers we knew, a retired 5th SF Group guy who did some of my gunsmithing, some of his SF cronies, a Force Recon Marine, two more Marines from another small and special East Coast unit but who weren't Recon, one Air Force pararescue guy who lost a coin toss with one of the SF guys to be lead medic... we'd be okay.

At some risk to operational security, I had a full sit-down meeting with Dave, Tommy, the full raid team of sixteen more guys, and a couple representatives from the intel section who were sitting in the back. With everyone in one room, we went over the full plan, so much as we had one up to that point. Most operations in our line of work are planned backwards. You know where to be, when, with what. Then you figure out how long it takes to get there, which gives you your departure time and so on. What we needed was a bunch of us chipping in on the plan.

First, we weren't having the meeting at the Hole. We knew some of these guys to a point, but we also didn't want them in the office and downstairs. Yes, I have trust issues. We used a little redneck barbecue joint over off US 41 just past the state line in Guthrie, Kentucky. We hired them to cook, set up a buffet line, then leave. And yes, I locked the doors and pulled the blinds with the CLOSED sign prominently visible after Morgan swept it for bugs and cameras. Again, trust issues.

Secondly, I wasn't explaining the whole job. The raid team would do the raid. The last that most of them, the temp hires from the on-call roster, would ever see of that container would be it leaving the objective on a truck and they didn't need to know shit after that. I had to make sure whoever did the job was cool with that.

Once we were all inside with the doors locked and everyone had a heaping plate of pulled pork, smoked brisket, and various sides in front of them, I opened. "Gentlemen, and I do use that term loosely, you were each lured here because you said yes to doing a Stateside direct action raid. One night's work. Cash payment to cover rehearsals and the job. Fifty grand with all expenses covered ain't bad for the warmup reps and a night's work."

The Air Force PJ threw his question out in my pause. "So what's the target?"

I snorted. "I'm not even sure all y'all are hired yet and you want me to pull up the skirt on all the secrets already?"

One of the non-Recon Marines cut in. "The target determines the risk. Risk determines the asking price and whether or not I feel like taking the chance. This ain't 2003 and I'm not a nineteen year old dumbfuck anymore. I have a wife and kids at home to look to. You have been around the game a long while, Prof and let's face it. You're rumored to have made some shitty decisions, if not so bad as Bam Bam. And you have definitely fucked over a couple people who trusted you."

I nodded. I ignored the personal gibe even though it was true. I knew this guy was one of the ones who'd turned down the Dallas job because of the bad odds involved. I couldn't fault him for that, but it also made me consider my next words carefully. "And the more details I put out there, the greater the risk of mission compromise and the greater the risks on the actual objective become if the defenders have a clue we're coming." I was playing hard to get like a chick on prom night. There was a method to my madness though. See, enough of the dozen-plus guys there were "my" guys. Dave. Tommy. Jake. Ben. When these other, newer guys started looking around at each other, enough faces would be watching me and not shaking their heads or calling bullshit that the herd instinct would probably kick in and they'd chill out.

I went on. "I'll put this much out there. There's an old farm one state over from here. On that farm there's a twenty foot shipping container guarded by a dozen cartel shooters. We want the container." Geography enthusiasts will note that in Tennessee, 'one state over' covers a lot of ground. And yes, that bit of vagueness was deliberate. Eight states' worth, tied for the national record with Missouri, which it also borders.

Kentucky comes in second, having seven border states. You know, if you care.

One of the other Rangers raised his hand. "So what's in the container? Cash or drugs?"

I answered honestly. "We don't fucking know. We hope it's cash."

He nodded. "And if it is cash, is that then up for being split?"

I shook my head. "We're paying you to get us the container. We don't know what's in it."

The Force Recon Marine slouched back in his chair, crossing his arms. "Bullshit. You know, or at least think you do, otherwise you wouldn't be going to all this trouble and hiring us to snatch the fucking thing." There were some murmurs of assent at that. That discontent was not good.

Freddie spoke up from the back where he and the five other Special Forces retirees were eating more than they appeared to be paying attention. "Gentlemen, we're all here of our own accord because we were offered work. The job is the job. Take it or not. We're getting paid enough for a few rehearsals and one night's work to not be greedy. Part of that professionalism is also keeping the faith afterward." The other SF guys nodded along. Even if you didn't know his record, there was an ice behind Freddie's eyes that kept people from crossing him. And there were enough long-tabbers at that back table to make a center of mass for the rest of the group to fall in around.

That was enough to shut the Marine up for a minute. I looked back over at the inquisitive Ranger and he merely nodded. The PJ also nodded, then gave a loud belch with plenty of pork grease in it before grinning. "I better tag along regardless, just in case someone gets shot. The 18Ds are only better if you have Ebola or the clap." One of the SF guys, the medic, gave him the finger.

We had very recent satellite images of the place. I had prepared one poster-sized version to brief from, stripped of all geolocating data. It could be anywhere from the Ozarks to Vermont and I wanted it kept that way for now. These guys didn't need to know where we were going yet, but I wanted them to see what was there. From orbit, it was merely a very clear view of a farmhouse up a long gravel driveway from the paved road, then a barn out past the house surrounded by a whole lot of fields to the north and west with woods to the east.

Dave stood. "You all know me, at the very least since I'm the motherfucker who invited you. I'm the ground NCOIC for this." That settled a lot of people down real quick-like. Dave had a reputation that far eclipsed mine in most respects. He continued. "Approach will be by land. We're going to move about two klicks from the paved road here, through the woods, wait here at the ORP for the distraction that knocks out the power to the entire road, then we move out in two large fire teams on night vision under full cover of darkness. One team is the support by fire, the other is the primary assaulters. Once the primary objective is neutralized at the barn by Team 1, roles reverse and Team 2 clear the house. Then both teams flow through to set out far side security. Site exploit team breaks off from the assaulters and checks the container. That team has already been identified. They call up what they find, then a decision is made. If it's a go, transportation moves in, hooks it up, it leaves, then everyone exfils. If it's a no-go, we abandon it in place, maybe demolitions are set, and we exfil. We'll have a minimum of two small UAVs overhead for coverage. Good commercial ones though. No armed overwatch, no Hellfires on call."

There were some chuckles at that.

I picked up in the pause. "So, now you see the job. Fifty thousand for the night's work plus some rehearsal time. Quarter mil death benefit and we cover your medical in full if there's a problem. We're going to put in a recon effort at some point and among other things, that risk assessment is going to determine whether we stick to a ground medevac plan or add an air option."

The PJ raised his hand. "If I may, if you have the air asset, go for it. Just because we have qualitative overmatch on the defenders doesn't mean one won't get a lucky shot off and that's probably kinda out in East Buttfuck for driving a casualty out by road to a decent trauma facility."

I nodded. "Can do." I supposed Adam would be up for a night on standby. If not, I knew another guy from that same unit who would do just as well. One of the advantages of still living here. "You up for being the flight medic instead of walking the mission?"

The PJ nodded his assent. "It's my core competency. You got a pilot?"

"Yeah, a retired SOCOM instructor. Still current on a few aircraft types. He'll do." That got me a look of approval.

I continued. "And while only two of you are going to see the inside of that container and the rest of you won't know where it goes, you may get Christmas bonuses on the back end depending on what we find. Fair?" Drinks were raised, heads nodded and somebody in back farted loud enough we all heard it. "Good enough then." The meeting then degenerated into dinner and penny-ante tactical details.

***

Now that we knew who they were, Dave and the rest of the raid force continued their planning and rehearsal process. They got into the weapons and the night vision gear from downstairs and made sure everyone had a plate carrier that fit. I stayed the fuck out of that. Despite having been one of Dave's first teachers, he had surpassed me long ago. There was no point in trying to micromanage somebody who was better than I was. And this wasn't the Son Tay Raid; it just wasn't that complicated. They only worked on it a couple nights a week since nobody wanted to quit their day jobs. Really, after a certain skill level there's such a thing as too many rehearsals.

That didn't mean I was useless to his process. At the first snag in rehearsals, when more overwatch and covering fire was needed to cover a blind spot, Dave asked if I had another good sniper I felt comfortable bringing in. Fortunately, I did. Troy had been an instructor at the Army's sniper schoolhouse on Fort Benning before doing an Iraq tour with me. Then he'd fallen down a couple rabbit holes behind tall fences until retirement. He had been contracting since, and wouldn't say no to a couple days of freelance work. He only asked if he needed to bring his own rifle. I told him he could have a nice fresh company 110 or something weirder from my personal collection if he didn't want to fly commercial with one of his. Him being sort of particular about equipment, he got in the car and drive three days, bringing a chassis-built .300 Winchester Magnum that was sort of an Army M2010 knockoff but would still get an angry thumbs-down from the authenticity enthusiasts in the cloner community.

After asking me for my opinion, Dave also consulted Eric. Eric then showed up without warning in my office. I mean I looked up from the file folder I was into and he was just *there* like he'd beamed in from the *Enterprise*, standing as still as a mountain lake with a slightly disapproving look on his face. "Hey, kid."

Fuck. I hope I look calmer than I am. "Hi, Eric."

"Were you planning on telling the Board about this little score you got in the works?"

I thought about my answer. "To be quite honest, no."

He shrugged. "All right. And the justification for that is…?" He flopped out on the big leather couch while he waited for my reply. Eric could get really pissed and never show it.

Warming up, I counted down on my fingers. "I know because it was my idea. Dave knows since he's the ground force commander. You already know because Dave asked my permission to tell you. Little John would have a heart attack from anxiety if he knew, but he already told me he didn't want to know. Mikey's dead. Big John is dead. James is retired. And coming in last, Greg has always held to not knowing about any shady gray or black-side shit we do with the other half of the company. He's neurotically law-abiding. You know that. You know him better than I do."

He visibly pondered that and then nodded once. "As a command decision, thinking about it, I see your reasoning and… I think you made the right decision. Okay." Crisis averted. Thank fuck. If it came to a fight, I'd probably lose. That old man was still a force of nature.

I threw an olive branch. "Dave's having a hard time getting everyone he wants for this. You want to suit up and play one more game?"

He sighed. "Kid, I haven't done a raid like that since the first six months in Afghanistan and that was twenty years ago. I was probably too old to do it then, only I personally knew the key players in both our local partner force and in the enemy units so I kinda had to be there. As much as I hate to admit it, my day may finally be passing for the hard stuff."

"Your knees may be going, but we could surely use your brain. Dave's perfectly capable of pulling this off, but a more senior set of eyes never hurt. You could probably be really valuable to him in the planning and rehearsal stages even if you don't want to be on the field at kickoff."

He slowly nodded. "Okay, that I can still do."

***

And those rehearsals hit another snag early. The container draw bar from Australia was only rated to move ten of our tons. We'd thought it was at least good for more. We found this out after DHL had already delivered the damn thing air-freight from Kangaroo Land. In our worst case scenario, it needed to move thirty. Even though the container was only rated for 22.5, we had to assume it was overloaded. I threw the draw bar under a workbench in the garage bay. We'd use it for something eventually. I told Steve to go think of something else.

The communications plan was going to be dodgy as fuck. We didn't have encrypted portable comms except the Black phones a few of us had. We could possibly get by with cheap handhelds for some of it, but since I didn't have an answer. I dumped it on Petey in IT. Once the signal officer, always the signal officer. We could just throw money at that one and buy whatever we needed to make the problem go away. Dave said he'd handle that.

Then Ben asked if he could go on the boat too. Apparently things weren't great at home again. Story of that dude's life. Anyway, he was looking to stay out of sight for a while and maybe make a few more bucks on the side. Sure. Why not?

Adam rented a used Bell Jet Ranger and the PJ set it up as an expedient medevac bird with room for two patients. Their plan was flying to a nearby field before the raid, then sitting until called in. When called, they'd come in, load any of our casualties, and then fly to Jackson, Mississippi. With Jackson's high murder rate, the city had several excellent Level 1 trauma facilities with helicopter pads. Better to have and not need, as Grandma used to say.

The backwards planning process continued. The cash gets to the *Ecstasy*. The cash goes aboard, the emptied container goes over the side of the crew boat. The crew boat would go meet the *Ecstasy* after having been loaded at Ocean Springs, Mississippi. Alternate load point was at Gulfport, etc. The cash would leave the farm in the container, that truck escorted by two trucks. Tentatively, one would contain Angel, myself and two shooters to be determined, the other containing Tommy, Dave and Ben. One of my other shooters would deadhead their car back once they boarded the crew boat to join the "two-thirds of the way around the world" cruise. They were already arguing over the deployment T-shirt design and I was hoping they weren't serious. Talk about shit we did not need…

So we had an idea of how to get the stuff onto the boat and some idea of how to get it onto the next boat. Now the next problem was figuring out how to get it out of the barn and onto the truck. We reasonably knew the container was in the barn. What we weren't totally sure about was getting the container out of the barn and onto a trailer. A straight drag out had been easy. This? No satellite could see through the roof. Ehhh... there was guesswork.

As a result, we may have overdone it with backup plans. We figured two chainsaws on the retrieval truck just in case something had to get trimmed out to allow the pickup. Carbide fire/rescue chains on the saws in case of metal. Two is one, one is none. A gas powered circular saw backed those up. There was an aluminum extension ladder in case someone had to go up high to trim overhead. The worst case scenario involved cutting out alternating poles of the barn, old telephone pole sections, lifting the container corners with the two heavy screw jacks we'd also packed and rolling the container out on the poles, dragging it with the semitrailer. That would get it far enough in the yard that the sideloader cranes would do their thing correctly.

Troy finally said fuck it, and that he was sick of listening to us argue and that he didn't trust our guesses whether or not it would work. He volunteered to do a one man insert prior to hit time to do some looking around. That way there was time to cook up an alternate option. Now Troy was a malevolent little fuck who'd racked up a kill count in triple digits over eight years of the war. I loved him like a brother, but I still told him no, he was not going solo. I told him to pick somebody else from the raid force to watch his back if nothing else. He picked Paul, since the retired Green Beret was also a former sniper instructor. The two of them drove off with a company rental. They were 'going to go recon a deer lease' if anyone asked about all the camouflage equipment in the car. They said they'd call if there was a problem, otherwise they'd report back in three days, tops.

He and Paul showed back up under forty-eight hours later, having done a full stalk in and out in ghillie suits. I think they essentially dared each other into crawling that far. Neither one was exactly young anymore.

First, Troy and Paul had dropped off a 'black box' the intel section had cobbled together that would collect all cell phone signals from the target area. We'd have their texts, we'd have their actual calls, regardless if it was a number we'd tapped or not. This way we'd have visitor's phones, disposable burners, changes of SIM card, whatever. That signals intelligence might give up follow-on targets.

The second matter was what they'd done the real close stalk for. Troy was up-front about the answer. "Yeah, we actually made it into the barn and verified the container was actually there. No fucking way are you getting the twenty-ish feet side to side you need for that sideloader crane trailer you were thinking about. That container doesn't have enough clearance around it to get that toy in there. The container just has to get dragged straight out before it can be picked up."

"Shit."

"Good news is that there is definitely something in there worth hauling off. In three hours, we spotted eight guys, light weapons. Mostly AKs. There were a few cheap ARs with bad setups. Fucked up slings, Chinese discount gun show optics, spare mags in back pockets. In all, kinda a sloppy operation by our standards. But it looks like they have been out there a while, the whole crew camping in the old farmhouse with a couple women for cooking and recreation."

Fuck. All right, I dumped that problem on Steve to figure out.

Surprising me a little, he just looked at me, shrugged and said, "That's easy."

He caught me short with that. "What?"

"I go buy ya a goddamn 80K-rated roller-bed truck like they use for specialized structural steel hauls and whatnot, pull the container right up the ramps with the truck's winch and we stop fucking around with portable cranes and shit."

I waved dismissively. "Great, go find one, talk to Accounting to pay for it. Handle it."

Shit, he was probably going to end up working here full time. I'd hide him in Roads and Grounds if I had to. But he was running out of leave days at his day job and I still needed him. He also knew too damn much even if I didn't. Netherton was another loose end, though I had no idea how to keep a lawyer occupied enough to keep paying him either. Last I saw him, he was studying for the Tennessee bar exam and thinking of staying in town.

Meanwhile, all the other terrain data they had gathered on their reconnaissance in was dumped over in the left side of the Intel department floor, where our Geographic Information Systems expert had her enormous computer desk and mapping tables. Zoey was a tiny little Alabama blonde in a Rocket City Trash Pandas baseball team hoodie. Kara had headhunted her out of the anthropology department at Vanderbilt and then paid off her student loans as a signing bonus. Turning in-depth 'human terrain' data into visual art was her abiding academic passion. Mapping GPS waypoints was a bit beneath her skills, but she was quite prickly about anyone else using her desk and her map printers. Freddie and Troy helped her convert their notes into the route plan for the night of the mission, just as she'd made the graphic for my briefing at the barbecue joint.

***

Dave and the raid team were still having fun in rehearsals and were working with Steve on how to assist in the container load. If the thing didn't get loaded and moving correctly, all this was for nothing. And we sure didn't want to dawdle on the objective a minute longer than necessary. We didn't want so much as one innocent sheriff's deputy rolling by.

One of the former Group dudes asked about helmet cameras. I pulled him aside for the conversation in case my opinion offended him. "I get that you're used to them, and they're great if we were going for full site exploitation and follow-on intel operations for the next night's raid like the old days in Baghdad. That's cool. Here's the problem. We're definitely going to have to shoot our way in, and maybe out. You really want to make 1080P high-rez video evidence of us killing a dozen people? Evidence that can possibly be electronically retrieved if we get caught then put on trial for multiple counts of capital murder, conspiracy, and armed robbery in a Southern state that loves to keep its Death Row full?"

That ended that idea real quick, and rightfully so, I think.

Jimmy called me from Tampa a week later to let me know the fuel blivets mostly fit in the drained swimming pool and with the hundred feet of hose and a transfer pump, with several spare pumps, they saw no issue with the fuel system. They'd bought a large freezer at each of a few big-box stores and those were secured at the aft portion of the main salon deck where the couches and outdoor dining table had been.

Meanwhile Steve found the truck he wanted to use in a bankruptcy sale in Indianapolis. He caught a flight to go pick it up. Once he had it, he was to move mostly at night, then park at the big truck stop off I-20 and wait for us to call him before he drove the ten miles further forward to the target.

We split up into several groups to move down to the target area in Mississippi. All cell phones and smart watches were confiscated and held at the office. The few Black phones going were bagged. Most of the vehicles were rentals from the Nashville airport, a collection of SUVs and such. We sure weren't taking our own cars. Dave and Tommy each took three guys with them. Troy originally planned on driving himself, then said fuck it. He threw an air mattress in the back of the van hauling the recon drone team and told them to wake him up after they got there. Another cargo van held the diversion team and pulled the box trailer of its gear. Then a 'small' 600-gallon gasoline trailer was piped together to refuel the whole circus train in a field or deserted parking lot so there was no traceable fuel stop for any of the half dozen work vehicles.

As much as I would like to go get one last good meal in Jackson or someplace before we lit this thing off, that was a terrible idea. The last thing I needed was the one in a million shot of somebody I had gone to school with thirty years ago recognizing me. I hadn't changed too terribly much. Complicating that, I didn't get along very well with most of them, so, quoting the late Charlie Daniels, *"the last thing I wanted was to get in a fight in Jackson, Mississippi on a Saturday night, especially when there was three of them and only one of me."* Well, two of us, since Angel was usually down with quietly stabbing somebody in a parking lot. But as the whole point was that we weren't really there in the state in the first place, better to not risk any unexpected nostalgia trips.

Chapter 20

"And when you walk in golden halls, you get to keep the gold that falls..."

~ *"Heaven and Hell",* Ronnie James Dio of Black Sabbath

Sitting back and watching this shit on a UAV feed was not, repeat *not*, how I prefer to do business. Then reality kicked in. Sometimes I forget how old and busted up I am, with the concurrent loss of the athletic ability to do what a much younger me once could. That was why Dave made the deal he had made. I had to tell myself that Colonel Charlie Beckwith wouldn't have been the first one over the wall of the Tehran Embassy if Operation EAGLE CLAW had worked either.

But the problem now was that I was *fucking bored.* Everything I could do had been done. Now I just had to sit here and not go nuts while everyone else did their jobs. If I had to start making decisions and giving orders at this point, something would have to have gone really wrong. Nobody wanted that. We wanted a nice, boring success. Meanwhile I read a book as we rode.

One of the first things we did upon arriving in the area was using the fuel trailer to fill everything back up. The nearly four hundred mile drive down 65 and across 20 from Nashville had drained most every fuel tank. Whatever happened next, having full tanks again was a good idea. Making credit card receipts or gas station video of us getting those tanks full again was a very bad idea. I preferred to make as little physical evidence as possible that we were anywhere but back home. We were about to commit so many felonies I'd need an Excel spreadsheet to track them all.

I was set up in the back of the rented van that held the UAV team's gear. There were two ground terminals for the pair of expensive civilian quadcopters that would be circling the objective looking for counterattacks, nosy neighbors, or passing cops. This gave me the best possible situational awareness of what was going on outside Dave's line of sight, and if something did pop up I could then warn him. He would then do what he was being paid to do and keep commanding the ground force without me bumping his elbow too much.

The communications issue had been solved by spending a bunch of fucking money and letting a couple of the radio enthusiasts among the IT guys go wild. What we had were distinctly outside of Federal Communications Commission regulations. They'd already begun as gray-market Chinese-made Baofeng ten-watt walkie talkies. The people I paid to be much smarter than I am had then modified the tuning software, making them more powerful and then adding frequency-hopping capability. Other modifications added a reasonable encryption package. Now while the SINCGARS family I'd used in my Army years jumped in milliseconds, these jumped in tenths of seconds, and the cryptography was nowhere near as good, but they'd still beat a civilian scanner and keep our comms secure. They'd passed every test we could come up with in-house and that had to be good enough. Counting the hike in and out, they only needed to work for an hour at most.

One of the UAVs ranged wide, spiraling out clockwise like a hunting hawk, while the other stayed close to the five big rental SUVs dropping off the raid element's two fire teams. It was Iraq all over again, no emotion to it at all. We just sat, watching little thermal blobs of pixelated humanity. walking around and doing their thing on a screen. Sixteen guys jumped out of the SUVs and went through the familiar dance of getting geared up. Five more had drawn the short straws and became the security element guarding the vehicles while the others pushed forward. They'd also drive the extraction in an emergency. Really, I didn't want to go putting any more sets of wheels on the objective than needed. Why make things easy on the crime scene guys?

In a vacant field half a mile past the target, the distraction team set up their little trailer-mounted surprise. That trailer also held the signal amplifier and retransmitter module for our hopefully secure radio network. I didn't want any black holes in the communication plan.

Further out, Adam and that Air Force PJ were sitting on-call with the medevac bird in another pasture.

To the northwest, in the county seat of Forest, a familiar black Yukon pulled up across the street from the sheriff's office building. It had a freshly made fake Mississippi license plate mounted to it and its black boxes were already warmed up. See, we would want a few minutes of radio silence while we worked. The cops might not even notice. But I had a whole van full of signals intelligence specialists on this. We were monitoring their radios, the lines into the county 911 dispatch office, and the local cell phone tower until then. Like Nimitz before Midway, an ability to see the other guy's cards is an enormous advantage. So is the ability to blind the other guy.

I kept watching the screen as the teams moved cross-country. Troy was moving off to the north side into his pre-selected hide site where he could cover as much of the farm as possible.

As they moved from the insertion point and the mission timer clicked down, somebody was humming a tune. Problem was, he'd bumped his headset selector switch from "push to talk" to "voice-activated", and it was automatically broadcasting to everyone else on the radio net. In a second, I picked up on the rhythm and knew who it was. My ground force commander was getting in the mood.

"All right, stop what you're doing, 'cuz I'm about to ruin The image and the style that you're used to..."

Dave had no-shit done the fuckin' Humpty Dance on top of the bar in dress blues at his retirement party. Now he was gonna ruin some more shit.

"Now gather round, I'm the new fool in town..."

They'd budgeted plenty of time to make the two klick insertion walk, following the route that Troy and Freddie had scouted and proofed on their recon trip. There were no gullies, impassable water obstacles, or other problems. They hit the last rally point, split off to their positions, and waited for the appointed hour to strike.

The diversion fired off first. This was half a dozen 81mm illumination rounds, basically big parachute flares, and another six black powder firework salute boomers. Each was in a four foot long piece of 3.5" high pressure steel pipe, the same stuff commonly used in oil fields. Close enough to a mortar tube for this since accuracy wasn't much of a factor. All of this was built into the back of a box trailer that had the roof cut and hinged. The whole thing could be parked, fired, and then driven away. That would happen either in an emergency or as part of the withdrawal plan. We certainly weren't going to leave the fucking thing behind as evidence.

The percussion primers in the illumination rounds were replaced with electric ones. The wires for those ran to a couple mechanical timers pulled from junked washing machines, with the whole thing being powered by a car battery. As the timer advanced, the electrical contacts would connect, and then the mortars would fire off. Parachute flares would blaze and salutes boom off in sequence, and all while none of us were anywhere near it.

For any of you Iraq War veterans, if any of that sounds familiar, I learned the tricks the same place you did, though I was too busy to build it myself. Fortunately I knew a guy, an EOD company first sergeant who'd been one of my PFCs once. He took a four day pass and I paid him twenty grand. When he figured out what was going on, he asked me if he could join up when he retired and I told him yeah, probably.

Lee was a good kid and had grown into a much better trooper than I had been.

Later, the SIGINT team told us that the noise and the lights in the sky had the neighbors calling 911 complaining about 'some gosh-damn UFO that was scaring their cows.' The important thing was the first two booms and the parachute flare had every eye awake at that hour of the morning looking the wrong way when the small cutting charge on the power lines went off. A quarter-block of C-4 stuck to the transformer on the pole would black out every farm on that road for hours, yet still be an easy fix once the line crew finally got out there. Transformers replace more easily than poles. No sense being rude about it and making their lives harder than necessary.

That preset time was the cue for our girl downtown (yeah, Angel took that job since I was running out of people) to flip the switches on the Yukon's jammers to TRANSMIT ALL. Downtown Forest, Mississippi became an electronic black hole, and would stay that way for fifteen minutes. Local law enforcement would be off the air. She would then flip the switches and drive away.

The blackout also was the cue for the raid team to do their thing. Really, it was the nearest thing to murder. The first of the two seven-man teams, with their high end night vision and collective century-plus of experience, killed all six armed bad guys in and around the barn with suppressed carbine fire in much less time than it took me to write this paragraph. The defenders got a few shots off, all wildly inaccurate. Dying men do strange things like twitch and accidentally pull triggers if their safeties are off.

I watched two guys move into the barn where the container sat, while another two kicked out to the rear corners of the barn for far-side security. I saw one security head turn toward the diversion site, as the mission timer told me another flare and boomer went off.

The primary objective being secured, Ben would be the man assigned to get into the container. His task was to get as deep into the pile as he could and then test as many bills as possible throughout the container in two minutes. His plan for that was slicing plastic and then using his handy currency testing marker, the same kind you see at the grocery store. Based on what he found, it was either pull out the raid force or send in the container retrieval truck.

Two minutes and one second later, he spoke over the radio. *"Jackpot. Frank. Load it."* Meant a good pile of at least mostly hundreds, ready to go. "Grant" or "Andy" would have meant mostly fifties or twenties. I was glad it was hundreds. After all, we'd already paid for the boat. Still, fifty dollar bills would have been worth it. Half a billion tops, but worth it. You just don't see as many fifties though...

I hit the push to talk button on my radio. "Redbeard, Redbeard, roll in."

Steve answered quickly. *"Roger that! Be there in two."*

The house was the secondary objective. The barn team left four guys on security, including Ben who was still in the container, while three more turned to be the support by fire element to the second team moving on the house. Plus Troy was still on overwatch from the woodline with his sniper rifle.

And this is where reconnaissance only got us so far. We really didn't know how many people were in the house, or how awake they'd be at two in the morning.

First answer: Way more than we thought.

Second answer: Really awake. I guess when you sell wholesale quantities of cocaine for a living, you then have enough around for a substantial amount of the night shift to be wide awake and living on vampire hours.

These answers were delivered via a substantial volume of full-auto AK fire from seemingly every back window of the house. The UAV turned and paused into a hover. My pulse rate picked up as the world started to slow down. I felt guilty for how good the adrenaline felt. One *sicario* bravely ran out the back door, rifle blazing, and about half a second later his head came spectacularly apart.

Troy clicked into the net. *"Sniper One, that one was me."*

Then another window-shooter went silent. At first I thought they had just stopped to reload. They never seemed to come back.

Troy clicked in again. *"Scratch two."*

Another voice clicked in. *"Hey, this is Two-Six, if you wanna get the rest of them for us, feel free. Make our lives easy, why dontcha?"*

Steve broke into the radio net *"Uh, I'm gonna hang out down here at the end of the driveway til you guys handle that part-"*

I hit my talk button. "REDBEARD, YES! YOU FUCKING DO THAT. SIT TIGHT!" This mission would be a sudden failure if the winch truck got knocked out. I should have gotten a spare truck. Two is one, one is none. Goddamn it, none of us thought about that part, not even Eric.

The important things are always simple. The simple things are always hard. And the easy way in always has land mines and sniper coverage on it.

I also didn't want to lose anyone from Team 2, and this was looking like way too much of a fair fight all of a sudden. One more *sicario* took a chance on running out the back door, and Troy's .300 WinMag took his head most of the way off too. Troy was obviously having fun, and that was great, but this also was taking time we didn't necessarily fucking have. Looking at the clock, this had taken almost five minutes from the blackout charge and the first shots fired around the barn. We were shooting suppressed, but they weren't, and even suppressed rifle fire sounds like something at a distance. There were neighbors less than a mile away, and we only had a fifteen minute radio blackout.

Dave knew this too. *"Base, this is Six. How much do we care about the house?"*

"Base Actual. Not at fucking all. I care about you not getting shot in the back while loading."

"Six. Good enough!"

Dave had a little extra glint tape on his gear and a compact IR strobe on his helmet doing a double *blink-blink, blink blink* pattern so we could tell him apart in the UAV's camera feed. His two team leaders were only doing single blinks. That meant I could tell it was definitely him when the crazy fuck stood up, unslung something stubby, pointed it at the house, then an upstairs bedroom gently exploded with a silent thump.

Huh. That asshole had borrowed one of the old M-79 grenade launchers from downstairs. Ah, well, it's always nice to see one of your dearest friends enjoy their work....

The defenders were enthusiastic, and putting a lot of lead in the air, but so far they hadn't hit shit. Personally if I had been planning the defense of a billion dollars in cash, I'd have gone big early on night vision gear and maybe a goddamn-

"MINIGUN!!!!" I couldn't tell who screamed it on the radio net, but here we were. On the camera screen, something woke up angry in another of the upstairs windows, and a whole fucking lot of tracers were pouring out of it. *Oh Holy Mary, Mother of God, what the fuck?*

Nearly as soon as that flood of fire started, it stopped.

"Sniper Two. Fuck you, One, that was me."

Nice work, Paul. Case of good booze for ya for that one.

Dave's vintage 40mm "bloop gun" took out another window and its occupants, while the others were ruthlessly sloshed with 5.56mm fire. *Goddamn, and for what ammo costs too, we just HAD to pick the premium shit.* With our guys shooting suppressed, it was much harder to see their muzzle flashes on camera, but I could only hope the guys were maintaining something resembling fire discipline. Nobody had packed that heavy on magazines- it was supposed to be a two minute armed robbery, not a bad day in the A Shau Valley.

Finally the house fell silent. Looking at the clock, we were still only seven and a half minutes from the first shot. Time flies at moments like this.

With Team 1 mostly committed to the barn perimeter and support by fire if needed, Team 2 then entered and cleared the quieted house. The women Troy and Paul had seen on the recon trip were apparently nowhere around. There were definitely a fair number of dead guys, including a couple that got finished off.

"Base, Six, this is Two-Six. EKIA count in Objective Two is one-four, say again, one four."

I hit my button. "Two-Six, this is Actual. Acknowledge one-four."

"Do we wanna keep the Minigun? It's got Jose's or whoever's brains all over it, but it looks okay."

"Bring it. Throw it in the truck, we'll get it after. Break. Redbeard, party's over, get up there and get loaded."

"Roger that!"

SIGINT in the next van over sent somebody to bang on our door. "We got another 911 call! This one's about machine gun fire into County Dispatch!"

I checked the mission clock. County Dispatch would be off the air for six more minutes.

The nearer UAV pulled back and circled. Everyone fell back out of the house and consolidated around the barn.

I turned to the second UAV terminal. The UAV teams were drawn from Morgan's people from downstairs in Intel. I legitimately couldn't remember the redhead's name right now, but she had a Banshee Troop, 2-17 Cavalry baseball cap jammed backwards on her head."Find me the nearest cop cars. We don't have much time."

She looked up at me and smirked. "Only two patrol cars out this hour of the night. One's running radar ten miles away on the Interstate, the other's cruising at the bottom end of the county and couldn't be here in less than twenty minutes if they wanted to."

I sighed. The load-up itself averaged three minutes in training. Now for nothing to go wrong.

The pole barn on that old soybean farm had been built to house great big combines, bush hogs, seed planters and so on. It had sixteen feet of overhead clearance and a clear span of twenty-four feet. If this had gone better and they had only put the damned container where we could more easily load it, this would go a lot easier.

Steve backed the truck into place. The load team broke off and kicked into the rehearsed plan. Two ran into the barn to set the attachment chains. Two more hit the clutch on the winch and began playing out the cable. One guy ran an electronic sniffer over the container, looking for RFID chips like Apple's AirTags, GPS beacons, or any other forms of communication or ID. The last two chocked the wheels in an effort to keep the truck from being pulled backwards by the inertia of the container's loaded mass.

That truck had been the second biggest individual line item on this project, second only to the *Ecstasy*. Without it, we were kinda fucked. I felt ice water churning in my guts. God, I hope this worked. *We should have had a spare.*

Rated at 80,000 pounds, it was basically a tank recovery winch, and it dragged the container out of the barn with pure brute force. A snatch block pulley upped the pull capacity to 160,000 pounds. Even through the drone feed, I could see the exhaust flare as he revved the truck to pull against the dead weight. It was a serious fight to keep the container from reeling him backwards as the chocks slid.

Pure math said the container couldn't weigh that much. The winch was gonna win.

Dave finally broke radio silence. *"We're gonna need more time, the fucking attachment chain snapped, over."*

Fuck. "Snapped?"

Dave's dry humor carried through. *"Nobody briefed these guys that they had to keep it light enough for us to load it correctly. We rehearsed this, we got spares, be cool."*

The one thing I am not capable of at times like this is being cool, no matter how well I fake it. Anxiety is my co-pilot. I'd rather be shot at. Goddamn it, at least Ulysses S. Grant would have had the courage to have a drink right now. Not me. I gotta be a coward and suffer in the professional manner in which I was brainwashed all those years.

It took less than a minute to re-rig it and get the winch going again. Finally it eased out of the barn and slowly up onto the truck bed's roller ramps until it halted. The raid team set a couple safety rails and ratchet straps to hold it in place; one of them running up to Steve's door to tell him it was set. Somebody else threw what was probably the Minigun and its associated equipment into Steve's passenger seat so they didn't have to schlep it back through the woods.

Thirty seconds later, he was rolling down the driveway with the load clamped in place. Its next stop was that public pier in Ocean Springs. The raid team then ran for the woodline. We were at fourteen minutes and fifteen seconds.

We cut it way too close.

Chapter 21

At this point, with the container clear, we began the scatter plan.

The first priority was getting the raid team and their collection of contraband firearms the hell out of there. Their string of SUVs on the side of the road was pretty damn obvious, but there'd been no better way to do it. They were to the east of the objective, that patrolling sheriff's car was south.

Adam got the medevac helicopter out of its standby position and headed back north. I wouldn't see him until we were back in Tennessee.

The distraction trailer was recovered. We might not need an unmanned pyro system again, but the radio retransmitter was worth keeping. And again, thou shalt not leave unnecessary physical evidence.

SIGINT had recovered the original black box the recon team put in. Their van was holding north near the Interstate where they could still eavesdrop and cover the withdrawal.

Meanwhile the UAV team would bring the drones down last, circling the farm looking for more cartel shooters or police cars until everyone was out of there.

Angel, knowing nothing of what was going on outside her jammer's radius, flipped her transmitters off on time, and headed to the meetup point halfway to the Gulf Coast. Bereft of electronic interference, County Dispatch came back up on the air quickly. And they were excited. Nay, they were quite fairly pissed off.

"DISPATCH TO PATROL TWO, PATROL TWO, RADIO CHECK! SAY AGAIN, RADIO CHECK!!!"

"Dispatch, Patrol Two. Read you loud and clear?" His confusion was understandable. Poor Patrol Two had no idea his headquarters had been deliberately blinded, deafened, and muted for the last quarter hour.

The dispatcher was clearly on her last nerve. *"DISPATCH, TWO, WE GOT A CALL ABOUT HEAVY MACHINE GUN FIRE OFF MUDLINE ROAD AROUND THE OLD SOYBEAN FARMS. NEED YOU TO GET CLOSE AND SEE IF YOU HEAR ANYTHING. STAY OUT OF THERE TILL WE CAN GET YOU SOME BACKUP, Y'HEAR?"*

While Patrol Two was turning north, the distraction trailer, the raid element SUVs, and the jammer Yukon were all heading away on other routes, routes that were empty and clear at this hour of the night.

I looked at both UAV teams. "You guys can operate while this thing rolls, right?"

They nodded. "Yessir, fully."

I called forward to the driver. "Get us the fucking fuck out of here then. And make sure that goddamn county mountie doesn't get near us or anyone else." I grabbed onto the ceiling rack as the driver took me literally.

Sorry, Patrol Two, whoever you are.

Ten minutes later, I jumped out of the back and into one of the SUVs. The UAV crew headed north while I was now heading south.

***

We planned on taking three hours to get to Ocean Springs. The crew boat had gotten the same text and they were coming in from Pascagoula. If something went wrong with the boat, we had preselected hide points for the truck until the boat was ready. But they were generally pretty reliable.

You may ask why we weren't just going to use the Navy paperwork to back the *Ecstasy* up to meet the truck since it was now "legally" contracted as a Special Warfare Combatant Craft unit training asset? Misdirection. I didn't want anyone on land accidentally watching the cash leave the container and go into the yacht. If someone was going to track the truck, the truck would be headed west toward New Orleans, then onto Lake Charles by land. Meanwhile the container would be heading east for Mobile Bay by sea. Then the container was going to get dumped ten miles offshore as fish habitat. That would be the end of that. But the Navy paperwork had made getting the yacht into US waters painless, which was good enough.

Before we got too far south, I pulled over, met Steve, and we got that goddamn Minigun out of the front seat of his truck. We had the battery, the power supply cable, the feed chutes, and the old .50 cal machine gun tripod it had been sitting on. I got it all loaded into the Yukon jammer truck, told Angel I'd see her at home, and that I'd take the SUV with Dave, Ben, and Tommy back north. With a little grumbling, she headed north too. .

***

We met the crew boat at the Ocean Springs pier at 0330. They were docked securely, stern-first and waiting on us with their heavy equipment ramps in place. Steve backed down the pier and down to the center of the deck, flipped two switches and as the winch spooled back out, the container practically unloaded itself back down the rollers. Specialized dollies were clamped underneath it before it settled all the way down, both to allow the load to be adjusted once the truck was out of the way and then to aid in offloading the container once it was emptied. Steve pulled off with a cheerful *beep beep* of the horn. I had no idea if we were going to keep the truck or not, but for now it was heading where it could be conveniently retrieved later. I high-fived Dave, Tommy and Ben as they got aboard to start their journey.

Tommy grabbed my shoulder. "My rifle, my NODs, two of the pistols and everyone's armor are all still in the Tahoe. We decided only two rifles, one pistol, two NODs and one bag of mags on the yacht, less shit to sink if we gotta worry about customs."

"Got it. Will even clean it all for ya." He clapped me on the shoulder and off he went.

I took a moment, went over, put my work gloves on and opened the container. I had to see this for myself.

It lacked the certain artistic flair of the Templar hoard's final discovery in *National Treasure,* or the shipload of golden riches in *Goonies,* or whatever. It was just green-bluish pieces of paper with the slightly frowning portrait of a long-dead Philadelphia printer's apprentice on them. But there were a whole lot of those pieces of paper. Giving the cartel fuckers credit where credit was due, the cash was fairly professionally done. Most of it was bundled and stacked on pallets, filling the container's floor almost completely and stacked over halfway high. It was probably technically overloaded if anyone bothered to weigh it. Depending how hard that corner had dug into the barn's dirt floor, no wonder the chain snapped on the first drag.

I had brought an empty Army duffel bag with me, one of the newer kind with the zipper and straps. I crammed six bundles, looking about a million each, into it. It mostly filled the bag. Dave and Ben were laughing. "What the fuck are you doing that for?"

I looked back at them with a completely deadpan look. "This way if the fucking boat sinks we don't lose all of it. I still gotta pay for that goddamn winch truck."

They stopped laughing and looked at each other, almost uncomfortably. "Shit, grab a couple more then." I did, filling the bag to the zippered top. We latched the container shut as the ex-Navy guys finished chaining it down and chocking the wheels. And unless I wanted to get stuck on the boat, it was my turn to get off.

As I watched the crew boat head out, I was overwhelmed by two emotions at once. The first was relief; we fucking did it. We had it in hand. The second was almost a crippling sense of powerlessness. I could bring absolutely nothing to the success of the project from here out, not until that cargo hit its destination. Even then it was iffy. But I would not be there watching the pallets go from the crew boat to the *Ecstasy*, praying none of them went over the side into Davy Jones' locker. I wasn't a sailor who could get the *Ecstasy* around the world successfully. I'd be watching weather radars and waiting for check-ins and all that good shit, but I was a spectator. Not a leader, not a participant, just a spectator.

The crew boat would meet the *Ecstasy* the next night over in Mobile Bay. They'd get cross loaded, hopefully not sending any of the cash to the briny deep, then get a clean departure.

***

I got home to Tennessee mid-morning, bringing up the rear. I had caught up to the UAV van around Huntsville- I think they'd stopped at the new Buc-ee's. The raid force had been hours ahead of us. Jake had supervised while they had turned in their weapons and night vision, then the guys scattered to their homes with their pay in hand. The distraction trailer got parked out behind the gazebo since it smelled like the Fourth of July. Letting the fumes air out for a while sounded great.

I met Angel at home for a long hot shower, a change of clothes, and a few hours of sleep before heading back into the Hole. We mostly planned to set up camp in my office until we saw how things shook out for the transport. Jake and the guard shack kids handled shuttling the rental vehicles back to the Nashville airport.

Late that night, Jimmy texted me on the Black phone. "Bump plan." This meant they'd literally run out of weight or space on the yacht and some of the cash had gone back to shore, which meant it would be coming north to us. Morgan had taken a large U-Haul load of supplies to Mobile Bay and was waiting for the *Ecstasy* there, so he would be in charge of getting that load back north. Sure enough, Morgan showed back up at the Hole with a pallet and a half of bundled money in the back of the truck. We hustled it down the elevator to the vault on the eighth floor. Cash would do her thing and get it counted and logged in.

That next morning, I was dozing at my desk when my phone buzzed at 0500. "Anchors aweigh." It would be a long way around Florida to North Carolina where they really planned on starting the trans-Atlantic run, but the voyage was on.

Meanwhile the fallout from the raid was beginning. A couple of those same tapped cell phones were active, one with new voices, and there was a lot of chatter about '*Abuela's* grocery money' coming up missing. Those phones called new numbers and so on. Cross-referencing that into some DEA records we could backdoor into, there were a lot of very unhappy people who knew they had been robbed but had no idea who did the job. Accusations were flying along with some bullets. But... so long as none of that came our way, it really wasn't our problem. Hit and run.

Chapter 22

"On Sunday I said fuck it
And told them they could suck it
And now I'm earning seven Gs a week at Lockheed."
                    ~ *"I Don't Want To*
                    Join the Air Force," Dos
                    Gringos

A couple days after that, my desk phone rang and I recognized the number on Caller ID by the area code. It was my kid brother. Well, not really, so let me explain.

William Tecumseh Bratten was the son of a now-retired lieutenant general I had once worked for. W had a rather familial relationship all through his West Point days and his five years' active duty as an armor officer, dabbling in intelligence. Up to when living next to a trash-burning pit in Iraq ruined his lungs and shortened his career, he was the closest thing I had to a kid brother and I often introduced him as such. We drank ourselves silly at sci-fi conventions and bitched about our love lives. We talked about wargames and our future plans for making pirate money. The good times never last though.

After the Army, he had given into the virus that infects some USMA grads and he had gone corporate-style legit, chasing the big pot of defense dollars you never make while still in uniform. The problem was that it suddenly made him very loyal to the establishment that paid him. He still had me blocked on Facebook the last time I checked. I'd blocked him back, including on my personal phone. I guess that was why he called the desk line. I didn't give a shit if he was mad at me. I was far more pissed off at the fat fucking neckbeard for how he'd suddenly treated several of our mutual friends, all of them people he'd originally introduced me to in the first place. These days, he was a project manager in somebody's intel services division, doing Pentagon contracting and specializing in... Latin America... *Oh, fuck.*

Obviously I hadn't looked far enough ahead. Bill did a lot of counter-narcotics stuff. We had just kicked over a fat anthill in counter-narc. For all the cartel's riches, even those guys would miss that pile of cash and we already knew it was making a lot of signal chatter and a certain number of dead bodies. No doubt Uncle Sam would want to know who ripped who off and for how much. Of course we knew that it was moving around the tip of Florida, out of the Gulf and into the Atlantic in the *Ecstasy*'s lower deck, but we sure as fuck didn't want anyone else knowing. Well, I hate lying to family, but God knows I have to do it enough. *Here goes,* I thought, as I picked up the handset.

"What the fuck do you want, little brother? Last I knew you still weren't talking to me."

"Hey, man. This is business. I'm still very anti-you because of your white nationalist conspiracy theorizing. But you used to live in Mississippi, so I need your brain." *Fuck. Right to the point. Thanks, asshole.*

Between the two Asian girls, admittedly my first ones as my first thirty years of dating history tended toward murderous redheads, my constant intake of foreign food, and the fact I don't like most white people either, I still don't see how I qualify as a white nationalist, but I suppose that's what the editorial board of *The Washington Post* had told him to call anyone who voted for the 45th President twice and thought some of that election was a little suspicious. Just saying.

"Yeah. I avoid the place like the plague ever since." True, actually. Until this, I hadn't done more than clip the state's southeast corner on I-59 en route to New Orleans in about ten years. I had a lot of bad memories from my years there. I live with enough of those without going and digging up more. You drink enough trying to forget shit and sometimes it actually works.

"You know anything about the drug trade there?"

"Not really, you know we mostly work the other wars."

He cleared his throat dramatically, thrilled he knew something he thought I didn't. "Not to blab much on an open line, but... fuck it, who cares since it's on CNN. Twenty-five dead Mexican guys on a farm in the middle of nowhere off the Interstate. Been dead a couple days at least. Forensics are a mess on account of the heat, coyotes, and vultures, but it looks like professionally applied gunfire. Short bursts of 5.56mm, military marked Lake City cartridge brass the crime lab guys say had been reloaded and reused. No fingerprints. Barnes hunting bullets in most of the dead guys. A few were hit with some kind of .30 cal from further out, but nobody has found brass or a solid firing point. A couple more in and around the house got done with 9mm."

And they won't find anything, because I made a point of hiring a fucking expert. But we only got twenty. Six in the barn and fourteen from the house. We didn't kill anyone in the house and there were no pistol shots from our guys anywhere. That's interesting.

I played dumb. "Who were the Mexicans?"

"Everyone they can ID is a known cartel associate. Not all were from the same cartel, which is the next weird point. Cooperation like that is rare. A bunch of felony records both here and there, everything from DUI and possession with intent all the way to rape and murder. There were a couple fresh AK cartridge cases, Chinese ammo, on the ground outside, but no weapons. Looks like someone policed up the weapons after it happened. Now inside the house is another story. Crime scene photos of the inside have enough brass to have been Second Fallujah. AK, mostly, and some seven six two NATO they are working on.

Wasn't us. We left the guns lying there except for the Mini. Between that and the pistol kills, guess someone came home later and got mad.

He continued. "Farm was owned by an LLC that goes back two shell companies to a PO box in Mexico City. State police guys say there was a shipping container moved out. Looks like someone did a rip and run."

Fuck. Which one of my friends didn't watch The Wire? But the fact they followed the corporate paper trail to Mexico City and hadn't caught the Atlanta connection yet was a good thing in my book. And note to self. Next time use a power washer or a leaf blower or some shit to get rid of the container's literal footprint.

I had to give him an answer. Might as well go with part of the truth. "Lots of Chicago gangs meet friends from down south in that part of the countryside. Makes for really good privacy for wholesale sites and it's been going on for thirty years. Wonder if someone ripped 'em off for the cash, the drugs, or both?"

"Apparently a whole lot of cash according to SIGINT. Like they are gonna have very serious liquid asset problems for a few months kind of problems." *Good, fucking assholes.*

I threw him a question. "Why would they put that many eggs in one basket?" I kinda knew the answer to this, but despite the awkwardness of the situation, Bill was a smart guy and I wanted his take on it even if I would never tell him why. He was never as unethical as he wanted to think he was. As our split happened before I came to work here, that also kept him off my list of people to hire. Once upon a time, I might have trusted him enough, but now? No fucking way. He'd trip over his own feet in his haste to sell us out to the Feds for good-boy points and his next job..

"Trust issues. Mostly because of an inability to move it and launder it as efficiently as they once could. Cash is as safe in a guarded container as it is in the bank, maybe more so. Physical cash guarded by trained and reliable gunmen is harder to seize than digits in a bank computer. It's the financial equivalent of burying it in the backyard though. No rate of return, no ability to make payroll or expenses with it without physically moving the paper and that leaves a trail when it's used. Moving a container is easy, but we have much better forensic accounting in Mexico than we used to so we can track bulk dollars when they get changed for pesos or laundered into Mexican banks. Stopping them from getting their dollars where they want them is how you hurt a cartel."

Time to turn this to other matters. "What about other banks than Mexican?"

"Not many people do big cash transactions in the States anymore because of the reporting requirements. We have turned into a debit card or credit card society anyway. But even before that, cash wasn't so much of a deal anymore; the IRS has been limiting big cash transactions for so long people are just used to it and the cartels have such problems physically moving the stuff to anywhere outside Mexico that we really don't bother looking elsewhere."

That made sense. Trying to sound as naive as I could manage, "Out of curiosity, where's elsewhere?"

"The Chinese own Canadian organized crime on the Pacific coast, the Quebecois French gangs own the Atlantic side. We own the Caribbean including Panama. They aren't going to try moving further south, for example Buenos Aires or Rio are both completely out. The Argies and Brazilians hate everyone, especially each other."

"Huh, interesting."

He went on, as prone to lecturing as I am. "Worldwide, the Chinese are sort of winning the financial game, but since you can't hardly tell Chinese banks from Chinese criminals after three thousand years of practice, nobody on our side cares that much since they're impenetrable to anyone not them. The Chinese immigrant community in Mexico has started washing money for the cartels now on a small level between there and China, but we get zero cooperation trying to make cases."

"Huh, well, not my field."

He laughed a bit. "Wasn't mine either. Gotta change with the times, old man. And stop watching Tucker Carlson."

"It's a brave new world, but I'm still the same old me." Despite the old Charlie Daniels lyric, maybe the joke was on him. We all knew I had changed more than I was usually willing to admit. When you are pretty much a freelance, government-sanctioned criminal, you are a long damn way from where I started.

Bill didn't bother getting a last word in, he just hung up.

***

The *Ecstasy* checked in from North Carolina. They took on a full load of diesel to make the long run to Gibraltar and would skip Bermuda and its customs agents. Based on their test run up Florida, they were sure they could do with a comfortable safety margin so long as they kept their speed at or below 18 knots. Made for a slightly longer trip, but they'd get over it. They had hauled enough groceries along that they'd be okay and eating fine for the scheduled ten and a half days. While the Navy kids they hired ran the boat with one of our guys watching them, the others basically took turns locking themselves in below decks. They counted their way across the Atlantic. The satellite phone text messaged something that looked like a phone number. (119) 384-6760.

Or, one billion, one hundred ninety-three million, eight hundred forty-six thousand, seven hundred sixty dollars. Guess there were a couple loose small bills. Really, I was surprised we broke a billion. But it wasn't all the way in our hands yet. It was still another day to Gibraltar and a long way across the Med, the Red and the Indian. And some had to go back to the Cayman Islands accounts to replace what we paid for the fucking boat in the first place, though we had the bump plan cash for that we hadn't finished counting yet either. Really, this whole operation had cost more up front out of pocket than anything else we had ever done, but oh, the payoff. Just so long as they make it to Singapore, God. Or maybe Poseidon in this case.

Chapter 23

"Just when I think I am out, they pull me back in."
~ Don Michael Corleone

The first refuel at Gibraltar went okay. The commercial fuel dock on the west side took American cash, as did the grocery store a block inland. The kid in the galley wanted to top off on things like milk and fresh fruit. Then it was on to the Greek islands and the world kept turning.

Now the *Ecstasy* was not rolling with a full set of Navy-style secure communications. That gear was potentially recognizable to the trained eye of customs cops and was therefore "probable cause" to be avoided, but we still had our ways. Jimmy had a map with numerous reference points marked to designate potential rest and resupply stops. They were NOT sequential just in case someone somewhere was listening. Gibraltar had been Q7, but Eliat was D3 if I remember right. There were four copies of the map, done by hand by Kara and one of her minions. Jimmy had one in his gear. Dave had one as well. At our end, Intel had one locked in one of the safes to translate the check-in calls from the *Ecstasy*. I had the last one locked in the arms room as a spare. It was in the desk drawer, tucked inside an old copy of *Penthouse* where it would take serious effort to find it.

The eastern Med portion of all this worried me. Sneaking around wasn't going to work forever and they needed a solid contact to help with that tricky, contested neighborhood. Ever since the first meetings, Eilat on the Israeli Red Sea coast looked a better option than trusting either Egyptian or Saudi customs not to come aboard and see things they shouldn't.

I dug in my phone for James' Black cell number. I hoped he still had it turned on.

It rang, it rang. He finally picked up.

"Hello, old man. Wasn't expecting to hear from you on this lovely afternoon."

"Call me back on the office line." I hung up and retreated into my office.

It took a few minutes, but the red light started blinking.

"Hey, James."

"Please pardon the delay, but I had to get the phone out of my lockbox and plug it in. I really was out of the loop for a time. I've rather been enjoying it. I made it around the Army-Navy Country Club course the other day in just under a hundred strokes. Not bad considering I hadn't gone eighteen holes in years." *That's great, James. Happy for you, don't give a fuck right now, but won't say so.*

I sighed. "Good for you, man. Seriously. Wish I had time to catch up and be social, but I am in a bit of a jam. You still got any of the Israeli buddies you used to talk about?"

He was thinking so hard I could hear the gears turn. "Seven or eight, I suppose, but you know as well as I do that the word 'buddy' with the Israelis doesn't always mean as much as we think it means depending on conflicting interests."

"Yeah, I got you there. Still. I need somebody with rank and clout to meet a boat at a marina in Eilat, make sure he doesn't see shit, make doubly sure no one else sees shit either, and then never speaks of what it was he didn't see."

He sighed theatrically. "Well, fuck. I don't suppose you would bother me in my retirement for something simple now, would you? What kind of boat?"

"A big white diesel powered yacht, about 170 feet."

His sarcasm dripped. "How tastefully understated of you. The absolute subtlety delights the eye. Now seriously, what are you moving?"

"Hey, you said you were out and didn't need the money, otherwise you would find out at Christmas bonus time." *Goddamn Ivy League WASPs.*

He laughed, some of the cultivated facade slipping. "Smart mouthed little fucker. Mikey really did rub off on you, God rest his soul."

"Yeah, but the old man didn't have the friends in *Mossad* that you do."

He sighed. "I don't know if I have the sort of friends in *Mossad* I used to have. Let me quickly make several discreet inquiries. What's the deadline for this?"

I literally counted on my fingers to make sure. "About four days."

"So one off the books customs clearance, maybe a night or two tied alongside for crew rest and I would wager you need a tame boat mechanic? They are rather maintenance-intensive as you know. My brother is quite the yachtsman and his repair stories are bloodcurdling."

"Sounds about right. But make this sound as unofficially official as you can. I don't want those guys thinking they can use my cargo as an ATM machine."

"Oh, come now, don't go giving into the moncy-grubbing Jewish stereotypes. Those fellows are professionals."

"That's what worries me. They are professional enough to know their total annual budget wouldn't buy a year of whiteboard markers or printer paper for Langley, so I don't want them shaking me down for their supplemental funding. And since it's their marina, they can rob me blind and get away with it. If I wanted that risk, I'd try floating through as normal tourist traffic."

"Eh, you may have a point there. But I know a couple gentlemen who are solid and who I trust to be mostly professional, so I will reach out."

"Keep me posted. To reiterate, I don't wanna have to try to blend into the tourist traffic in and out of Sharm or Jeddah with what we are hauling, but I don't wanna get hemmed up by the Israelis either."

He sighed, his *Haaahvaad* composure again slipping a touch as he got impatient. "I've got it, I've got it. You just hang tight and do your best to remain calm. Keep the faith, old man."

"Wilco." The line clicked dead.

***

James called back by lunch the next day. "I got hold of a friend who can help."

I sighed. "How good a friend?"

"Well, you know how these things can go. You can trust them with your life, but not your money or your wife as a wise man once said. But he's arguably the number three in *Shabak*, which most people outside Israel still call *Shin Bet*. He assures me he will come down south for a little fishing, assure a trouble free refueling and that there will be no issues with a bit of shore leave and grocery shopping for our people."

"Lovely. Will this cost me anything?" I was really trying not to sound sarcastic, but I had very little experience with Israeli spooks. When they are functioning as your concierge and valet service, is tipping expected? Is it a social *faux pas* to offer? Neither Emily Post's book of etiquette or *Military Customs and Traditions* were a bit of help on this.

"Yes, we did talk about that. He did say the on-site quick reaction force in Eilat were all volunteer reservists. Some are even retirees from other special operations units, so a little something for their time would be nice. They'll all go out to dinner after your crew clears the port or something, I suppose. I'm as much in the dark as you are. Nine business trips to Israel over the decades and I have never been south to Eilat."

"So some money for their time. Sure, why not." Should we write checks? Maybe I could have Jimmy pass an envelope of cash to every one of them like it was a goddamn Sicilian wedding. Maybe Adam was right and next time we ought to just charter a fucking airplane. Fuck. My nerves were definitely fraying a bit.

Detour Two
"L'chaim," or "To Life"
~ Very old Hebrew toast

Later on I asked Jimmy what the hell had gone on with the Israelis, since I was deeply curious and a couple curt text messages from him while at sea had not assuaged that. Singapore has a reputation as a very serious surveillance state, so we didn't really unpack the details until we were both home in the States a couple months afterward.

Without a couple drinks in him, Jimmy is not much of a storyteller. He's from that older generation of SEALs that didn't really go for book deals. He's also half Italian from a neighborhood in Noo Yawk where even the guys who aren't formally mobbed up still have enough friends that are that you're expected to stick to the *omerta* and keep your mouth shut anyway. But at first in Singapore, then later back at the house, with steaks and good booze, we started digging into the untold bits of story.

"So we pull up to Eilat. We're threading a needle up the Gulf between Egypt on the left, Jordan on the right and the little bit of Israeli coast in the middle. And really, there's marinas and dive shops on all three beaches. We had options. But we knew you were gonna try having us met, so because of the cargo, we stuck to the plan. Dockmaster was on channel 16 VHF, so we called in. Had their phone number to book a mooring if we had to. Because of our size, they tell us we have a mooring on the jetty at the channel mouth. Guess they didn't want us trying to thread the big girl down that canal into the small craft basin. Lots of boats, mostly smaller than us. That got us a lot of attention, really. Hot chicks in small boats and smaller bikinis were edging up close, yelling "When's the party?" in several languages. But rather than a couple of the uniformed customs cops meeting us, it's one old guy in a seersucker suit, no tie."

"Huh, guess he went low profile. Some friend of James'."

"Yeah. Told us his name was Joni, pronounced Yoh-Knee, and he was 'a friend of a friend.' Didn't explain who he really was, just asked what we needed for supplies and spare parts. Told us he had a couple Israeli Navy mechanics on standby if we needed the backup."

"Oh, so he didn't tell you he was a 'retired' two-star and was chief of staff for the *Shin Bet?*"

Jimmy snorted. "No, but I had a feeling he wasn't just somebody's uncle from Brooklyn, either."

"Why Brooklyn?"

"His English didn't sound Israeli, sounded like a fellow New Yorker, so we talked about it. He seemed more a spook than a soldier, but everyone else we dealt with through him definitely took what he said as orders even if nobody stood at attention or saluted."

"Did you need the mechanics?"

He shrugged and took another pull at his Scotch. "Need? Not really, but we didn't want to be rude so we let them help out. Four pairs of hands are faster than two and they did bring a maintenance truck down. We checked the oil for any metallic contamination that would indicate an engine wear problem. Then it was oil changes, filters, fuel samples, and so on. We let the engineers worry about that. Everyone else either slept or stowed supplies, so that's what I dealt with. A couple of the grocery stores advertised pierside delivery so we went with that. Yoni offered us an Israeli Navy commissary truck if needed, but that struck me as just another complication to avoid."

Now my big worry. "You think they know what we were hauling?"

Another shrug. "Near as I can tell, and we did keep one of the four of us watching the cargo at all times, none of them ever came below decks anywhere except the engine room and they used the aft hatch for all that coming and going. I'm sure the *Mossad* has a couple ninjas on staff, but if they made it below decks to where the money was, they're much, much better than we are and we ought to try hiring a couple."

"As if we could afford them."

Jimmy was a consummate pragmatist. "Eh, afford, yes, need to? Probably not. But we rotated ashore for restaurant chow and the simple joy of walking around on dry land. We caught up on some rest... basically just gave ourselves seventy two hours to recock us and the boat. There was a pretty good Italian place on the coast road. I picked up on Joni's hint that we 'buy dinner for his troops' and so I gave him a nice bundle for their time and trouble. Half a mil, more or less, since he told me he'd handled our marina paperwork and fees. I used the loose bills from the edges of the pile. I don't know what he shared out from there to his guys. Then... we cranked the engines and sailed with the tide."

"So what about getting to India?" I'd worried hard about that despite them telling me they'd handle it. Eilat to the Indian coast was a long way across a deceptively long stretch of water; it was within 400 miles of the trans-Atlantic run and there was no accepted landmark in the plan to aim for like Gibraltar had been.

"Shit, that was way easier than even I thought. We had a little drama down below the Mandab Strait before we even really hit the Horn of Africa, but after that?"

"Wait, what do you mean drama?"

Jimmy took a long swig on his Scotch. "Okay, so I shot a pirate wannabe in the ass."

"What the fuck?"

He shrugged. "I didn't have time to pull him aboard and hang him, and it was just a couple of idiot kids in a shitty boat so I wouldn't have wanted to. I have morals. Fuckin' Captain Teach was maybe fourteen and his brother or cousin or whatever was less."

My control freak nature popped up. "Why am I only hearing about this now?"

He laughed. "What the fuck was I gonna do, put it down in an email or bust out the satellite phone? We handled it. "

Drinking myself empty in useless frustration, I poured myself a refill. "So what happened?"

He shrugged. "Two teenagers in a speedboat with a rusted-ass Tokarev pistol tried pulling up on us. We hadn't made that big left turn out of the Red and into the Gulf of Aden yet, and we're cruising at a nice leisurely ten knots. I instead did him the professional courtesy of just shooting him in the ass."

I shook my head in disbelief. "Really?"

He grinned as he refilled his Scotch. "Man, if I was going to make this shit up, there would have been at least a dozen of them, and a good looking female hostage with bigger tits than Cash's." I groaned. Though he did have a point. Somali piracy was not what it was even four years ago. He continued. "Oh, wait, I forgot. Dave copied the video to my phone."

Jimmy whipped it out, fumbled around in the Gallery folders, and then there was video of him standing on the *Ecstasy*'s salon deck at the rail with one of our upgraded M4A1 style guns slung across his chest, watching a little shitbox of a boat struggle to catch up.

If they'd been further offshore, that boat never would have gotten near them. Idly, I asked "Why were you guys so close to the coast?"

He shrugged. "Fish were biting. Cook had four tuna lines off the stern and there were yellowfin tuna up shallow working on a school of baitfish. We made a few loops trolling through, which isn't easy with a boat that size. He wanted a couple midsize ones to cut up for sushi night and to fill up the freezer. Kid does a mean poke bowl too."

On the screen, the boat was struggling to get near. We could already see the young man in the bow waving what, yep, looked like a rusty Tokarev pistol in the air while an even younger guy milked the overworked outboard motor for all it had. Between a lot of time around outboards and chainsaws, I know what a small motor sounds like when it's pushed too hard. Those dudes were in danger of killing the engine and having a long paddle home. I could hear Dave laughing off camera. "You gonna shoot these pricks?"

Jimmy was cool as could be. "Not unless I have to. Two barely-teenagers aren't a *jihadi* rape and murder gang. They're out for glory or out for a meal, and neither one should automatically be a death sentence at that age."

Dave's recorded voice turned philosophical. "Huh. Kind of you."

Jimmy shrugged. "I remember my older boys when they were that age."

The boat finally got within easy shouting distance of the *Ecstasy.* Captain Tokarev yelled a torrent of Somali, waving his garbage pistol in the air.

Dave asked "What's he saying?"

Jimmy shrugged. "No idea. That was thirty years and three theaters of operation ago for me. All I remember is-" He then yelled back another short phrase in one of the dozens of languages I don't speak.

I heard Tommy off camera as well. "Huh, what was that one?"

Jimmy didn't take his eyes off the boat, relaxed but ready. "Drop the gun or else I blow your fucking head off."

Off camera, a voice I didn't recognize called, "Skipper wants to know if you are gonna cut the fishing lines so he can give her some gas and lose these guys."

Jimmy turned toward the unknown. "Nah, this will be over in a minute. Don't want to mess up the menu planning by losing the tuna.

The camera swung back out to the boat. Captain No-Beard was jumping up and down angrily, yelling in his language that no one else understood, but his pistol was very carefully not pointed at our guys.

Dave quietly asked from off-screen "How much longer before you think he loses his shit and tries shooting that thing?"

Jimmy calmly brought up his carbine into a classic standing offhand position, visibly concentrating on the gentle roll of the deck while peering through the Nightforce variable. "Haven't made a shot off a moving deck in a while", he remarked to no one in particular. He then gently squeezed the upgraded trigger and the shot rang out. Dave swiveled the camera to where the Pirate King was now holding his hip, the cries now of shock and pain more than rage.

Tommy said "Nice shot, and I think he dropped the pistol overboard."

"I was trying to get more of his ass cheek, but he wouldn't turn far enough."

The look of horror was plain as the younger kid pivoted the boat around and headed for shore as fast as they'd come. The video then cut off.

Damn. "So then what happened?"

"Those two little pricks took off, we got the tuna on board, then we went to max speed for about an hour while we pushed further offshore. We helped the cook deal with the fish, I had a poke bowl for lunch, and then it was my turn to get some rack time."

"Okay, so India. That leg scared me. Their west coast doesn't seem to have any big ports."

"Easy. We didn't need any big ports. And I'd picked one of the Navy kids because they had a last name I couldn't spell and they supposedly spoke really good Hindi. I turned them loose on the satellite Internet connection. They then took the satellite phone and started calling random tanker operators from the local version of LinkedIn or whatever. Finally they found one willing meet us offshore to pump sixty or seventy tons of marine diesel for straight cash. It took longer to get a seller on the phone than it took them to pump it."

I had to shake my head in disbelief at that one too. In the other room, Angel and Cash were laughing with Jimmy's wife as they played with the kids.

He continued. "It was easy. Sea state was pretty calm, so we simply tied up alongside this rustbucket coastal tanker, Tommy went up a bosun's ladder with some cash and they passed a couple hoses down. One of the machinist's mates got a fuel sample, called it good, and so we filled up."

"I figured that part was gonna be voodoo and guesswork."

"Nah, the Internet makes a lot of things possible and good satellite Internet makes some things possible that you couldn't do even five years ago. Guess that was Elon Musk's contribution to the mission. So we figured out what we pumped, Tommy gave the head wallah a stack of Ben Franklins, and it was on to Singapore."

Chapter 24

"Finally, I know now what it takes, it takes money and aeroplanes..."
~ The Wombats

At the time, all I knew was they had cleared the Horn of Africa passing into the Indian Ocean, and it was now time for us to get moving. Flashing back a bit, Angel had previously appointed herself the travel agent for the three of us. Having family in Taiwan, Angel had crossed the Pacific more than any of us and was a seasoned veteran. She booked us first class on Cathay Pacific to Hong Kong. It was in the same time zone as Singapore, so we would sort out our jet lag there, taking several days to relax before moving south and getting down to the heavy business of banking our ill-gotten gains.

There was a method to this madness. I'd discussed it with Chris since again, he'd been there before. The Chinese spied on political dissidents, serious criminals, and foreign intelligence services. The government of Singapore, spending way more money and using better technology, spied on every fucking body. Given a choice of a place to kill time waiting for the boat, he recommended Hong Kong over a prolonged sojourn in Singapore. Show up, do business, leave.

Angel and I had discussed the hotel choice over dinner. I kinda wanted to stay somewhere historically interesting, but I also wanted a pool, a hot tub, and a massage spa when I got there. However, the Peninsula was booked solid for 'the high profile wedding of the season' between rich people from there that I'd never heard of. Past that, options were thin. Hong Kong is extremely crowded. Pools take up space and cost more, so they are scarce. So we ended up in the Ritz-Carlton.

The hot tub was really the critical bit. Eighteen hours in the air across the Pacific to Asia had been a literal pain in the ass the last time I had done it, and that had been over twenty years ago. I was young and healthy then. I was much less so now. Even with going from government charter coach-class seats to decadent first class mini-cabins with actual bunks, this flight was probably going to injure me badly. I didn't want, nor could I professionally afford, to be bedridden for days with back problems once I got there. Fuck parachuting; at this point I could and had fucked myself up that badly several times just working in my yard. A bad sneeze or the wrong kind of sex would do it. Remember, Angel and I met when she was my actual massage therapist.

Now Cash, with Angel playing the role of her loyal briefcase carrier and ambiguously lesbian companion, could probably do this without me. I didn't want that. It was my job to play the cultured thug following those two around, never mind my supervisory responsibility for the financial future of what was basically my company. I couldn't do that if I couldn't even walk correctly. Besides that, it hurts. Chronic pain is corrosive to the soul.

So we flew our usual Lear into Van Nuys. Matt wasn't the pilot. The broker said he had something with his kids that night, so he had found a temporary replacement, actually a pilot and co-pilot team. We didn't know these guys at all, so we were way less reluctant to talk about anything resembling business in the cabin even with the door closed. But there were other ways to pass the time. Instead, Angel and I had initiated Cash into the 'Mile High Club' somewhere over Nebraska. Personally, I had wanted to fly into Chino and see Ed Maloney's Planes of Fame museum again, but there just wasn't time. Maybe on the way back. We bailed out at Signature Flight Support and we had laid on a limo (actually a Chevy Tahoe) to get something to eat before we hit LAX.

I insisted on going to the nearby 94th Aero Squadron, which is sort of like having a steak dinner in an air museum.

Cash sulked a bit. The neighborhood was full of small Asian joints and she wanted to explore since she was out of her basement. I reminded her we were going to be in actual Asia 'tomorrow' so I wanted American food in an all-American setting before I trusted my ass and theirs to the airline industry. That cheered her up. Angel, who has a bit of a militaria kink, loved it. There had been a 94th near where she and I had grown up (fun fact, America's original military airfield had been at College Park, Maryland), but it had flooded out after a particularly bad set of storms and never reopened. Great dinner though. Their French onion soup sets up the ribeye well.

Then it was a straight shot down the 405 to LAX. To make our flight time sort of work with the rotation of the earth, time zones, and the International Date Line, we were scheduled to break ground thirty minutes before midnight Friday and arrive before breakfast local time on Sunday. I will say this. Cathay Pacific's customer service was amazing at that level. VIP lounge passes, private express-line check in, and no standing in line with the rest of the herd of cattle. LAX isn't anywhere near as crowded in the middle of the night, but any relief from that was still welcome. Now in those surroundings I was throwing tip money like it was Las Vegas, but it was worth it.

The problem is we had budgeted two and a half hours to get there, through security and to the gate. I was also trusting our guy at DHS that none of our passports were hot; especially Cash's fake. Instead, with that express lane treatment, it took us forty minutes. No issues with the passports. With so much time to kill, we explored Cathay's VIP lounge, including the shower rooms and snack buffet, and had a couple free drinks each to settle the nerves. Their whiskey selections were pretty common. It was a menu for Asian business travelers who think Maker's Mark is a rare treat. They had a fresh-squeezed juice bar, so with the free vodka it turned into Salty Dogs or Screwdrivers for everyone.

I was hoping we'd relax enough to sleep most of the way across. If it's going to take me fourteen to sixteen hours to get somewhere, I prefer car trips where I can stop, stretch, then hit random flea markets and eat local food. But you can't drive across the Pacific, so vodka and fruit juice would have to get me through this pending discomfort.

It sort of worked. It was a really long airplane ride, taking longer than any of us could successfully sleep at once. I don't care if you have a little pod cabin with your own bunk, bespoke food from the onboard galley, and the entertainment library or whatever, it's just a long fucking time over a whole lot of water. Because you're above several layers of clouds and that whole lot of water, there's zero scenery. Until someone pisses off the environmental scammers and gets back into the supersonic airliner business, nothing is going to change that fact. Cathay (and Emirates and Lufthansa, etc.) all do their best, but their best takes time.

Plus, we were all in our own separate pods. We missed each other. After some *Game of Thrones* highlights and rewatching parts of *Battlestar Galactica*, I was actually bored. We actually resorted to sending dirty text messages over the plane's wi-fi to each other when we were actually awake. If some airline wants to make a ton of money, have a family-size pod. We couldn't book the "couple's pod" since there were three of us. Cash told me via text message that next time we decided we had to go across the Pacific, we could get a chartered Gulfstream 6-series.

"How much?" I messaged back.

"From $75,000 to just over 100, depending on which firm we use." I damn near choked on my chef-made dinner. These seats alone had been almost four grand each and I had thought *that* was fucking extortion. The Szechuan beef was really good though. Reminded me of the nearly sauceless version they do at Trader Vic's in Atlanta. That reminded me I was in need of another cocktail, so I pulled up the onboard drink menu to look for a Gun Club Punch while I thought of a good answer. I gave up on trying for clever.

"For that kind of money, we can wait for the hotel to cuddle."

"We can afford it, sir, just saying."

Doing this kind of thing, there were times I had to mentally hold onto the old times in college when I was digging in my couch for enough lost quarters to pay the electric bill. I really did. Having nearly unquestioned access to enormous sums of money can be highly corrosive to your judgment. I also knew my naturally learned inclination to be a cheapskate was a roadblock when we were pretending to be who we weren't. I just couldn't bring myself to spend with the unthinking nature of the truly world-class wealthy. The company could afford it, but that meant we could afford less of something else. I would rather put that excess sixty thousand dollars a charter G6 would cost above and beyond regular airfare toward three more pairs of high end night vision goggles, or upgrades for the IT department. We weren't building the company treasury to live like rock stars; we were building it for prolonged war. And I'd worked on nationally important stuff for poverty wages in the Army, so I already felt awkward about making good money now. With that in mind, I had another drink and fell back asleep.

Finally, we debarked at Hong Kong's airport- the new one out on the man-made island that I never remember how to spell. Thanks to Cathay's luxury, my back only partially felt like shit, so I only limped down the jetway instead of needing crutches or something. Their service on arrival was as comprehensive as it had been at departure. There was a nicely appointed Mercedes van to get us and our bags to the Ritz, which was built in the top levels of the International Commerce Center across the street from the west harbor. We took an express elevator a hundred floors up to the Ritz's real lobby on 103 and got checked in by five AM local time.

Once we hit our room, a corner view suite on 116, we pulled the blinds shut and went back to bed just around sunup.

With another couple drinks and some prescription chemical assistance, I slept maybe six hours. It was just after eleven local time when I finally got out of bed. I still felt like shit. Not the screaming pain of a locked-up sciatic nerve. That felt like a red-hot wire strung between nails pounded in. I just felt mentally fuzzy from the booze and the sleep meds while my back was a barely survivable level of stiff and achy. It was the sort of pain I could handle and knew how to fix. The girls were still blissfully passed out.

Retrieving a swimsuit from my carry-on bag, I went and spent an hour in the hot tub and the pool, going back and forth in five minute cycles. That helped a good bit. The pool was indoors on 118, with an LED ceiling screen to give the illusion of being outside. It was pretty trippy in a luxury cyberpunk kind of way. A plaque on the wall said the pool was in *The Guiness Book Of World Records* for the highest hotel pool in the world at 1,588 feet. That got me thinking 'international commerce' sounded a lot like 'world trade', and I reflected that I was up higher than I was in my childhood picture atop the long-lost South Tower. That sent a nasty shiver up my spine, which sent me past their bar for a drink then back to the hot tub.

After I woke up some more, I then called the spa from the pool deck's in-house phone and made a massage appointment. They said they could get me in at half past two. Returning to the room and finding them still out cold, I decided I still needed to eat something. So I showered then dressed in a manner I hoped wasn't too glaringly Southern American in a polo shirt, khakis and my boat shoes. I then went down to the lunch buffet at the 103rd floor's cafe. I almost died when I saw the $399 price, but then remembered it was in Hong Kong dollars that were just under a dime each. Still a steep lunch by my standards, maybe fitting the surroundings, but their prime rib was really good and the seafood really was worth it. I don't know where they got their scallops, but they were near perfect. The whole meal beat the Bellagio's Sunday brunch in Vegas that held my previous record for "most expensive buffet," but I didn't feel ripped off since the food was even better. Five years ago I could have handled a third plate, but I stopped at two. I just don't eat that much anymore.

A man could get used to living like this. Problem was I shouldn't.

I went back to the room and found the girls slowly waking up and picking through a room service appetizer platter of *dim sum*. I played with the sightseeing telescope in the corner of the room while they got ready to go to the pool. I said the hell with it and decided that was as good a place as any to kill remaining hour and a half until my massage appointment. I went back with them for a while, then went downstairs and across to the spa while they continued to splash and lounge, attracting attention in matching metallic black bikinis.

The masseuse was really good. Early twenties and cute. Not as cute as Angel or as porn-star hot as Cash had made herself into, but extremely professional and with hands that were probably strong enough to crush an unopened Coke can. Afterward, I sat in their steam room a bit, then I stumbled back to the suite and mostly collapsed in the shower while drinking more ice water I carried in with me. I'm told that's always important after a massage, otherwise toxins get broken loose in your system so you have to flush everything. Angel assures me horrible things will happen otherwise. Anyway, the girls wandered in from the pool eventually. Their bikinis came off and we all fooled around a bit before we started debating the subject of dinner.

There was a joke personal ad on Facebook once. "Couple Seeks Third; Not Sexual, Just Need Help Deciding What We Want For Dinner." Let me clue you in from experience. If you have a third involved, well over half the time their opinion is not a tiebreaker, but instead merely another complication in the process. Eventually we just ended up wandering to the lounge for their complementary-with-your-expensive-ass-room cocktail hour snack layout. From there we went on to the upstairs bar for more light food. We were planning on drinking ourselves sleepy by 'bedtime' since our bodies thought it was still before lunchtime yesterday.

We woke up the next morning well before dawn, our body clocks not greatly aligned with local time yet. We sort of dozed until we could wander back to the club lounge for the allegedly free breakfast. Suitably fortified, we returned to the room to plan the day.

Chapter 25

"The most outrageous thing I could imagine ever doing would be going to the shopping mall for lunch."
~ Brian "Marilyn Manson" Warner, the Gothfather

The plan was apparently shopping. Cash had brought a fair amount of money in her luggage from the pile downstairs in the Hole. She had stuffed a few hundred thousand in Angel's luggage as well. For some reason Hong Kong Customs hadn't cared. I suspect the cops ask fewer questions of well-breasted Asian girls who speak the language and are in the private customs lines for first class passengers than they do of other people, say large corn-fed white boys without local language skills and who basically radiate 'PROPERTY OF UNITED STATES GOVERNMENT.' I was surprised I didn't get fucked with on the way in. Of course then I opened the bottom half of my main suitcase that Cathay's valets had whisked through Customs for me and found half a million dollars in it. I about shit myself and told her so.

She sighed at me like the clueless provincial I really am at times. "You don't have to declare cash coming into Hong Kong, sir. They want you to bring it and spend it." Wow. Would be awesome if our own government was so enlightened, but that way the Feds wouldn't get to legally harass minorities at airports with the asset forfeiture laws leftover from the 'War on Drugs' we lost. Well, that was a wasted panic attack. Probably what I get for letting the girls mostly pack for me. Of course I also wondered why they sacrificed suitcase space for cash. I couldn't wear money...

Oh, the fuck I couldn't. The ladies had planned this in depth. They had already criticized the suit I had laid out for the lousy thirty minutes I figured we'd spend in the commercial bullion depository in Singapore. Shit, I can go an entire calendar year and literally wear a tie once, usually when crashing a reception at the National Rifle Association convention. And I have one decent suit, a medium gray one, that I bought for a wedding a few years back. Wait. Fuck. More than a few years. How old is my nephew? Okay, add two...that was...twelve. Huh.

Anyway, since I bought fairly well, have a good dry cleaner, and it doesn't get worn more than a few days a year, it has held up. That suit was now deemed inadequate. It wasn't even in my suitcase, so I assumed it was still in my closet in Tennessee. Now the ladies were conspiring to improve my wardrobe. According to some, Hong Kong allegedly had some of the world's best shopping, so now we were going to spend a bunch of money to look like what we weren't.

Elements Mall was downstairs and across a skybridge from the hotel and is what happens when the architects' desire to make good art gets in the way of my desire for an efficient retail experience. This mall? To my way of thinking it was incredibly disorganized with a confusing floor plan. The brochure told me it was thematic and based on traditional Chinese alchemy. Yeah, whatever. Wood and Metal looped okay, Water sort of made itself into a figure-eight, but Fire was this dangly trail that didn't get you into anywhere else. It mostly had the same high-end multinational chain stores as you got at... say in Vegas, like the Forum Shops at Caesars Palace, just scattered weirdly.

Look, I have definite opinions on shopping. I am basically a redneck by choice if not exactly by upbringing. My idea of an efficient retail non-grocery retail experience is something like Bass Pro Shops. Ammunition to socks all under one roof. Anything you can't get there? Hardware store or Army surplus. Done. That's it, that's my hick life. Two minutes into trying to plot a sensible walking route to get what we needed in one shot, I groused we should have just fucking stopped the Lear at McCarran, taken an Uber around in Vegas, done what needed doing and that way we could have shopped in the States.

The girls just stared at me like the barbarian I am.

Undeterred, I started warming up to a proper rant. "Seriously, do you think I can get an off the rack 52R that will meet your tastes in an Asian city? We don't have time to dick around with custom fittings or made from scratch and I am too cheap to pay double for all night tailoring. The boat is maybe a week out," I carefully did not say from where, "and we are on a deadline to get our shit together and get there." *Sigh.*

They just told me to relax.

I don't relax well. At all. Have you gotten that much from the story so far?

Anyway, I was right about the suit, a 44 was considered the big end of the rack in every store since Chinese men generally don't come in my size. Brioni had a couple of 46s. Then the assistant manager in Brooks Brothers slipped Angel a business card for his uncle who ran a 'traditional men's tailor with all-night service' across town. I was told we were going there next. Told. Not asked. Told. Okay, sure. I can be patient. But them giving the orders wasn't the usual method for us.

So as not to waste the trip for me, I went into one of the shoe shops, turned up my drawl and told a clerk sort of the truth; I was in town on the way to a business meeting and didn't need to look like I was from Texas. Yes, I assumed the clerk didn't know one flavor of Southern accent from another and I was right. With their efficient help, I picked up three new pairs of English-style dress shoes, two black, one a medium brown. I then wandered into another element's hallway while the ladies did their thing in YSL.

OK, so Cash and Angel sneered at the idea of me wearing my 'dress' watch, a steel Seiko diver I kept on a ten dollar nylon NATO strap. The strap itself was the old James Bond *Dr. No* movie color scheme, the fictional colors for Her

Majesty's Secret Service. Twin olive drab regimental stripes edged with maroon, all on navy blue. It was just another joke I told to myself. Some of my fellow delinquents had recognized it for what it was over the years and giggled along. But that was my 'dress' watch. It was that or nothing. I hadn't even brought my old Casio G-Shock I wore most days. At least in this respect, I could re-equip myself without female supervision.

Yeah, I had a wish list of expensive watches I meant to get someday for fun since I knew a bit on the subject, but I never had dropped the money. A few of my gun nut acquaintances are serious watch guys. Some of them can afford to be. Trey got rich selling railed forends, suppressor cans, and then sniper rifles to the DOD. Duane went from flying Hornets for the Marines to making polymer rifle parts and magazines by the multi-millions and so on. Me? I was just getting used to making a comfortable middle six figures. Five or six years ago I was having to call-block my credit card company. When I did start making good money at the firm, I was paying off old bills and buying a few guns. Well, maybe more than a few guns. Maybe it was a lot of guns depending on your standards. I just hadn't gotten around to the watches.

I entered the Rolex store and was confronted with about five thousand watches at varying price points from 'a nice used car' to 'a new house.' I suddenly remembered why I hadn't ever actually invested. I'd hit sensory overload after two minutes of looking at *all this shiny stuff*. Making an actual informed decision like a responsible adult was hard. Instead I turned my inner eleven year old loose in all his ADHD *ain't-this-cool* energy.

I poked around in the 'certified pre-owneds' and picked out an 'it's-sort-of-vintage-now' mid-1990s GMT Master II. It was just out of a dealer rebuild with a replaced red and blue bezel and a fresh polishing. Chuck Yeager had worn that same model in Rolex's ads in *Air and Space* magazine when

I was a kid, cashing in on the fiftieth anniversary of breaking the sound barrier. This is proof that good advertising makes a lifelong impact. I tried it on, admiring the look while humming Bill Conti's majestic closing theme to *The Right Stuff*. My inner child was now happy.

Then Grown-Up Me saw the price tag and about fucking died. Even converting for Hong Kong dollars, it was a bite. Yeah, since it was heavily rebuilt, which ruined some of the collector value, it only worked out to about seventeen grand in American dollars after I haggled the guy down and paid cash. But, I figured I had a lot of money to burn through for this and Merry Christmas to me or something.

The girls weren't holding back on themselves either. They planned on making an entrance when it came to getting our ill-gotten gains into respectable brokerage. Cash and Angel had gotten out of Christian Dior with a dress or three slung over their shoulders when I caught up to them. Cash looked at the Rolex on my wrist that I thought looked pretty spiffy and she just snorted derisively. "Sir, you might as well just wear your dive watch then."

Sigh. "What am I supposed to wear then, dear?"

Her look was one of loving disdain. "Something not steel that is not worn on the job by fighter pilots or scuba divers."

Double sigh. There goes my entire taste in watches, really.

Cash took pity on me and decided to explain. "Trust me. I worked on the Street and followed some of the major players in and out of the *important* conference rooms, sir. There are times a steel watch will not do if you want to be taken seriously with high end business meetings. White gold, yes, platinum sure and yes, they can tell the difference by the reflection from ten feet away, but not steel. To them, that just marks you as a hick to be taken advantage of." That was accurate enough that if anyone else had said it, I might have gotten offended.

Okay, so I guess I needed something else. *Time* to add something else to the collection, pardon the pun. We wandered down the wavy Fire hall to another watch dealer that handled multiple lines.

I went back to looking, with the girls helping. Cash quickly picked out a delicate little white-gold Cartier watch for herself, then a rose gold IWC-Schaffhausen with the neat little phases of the moon dial. Angel also decided she wanted two; a men's steel Omega Seamaster dive watch (yeah, it was one of the James Bond movie commemoratives, too) for daily use and something French-Swiss in yellow gold I couldn't correctly pronounce for dress wear. Then I made the mistake of mentioning to the salesman helping her that I'd love one of the Omega Speedmaster commemoratives from the Apollo landings. If there was one sitting in a display case anywhere on Earth it was Hong Kong, but I didn't have time to rummage about looking for one.

He smiled serenely, with only the barest trace of smugness. "I only have two. One is steel and used. Came as a trade-in. No case, either, which kills the resale value to the collector market and they are not popular as daily wear items here. I was getting ready to list it online, so it is in the back. One is new and it is right over...there." He pointed across the shop to the side I hadn't looked at previously, the side where all the yellow gold was. I'd stayed away from that.

It laid in its presentation case like the reliquary of a saint. It was the 45th anniversary Apollo 17 commemorative from a few years ago, the yellow gold one with the blue ceramic dial. I knew it from online drooling. Less than three hundred were made. Cost more than my truck had when it was new. Shit. No way. I was not spending that kind of money on a watch. Just no. Maybe I would do forty-eight grand on a really rare rifle, or a new truck....

Angel had none of my reservations. "He'll take it."

I looked over at her, probably with a look of abject horror. "I'll fuckin' what?"

Cash nodded. "Still a bit space-nerd, but it's pretty. It fits the aesthetic you need for this."

Angel patted me on the shoulder. "Happy birthday early, love." Maybe from her and Cash both. I didn't pay Angel *that* well.

My stomach was slightly knotted. I just wanted to go sit in the woods in dirty fatigues with a rifle until the sticker shock went away. Sure, we'd spent just shy of thirty million dollars on the boat and the other mission prep, but it was bigger than a World War I subchaser and it actually worked and did things. A forty-plus thousand dollar watch? This was completely antithetical to my upbringing. I don't know how much of my inner turmoil showed on my face. The salesman merely smiled as he returned from the back with the other watch. The steel Speedmaster was the 40th anniversary Apollo 11 with the coin-style mission patch insert on the dial. Damn. Another of my watch goals.

Angel then turned on the salesman, her eyes predatory. "I assume there will be a package discount on our purchases?" The conversation then switched to Chinese, with some hand waving, but they finally nodded and shook on it. Cash and Angel rummaged in their purses and handed over what looked like enough hundred dollar bills to buy a couple new Porsches. We probably got a fair deal, but damn, that was a large stack of cash to drop. More than I would ever spend in other circumstances. If he was on commission, the sales guy was probably going to go home early and celebrate.

I sat down on a bench and started flipping through the library on one of my phone's book apps to relax from the sticker shock. I found a gunfighter novel from an indie Texas writer named Seth Bailey that looked good and calming. Meanwhile the girls rampaged on more dresses and Louboutin heels *and so on and so on and make it stop please God this is more than I can take* and it made my eyes figuratively bleed.

Let me put it this way, when you are watching the two hot Asian girls you are sleeping with drop five thousand dollars on a few bags full of Agent Provocateur and La Senza lingerie and all you can think is, "God, please get me out of this labyrinth," yeah, you have been at the mall just too fucking long.

Getting everything back up the sidewalk and up into the hotel was a bit of a chore, but it was done with some help from the bell staff who earned their tips. At this rate, we were going to need more luggage just to get to Singapore, let alone home. Well, hell, they sell luggage here too. Solvable problem. Then it was a light snack in the lounge and for me, a good stiff drink from their Scotch menu. Well, then a second, just to settle the nerves. The girls were clinking wine glasses with a giggle and having a ball. Me, I had been less stressed than this after incoming mortar fire. That realization made for a third Scotch.

Back to my wardrobe issues for this little jaunt. Over the years, I had ordered a few unit ties from the British regimental museum gift shops in the UK. They're a British thing that never really caught on with most American units. But with cross training, there were a few I was kinda-sorta entitled to and therefore could wear without feeling a complete fraud. No SAS or Royal Marine Commandos for me; not my field of endeavor. But the Royal Scots Dragoon Guards and the Black Watch from our shared Balkans trip, 1/7th Gurkha Rifles, long story, the old Green Jackets, oh and I brought a couple American offerings from my old units and associations. This was good. Corporate-style anonymity truly didn't suit me and where I usually did business, that bit of style mattered. Where you had been and what you had done usually mattered more than the cut of your suit or the knot in your tie. But I didn't wear ties often, as I mentioned, so not knowing what I would need this trip, I brought my best half dozen. I figured I would carry them to the tailors to see what fabric looked good with what I had already resolved to wear.

After drinks and snacks, it was off to get measured. The shop was apparently an old north Kowloon landmark; neon signage, vintage "modern" chrome-framed vinyl-padded furniture, and a staff that looked like they'd been there since when the Vietnam War was still bringing in planeloads of GIs spending their R&R money. Angel and Cash were parked in comfortable chairs and brought complimentary drinks while I was up on a podium being assaulted with a tape measure. It was nearly seven in the evening, but the shift on duty moved and measured with the speed of a NASCAR pit crew. The only apparent concession to the modern world was the numbers were recorded on an iPad app, not on paper. I was told their experienced crew of magic gremlins in the back would have what I needed ready for fitting after lunch the next day.

Then the senior of the fitters, a wizened gnome of a man, looked at me knowingly and asked, "I am surprised you have not yet asked us to tailor around your weaponry. Poor idea here in Hong Kong with its laws on the subject, but in America or elsewhere, of course..."

I sighed. To be honest, I was only planning on one suit for this one meeting and had not thought further ahead. "What gave me away?"

"You are a large *gweilou* with two quite beautiful Asian lady friends." He looked back over his shoulder at them and dropped his voice a bit. "Though the one who speaks Cantonese does so with more of an American accent than she thinks." He chuckled and continued. "They are not merely hired escorts since they are picking your clothes as a wife would. Your *chi* is obvious. The knuckles on both your hands are calloused and deeply scarred, with a distinct bump inboard on your right thumb from many hours on a rifle selector switch or pistol safety. Most likely both. Then your accent makes you sound like the actor with the crossbow on

The Walking Dead. I liked that show very much for its first few seasons. Now what will you normally wear for a pistol?"

"There's a book called *Irregular Scout Team One* that's much better than that show if you're a zombie enthusiast. Guy named Holmes wrote it."

He rather charmingly stopped what he was doing, opened his phone's Amazon app, and looked for it. Smiling, he spent $2.99 to humor me.

That done, I continued. "Now as for pistols, I prefer a 1911A1 pattern .45 automatic, behind my right hip."

"A classic choice, if a bit dated." Great, I was getting called a Boomer Fudd by a guy who looked old enough to have been in the *two world wars* of meme legend. "Inside or outside the waistband?"

"Inside. Outside the waistband events with dress guns are usually not dress trouser events."

"Appendix carry is popular for a reason. Now, where is your spare ammunition?" Man, I really was dealing with experts.

"One magazine, horizontal to the left of my belt buckle, base out, bullets pointing up. If I feel I need more than that, I add a second magazine carrier behind the left hip or switch to the Glock 19 for capacity."

"Medical equipment?

"CAT tourniquet, kydex flat pack on the belt behind my left hip, combat gauze in pockets."

"You may wish to upgrade that. Another nephew runs an Airsoft and military simulations shop over in Quarry Bay and believes he has made a breakthrough in discreet medical carry. Very well, we shall have inert stand-ins for your kit here at the fitting. Will you be wearing soft armor under any of your jackets?"

"We will set another one up for that, I guess. I prefer to work in less formal garb with more pockets and more damage resistance."

He nodded. "As you can tell, we tailor for quite a few professional gentlemen from around the world. I see you are in need of such modifications for several of your suits."

"Wait, several?" Angel and Cash nodded. Cash held up four fingers as she delicately sipped her coffee.

Why the fuck I needed four new suits, I don't know. I have a couple friends who are clotheshorses. Me, I am not. But, a different kind of warfare, so different uniforms and therefore I would shut up and do what the girls told me. Not the way things usually went between us, but sometimes you have to let them do their thing.

The old man chuckled. "See, as a wife would. We use a thin Kevlar reinforced nylon material for the lower lining of the jacket to prevent equipment from abrading the fabric but also to reduce printing without bulking the jacket. Sixty years ago we used actual sail canvas, but as sails have smartened, so have we. Crotch and armpit gusset reinforcement. Stronger knees and elbows. Pockets are subtly reinforced for load carriage while maintaining flatness, there is a protective tab for knife clips on the front pockets, and so on. The belt loops will be one and one half inches to accommodate working belts versus dress, the belt loops strengthened and set to aid with gear retention, and some extra concealment pockets can be added."

"With that in mind, I think I will need six suits, not four. It is a long airplane ride back if I ruin one working in it. Two navy blue, two in that lightweight gray wool I liked for the one suit I originally thought I'd come in for-"

"Richmond dress gray, you called it, though I am unfamiliar with the term."

"It's an American Civil War reference; it was a specific uniform shade from the losing side."

"Ah. I shall look for an appropriate documentary on YouTube."

"And I'll take one each in the light gray and the charcoal pinstripe. Oh, hell, two black as well. We'll go armor tailoring on one blue and one black and concealed weapons tailoring on everything except one Richmond and the other navy blue. There are places I cannot carry, so no sense looking baggy at those times." I shrugged. "And I appreciate your assistance, sir." I slipped him a fat wad of folded bills as we shook hands. I was going to have to put Bun Bun onto this place. He'd hate the flight out, but these guys did amazing work and the big man was harder to fit than me.

"The pleasure is ours, sir. We do enjoy our craft. And I think you will find the meeting with my nephew interesting. We will see you tomorrow."

We got out of the cab about half a mile from the hotel just to walk through Temple Street Night Market. It was an open-air food court and flea market that opened after sundown and went much of the night that I had heard of over the years. We walked and ate, shopped, ate more. I looked past a bookseller or two and found a vintage clothes stand with some old US and British militaria to eyeball while the girls looked at anime merch.

As we walked and nibbled, I gently bumped Cash. "See, I told you we'd be eating real Asian food in Asia pretty soon."

She giggled around a mouthful of steamed pork dumpling. "I know, sir. It's just rather unreal to be here. Let alone here with you and Angel like this."

"Beats the shit out of working late on Wall Street, doesn't it?"

"You have no idea. Independence, the money, the travel, having you in my life and even her in my life too..."

"Interesting arrangement, eh?"

"Well, I think she used to be straight, but I think it's obvious I'm not."

You know, despite the highly diverting subject material of hot twentysomething Asian chicks making out frequently and how that fueled my own fun, I never had gotten completely used to Cash's habit of referring to her old life in the third person. The subject rarely came up, but at the same time there was a fine line between reinvention and dissociative identity disorder. She was too important to the company, much less to me personally, to lose her to a long term fit of craziness. Oh, well, one more thing to keep an eye on. I had so many things I worried about, what was one more? Even my anxiety has anxiety.

Angel probably picked up on that. She laughed wickedly, saving the moment with humor and erotically teasing her ice cream cone with her tongue. "Spaghetti is straight too, until you get it hot and wet enough. After that? No such thing."

We eventually wandered all the way back to the hotel for a nice night's sleep.

We were up early the next morning, our body clocks still somewhat jangled. After a casual room service breakfast, Cash had another idea. Some of the jewelry wholesalers would sell ounce or kilogram bars and other places in town advertised vault storage. Maybe a couple years ago I would have jumped at the opportunity. But anything we stashed here was too close to mainland Commie China for my long-term comfort. The Chinese military had nearly overrun the place twice in the last decade and had already imposed some heavy political changes at bayonet point. I just had the impression Hong Kong was on borrowed time that way. I didn't want to store things here just to have it become loot for a ChiCom armored brigade.

We caught a taxi to lunch at a gourmet hot pot place courtesy of Cash's research, then after lunch it was time for my first fitting. The nephew was there with a gear bag, the London Bridge Trading Company version of the classic aviator's kit bag. I had two of them myself and half a dozen of the standard issue sort. I had tried for more on eBay over the years, since they're stitched better than the GI contract ones, and always lost the bidding to various Asian airsoft kids who had a hard-on for anything from LBTC. Their reputation as gear makers to the East Coast SEAL teams gave their stuff a marketing push and secondary market demand through the early 2010s that you didn't get with Paraclete (Army SF), Eagle (75th Rangers, some Marine units), California-era Special Operations Equipment Inc (West Coast SEALs and Recon Marines), or High Speed Gear Inc (East Coast Recon Marines, some of the 82nd Airborne) stuff. I might have bid on this very bag and lost. He stuck his hand out with a smile and said, "Good to meet you, man. Call me Bobby." Uh, sure, we'll go with that.

He unpacked the bag. It was loaded with stuff. A low-profile ammunition chest rig, looked like a Haley Micro knockoff. An interesting Airsoft 1911 in an old leather Milt Sparks "Summer Special" inside-the-waistband holster. An Airsoft Glock in a Raven kydex holster identical to my one at home. Several styles of magazine carrier. Several knives and multitools. Body armor. Then he handed me his breakthrough.

A narrow plate of thin steel was mounted in a kydex belt slide. Extremely strong neodymium magnets worked through the cloth waist of the trousers, securing a thin flat pack of medical gear inside the waistband in the small of the back. Looked like 500D Cordura nylon with a flannel patch for comfort where it would lay against your lower back. CAT tourniquet, two packs of combat gauze, a pair of chest seals, a flat roll of tape and so on vacuum-bagged together like Dark Angel Medical or Dempsey at SoLaTac in Lake Charles had pioneered. But you merely had to reach back under your suit jacket, grab the tab at either corner and pull hard. Until then, the magnets kept the pack from either falling down your pants and down one of your legs, or working its way uphill and out. It was also convertible for outside the waistband carry, where it was still a discreet package that wouldn't show below the hem of a suit jacket. I really was impressed and told Johnny so.

"How long before you have these ready for sale?"

He hemmed and hawed a bit. "I'm still in beta testing."

"I need twenty in gray, ten in black and another ten in ranger green, smoke green, whatever you want to call it, by late November. You just made my Christmas shopping for this year much easier."

Bobby laughed. "Okay, that I can do. I was afraid you were going to ask for a few hundred for an agency order."

"I'm not a very big agency. Hell, I wish you had more than one ready to go now."

"That one isn't really ready to go."

"It's for sale, right?"

He sighed. "Yeah, man, you can keep the gray one. I have a couple more. The QuikClot is fresh and that CAT tourniquet is genuine, so it's ready to roll."

Once we had finished playing with the medical pack, they had me into one of the suits and with a semblance of my usual weapons load with the medical pack in place, all within five minutes. I was quite impressed. Then it was off with that one, on with an adjusted weapons load and I was throwing on a simulated set of soft body armor and being fitted to conceal that well. Then, "jacket open, ammo rig on" and so on. And so on and so on with varying combinations of the suits and their appointed roles.

I was going to need a bigger closet.

When we finished with those suits, I expected to have to repeat the process with the rest of them. The old man smiled. "With laser measuring guiding the cutters and fitters and a bit of computer assistance on the sewing machines, what is done for one is duplicated for the others once we have the numbers."

All right, better living through technology.

While Bobby and I were figuring out what he was going to sell me for add-on accessories, Angel was playing with some of the knives and Cash was on her phone trying to figure out what sounded good for dinner. I picked up the Airsoft 1911. It was an insanely accurate reproduction of a 1970s Bob Chow custom gun, down to the GI surplus

National Match part numbers and his own maker marks. It would be pretty cool for shooting in my office when I was allegedly supposed to be working.

"Bobby, where did you get that?"

"Oh, one of the Japanese Airsoft companies makes knockoffs of some of the old American .45 custom smiths. You know, for us gun-obsessed Asians who aren't legally allowed to own the real thing. There are Japanese who obsess over Armand Swenson or Bill Wilson the way American sword nuts go crazy over Masamune, Muramasa, or Amata."

I nodded. "An apt comparison, the famed weaponsmiths of one land and time versus those of another land and time. You have another one of these Airsoft ones for sale? I have an actual Chow pistol, but I can't shoot it in my office."

"This one's my personal one. I have a new one still in the box back at the shop. Cost you nine hundred American though; they're highly collectible."

For a high-end, steel-frame Japanese reproduction, that sadly wasn't that far off the market price. Most places in Asia, a metal 1911 airsoft gun or display dummy cost as much as a real live one would in the States. "Fair. Stick it on my tab with the rest of the stuff. You have my shipping address."

He nodded and stuck his hand out. "Pleasure doing business with you. Come on by the shop if you have time, there may be more interesting things I can send you home with."

"You'll be shipping them to the States for me regardless. I am going on to Singapore for business after this and you have heard stories of how cheerful and understanding their customs personnel are."

"I've been there. They aren't so bad as all that, but I do see your point. Shipping is pretty easy to the States though."

I resolved to swing by the shop. I had cash to burn and I do love my war toys. In some respects, yes, I am a large child.

After playing tourist at the Kowloon Ferris wheel, we went back to the hotel to get cleaned up before dinner. Checking in with the office told me nothing was happening there. At this point the few folks in the company who really knew what was going on were hunkered down waiting for the news that the shipment had arrived.

That actually annoyed me. The boat was either going to get there or not. The rest of the world wasn't going to stop turning meanwhile and we didn't need to go missing things while we were distracted with this shit. Funding the company's future would do us a shit bit of good if we fucked up its present. Doing their self-appointed jobs, the girls dragged me out to dinner in an effort to make me calm the fuck down. It partly helped. I am sometimes a simple mammal that can be placated with treats.

The next day, it was south across the bridge onto Hong Kong Island. First it was west to the Victoria Peak tramway and some wandering in the Aberdeen wilderness park before we headed back east to another expensive shopping district that lay between me and the Airsoft place in Quarry Bay. The girls wanted to eat lunch and hit Jean Paul Gautier before I got to my toy guns.

I need to stay out of some kinds of toy stores when I have money. Really. Making a long story short, I went in for one Airsoft gun and Bobby ended up selling me, uh, seven, including two different Thompsons and a full-size full-auto M240B light machine gun like a younger me had once carried in the 101st. He laughed as he rang me up, assuring me they'd be boxed up and shipped to the States. They were going to be there before I was, probably.

After snacking on more street food as an early dinner, we ended up at this deliberately-Eighties styled cyberpunk theme bar over in Quarry Bay. Funky neon and lasers lit the place, which was otherwise dark corners and black pleather couches. A DJ was "spinning" retro synthwave music off a laptop until ten. Perturbator, Scandroid, Dance With The

Dead... I knew a lot of it. I had a 46 hour YouTube playlist of the stuff for when the mood struck me. At one point when the beat was really hitting, it seemed half the girls in the place were dancing on tables, customers and staff alike. Cash and Angel were up there too, grinding and kissing.

Then we got the main attraction, for certain values of the term. The stage curtains at the back wall opened and out came five adorable little Chinese girls, eighteen or nineteen tops, dressed somewhere between a young Lita Ford and the worst of Motley Crue's leather-and-eyeshadow androgyny days. Two songs in, I had figured them out as a really bizarre mix of California punk rock and old pop. Unfortunately they had the rather horrific Chinglish name of *Monsoon Poon.* The drum and guitar work was pretty solid, but I couldn't understand a goddamn word they were saying. Even their clearly recognizable American cover tunes were translated. "I Hate Myself For Loving You" by Joan Jett and the Blackhearts sounded like a carry-out menu read over the familiar guitar riff. The girls were singing along as best they could.

I elbowed Angel during the next song. "What the hell are they singing about now?"

She shrugged, half-yelling back in my ear. "Beats me, there are six hundred kinds of Chinese and I don't know this one." It didn't matter; it was ninety minutes of pretty decent rock and it took our minds off things.

In the cab back to the hotel, Cash and Angel were both pretty happy. Angel said, "That kinda makes the trip for me. I listened to them in high school."

"Those girls looked like they were in diapers when you were in high school. If that."

Cash laughed. "It's not like those girls tonight were the original lineup. They're like that country band you like that had the plane crash, no original members are left but they keep playing the same songs while keeping the same name."

Angel nodded agreement. "Yeah, I don't think anyone from the Monsoon actually died, but yeah, they're definitely the Lynyrd Skynyrd of Asian pop." Now that was an analogy I got. I'd never heard of the band prior, so otherwise it was kinda lost on me. Shit, Angel and I'd seen Skynyrd live on their alleged retirement tour back in '19.

***

The next morning, it was on to the second suit fitting. The manager informed me that they would be completed by dinnertime tomorrow, bagged and sent over by their courier to the hotel. There were also dress shirts and a couple pairs of khakis with various modifications and hidden pockets. They were similar to ones 5:11 made a decade ago, but I hadn't seen anyone else try in years. I bowed in gratitude and tipped heavily before it was off to dinner.

Chapter 26

"Good times for a change, See, the luck I've had, Can make a good man turn bad,
So please, please, please, let me, let me, let me, let me get what I want, this time."
~ The Smiths, though the Dream Academy version is better

I woke up about two in the morning for no real reason. The girls were still asleep. I slid out from the bed and out to the chaise lounge by the sitting room windows. This hadn't happened in a couple weeks and I was way overdue. So, I stared out over the lights of Hong Kong, a thousand thousands of neon jewels shifting around as in a giant fish tank and just marveled at the sight for a while. It was kind of hypnotic, watching cars and boats and the neon-trimmed skyscrapers of Kowloon...

I sat in a thousand dollar a night luxury hotel suite on the other side of the world, with a belly full of expensive food and drink and with two beautiful women who loved me back in the bed. What the fuck on God's Earth did I have the right to complain about right now? You know, except for the job stress, the fact we had a literal billion dollars coming this way on a boat trying to complete the theft of the century, worrying about a pissed off drug cartel, and so on and so on.

I was pretty far lost in my thoughts, so much so I didn't notice anyone behind me until hands slid over my shoulders and long hair brushed down my back. I looked up and Angel had that disapproving look on her face. It overshadowed the fact she was naked. "What the hell are you doing out here by yourself, sir?"

"Eh, woke up in a mood and you two were out cold. I figured I would leave you to it."

She sighed. "You know the rules, sir. You wake up in one of your moods, you are to wake one of us up, preferably both of us, and we take care of you until you are okay again."

"You two need your sleep."

"So do you, which is one of the many reasons we are around to help keep you stable."

She had a point. "That's a hard job sometimes, isn't it?" I sighed.

"Made harder by your stubborn refusal to let anyone help you, even when you need it."

She really had me there. Unfortunately I read *The Eagle Has Landed* when I was ten; no, not about the Apollo 11 landing, I mean the novel about the probably mythical German assassination attempt on Churchill in '43. The phrase Jack Higgins used was *'an arrogant self-sufficiency bred from the hazards of the calling.'* Because Ten Year Old me was an idiot, I decided that was a perfectly reasonable personality to cultivate as I grew up. I even met the old guy once at a book signing and we discussed the matter. He never did release the third one in the series he'd promised Nineteen Year Old Me, either. I remain bummed about that. Still, heroic fiction can be as bad for your mental development as drugs, kids. Believe me, I learned the hard way.

She looked over my shoulder, out over the kaleidoscopic wonderland. "It is pretty." She nuzzled my neck for a moment, feeling me relax. *Hey, cool, about to get laid...* Then she pinched me by the earlobe. Hard. She was not fucking around. Then she twisted it and pulled, yanking me to my feet. "Now let's get your ass back to bed where it belongs at this fucked up hour of the night."

***

We slept in pretty well that morning, well, we were in bed for a while. Then it was off to the pool. Later, we were walking out of the lunch buffet on 103 when my phone buzzed. It was a Facebook Messenger text from Jimmy. "96 HRS". Not secure, but the *Ecstasy* did have that quite expensive satellite Internet and onboard wi-fi. It was probably easier to get a fast message out that way than pulling out the satellite phone. Yep, time to start wrapping up Hong Kong and get along to Singapore. Angel whipped out her phone and started going to work as our travel planner. When we got back to our room, I called the front desk and let them know we would be checking out the day after tomorrow. After that, it was off to the pool again.

As we walked upstairs, the next hotel was a point of contention. I wanted to be a traditionalist and stay at the old Raffles. Named for the first British colonial governor like half the things in Singapore, it was a landmark of British imperial-era opulence. Cash and Angel were insisting on the Fullerton, which was waterfront in the old colonial-era post office headquarters building and more highly rated. That was an acceptable compromise on being historically interesting. Angel booked a loft suite for us and to serve as a local headquarters so much as we needed one. Singapore's government being what it was, we'd have to assume it was bugged though.

Then where to put the ship and crew? Under one of the company accounts, we booked five nice rooms over at the Raffles Marina for the guys on the *Ecstasy* to rotate in for some shore leave. The place was basically its own country club anyway. Now Singapore was far more straight-laced than Thailand would be after their long haul halfway around the world, no blow-job bars or blatant public nudity, but they could deal with it a little bit longer. This was still a better deal than they would ever get while still in the Navy.

The next matter was getting ourselves there. First, we had WAY too much stuff. We'd picked up more luggage to repack all our new goodies. I didn't want us trying to get four or five suitcases each back across the Pacific when we finished in Singapore, but I didn't want to ship back anything we'd need there either. I knew I was going to end up overpacking for Singapore. I managed to stay at two very full suitcases and the girls three each. Angel and Cash told me that would be normal for upper-class Asian ladies on a long business trip. The rest I got into three decent size boxes and sent those back to the States on DHL through the hotel concierge. I tried not to puke at the price.

I stood in the middle of piles of boxes and wrapped clothes. I just looked at the ceiling and asked "Why, God? You there? Why the fuck did we do all this?"

God didn't answer. Cash did. "Because we need to look like the sort of people who have a billion dollars to bank. Book covers do matter. That's why they're the judgment material. If we don't want to get laughed the fuck out of the offices, regardless of how many pallets of money we have waiting offshore, we need to look a certain way, dress a certain way, and, as much as the idea terrifies me, I will have to do way more of the talking than I want to. You simply don't have the technical vocabulary to deal with it."

I couldn't argue with that. I wasn't the one with a *summa cum laude* MBA from Harvard.

In an attempt to comparison test the long-range Pacific Rim first class services, Angel had us on an early evening flight on Singapore Airlines from Hong Kong to Singapore. After a VIP check in and snacks and drinks in the lounge, it was an easy flight on a Boeing 777. The whole thing took a skitch under four hours, so it really didn't stress test the convertible sleeper chairs. The food was great; I had the grilled veal, Angel had the black pepper beef with fried rice, while Cash went for lobster thermidor. We all traded a few bites as we flew along. We were on the ground an hour after dinner and caught a car service to the hotel. Whoever Angel used had sent an actual Rolls Royce to pick us up. Damn. Color me impressed. I'd never been in one before and tried not to gawk.

The city was lit up like a theme park, even more than Kowloon had been. It wasn't quite a *Blade Runner* level of cyberpunk, for that you gotta go to certain neighborhoods in Tokyo or Manila, but definitely not like much back home in the States except parts of Las Vegas. That thought had me sort of humming Vangelis' theme from the film's end credits, which then shifted to me whistling something appropriately Edwardian England as we pulled up to the front of the Fullerton.

Later, when I thought of it, I looked it up and realized I had been twenty years off. Holst's *First Suite for Military Band* didn't debut officially until twenty years after Edward VII's coronation and nine years after the old boy had died. Oh, well, George V would overlook my error on account of his also being dead. I was pretty close to when this formidable pile of rock was built though.

Again, it really was possible to get used to living like this. The bell staff whisked us away to our suite and probably would have unpacked for us had we not made apologies and herded them out with a nice tip. We still had a whole lot of cash in there I didn't want them seeing. And it wasn't like we bothered with pajamas as we fell into bed. Angel was out like a light in thirty seconds. Cash, being anxious about the upcoming dealing, well, she took some 'comforting' before she dozed off as the middle layer of the sandwich. That left me contemplating the ceiling again as I thought about things. The *Ecstasy* was due sometime in the afternoon, the day after tomorrow. Get it in, docked and the guys rested. Figure out the maintenance needs and then we worry about unloading. After it was unloaded and we didn't need to worry about the boatyard guys seeing anything they shouldn't, then repairs could start. Getting the money put away was mostly Cash's project at this point.

What to do with the damn boat was my next big concern. I was just tempted to sell it locally because really, who the hell wants a yacht when the company is 300 miles or more above the high tide line? There was no damn way we could ever bring it up the Mississippi and then the Ohio Rivers without it attracting more attention than we ever wanted. I wasn't even sure if it would make it up the Cumberland. Leaving it in Florida, or maybe Mobile Bay, were options, I guess. But getting her home across the Pacific...that I was iffy on. I figured I would discuss it when they got in. I wanted Jimmy's input since he had just spent a month aboard in command.

And about then was when I dropped off.

***

The week of adapting our body clocks in Hong Kong helped. We were up early and caught a relatively English style breakfast downstairs before helling off to the Botanical Garden then the Toy Museum to play tourist and do some subtle reconnaissance of the town. We wouldn't have the time after the boat came in; at that point it would be serious work time for a while.

I took some time to think about it while eating lunch at the visually spectacular McDonald's at the Ridout Tea Garden. At first I was distracted by the fact their version of McDonald's is way better than ours. Once I got past that part, I slowly noticed that the entire city had more surveillance cameras than a casino floor in Las Vegas and that there was a lot of blatantly obvious wealth. Probably as many Ferraris as Kuwait City. A couple privately owned Rolls-Royces, at least one Bugatti, numerous high end retail stores and so on. People were definitely doing well here, but the recently-built-theme-park feeling of the whole city I'd noticed on the way in the night before was also holding true. Maybe the outskirts of town would feel differently if I had the chance to wander, but that just wasn't my focus.

The cameras weren't the only thing staring at us. Every now and then we'd pass an attractive female, mostly

Chinese-ish as was most of the population, staring daggers at Angel and Cash. I thought it odd and mentioned it. Angel snickered. "Since you're pretty obviously not from here, my guess is they're local hookers who think the competition stole a prospective client. The Internet says there's a lot of that here."

***

Jimmy called the next afternoon when they were in the marina and he had cell phone signal. Since we were in the water park having fun, we made arrangements to meet at the hotel's Lighthouse Bar in time for their Happy Hour. It was just Angel and I. Cash had stayed back in the room, nose-deep in her laptop going over her final financial planning for gold buying and bank deposits over the next week. I had to walk a line between letting her work without interruption and not making her feel abandoned which would worsen the stress.

Angel and I were only one drink in when Jimmy walked in. He had cleaned up well for the occasion and was looking way more tan than usual; I suppose a month at sea does that to you. He also had the rolling gait of someone who hadn't been off a moving deck in a while, only slightly staggering across the polished marble floor. Still, he blended in better than I did. Handshakes turned to bro-hugs. "Crew got ashore okay?"

"Yeah, they all came ashore as far as the marina rooms, leaving two back for anchor watch. Three of us will always be back there too, either aboard or close by the dock. One ashore to wander a bit. Me first. Dave next, then Tommy. Ben said he would take the last turn so long as he got to go hit the Games Workshop store." Good old Ben. He was predictable in his own way. Most of us were by now. Jimmy grabbed a double of Glenfiddich; the 18 year, since we *were* celebrating. I grabbed another Gun Club Punch, me having taught the bartender how to make one, and we sat back down and clinked glasses.

I figured if there was a problem, he'd say something, but I had to ask. "Any customs issues?"

He shook his head. "None, which shocked the shit out of me, knowing how strict these guys are by reputation. You get an agent first by phone or email. We used the Raffles Marina agent since that was what you told us to use."

"Looked like the best boat yard and shore facilities for the guys."

Jimmy nodded in agreement. "Yeah, it's a pretty classy place. The kids are all impressed. Anyway, we met the little gray Customs boat out in Western Anchorage. They have you send over all your document copies in a waterproof bag they grab with a boat hook, then they have everyone basically man the railing so they can match faces to passport photos. The guy on the boat stamps everything, you get your bag back and then you are cleared into whichever marina your agent got you, again, Raffles. Then if you actually dock during business hours, the skipper goes to their central office and finishes the papers, otherwise it waits 'til they reopen on Monday."

"Huh, that's pretty cool." I had looked up the process, of course, but hearing it described was kinda fun. I wish I had the freedom to vanish out to sea for a month and sail half the globe or something liberating. I didn't want to be a slave to the game until the day I died the way Big John and Mikey had been.

Jimmy continued. "We did declare cash in excess of $20,000 Singaporean aboard, told him our employer was going shopping, but the guy said that was great and since the law did not require him to ask how much in excess, he wasn't going to."

"What about the spare parts?" You may recall they had kept two good ARs and two NODs aboard for running the Red Sea, Horn of Africa and Malacca Strait. Piracy was still a thing, as I found out from Jimmy much later. The goggles were also good for stargazing or finding blacked-out rustbucket freighters with inattentive bridge crews that wanted to run you over in busy shipping lanes after dark. Radar was imperfect sometimes. The *Ecstasy* had done some of the world's busiest waters on the way over, Malacca being perhaps the worst. Getting out of here wasn't going to be a picnic either. It took situational awareness in traffic not to get run over by something way bigger than you; ask the ten sailors who died on the USS *John McCain* a few years ago just southeast of here. As our hired captain had formerly commanded one of the sister ships, that had to have weighed on his mind when planning all this.

"Stored deep. They could have stored them for us, again, useless if we need them. Goggles count as safety and navigation gcar."

"Gotta watch that one. Singapore's national motto should be 'fuck up and find out'."

He chuckled. "Yeah and I wasn't going to trust the Navy paperwork there either."

"How's Ben holding up?"

"Got some miniatures painted, even with the occasional pitching and rolling and also set a new situp record for himself. That crazy fucker is as happy as he ever gets." Jimmy thought Ben was nuts. To a certain extent, he was right, but like me, he was also too old and set in his ways to change much. Shit, I'd known Ben longer than Jimmy and that was saying something.

After more sea stories, we strolled across the atrium from the bar to the restaurant and looked at the dinner menu. It was a very avant-garde Italian menu. Long on art, short on mozzarella and tomato sauce. He stared hard, his lip curling in a native New Yorker's sneer. "Dude, I've spent more time in Little Italy than most people. You know I'm half Italian. This," he waved a hand at the board, "this is not what I call Italian food."

I'd thought much the same. "Thought it looked a little high end myself."

"We'll find a good traditional red sauce joint when we get home. Stick to the appetizers. It's hard to fuck up calamari."

"I had their antipasti platter yesterday. That was good. They fly in good prosciutto from somewhere. Snack here? Or we can hit the Japanese buffet downstairs for actual dinner. I haven't eaten there yet but it looks good."

Jimmy visibly thought about it and his New York prejudices won. "Let's go with that then. Asian food in Asia." Angel was into her third Singapore Sling and eminently agreeable either way. I wondered if the buffet downstairs had a 'My girlfriend isn't hungry' menu option.

Spoiler alert; they didn't. But the waiter politely ignored her smiling, giggling, and snitching off my plate while nursing her Coke. I made the call that three Slings had been enough for her. The place was only a third full and only *maybe* bugged, so it was safe to talk a little more so long as we were careful. I asked Jimmy the question that had been on my mind. "So after we get her unloaded, is it worth keeping her or should we sell the damn thing and fly home?"

Angel giggled. "Get me unloaded or the boat?" She then went back to stealing a few more pan-seared scallops and a couple steamed dumplings off my plate. I'll say this for the bar, the drinks here cost as much as some American entrees, particularly with the exchange rate we were on the downhill side of, but they did not stint on the liquor and it was all top shelf brands.

Jimmy looked horrified at the thought of selling his first command. "She needs a little routine engine maintenance, even after the oil changes and tune-ups at that stop, but hell, we didn't so much as burn out a light bulb on the way here. Boredom and a little weather aside, it was a really easy run. We can top off provisions, do all our routine maintenance, rotate for shore leave and be good to go in a week if we push it, two if we want to be bored of the town and want to get somewhere else with better night life like Bangkok or Pattaya Beach in Thailand, or maybe Subic Bay over in the Philippines."

"You are fucking serious."

He just stared at me. "Of course I'm serious."

"First, scratch Bangkok off your list. The city itself is thirty klicks up a polluted-ass sewer of a river from the actual Gulf of Thailand and there ain't no way in hell she is gonna fit up there. Maybe the Zodiac, but not her. And you really want to take my most of thirty million dollar boat to Pattaya to get stolen?"

He waved it off. "Well, I hadn't checked that chart yet. But anyway, I have estimates from two commercial companies to ship her back as deck cargo from here. We can do that. It ain't cheap. But selling? Hell no. She's a good cruiser. Worth keeping, dead serious. A maritime option is a good thing long term, I think this proved it and we would have to look hard to find something this good on the market if we needed one again. Your girl got lucky."

"Yeah, my inner cheapskate rebels at the prices involved, but then I ask myself if I were doing this with Uncle's money instead of our money, would I want to preserve the asset and the answer is yes. So at that point I just tell myself to shut up about it and let Accounting write the checks."

He laughed and toasted me with his glass. "See, you are improving at this command shit already. Well done. But, also an option, depending what we get into here in terms of buying stuff, it's less than a week to the Philippines, then a week up to Japan and a fairly easy run this time of year across the north Pacific to the Aleutians then back down the coast. Then it's the Panama Canal and up the Caribbean and the Gulf to home."

That was kinda ambitious. "You really feel up to taking her around the world?"

Jimmy nodded. "I'll talk to the guys. I'm good for the job. Pretty sure the skipper is. He's divorced and trying to stay offshore as long as he can, since he's working under the table for cash his ex won't know about. I won't need Dave or Ben, so they can fly out. Tommy, yeah, I could use. He was an honest sailor once and he's having fun. The other blackshoe Navy types? Some of those kids will be down for whatever; they're just in it for the money and the certificates."

"Certificates? You mean..." Despite my personal background being Army infantry, mostly air assault and airborne type, I had read more than enough naval history books to know where this silly shit was heading.

He grinned. "We are only ninety miles north of the Equator here. We had hooked south yesterday and did a short Shellback ceremony this morning before we made the final turn north. We had a few ex-Atlantic Fleet kids who'd never been south of Cuba, then of course I had to fuck with the two Army guys while I could. Going back, we can knock out the Order of the Golden Dragon at the Date Line, or qualify for the Golden Shellback upgrade if we cross the Date Line at the Equator. Then we make the Order of the Ditch for doing the Panama Canal and if we get all the way back to Mobile Bay, we join the Order of Magellan. That one is a bitch. Doing it right is actually going to be a rare feat."

I took a sip of my overpriced Coke (seriously, they gave free refills but it was still American movie theater prices for a much smaller glass) and chewed on a very nicely done black pepper shrimp. They were going to joyride a yacht around the Pacific hitting navigational checkpoints to earn the right to hang pieces of paper on the wall. And I thought some of my *Star Wars* costumer friends were weird. "Whatever amuses you guys, man. Far be it for me to fuck with the customs of the Fleet on that alleged auxiliary vessel. But Holly is gonna come after me with an ax if I keep you gone another month."

"For what this job paid, she'll calm down a little."

"Yeah, well, you earned it. This could not have been done without you." Really, I had been calculating splits and bonuses for full time employees who had made the full trip, leadership kickers and so on. Jimmy and Dave were going to bank enough to buy new cars and to put their kids through college. Tommy not far behind, Ben not far behind him. Bonuses for the intel staff and so on.

Then Angel and I stumbled back to the room to go make sure Cash wasn't too high-strung.

***

I had kicked all the guys who made the trip a decent bit of walking around money so they could enjoy their leave even with Singapore prices. Ben being Ben, I think he spent at least five grand of it on miniatures and paint to get the rest of the way around the world even after he was given the option of flying back instead. Dave was shopping for art and antiques that would keep his wife happy back home, while Tommy seemed content to either hit restaurants or sleep. He took us up to a pork and noodle shop that was in the record books as the most inexpensive Michelin-starred restaurant in the world. But we also started getting the real work done.

We were breaking up the transactions into bite sized pieces, the same way you proverbially eat an elephant. Our first stop was the smallest, though it had been first on the list of places recommended by Jack's cousins in Vancouver. We planned on dropping maybe fifty million depending on what the deal was; sort of a practice run for us. But by the look of the place, Silver Dragon Brokerage didn't have the fifty million. *Oh, well*, I figured. It would sort itself out. Two guys answered the door when we rang. The younger one did the talking. The older one reminded me of Toshiro Mifune's portrayal of Admiral Yamamoto. Iron posture, slightly grave demeanor. Didn't say a thing, just stayed out of the way. The much younger of the pair ushered us down a shabby hallway as a radio blared some strange music. Really, it looked like the back room in DC's Chinatown where I used to buy cheap switchblades in college.

Things got off to a poor start. Their variety of Mandarin did not quite track with Angel and Cash's variety of Mandarin. There was a lot of repeating themselves on both sides. Then the younger of the two, a chunky fellow in a *Neon Genesis Evangelion* shirt, began arguing with his older partner. Switching to English, he then asked Cash if she wanted to put ten percent into cryptocurrency. Cash is not a fan of crypto, believing it full of scams and bubble-to-bust cycles. Me, I am inclined to agree with her. Some people have lost piles of actual cash in Bitcoin and its rivals. She just stared at him distastefully until he gave up the idea.

Finally the old guy dismissed the younger one and also switched to English once he had closed the door behind him. He was quite fluent and faintly British accented. "I see you are judging the food by the condition of the kitchen."

"Perhaps the book by its cover," I interjected.

He nodded in my direction. "I suppose none of us here is truly what we appear to be. You are not merely the guard and briefcase carrier for two Asian girls who are adorably close friends and probably share a bed, just as we are not merely a down-market goods and metals exchange. I believe the term from the *Horatio Hornblower* novels of my youth is that we are all flying false colors at the moment. The names don't really matter, but things will go much more simply if we lay some of our cards down."

I snorted a bit. "If I didn't know better, I'd say you had been watching us, or at least had a friend who was." Me, I was watching his eyes. If this guy didn't have some idea who we were when we walked in, I'd get my beret out of the closet back home and eat it. He'd probably been warned by Vancouver, either for good or ill. No doubt Mad Jack had to share some information with his cousins as the price for a couple contacts and information moves both ways.

He chuckled. "Singapore is a small place. Past a point, everyone knows each other."

"Pull the other one, it's got bells on it."

He laughed at that one. "I had forgotten how much I missed bullshitting with Americans."

I chuckled in turn. "Who said we were Americans?" He *really* laughed at that one but said nothing else. I looked over at Cash, she nodded at me. "One is my finance chief first and foremost, the other is my longtime companion and assistant."

He lifted an eyebrow. "Assistant?"

I smiled a bit. "With eyesight as poor as mine, finding your glasses in the morning can be a struggle, not to mention putting the spine back in place after a bad night's sleep on an airplane." He also smiled a bit in return as we mutually thawed out somewhat. I continued. "Fortune has smiled. We have a windfall we would like to put aside for a rainy day in bulk gold or silver. And while you are supposedly one of the smaller firms, yours was the first name on the list given to us by friendly acquaintances in Vancouver, so I am sure you appreciate the need for some secrecy."

He nodded. "May I inquire as to which friends in Vancouver?"

Angel smiled faintly and interjected. "You know as well as I the *enlightened, honored grandfather* would not like his name or that of his family bandied about, but I think it safe to say we would not take his gesture of goodwill lightly."

The old man nodded. "Your discretion is appreciated and so I shall return it in kind." That was good. Mad Jack had never actually given us the guy's name, just his title.

Cash picked back up. "We are grateful. My government treats certain financial movements and structures as illegitimate, regardless of the source or the intention, so we must find older friends with older methods with which to store some of it. Hence our situation. We seek to do good works with the money over a long term, but must follow an outlaw path to do so in the shorter term."

He turned his attention to me again for a moment. "You have a warrior's eye. I sense you are preparing for a long campaign."

I nodded. "Very long. Very unlikely to be finished in my lifetime."

Cash slid back to the forefront. "As my employer states, we have a large number of US dollars and we do need them out of dollars and into precious metals."

"Will you be storing them with us or taking them with you?"

"That depends how secure your storage arrangements are."

He smiled broadly for the first time. "Secure? Come downstairs. I don't normally give a tour, but for some reason I like you and your employer there may find this historically interesting."

Chapter 27

"Down, down, to Goblin-town you go, my lad, ho-ho, my lad..."
~ *A former British lieutenant, a guy by the name of Tolkien...*

It was a lot of stairs. Deep rock-hewn cellars with some old, old brick work. "We, meaning our family business, have had these cellars since the colonial days. Our Japanese guests stored some things in them during their brief ownership of the city and before their surrender in 1945. We have added to that."

I dropped a hint that showed I knew a thing or two myself. "There was one version of the story that the Japanese shipped much of their looted gold here rather than to the Philippines where all the Yamashita rumors placed it."

He smiled. "I wouldn't know anything about that, of course." His comedic timing was perfect. A six foot tall gold Buddha gazed serenely from an alcove as we passed it. "Well, we are donating that to a temple that is being rebuilt. Regardless, we may have some quality vintage product on which we can do business."

The bottom cellar resembled nothing so much as the common area of a jail. It was a big square room with a barrel-vaulted ceiling and perhaps a dozen alcove cells of maybe eight feet square coming off it. The illumination was bare LED light bulbs on extension cords. It would have been hellish in torchlight. In each cell were several pallets, usually two to four. Stacked on each were varying numbers of gold or silver bars. One "cell" caught my eye. The bars in it were big ones, substantially larger than the 12.5 kilo "London Good Delivery" bars that were the international standard these days. "Found some prewar twenty kilo bars, eh?"

Our host nodded. "Japanese-made during the occupation and left behind afterward. Been down here ever since. Coin bars, too. None of the twenty kilo bars ever assayed out at better than point nine, most closer to point eight-five. Too heavy to easily steal, bigger than our friends in the jewelry business care to deal with, and they can't be explained as a hard asset on the legitimate side of the business. We have just over two metric tons of them left. 119 bars, I believe. They haven't moved in years. The last ones sold thirty years ago. Someone wanted to make alleged vintage coins to sell to the credulous and since it was already coin alloy, they took two dozen. Everyone else buying these days wants at least three nines fineness or expects us to eat the refining costs."

Wheels started turning in my mind. If the *Ecstasy* could move twenty-five tons of paper halfway around the world, it could surely move…math, math, okay, just over two and a half US tons of metal. And there were some of the world's best gold refiners in Canada; some electrolytic process Debi had read about in the *Wall Street Journal* and found interesting enough to tell me about. She accumulated a lot of odd gold in her profession. Jewelry gifts from clients she didn't always actually like, the occasional foreign coin, and so on. I nudged Cash. She shrugged. "Since they assay out at point nine or a bit less, does that make the price on them a bit more negotiable?"

He shrugged. "Perhaps."

"Does your freight elevator work?"

He made a coughing noise that may have been a laugh. "Not in several months. We move things from one pile to another sideways as in a bank, not up and down very often, so we have sadly procrastinated."

"I would suggest getting it that way and I will pay for it as a gift to a new friend."

He looked at me strangely. "And what would my new friend like to move in that elevator?"

"One hundred bars or so of your coin gold up. I have a good home for it. And depending what other bargains we find in this city, we might need to bring things down."

"Deal, but you have to take all of them except one. I need the space freed up, but keeping one for a souvenir appeals to me, since all the Japanese military stamping is interesting. And secure storage is definitely negotiable depending on what else you find appealing."

"Deal." We shook on it.

Cash slid back in. "So twenty kilos per bar, individually weighed of course, call it 80 percent of spot gold at Singapore price to account for the coin gold and a slight bulk discount?"

He eyed her. "Genuine US cash or wire transfer?"

"Straight cash, delivered in person."

"The coins originally melted to make the bars were probably British or Dutch. Maybe a bit of French from the fall of Hanoi or Saigon. Point nine was a reliable number for content."

"And God knows what the Japanese or their slave labor threw in there at melt time. If you wanted to assay each bar individually, your organization would have done it fifty years ago and they wouldn't be gathering dust in your basement. Point eight five is a generous offer."

"Point eight eight is a fair compromise since I have to trust your paper dollars."

"Which are far more liquid than your dusty Japanese war surplus gold bars."

He looked over at me and laughed. "I like this one. Young lady, should you ever need another employer, a place would be made for you here."

She bowed gracefully. "For that I am grateful. But I am still rather careful with my current employer's money, so don't think I will cave to point eight seven."

"Who said point eight seven? I certainly didn't."

Cash was losing the azimuth. The point was to get rid of as many of the dollars for metal as fast as we could, not pinch every nickel til the buffalo screamed in pain. Point eight five versus point nine was hardly worth arguing over for long, considering we had over one thousand, one hundred million on the *Ecstasy* to make vanish. I was not going to quibble, not when these dudes could be long term useful. I was not above buying influence in a town where we didn't really know anybody but now had business interests.

Cash was smiling like she rarely smiled. "And I certainly didn't say point eight seven either, since anything past point eight six is high seas piracy."

I had to cut in, even though both of them were grinning and having a lot of fun. "She is as ruthless as she is beautiful and for that I will keep her, but I also hope to have need of your good offices in the future as well. For that I am willing to pay up front now for some goodwill later. Cash, darling, remember how much future business we have to do, so for that..." I banged away on my cell phone's calculator, "let's meet in the middle at point eight six five then round up to the nearest million in the interest of simplicity." Fortunately with gold's climb on account of the world's inflation problems, we were getting rid of some paper on this deal, by my math... "Rounding up, I call it a hundred and fourteen million." She just looked at me with the same look a teenage daughter would have, a *But, Daaaaaaad!* face. Angel hugged her and patted her on the butt reassuringly.

Our host smiled. "You are fortunate in your companions."

"That I am." I handed over two wrapped stacks of hundreds. These had come over with us from the eighth-floor vault and survived the Hong Kong Shopping Massacres. "Twenty thousand dollars to get your elevator mechanic going as soon as possible. I am certain none of us want to walk all those stairs twenty kilos at a time."

"No, we would not. Now would you have other investment needs?"

"Several. First we would be interested in further gold investment."

"Here I am somewhat hampered by lack of new inventory. Perhaps a thousand kilograms maximum of London Good Delivery bars are available from us and I know where to get another three thousand fairly easily. In exchange for your storage here, that also at a reasonable fee per year, we can assure a favorable price and guarantee your security. Past that, there's just not much there." But I did some cell phone math and looked at Cash. She nodded. A shade over two hundred twenty-five million. Not bad. He sighed. "Much of the bullion market here in Singapore has been absorbed by large commercial interests that broker sales and storage. However some of these are ones in which our organization or our allies hold legitimate financial positions, so then we can offer some recommendations."

"Quite fair. I know some of the Australia mining output comes north, but I didn't know how much of it entered a shadow economy."

He sighed again, wistfully, as we old men do. "A lot less than thirty years ago, I can tell you that much. And much goes on to China or Japan to launder and store others' wealth. The shadows here are not what they used to be."

"That's true most places."

He nodded. "And I must say, you played it well going from the airport to your hotel and playing tourist for a few days. Getting off a plane and going directly to business always seems to attract police attention. The integrated surveillance systems here have become quite chafing."

I knew somebody had to have been watching us. It was nice of him to admit it. "Yeah, I saw that article in *Wired* too. I preferred to learn from the CIA's mistakes."

"It is always wiser to learn from others' errors before making your own."

I nodded as well. "That is true, one reason we are being circumspect in our hotel room as well. Oh, well. On to Plan B. Building on that, I am sure you also have friends in one or more of the local banks, or a branch or more of the international ones?"

He grinned like a wolf. A Chinese wolf, but a wolf. "You could safely assume so, yes."

I dramatically sighed. "Sadly, the modern world does not move on gold alone. Some of the cash will need to be banked with a minimum of fuss in the offices of Credit Suisse, UBS, HSBC, Royal Bank of Scotland, or whoever. We have accounts in these, at least their other branches, we just require friends in the office to smooth things. Compliance officers, regulatory liaisons, internal auditors..."

"This can be done relatively easily, also for a modest consulting fee. Ten percent, fifteen at most. That is merely traditional. Really, now since we are friends, I will confess that you have my gratitude for buying the coin bars. We could be termed asset rich and cash poor in some respects. This clandestine infusion is welcome."

If he hit us even for a ten percent consulting fee on that remaining billion, he was going to be positively flush.

Cash smiled. "You need to diversify your assets."

He sighed again, then shrugged, a heavy air of resignation on his face. "We did. That's the problem. Everything from restaurants and dry cleaning shops to a water park, several shopping malls, and a couple very nice hotels. Not the one you are in, but the next time you are in town, we can arrange something very nice and quite highly rated if not quite so heavy on the harbor view and historic architecture. But as I am sure you have learned yourselves, going legitimate creates a whole host of problems and extra expenses. Mixing your off the books dirty money with your on the books legitimate income is never a good idea."

Cash bowed her head in assent. "This I have learned. But the game is fascinating."

"And playing worldwide, you have more flexibility in your rules. Living here? This is a town of strict and scrupulous legality until you go down a great many layers and all those layers have expenses. Some of our traditional methods of income are not worth the intense legal risk here any longer. Drugs? Not with Singapore's death penalty laws for such and utter willingness to be generous with such sentences. Women? Certainly. It is nearly legal here, but so common that there is no profit in it. Ladies make their own arrangements over the Internet with minimal need for houses, house mothers, or management. Male talent, the same, for those who go that way. Street loans? Minor gambling? Yes. But in major gambling, we cannot compete with Marina Bay Sands the way our cousins could not compete when the casino corporations came to Macau and turned it into the Las Vegas of the Pacific Rim. Money laundering? For the most part, the multinational corporations do it bigger and better. My generation and the ones before, we were tutored in the streets. Now we pay for private schools and top-tier MBAs and the grandchildren go legitimate since that is where the real work is done now." He sighed again. "It is hard being a pirate in a modern age."

I laughed a bit. "Do you know an American song called 'A Pirate Looks at Forty' by Jimmy Buffet? Sums up your dilemma and mine, friend."

He chuckled. "I know it well. Before I returned to the family trade, I spent ten years as a naval officer here, with a two year exchange tour aboard Naval Station Key West in Florida. That was why I laughed when you asked how I spotted you as American military the second you walked in my door. You're quite obvious even if we didn't know you were coming. That was way back in 1979 with Patrol Hydrofoil Squadron Two."

"Really? The *Pegasus* class? Those were the coolest little go-fast ships. Before my time, sadly. I wanted either one of those one of those, a *Des Moines*-class heavy cruiser, or an *Iowa*. The Navy got rid of everything I wanted to be on, so I went Army instead. Hell, if I had the money to work with then that I do now, I might have bought the damn *Des*

Moines and turned pirate. So sad to see a beautiful warship scrapped."

He nodded. "And I would have sent my resume if you had done so, or if you find something suitable in the future. I miss the peace of the ocean and am not as important to the family business now that there is a younger generation or two aboard. But I was on the *Aries,* before I went to the Squadron staff. She endures as a museum."

"Yes she does, up a river in Missouri, I think I took the tour ... three years ago?" It had been a rare weekend off for me at the time and not even a day's drive.

"So yes, yes, two years in Key West, so I know some Jimmy Buffet and have kept up my fondness. Even though 'Jimmy Buffet, he don't live in Key West anymore.'"

Damn. This was getting deep. "David Allan Coe. I am doubly impressed."

He thoughtfully nodded. "Many outlaws have not heard of Coe. I know of few who, once having heard of him, haven't liked his work. Do you find it strange I have?"

"Hardly the weirdest conversation I have ever had. So, how shall we do this?"

He patted me on the shoulder. "Slowly. Getting that elevator fixed over a weekend isn't going to be easy, but we have time. This is a beautiful city. Go enjoy it as the work is done. That also gives me time to consult the cousins and nephews in the banks. We will get the gold to the surface once the elevator is fixed. In truth we are almost a full block away from the office where we began. Then we can move the gold out in installments and your dollars in. Easily done. Almost enjoyable. And it has been too long since I have truly enjoyed my profession."

***

When we got back to our suite at the Fullerton, I stumbled up the stairs to the sleeping loft and merely flopped face first on the immaculately made bed. That had been a somewhat exhausting process with a lot of numbers. Not really my thing. Angel was shedding clothes and talking about the pool. Cash, well she was practically bouncing with manic energy. "Sir, I know I could have gotten him lower, I hadn't even popped the top button on my blouse yet."

"Dear, one percentage point was not much difference. Time is money, baby." I also shook my head and pointed at the walls. We still didn't know if the place was bugged and it wasn't like we could have brought one of Morgan's sniffers in through Customs.

We collapsed into bed and hugged, dropping our voices. She sighed. "Yes, sir. But this is the biggest thing I have ever done and I just want to be sure everyone is proud of me." She was still faintly quivering.

Angel and I both hugged her while I did my best to calm her down. "We are proud of you. You're doing great. We couldn't do this part without you. This is your time to shine and you are."

Cash actually shed a tear. Just one, but a tear. "I love you both so much." With that, we all got up and went out on the balcony where there was less chance of a casual microphone. The wind was coming in hard off the harbor and that would help a good bit. Cash continued. "I guess the question now is how much do we trust our new friends?"

I laughed. "Not a fucking bit, past a point."

Angel shook her head. "You can trust them a little. They know we got their contact information from Vancouver. They won't randomly rob us, not wanting to offend Vancouver, at least not until they talk to Vancouver." You know, despite her complete lack of military intelligence or law enforcement background, I really did instinctively trust Angel's insight into people and especially the cultural nuances of Chinese organized crime. If you asked me a year ago, I would not have predicted her expertise on the subject.

"And Vancouver will just tell them we are random friends of their redneck cousin they don't much care for, so game on."

It was Cash's turn to disagree. "They want repeat business more than a gunfight. They start something like that, then the Singapore cops make an example out of everyone. The cops here have a no-shit reputation to uphold. The Chinese mafia, whatever they call themselves here, wants future business. And we are holding the potential for some big future scores in front of them."

Ugh, my turn again. "Depending what else we find to bring back here, bank through these guys, and keep renting their loyalty."

She shook her head. "Word will spread if they start robbing potential customers and the money will go elsewhere so they lose their percentages. Ten or fifteen percent of a billion beats ten percent of jack shit."

That night, I slept. Long, deep, and dreamless. Still down in the dark, I felt hands stroking my hair, then a gentle kiss on my forehead. "Wake up, babe. Come on." I couldn't even twitch. I was somewhere between dusk and dawn, as it were. Slowly I came up and out of it. I realized Angel on one side of me, Cash on the other. They looked at me strangely, but almost amusedly. "You were down for eleven hours straight, sir. You didn't even roll over," Cash reported. I slowly tried moving. It didn't work all that well, like the sleep paralysis was taking time to wear off.

Except for my last prescription drugs phase, courtesy of the VA, I hadn't slept that long uninterrupted since Bush 43 was still President. "Seriously? Eleven hours?" My voice sounded weird in my ears.

Angel nodded. "You were out cold before I was and we've been up for hours. We went downstairs and even ate already." Eh, I'd live. The breakfasts done in-house were fancy and all, but I'd kill for a Waffle House in this neighborhood.

"I need a Coke or something," I croaked. Cash handed me an ice-cold can. God knows where she got it. Slowly they helped me sit up and guided me toward a hot shower. I was kinda unsteady on my feet. "I wonder what the fuck happened to me?"

Angel shrugged. "Maybe with this part of the job done, you finally relaxed for once."

I hate being insane.

Chapter 28

"Clean shirt, new shoes, I don't know where I am going to..."
~ "Sharp Dressed Man," ZZ Top

Our friend was right. Not much happened over the weekend. We played tourist, much as we had in Hong Kong. We were on our way back from a Sunday dinner with Dave when a member of the concierge staff approached us with an envelope addressed to 'American Friends' and our room number.

I sighed in defeat. They definitely had someone, or several someones in rotation, watching us. There wasn't a damned thing we could do about it. We were the strangers in a strange land. When we got back to the room, I opened it and read the note informing us that we had a 10:00 appointment on Tuesday at a particular address to meet our friends' 'friends.'

With Singapore's reputation as a surveillance state, I didn't even want to Google the address on my phone. I went over to the concierge desk and used one of the public touchscreen maps instead. I saw what I figured I'd see, and scrolled away to several other imaginary destinations.

Knowing the day would be meetings, and formal ones, we got booked for serious spa maintenance on Monday. Angel was usually capable of working on everyone, but of course she didn't have all her gear while we were traveling. And yes, I got booked in too because the girls insisted. First, the most expensive haircut of my life. My rather shaggy eyebrows were painfully fussed over by women with tweezers. My wide Irish nose was inspected pore by pore for blackheads, my neck was massaged and I got my first straight razor shave since Ranger Joe's at Benning two decades ago. I got exfoliated, polished, folded, spindled, and mutilated. To be quite frank, most of it fucking hurt.

When the appointed hour approached, I picked the Richmond dress gray suit, the one without the combat modifications since I was rolling out completely unarmed except for a Swiss Army knife. I then unwrapped a white oxford shirt, touching it up with an iron. Fortunately, that made me look at the cuffs. Unfortunately, I wasn't used to needing cufflinks and didn't have any handy. Fortunately we were staying in the sort of upscale neighborhood where that was fixed with a walk across the street to buy a pair. I went with the dark blue silk tie with the jagged gold stripes of the Royal Scots Dragoon Guards and the (to my mind) really far-out-there gold Apollo 17 watch with its dark blue dial and brown band. I then matched the shoes to the watchband. I knew that much. Then someone on the tailor's staff had thrown in half a dozen assorted 'pocket squares,' handkerchiefs that weren't really handkerchiefs but served as decoration, each one coordinated to but not matched to one of my ties. Matching is apparently a *faux pas*. But the guys in the tailor shop knew I knew precisely less than dick about all this. Everything was carefully bagged and tagged with handwritten notes so not even an idiot on the subject like me could fuck it up.

The girls were in nearly matching Dior black silk dresses with classy four-inch heels they made look easy and Italian sunglasses that cost more than the car I drove in high school. It was a long walk through the lobby, but we didn't stand out too terribly much. The girls got some admiring glances, but I seemed much less remarkable to our fellow guests in a suit and tie than I had earlier.

We'd set up a car service to arrive appropriately at the 'friend's' office in a respectably sized Mercedes. When we did arrive at the provided address, my map check had been correct. It was a side entrance for one of the major multinational banks. I won't say which out of deference to our contacts. We were met on the sidewalk by two rather cheerful fellows in very nice suits and extremely expensive looking silk ties. Neither one was much over thirty by the look of them. Since they were Chinese, they could be pushing fifty for all I could tell. Yeah, it's a stereotype but there's truth there.

The one on the left smiled and stuck his hand out. "You must be the friend who needs consulting." His oh-so-British accent screamed an Oxbridge education.

I shrugged as we shook. "Is it that obvious?"

"We were told we needed to look for a tall American with glasses, followed closely by two Asian beauties who were not to be underestimated."

"And this message came from...?"

He chuckled. "'A new friend who has a large basement' would sum him up nicely."

I nodded deeply. "Forgive my caution. I am a simple traveler far from home."

The other one snorted a short laugh. His accent was pure California surfer. "Says you, man. You have shaken things up for the family, which is a good thing for us. Please, come on in and let us see what we can do to assist your financial needs in our fair city." He was hitting the formal notes, but his grin and his tone were clearly letting me know it was just part of the ritual.

We went in through a fire door that had been propped open. They closed it behind us and down what looked like a maintenance corridor. It could have been a junior high school in the States. Simple painted walls, linoleum tile floor, buzzing fluorescent lights. We were definitely not getting the red carpet VIP treatment. We went up two flights in an echoing concrete stairwell, through one of three doors and found it was a side entrance into a large sunlit office paneled in dark hardwood with about a two inch thick emerald green carpet.

Oxbridge was eying my wrist. "Nice watch", he idly commented as he ushered us in. At that, Cash shot me a sideways look with a wink and the barest hint of a smirk. I conceded she was probably right. The furniture had that old school British Empire feel that matched the walls, all age-blackened wood. We were gestured toward leather wingback chairs around a very nice walnut coffee table and they sat down facing us.

Oxbridge began. "Our apologies for sneaking you in the back door, but there are no functioning cameras on that hallway. The rules are somewhat different for customers who require the utmost in discretion and for whom the normal rules cannot apply under any circumstances. This is why we are very carefully not introducing ourselves either. I am merely a junior account executive and my cousin here is... what the hell are you calling yourself these days?"

"Officially I work in Small Business Loans. As you can tell, our titles don't match our actual duties. Particularly where the interests of the family's business align with those of our legitimate employer. We have a certain amount of off the books power to make arrangements to the benefit of both and in this case to help get your deposit made with a minimum of fuss."

"Excellent. Seeking a lack of fuss is what brought us here."

Oxbridge nodded. "And with luck, that is to the profit of us all. Coffee, tea, sodas, anything stronger? And then we can then get started?"

The girls took tea, Chinese green, and I asked for an ice water as well.

Somehow, within two minutes flat, a female assistant of some variety who was almost as dolled up as Angel and Cash brought in the tea tray and then excused herself near-silently. Oxbridge poured for us all.

As we all sipped, the California surfer of the pair smiled. "So, we need to make a large cash deposit without setting off any alarm bells."

"That sums up the situation nicely, yes." This really was good tea, not that I was a connoisseur of the stuff by any standard. Angel and Cash, who were, were definitely impressed.

His buddy smiled. "We are somewhat fortunate. As our uncle hinted, a small number of the bank branches here in Singapore fly international colors but are still under strict local control. In this case, the control is ours. As long as we preserve the broad appearance of legalities under local and international law, we may continue to conduct our own traditional business arrangements under that degree of cover."

"So long as no one does anything stupid or gets too greedy," I said.

"Exactly so."

"That makes sense. Pigs feed, but hogs get slaughtered."

They both laughed. Oxbridge nodded. "I had not heard that one before. I like it. I may have to steal it from you."

"Ha. Go right ahead, I am certain I stole it somewhere myself. So the Oxford or Cambridge accent is obvious, but you... who tries to sound like a California surfer... I am going to guess Stanford for your MBA."

Oxbridge laughed. "Oh, you *are* good. Oxford for both undergraduate and graduate school, though different colleges respectively, while my cousin here was Stanford for both undergrad and MBA."

Surfer Dude echoed the laugh. "I thought about USC for my first few years, but I'm not the Hollywood type. I went to Stanford when it was still weird. The pod people didn't take over the campus until later. And NorCal has better weather after growing up in a Malay jungle town."

Cash smiled demurely. "Nice to be among academic peers in such matters."

Oxbridge looked at her inquiringly.

She let her accent come back. "Harvard."

Surfer Dude groaned. "Great and here we were hoping your crew was all looks and less brains." Cash just stared back at him. He withered under the glare. "Actually we knew better. Uncle already warned us he wants to hire you if you ever become professionally available. He said you'd be fierce competition."

They then turned their gaze to Angel. She chuckled. "Leave me out of this, gentlemen. I was a theater arts major. I'm the one who's just here to look cute." Everyone had a polite laugh at that.

I looked back over at Surfer Dude. "Long way from California, huh?"

He grinned. "Yeah and I actually learned how to surf pretty well, too. I miss it, but you know how it is when you start losing your hobbies to things like work and sleep. I try to fly down to Australia for a week a year, rent a board and keep my hand in, but then the lockdowns..."

I nodded sympathetically. "I definitely know the feeling. It kinda sucks to have resources to finally play, but never have the time. So, laying cards on the table, what are you offering to charge us for this consultation?"

"For ten percent of the gross deposit, which we will slice off and deal with ourselves, we offer both a trouble free deposit at this bank and immediate pass-through into several of the other large multinationals where we also have family members emplaced. We can also break it into phases to further disguise the total amount. All transactions are verifiable electronically and in person at the branch before and I repeat before, we collect our cut."

"Account sequestration or physical escrow of your cut?"

"Physical is more certain for both of us, and of course we have an excellent storage location as you have seen. Our uncle spoke highly of your courtesy and generosity. Few metal buyers wish to round upward. He found that unusual."

I shrugged. "Few buyers are looking forward toward repeat business if all goes well."

"He did mention that. Uncle insisted to the other elders that he had said ten, or fifteen at most, and his word counts. Besides, you were referred to our distant relations in

Vancouver with a note that you were a good friend of the extended family. Still, there was talk of gently squeezing you a bit for at least twenty. That's much closer to our usual going rate. Some customers are charged a good bit more than that based on risk or, frankly, how much we like or dislike them. It's complicated, really. We charged some Russians seventy percent once because it was an extremely rushed job on some very dirty money and they still thanked us for it."

"That would have been unfortunate." I tried to keep the relief off my face, but shit, I would have lived with twenty and not felt bad. Price of doing business. Eighty percent of a billion is still a metric fuck-ton more than I ever thought I was going to make the day I signed off active duty, even if it was technically the company's money and not mine.

He nodded. "Precisely. Still, with large amounts you are restricted in options these days. You just can't fly a cargo plane of cash into Switzerland. It's not the 1970s anymore. Not if you're American, at least. Lichtenstein, maybe, if they like you and then a few places in the Caribbean, but there are limits to what they will handle secretly. Or even *can* handle secretly. Rumors abound that your NSA and your allies are into their computers."

"Are there restrictions on size here?"

"We prefer to think of them as challenges to be overcome. So we may gauge the size of the task, how much of a windfall do you wish to secure?"

I grinned over at Cash. "Dear?"

Cash grinned like a predator, recrossing her legs and teasing up her hemline a bit. That caught their eye as much as the enhanced cleavage. She lingered a moment, enjoying her distraction before the strike. Cash loved to flaunt her looks at moments like this. It was simply her nature. Now these guys were professionals to whom it wouldn't make that much difference financially, but we could all tell they admired the show as much as anyone. "We are pulling a bit back for local expenses and maintenance. We then have a pending delivery of one hundred fourteen million dollars to your uncle for the initial bullion purchase. There is follow-on buy of over two hundred million, also through him. The banknote deposit will be approximately eight hundred million dollars in US one hundred dollar bills. Used, non-sequential."

Even Oxbridge, the quieter of the two, let his dispassionate mask slip a bit. "That is... a little more than we figured." He looked down, contemplating his tea. The jolly surfer slouched forward with his head in his hands. I had seen enough reruns of *Firefly* to recognize some cursing in Chinese when I heard it. I figured that might leave us maybe seventy million aboard. We could deal with that. If Jimmy was going to loop the northern Pacific, we still owed Vancouver a taste anyway. No sense offending them after they'd been helpful.

Cash enjoyed their discomfort. I could see the same subtle sadism she and Angel reveled in when... never mind, maybe I will tell that story another time. "We are spending with your family on precious metals, through your uncle or at least with his counsel, but that eight hundred still makes a considerable sum for you in consulting fees." We gave them a moment to catch up.

Oxbridge looked up from his tea, drained the cup, and then refilled it. "And future business may be of similar scale?"

I shrugged, drained mine and refilled as well. "It is like hunting or fishing, sometimes you get what Fate chooses to give. But we have hopes. There are numerous windfalls to be had out there in the wide world."

Surfer Dude shrugged. "Well, we hope to earn your future business with how well we handle this for you. And to be frank, make nice money for ourselves at the same time. So the next time you need to hide another windfall, please remember that we played really nice and treated you like family at ten percent rather than screwing you for thirty or more the way we do most everyone else. You got very lucky that Uncle likes you. Is the material already in Singapore?"

"Yes, but you will forgive me if I am slightly circumspect as to where."

He laughed a bit. "I would be more worried if you weren't, man. But I doubt it's at the airport. Too many eyes. Probably came in by water. Is your ship docked somewhere where a truck can reach it?"

"You may assume so, yes. The cargo is already on pallets. Heavy pallets. Most of the first one of those will be for your uncle, with two more heading that way afterward for a follow-on purchase."

Oxbridge drained another cup and sighed. "We will find you a trusted truck, driver and security to assist you in making that delivery yourself. Uncle said he very much enjoyed the company. He is very traditional in ways, but, well, he doesn't get out much anymore since he lost his wife to cancer. He just reads naval history all day or yells at our slacker cousin when he isn't in that basement of his moving things around."

Cash pursed her lips a bit in a light scowl. "Is your cousin the crypto-currency enthusiast with a fondness for anime t-shirts?"

Surfer laughed. "Ah, yeah, you did meet him briefly, didn't you?"

She rolled her eyes. "I did. I still think crypto is for gamblers and college kids, but I slightly admire his enthusiasm."

Surfer snorted. "Not to sound like more of a male pig than I admit I am, he was probably admiring other things in your case."

Cash and Angel both grinned. "Let the boy dream," Angel snarked.

Oxbridge nodded. "Still, you will be quite well taken care of. For our high-confidence accounts, nothing goes into a computer that hasn't been carefully crafted. We could go with completely paper records the way the Swiss still do for some customers, but you would have a hard time accessing funds without returning here to do it. That data wouldn't share with the other branches, so Zurich, New York, or London would never have heard of this."

"And no matter how much we like doing business with you guys so far, or how good the food is here, that is a mighty long airplane ride even if we need to so much as cash a check."

Surfer Dude chimed in. "Agreed. Still, we have a few family members in Los Angeles who can arrange access to some of those funds, slowly, as a reciprocal matter where it will not flag as a foreign transaction. Your government is simply another obstacle with which to cope." He sighed. "But, that's the game and we all play it."

***

We were not the first people to show up with a boatload of something heavy that needed to be moved to a bank. Or be moved to a nondescript warehouse door in a northern suburb that had a freight elevator behind it. As we moved just north of three hundred million in and down, we took ownership of a large pile of London Good Delivery gold bars that would be stored for us in that basement. We also hauled out 118 twenty-kilo bars of the Japanese war surplus coin gold which was carefully distributed as ballast aboard the *Ecstasy*. Other deliveries took us through the back doors of several other banks. We were in and out of that bank and four others as their guests several times in the few days that followed. We slowly whittled away the pallets of cash over a week and a half of work, carefully checking and rechecking that we weren't being robbed of what we'd rightfully stolen. But sometimes when enough money is being made, everyone stays honest enough to say there really is honor among thieves.

Once all the arrangements were made and it was merely a job for unmarked trucks and forklifts, Cash quickly became bored and was Googling. "Do we want to stop at the Hong Kong Coin Show on the way back, sir?" Angel was way less fidgety. She was hanging out on the veranda taking pictures of things to paint later back home once the winter weather hit and she needed her inside hobbies.

Me, I was sorting some of the luggage filled with the girls' purchases from Hong Kong and the half a business wardrobe they'd bought for me. I was looking at making a second shipment back to the States. Hell, I might lock up some of it on the *Ecstasy* since it was going that way anyway. Didn't much matter how fast some of it got there and it saved on postage.

"That depends, do we want to go back to Hong Kong or do we want to get home? The pets are probably missing us. We've been gone for three weeks."

Angel scoffed. "Jeanie says Odin is sleeping in her bed in the guest room, the cats are fine, and Kara's taking care of Rockefeller. Face it, sir, you're just sick of this shit and want to go home."

She wasn't half wrong. I simply wasn't meant to live at this level on a constant basis. But until the *Ecstasy* was unloaded, everything had cleared the bank, and Jimmy's pirate gang had departed the harbor, I sure as hell wasn't leaving.

Cash was unthrilled. "Ugggghhh. Rock has always been cheating with her. I find him upstairs in the intel hall playing with one of their cats or bumming tuna fish and cat treats at least twice a week. He's getting fat."

"Cash, you get credit for starting the company cat fad. We'll never have mice. Now back to the main point. We already did Hong Kong on this trip. Shit, why don't we do Tokyo?"

"Their big coin show isn't until November, sir. But we could always come back over."

I shrugged. "We bring some coins from here and a nice suitcase of money, declare it as en route to the coin show and we might be able to beat Customs with it. Hell, we could coin shop Tokyo anyway, but their declared cash limit is less than the States and I don't know if there is a decent percentage in it."

Cash shook her head. "The Japanese are much stickier about that than Singapore. They have limits. So we throw it in one of the big international banks here where we have friends now-"

Angel laughed. "Where we rented friends is more like it."

Cash nodded. "I concede the point. But again, we don't want to fuck around with the Customs cops in Japan. Rather than humping a load of cash in, how about we just put a few million in an account where we can then draw it out in Tokyo if we go?"

***

I had another working lunch and some casual afternoon drinks with Oxbridge and Surfer Dude, this time at a local version of an English gentlemans' club. I did know their names by now, but I'm deliberately not using them. It had really been old-school, so casual was a stretch. No female guests were allowed into that piece of the British colonial legacy, so the girls had the day to themselves. It had been a bit much. I was personally more accustomed to 'gentleman's club' as one of the American euphemisms for 'strip joint'. Also, I preferred having Cash around because she's a lot smarter than I am. I didn't want to have to keep track of that many numbers by myself, which made the whole thing way less enjoyable than it might have been. It was a relief to get out of there. I walked back into the suite and undid my tie, this one a regimentally striped 101st Airborne Association tie.

It was still worth it. There's a Chinese word I'd picked up on from a retired colonel buddy of mine and Angel had put some effort into explaining in more depth. *Guanxi;* "the system of social networks and influential relationships which facilitate business and other dealings." These guys wanted to be personal friends to a point, since they were making eighty million dollars off helping me hide my money in addition to whatever profit their family business made off the gold purchases. Being friends, or at least being friendly, and me being one hundred percent cognizant of the difference, fostered the trust that made the deal work. They wanted me calm to ensure I wouldn't back out and them lose out on their cut. They wanted me happy to ensure I brought them more money in the future. They probably wouldn't say no to me discreetly referring other friends to them for their laundering needs as well.

I then got distracted. *Brain paused on account of hot chick.* Out of deference to the conservative local mores, Cash had dragged one of the patio lounge chairs off our balcony back through the French doors into our room and as the sunlight was coming the right way, was tanning there. Naturally she was minus her suit. Her pricy Italian shades on against the equatorial sun, she was further shielding her eyes with an iPad, on which she was scrolling through... looked like *The Wall Street Journal.*

I snorted a bit. "Why can't you just read novels or play video games on vacation like normal people?"

She looked up at me with a bit of disdain. "What? I'm working! Sir, the markets are open and we're actually ahead over here. I haven't gotten to play from inside their time zone before, so I'm looking at some interesting options calls."

"Baby, you know how your eyes glaze over when I start talking about expensive custom gun parts off the Internet?"

She nodded. "Yes, sir?"

"Yeah, all these years and I still don't know how options calls work. That's what I hired you for. You know that shit so I don't have to be bothered."

I could practically hear her eyes rolling behind the sunglasses, but she dropped her voice to a breathy little Marilyn Monroe flirt. "Awww, sir, I thought you hired me because I was one of the best fucks you ever had in your life."

"Ha! I didn't know that when I hired you!"

Angel, equally underdressed, swept in with a glass in each hand, giving one to Cash. "He's got a point there, babe. You didn't rock his world until later."

"Mmmmm, or yours," she purred.

Angel slid her free hand into Cash's hair and looked her in the eye with mock ferocity. "Who rocked who, bitch?"

Cash grinned, "Okay, we rocked each other."

Angel shrugged. "Better. Good enough, at least. Slut." We then allowed ourselves to be further distracted by cocktails and other fun for a bit until it was time for lunch.

***

Long story short, after the last of the cash left the *Ecstasy,* she was fueled, provisioned, loaded with the gold and out to sea. Dave had flown out for home two days before, while Ben was staying aboard for "the around the world cruise". We then had a last lunch then got on a Singapore Airlines A380, a whale of an aircraft. We spent sixteen hours first-classing it in three little mini-suites to Los Angeles and regaining the day we'd lost on the westbound leg of the voyage. Invading Japan would have to wait for another time.

Chapter 29

"Tennessee, Tennessee, there ain't no place I'd rather be..."
  ~ The Grateful Dead

I didn't bother trying to get a charter from LAX back to Nashville. With a planned mid-afternoon arrival, we'd allowed ourselves several hours for customs, luggage and such. Angel short-circuited that by paying heavily to get us through the VIP terminal down by the South Cargo hangars. We got off the plane, went down the jetway's side staircase into a large BMW, then off to a tiny private arrival lounge with very polite Customs personnel. They were used to billionaires and other celebrities. We were just impatient people who could afford the additional expense.

I was quietly making irrational deals with God that our passports remained good to go. I was fairly certain that someday Cash's fake would pop in the system and it would be really, really bad for it to happen right then. Being that far from home turf and any possible support from the firm while being surrounded by government employees was just stressful. But we got through it. From there, we largely reversed the process to get onto our flight to Nashville. That flight was probably the last departure of the day heading there.

Jake had my truck waiting outside the terminal when we got in. He had pulled my spare set of keys out of my office. The suitcases went into the bed and we didn't even have to drive. Damned nice of him and I told him so.

"Jake, I think you're sucking up for your annual bonus, but I'm still grateful."

"Hey, I got the raid money but I didn't get in on the cruise money kicker, so I'm trying to make what I can. You know, Christmas and all."

I snorted a short laugh. "Yeah, you did fine this year, man. You know you'll be taken care of." And he would be. Shit, I tried to take care of everyone on the team.

We all went to my house and unloaded there. It wasn't worth taking a detour past the office to drop Cash off at her basement apartment. I threw Jake on the couch since with Jeanie still housesitting, I was out of guest rooms. We had dozed on the plane, but just being home, we all mostly slept the dreamless sleep of the mostly dead. And Odin was really happy to see us, no matter how much people food he'd wheedled out of Jeanie. The cats were slightly annoyed with us though.

The next morning I called Mad Jack to thank him and told him I was going to need a bit of help on something else in a few weeks. Really, I was thinking of his cousins in Vancouver. I figured I was going to need their help getting the two and a half-ish tons of gold bars off the *Ecstasy* once she got there. I'd also designated a bit of the leftover cash (well, about fifty million dollars) as a thank-you gift for their good offices in referring us to the Silver Dragon. Without that bit of good fortune, we would have been screwed. Mad Jack? Eh, I'd find him a couple more old 1911s and a few rare bottles of bourbon for the next four or five Christmases and he'd be happy enough. That turned into me having to go out there to securely talk business.

It was a few weeks before Jimmy called me from Vancouver. "Our friends met us at the dock. Low stress unload."

"Really? That was nice of them."

"Yeah, well, we didn't want to have to get that stuff up from below decks ourselves."

I laughed at that. "Don't blame you a bit."

"Well, I kept you one of the, uh, pieces, one with more and better markings than most."

"Jimmy, thank you for thinking of that. I was going to say something but I forgot."

He laughed. "They were in a real good mood. They even gave us a receipt."

I laughed even harder at that. "No fucking shit?"

"No shit. It's impressive looking. It's done in ceremonial Chinese calligraphy I can't read with a couple wax seals and a few dangly ribbons. I think they made it just to fuck with us. Will show it to you when we get back. They said it would be a while before they got it done and delivered."

I made a mental note to have Angel translate it if she could. With my luck the note said, "Fuck you, round eye, we're keeping all this shit. Eat dog dicks."

Chapter 30

"Look around, leaves are brown and the sky, is a hazy shade of winter."
~Simon and Garfunkel, though I think the Bangles did it better

A couple months had passed and we were into a wet and gloomy December. I was back around DC, visiting family. It wasn't going all that well. Not even the Christmas lights and hearing *Rudolph the Red-Nosed Reindeer* were really perking me up at the moment.

It wasn't work that was eating at me. Yeah, we'd been tracking a fairly high number of gang-related homicides. They all went back to the missing money, like a spreading infection. From the initial two dozen dead at that Mississippi farm that happened during and after the raid, on to a 'Mexicans vs blacks' gunfight in the New Orleans suburbs and so on and so on, there'd been dozens of shootings from Boston to St. Louis. Methodical network-mapping traced them all to the fallout of the missing billion upon the American drug trade. I didn't feel that bad about it. If it hadn't been us lighting that fuse, it would have been someone else. But since we didn't have the strength to pacify a small town, let alone a big one, we just dropped a lot of illegally gathered tips to every homicide detective and narcotics guy we could find. It was probably still a losing fight.

The good news was we'd been able to give healthy Christmas bonuses to the raid team in nice untraceable hundred dollar bills just from the pallet and half of 'bump plan' cash that never made it to the *Ecstasy*. Another fifty grand per man doubled their take-home on the job. It bought some good will in those social circles. More was used to handle internal bonuses for our own people. Enough was left that we were able to do some nice charity work that year.

My real problem was that I wasn't at work, so had a little more time than usual to think about my own problems.

First, I was lonely. I couldn't always travel with one or both of the girls. Angel liked my sister well enough. She'd normally be quite welcome at a family Christmas. But in a twist of fate, her parents lived nearby, like 'ten minutes away' sort of nearby. After we flew up commercial, instead of cuddling me through my mood swings and seasonal depression, she was off with them pretending to be a dutiful Chinese daughter again. Since she wasn't the computer scientist or CPA her brother and sister were, the parents were pissed she'd both moved out and left town rather than be cheap domestic labor for them. And no, I didn't get to go home with her and meet her parents either.

At the same time, Cash had stayed home in Tennessee. She avoided the major cities on the East Coast whenever possible. She didn't want to run into anyone from her old life, since most of her former Ivy League classmates lived and worked in the 'Acela Corridor' between DC and Boston. Odin didn't travel well at his age, and I couldn't even bring one of the cats to snuggle. Most of my family is allergic.

Second, I had some family tensions anyway. Between my divorces, the unanswered questions and a three decade parade of unusual girlfriends, I was often disapproved of. Every family needs at least one black sheep and since my uncle, Mom's middle brother, had passed, I was now it.

Third, my sister was specifically annoyed with me again. See, I'd bought my ten year old nephew a four hundred dollar, screen-accurate, stunt-durable lightsaber with the color-change LEDs and the digital sound system. My sister wasn't happy about it at all. He, on the other hand, was thrilled. It's the sort of extravagant gift you get from a well-off uncle who's still a nerdy juvenile delinquent at heart. He was running around with it set for Sith Red, the flash-on-crash mode turned up and the *whooshing* noises announcing every swing while he fought the furniture and chased both their dog and his little sister.

The joke was on him though. FedEx tracking told me his sister's equally tricked out neon pink saber would be there tomorrow morning and she was the sort to give him a good fight right back. It was a good thing I was leaving town the day after.

So while this went on, I was taking an evening off from being around housefuls of relatives. I was minding my own goddamned business sitting in a back corner booth at a little strip mall Chinese place. It was yet another cramped little joint that smelled of hot grease, where the hiss of woks and yelling of cooks was audible in what passed for the dining room. It reminded me of one of Mad Jack's 'family-owned businesses.' See, I loved little holes in the wall like this. They usually had the best food and if you tipped well, they didn't care if you lingered. I was munching on an egg roll and reading Aaron Dembski-Bowden's latest *Warhammer 40,000* novel on my phone. Then the guy I thought was heading for the bathrooms instead sat down across from me. Mid-fifties, mediocre suit. Standard issue DC bureaucrat.

I just sort of looked at him. "The place isn't so crowded we need to share tables in the European manner."

He smirked. "If I were a cartel hit team, you would be so dead right now."

"If that is your idea of a pickup line, you must not get laid very much."

He was still smirking. "Your file says you're an unlikeable smartass."

"Which one? I probably have records everywhere from the ATF to the National Zoo. And since you walked right up on me, when the car I am rolling in is a rental and the only phone I have on me is Fed, you must be part of the extended family and know who I really am."

"I know a fair bit. There are a lot of things I don't. You have done quite the job of muddying your tracks for a guy who allegedly isn't a real spook."

I rolled my eyes. "Oh, thank God, you scared me. For a minute I thought you were from the IRS or something."

"Maybe I can ask them what the back taxes are on a billion dollars and change?" He flung his metaphorical bait into the water and commenced fishing.

Mother. Fucker. "If I ever make a billion dollars, I'll let you know."

"What if you made it the old fashioned way and stole it?" His expression was smug, expecting me to crack and give him a tell.

"You're a Fed of some sort. Stealing a billion dollars is your job, not mine."

Now he was getting pissy. "Listen, asshole, think of this as a casual warning. You and your little redneck pirate gang need to know your fucking place in the world."

"Somewhere north of Nashville. And we prefer the term Appalachian-American."

"You think Big John, as he liked to be known, was in charge of jack shit? He was a foot soldier. He did what he was told. His little boutique spook shop existed to serve higher interests."

"I can't imagine what those interests are. You seem a little power-mad to give me a lecture on the Constitution and a little-r republican form of limited government."

"Yeah, yeah your file says you think you're a patriotic anarchist of some kind."

I sighed. "Depending how far you got into my file, you know I am eligible for the Society of the Cincinnati and will probably be in when a rather elderly and very distant cousin of mine passes."

"The what?" *We need a better class of aspiring Gestapo chief in this country.*

Great. I was going to have to reteach what used to be American History 101 to this guy instead of finishing my dinner and then spoiling its digestion by going back to argue with my sister about loud toys. "Washington's regular line officers and their descendants. The ones who made a compromise in March 1783 while in garrison at Newburgh, New York, in which they agreed not to move on Philadelphia, round up and then probably execute the Continental Congress over the matter of overdue back pay. Some of the more hotheaded ones had wanted to install Washington as king of the newborn nation, not bothering to have asked his opinion on the subject. He talked them down rather than accept the metaphorical throne."

Still pissy and smirking, he shot back. "I always preferred Henry Kissinger's observation that soldiers were dumb animals whose job it was to die obediently for foreign policy."

I sighed. "Yeah, those were big words, since they supposedly came from a former private first class who narrowly survived the Bulge in the 84th Infantry Division. More likely Bob Woodward was just making shit up again. He does an awful lot of that if you look closely. Regardless. The Army made a deal with the Congress. And the upholding of that deal is a calling. The further we as a nation stray from the original intent of the Founders, the greater the likelihood the deal will be called off. When that happens, a forcible reset of the system is inevitable."

"Lovely. Advocacy of treason. Hope I get to sit on your next security clearance review."

I continued ignoring his weak jabs. "Point being, I take American governance as a fairly serious project, no matter how doomed and futile the whole thing is. Mainly because the work of governing other people attracts people like you. Now you were saying something about higher interests?"

"There are bigger fish in the ocean, you pissant. You can't be doing whatever you feel like doing. There are balances of power between the people who matter."

I dramatically sighed. "It's a free country. Or at least it used to be."

"It's a free country if you shut up, do what you are told, buy what you are told to buy, and pay your taxes, both seen and unseen. Otherwise you become an inconvenience to the machinery. The machinery doesn't like being inconvenienced."

"See, we can agree on things. Difference between us is that deep down I want most of that machinery gone."

"Do you know what you did?"

Sigh. "No, please tell me."

"A billion dollars in cash vanishes completely one state away from your little operation and you are going to tell me you don't know about it? Some people think you did it."

"If anyone who mattered thought I did whatever silly shit you are talking about, they wouldn't be sending a weirdo like you to interrupt my dinner. Those people know our legitimate contracting business does not include any form of domestic operations. But tracking me down to a particular table while I am traveling, probably by what is alleged to be a rather secure electronic item, is a fairly impressive feat. So I will pretend you are some kind of legitimate. Therefore I won't lean across the table and put this fork into the side of your neck to puncture your carotid artery. See? I can be very reasonable."

"You can't just threaten me like that." He appeared indignant.

"I didn't threaten you. I told you what I wouldn't do. Hang on." I stretched and twisted in my seat, digging both sets of knuckles into my spine while I winced in well-simulated pain. Don't get me wrong, I hurt, I almost always hurt, but I just needed a reason to get my hands off the table and not bring one of them back up. I then hooked my ankle gun. Better to have it in my hand than a holster if this guy got stupid. *And this is why you always practice your weak hand shooting.* I drew with my right, but shifted it to my left as my right hand came back up. I then conspicuously drank with my right hand, while my left hand stayed below.

Lecture time again. The easiest draw for an ankle weapon, be it knife or gun, is the inside of the opposite ankle. Not the outside like you see with big knives in the movies. Touch your ankle and try it. Some people use a small semiauto. Some small semiautos are finicky if limp-wristed or otherwise mishandled. That is easy to do with a small backup piece under stress. Revolvers can be far more certain to go bang on command, with the tradeoff of a shot or three fewer.

I have been well coached on the subject over the years. When I bothered with one, my ankle gun was a vintage Colt Detective Special with a shroud over the hammer so it wouldn't snag on the draw. I had two of them. This one and its holster lived in a very well-concealed hiding spot at Mom and Dad's for the times like this where I had flown up commercial and didn't want to fuck around with flying with a gun in my checked baggage. I had more than that stashed up here, but different tools for different jobs.

Normally I loved Smith and Wesson wheelguns, since I find their push-style cylinder latch faster on the reload than Colt's pull-style, but until Smith makes a six-shot .38 on the small J-frame, I was cheating on them. That extra shot transcended brand loyalty. It was loaded with Speer Gold Dots, the custom NYPD 135 grain hollowpoint load that was designed to expand reliably from short barrels. I had boxes of the stuff stored. *Thanks, Uncle Pat.* It would do rather nicely to end this fellow should I decide it necessary. The spluttering jackass opposite me wasn't paying attention to my hands at all. He was too busy trying to stare me down eye to eye. Bad technique. *Hands kill. Watch them.*

"You need to pay your taxes on what you took. Put you in your place. Give me... say a hundred million in cash and I might forget your offense against the rules of the game. A tithe to the Powers that Be." I could hear his capital letters. What a fucking weirdo. Guys like him are the reason people think the Illuminati or the Lizard People run the government instead of just too many Ivy League educated liberal-lefties with pretensions of aristocratic grandeur.

I shook my head in disbelief. "Give you, personally, a literal million pieces of paper? Do you have a large truck handy?"

"Wait, what?" I don't think he could have looked more confused had I put a baseball bat across the bridge of his nose. Not that I was opposed to doing that, but I didn't have one with me.

"I don't know what you are talking about with this billion dollars, but do you know how much paper that is? Literally tons. Cubic yards. A hundred million, ten percent of that, is still literally several tons of paper. You aren't putting that in a briefcase like the movies."

He was looking suddenly crestfallen. "I don't get it."

"That's because in addition to being a creepy weirdo with no people skills, you're dumb. Do some math. How many hundred dollar bills in a hundred thousand dollars?"

"Uh, a thousand."

"How many thousands in a million?"

I swear by the Archangel Michael, patron saint of the Airborne, he subtly counted on his fingers. "A thousand."

"Almost there. Now think of the bills. How many pieces of paper are a thousand thousands?"

He slumped and sighed. "A million."

"Or, a hundred million divided by one hundred is one million. One million bills."

He looked at me like I was Einstein reborn. "You're really good at math."

I snorted. "Actually past a point I am terrible at it. Failed College Algebra four times. But raw brute force arithmetic? I'm not bad at it just because I played so many pencil and paper wargames growing up that I learned to do some of it in my head."

"Oh."

I continued. "So you are looking at maybe two cubic yards of paper. How many cubic feet to the cubic yard?"

He thought about it for a minute. "Three feet by three...Nine?"

I shook my head. "Not square feet, you're thinking flat. Think cube and come up three layers. 27 cubic feet. Double that, it's 54, in other words a block of stacked paper three feet high, three wide and six feet long. Like a refrigerator box."

"You really thought that through."

I waved. "I'm not done. That's for just the hundred million. Multiply that by ten."

The light bulb went on in his head. "Ten refrigerator boxes full of paper, weighing two tons each. Twenty tons."

"You are starting to get it. Moving bulk cash is a serious industrial process, which is why everyone in banking wants everything done digitally now. Less manual effort and billable labor. Never mind the fact it's all highly traceable."

He sipped his Coke. "I never thought of it that way. Why don't they have bigger bills anymore?"

Lecture time. "Since 1969, the official concerns were tax evasion, illegal activity, and money laundering the profits of illegal activities. So despite inflation making the hundred worth less now than the twenty was then, we'll never get bigger bills back, not even a five hundred or a thousand. It's all about government control, which really means the big banks and the Federal Reserve, with the IRS taking their cut."

"Oh, good, I was starting to think you were way more normie than your file indicated."

That was sigh and eyeroll time. "Dude, you just tried walking up on me like an asshole then bluffing me into giving you a hundred million dollars of stolen money that I haven't heard anything about so don't have. Nothing about this is normie."

"But you figured it all out?"

I sighed in frustration. "While I was sitting here. Some of what I did in the Army involved knowing how to pack up and move the unit a lot, so you have to be able to think in cubic feet. And paper is heavy as shit. Almost eighty pounds a cubic foot. When I was in Headquarters Company, we took fifty boxes of copier paper with us to Iraq the second time because we were afraid we wouldn't be able to get more while we were there. That takes up a lot of weight and a lot of space."

He looked even more confused. "Really?"

"Yeah, you need forklifts and a place to work and all kinds of stuff to move that much weight around. Look at the web site for the Bureau of Engraving and Printing sometime. They only pack 64,000 bills on a pallet, so think how many pallets that takes to add up to a million bills."

If someone were to look up and confirm what I just said, you would realize I cut that number by ninety percent. Per their own web site, they put 640,000 bills on a pallet. He didn't need to know that right now. Again, never give a sucker an even break. I still had my gun on him under the table with my left hand, and while he was lost in thought, I snapped a pic of him with my phone with my right. I was going to figure out who this guy really was, even if I had to kill him tonight out in the parking lot. But he didn't seem to be playing with a full deck of cards. He'd gone from being the megalomaniac ambassador from the Secret Lizard People to being a confused math student or a guy who would fail the Unit Movement Officer's Course.

He was still shaking his head. "Damn. My boss was so sure you guys did it."

I was confused too. I was just hiding it better. "Who's your boss? Fuck, I don't even know who you are."

"You aren't supposed to. Apparently the factions don't talk between themselves at our level."

"Our level?" This was about to get weird. I just knew it. And except for arguing with my sister, today had been going so well.

He kept going. "Different power blocks have different allegiances and different rosters of contractors and subcontractors, different go-to players and so on."

"So what, the Illuminati call Blackwater, the Trilateral Commission call Triple Canopy, then the Bilderbergers go British?" And yeah, Blackwater wasn't Blackwater anymore. I know. Don't get too far into the weeds, people.

This guy had been up too late reading the cut and pasted work of paranoid schizophrenics on the Internet. I recognized the symptoms. I had done way too much of the same shit going back to when it was .txt files and dial-up bulletin board servers. Searching for meaning where there really was none was an addictive hobby if you have a certain inquisitive intelligence. Some people fall into that hole and never get back out. Look at 4chan's politics board if you don't believe me. But I still had something resembling a functioning bullshit filter. It had been strained over the years, and in some cases ripped, but it was there. Buying two metric tons of long-missing twenty-ish karat Japanese war loot and knowing one of your brokerage accounts controls 800 kilos of genuine Nazi bullion will do that to you. But at some point you still tell yourself you're still a skeptic, that there are no clumps of self-styled elites pulling puppet strings on the world, that it is as much bullshit as the monster under your bed when you were three years old.

You pretend the world is still what you were told it was, even though you know better.

He looked back at me a little too calmly. "I know you think I am nuts. But there are a lot of things you don't know."

"I know there are a lot of things I don't know. There are even some things I probably don't want to know."

He was back on his bullshit. "But what you don't know can kill you."

"All right, try me." I figured it was going to be a while before I got out of here. I waved to the waitress for a refill.

He opened with a question. "What is the common factor between the Royal Institute for International Affairs and the Council on Foreign Relations?"

Yep, Internet schizophrenia. "Cecil Rhodes' will, well, one of them, several drafts existed. Then there was his buddy Milner who executed Rhodes' monetary gifts to the Round Table Society which then became the Royal Institute." Just because the guy was nuts didn't mean I didn't know some of the iffy and speculative history he was referring to. All those sleepless nights online, you know.

"Who was Colonel Edward House?"

I knew this one too. "Not a real colonel. Texas politician turned DC power broker. Crony of Woodrow Wilson and supposedly his liaison with the New York banks when they were setting up the Federal Reserve."

"What if I told you Wilson and House's work was still going on with money Milner arranged and that despite being dead for a century, Rhodes' trust funds support the idea of global government?"

I sighed again in irritation. "You'd be telling me shit I knew thirty years ago."

He seemed uncertain I believed him. "I mean the real facts and real evidence. Not the rambling on the Internet, which no one believes even though it's actually true."

"You're going to tell me it's out there for disinformation, to hide the truth in plain sight, so the Council for Foreign Relations can go on with the Trilateral Commission and the others then rule the world in plain sight for the benefit of big corporations."

He just looked at me. Then the waitress stopped back by the table with her pitcher to refill my Coke. I nodded my thanks and pointed at my guest. She quickly brought him one as well.

He looked at it then looked at me. "I didn't really want this."

"Shut up and drink it. We're in the business of being inconspicuous and polite. Remember, most of the staff here has been off the boat from China for about ten minutes and are still paying off the snakeheads who trafficked them here. They don't care if we kill each other here or in the parking lot except so much as it disrupts their earnings."

"That's pretty harsh."

I rolled my eyes at him. "It's also accurate." I took a long drag at the Coke before I continued talking. "Now do you think I just fell off the back of the pumpkin truck with the rest of the rubes? Come on. I may not have the recordings of the meetings, but the idea that there is a multinational gathering or three of the ultra-rich and influential who run the world is not a new or shocking idea at this point. Sometimes it makes the social pages. You aren't going to surprise me. But the biggest argument against it being completely true is the horrible inefficiency of the whole thing. No matter how slick the World Economic Forum makes their PowerPoint slide decks, whoever is running the world behind the scenes is completely fucking incompetent since it's a mess. Calling the world a dumpster fire is an insult to flaming garbage. You think the men behind the curtain are actually steering this wreck?"

"They have meetings. The wars and such are because of the deadlocks at the meetings. It's like tectonic plates. No one can agree and subtle wars sometimes become open ones the same way earthquakes happen. Tension has to go somewhere."

This was going to annoy me. "They don't have enough little wars. Iran has been an open ulcer for forty years and the North Koreans are only tolerated because no one wants to be the new owner of twenty-odd million malnourished and brainwashed zombies who still have at least half a dozen working nukes." They had more than that, but quality control was a bitch and a couple of their tests had been fizzles. Nobody wanted them launching and then rolling dice to see if they worked.

His face was lighting up as he thought he recognized a fellow crazy. "And because there is no short term profit in either war. They're too one-sided to be interesting unless they can arrange a long and expensive occupation. But after Iraq and Afghanistan, that doesn't sell politically."

Time to dampen his enthusiasm. "Or there is a greater long-term benefit to the national security state by having those 'sponsors of terrorism' to keep pointing at. Heart disease and car crashes kill more Americans in the aggregate than terrorism ever will. Let alone the occasional barely lethal virus from a Chinese lab."

He looked at me strangely. "That is a shocking statement for a guy with your background."

I shrugged again. "Doesn't mean we should ignore the problem either. Besides, I like the work. I'm not smart enough to be a cardiologist."

He went on. "So if I told you the Germans and other European intel agencies cooked the books on the Iraqi WMD intel to embarrass and then tarpit the US, and the CIA under George Tenet swallowed it all up without question, you would believe me?"

An unpopular theory, but…. "The measure of a man's intelligence is how much he agrees with you, and I came up with that while we were still invading the place. After the first two months, I had way too much free time to think while waiting for shit to happen. It was either that or obsess over an ex I had. But there were reasons the Germans wouldn't allow direct access to the primary human source on WMD programs, who was a dishonest little shit trying to get whatever the Germans call a green card."

"Damn, you did pay attention."

This was an easy one. "For the European Union to rise to preeminence, the US has to fall and they consider us upstart bumpkins with no culture anyway. They want us gone. Using our gunslinger tendencies against us is the sort of devious bullshit you would expect out of a social club run by the Germans and the fucking French. But writing the whole thing off as a lie also ignores the fact that lots of Russian 'commercial' flights were hauling loads out of Baghdad Airport and long convoys of eighteen wheelers went into Syria. They were moving weapons material out the back door that some people didn't want found there after we fought our way in the front door. They knew the Iraqis couldn't stop us. And the Iraqi general who ramrodded the effort wrote a book too."

"We?"

I sighed. "Yeah, I was there at the time. Ask me about five thousand OD green barrels behind two fencelines on an Iraqi military base that tested positive for VX nerve gas and were then were dismissed as 'pesticide ingredients'. Or a whole bunch of yellowcake uranium that was recovered then shipped to Canada for commercial reprocessing later. Which is still a long way from how John Rockefeller's father in law, Senator Nelson Aldrich, worked with Adam Schiff and J.P. Morgan to set up and then sell us all out to the Federal Reserve Board of Governors and through them to the European banks that bought in to the Fed through intermediaries."

He was slipping, I could read it in his eyes. "But if you go back to the beginning, through Rhodes and the Round Table groups, it explains all of it."

I shook my head. "No it doesn't. It throws a thin veil of historical argument over the top of loose ideas that try to make sense of a chaotic world."

He was undeterred. "But I am telling you, evidence exists. It can be proven that we're all in the hands of dark forces conspiring against us."

I scoffed. "Look, there may be a few British bankers who think they run shit, but I seriously doubt the lawyers of the planet are running things out of the Temples of Court in the City of London proper. Yes, I saw that idea too."

"But the Templars-"

My personal belief is that invoking the Knights Templar into a conspiracy theory is usually just lazy writing; they were fighters and eventually a few survivors became bankers, but they weren't omnipotent boogeymen. "You are looking for too difficult a solution. To quote John le Carre, never underestimate the capacity of the British ruling class for reluctant betrayal and polite self-preservation"

He looked disappointed. "Really?"

I continued. "Yeah, a substantial chunk of the British upper classes hate our fucking guts. They thought they were destined to keep ruling the world, but after winning both World Wars they ran out of blood and treasure by '45. Then they lost the *jewel in the crown*' when India went independent. Sure, they did a bit of Korea for old times' sake, but then Ike made them his bitches over Suez in '56 and they had pulled home by the Sixties when they gave back Singapore. They never would have managed the Falklands without our help, and then the last real gasp of the Empire was the flag coming down in Hong Kong in '97. While they will stumble into Iraq or Afghanistan to back us up and pretend they are still a world power, they are a second or third tier one, even with a couple really nice ballistic missile submarines. They overpaid and underbought on the two new carriers though. Some of them can admit that cruel fact to themselves while still hating us because Britannia doesn't rule the waves. Shit, if SEA LION had worked and Germany had invaded, the Brits would have been more Nazi than the Germans in about ten years. A thousand-plus years of monarchy makes a nation of born followers."

"Sounds complicated."

I raised my glass in a mock toast. "Yes, which is why it's best to have as little to do with the bastards above a certain pay grade as possible. They will fuck you over for King, Country, or personal gain, guaranteed. But see, you come running in here trying to explain things to me but now we have flipped the script and I am tutoring you in all this. You're wasting my time."

I'd almost said Queen and Country out of habit. Elizabeth II hadn't been gone long at this point.

He took a deep breath. "Okay, let me get back to the point so much as it is relevant to you."

I sighed again. "That would be nice."

"The US government and major socio-political blocs worldwide are engaged in a long term cold civil war against themselves and each other. They have their fingers into everything from Hollywood to the drug trade, fighting against themselves for wealth and power."

"Again, not telling me anything I haven't known. The State Department's been off the reservation working their own agenda since World War I at least and since 1933 doesn't even pretend to work for our team much of the time. Secretaries come and go, the Foreign Service is forever."

His enthusiasm was coming back. "You're not getting it. You're not a spectator anymore. You're not terrain, or an innocent bystander. When you went to work for Big John, you became a player in the game. More so now that you are sitting in his chair."

I wasn't buying it. "If I am anything to people like that, I am a chess pawn."

"The hell you say. You have a dangerously competent freelance intel shop that hears things that some people don't want heard. Maybe more than one shop, depending on the rumors. You make a specialty of getting dirt on people who don't like other people knowing their dirt."

I chuckled. "Oh, yeah, Senator whatever his name was with his fondness for really femme twenty-something Hispanic twinks. And the other one with the dominatrix he stashed at the Watergate. Don't get me started on that bitchy old queen from South Carolina. Definitely a 'confirmed bachelor' as they used to say."

"You think you could piss off two or three sitting US senators and get away with it?"

I drank deeply. Talking is a thirsty business. "Hey, those were completely amicable transactions."

His turn to scoff. "Yeah, whatever you tell yourself. But you personally have gone to war on the side of some of the Texas oil money faction, so some people assume your group is allied there."

"Oh, really?"

"Come on, *Professor*, DHS didn't do that good a job losing all the news footage of the East Dallas Massacre a few years back."

I snorted. "That what they call it now?"

"Some do. The other team's dead included a lot of people with long grudges and who take their orders from people who would like to peacefully integrate them into the Big American Melting Pot for votes while taking in a percentage of revenue off their drug trade. And there's no statute of limitations on murder, which is what some people think you guys did despite the DHS contractor badges and the FBI support that you got under the table."

Well shit, this was an unwelcome surprise. I was really surprised this guy knew anything about that.

He continued. "Your old Army buddy down there? We know which team pays his bills and you're considered a known associate in a couple of very obscure computer databases."

"That's interesting. I haven't even seen him in person in a couple years."

"Doesn't matter. Once in, never out."

My historic pedantry buzzer went off. "That was the Irish Republican Army."

"Yeah and your hands aren't clean there either. Don't you have a couple friends in Belfast?"

Fucking wonderful.

He stood. "Anyway, I just wanted to find you and let you know where you really stood. I'll be in touch, of course." As he walked out, I reholstered the Colt and kept sipping my Coke as the tension bled off.

***

Angel and I made apologies to our families for Christmas itself, citing work emergencies and we whistled up the Lear. I didn't have time to hide the Colt again at Mom and Dad's two hours away, so I'd have to remember to bring it back up the next time I drove.

Catching a ride out to a small local airstrip with one of Angel's old friends, we left around 2300. In the interest of time, Matt dropped us at the Clarksville airport instead to save us some time driving home. Cash was awake and working in Intel, so she came and got us in her Mustang. We were back in the office the next morning. One of Kara's kids ran the pic of the guy through a fairly sophisticated facial recognition software system that Uncle Sam maintained and to which Athenaeum had a user account. That didn't mean we used our account, no sense autographing our work, but we needed the result regardless.

The computer spit out the name and driver's license photo of one Donal (not Donald, that would be too pedestrian) Cuthbert Rife, of Bethesda, Maryland. His LinkedIn told us he was a former Deputy Assistant Secretary of State two administrations ago and was mostly a lawyer by profession. He specialized in the exciting field of international copyrights and patents. That had put him in the middle of a lot of commercial negotiations with various Third World sweatshop countries. Those countries invariably had interesting payoffs to and from assorted US corporations and politicians, so he was quite possibly in a position to know who got paid to do what to whom and where the bodies were dumped afterward. Nobody has more dirt than gravediggers. It was... interesting.

Two days later, I went downstairs to my office to begin the day as usual, Angel in tow and Morgan was waiting for me since he'd held down the overnight watch. He handed me a clipboard as Angel brought in another Mountain Dew from the break room fridge. "Guess what? Our new buddy Donal Cuthbert Rife is now the lead story on every goddamn channel of the DC morning news. It seems he jumped in front of a subway train and shut down the Blue Line in the middle of rush hour. That's fucking up a lot of people."

I groaned. "How convenient for somebody."

Cash walked in from downstairs as I took a long pull at the can. She blew me a kiss as Angel slapped her on the ass. Morgan didn't even bat an eye. While I didn't rub my personal life in anyone's face, some people like Morgan had known me for twenty years and weren't going to be shocked at anything I did or who I did it with.

"Yeah, witnesses say he was literally screaming about the Lizard King as he jumped."

I shook my head ruefully. "I really miss the days when people could go batshit insane with some form of dignity. Truly we live in a decaying civilization on a fallen world."

Cash laughed. "So much more money to be made that way. Peace is boring, let it collapse."

Well, somebody woke up in a mood. I looked at her pointedly. "We aren't really set for civilization to implode. You cannot eat gold bullion, nor shoot it at people. Should we really figure out it's going to collapse and we need to run

Galt's Gulch, we're in the wrong location with the wrong inventory."

Morgan was looking for something to throw at me. "Knock off your bullshit. Civilization isn't going to collapse this morning, or so quick we can't adjust. Try to focus on the here and now, boss, goddamn it."

I did my best to get back on track. "Okay, here and now, our one name for the people who is now dead, but even the dead can be tracked by the footprints they left. We need to trace this fucker back to these people sniffing around our business. Fire up a couple of our best scumbags and turn that dude's life inside out. A complete lack of subtlety is now authorized. Find who he moved and sat with, find who they move and sat with, emails, phone records, anything."

He nodded. "I got just the people. One's admittedly a nineteen year old with a juvic record even longer than mine, but she's really very good at phone records."

"Morgan, I love you like a brother, but I don't even have the mental energy for details until I drink two more of these."

Angel said, "And you won't, because you know two a day is your limit for daily operations."

Being fussed over is hard sometimes, but as you get older, unless you want a case of the Type II diabeetus, you just can't open a two liter of soda and throw away the cap the way I could when I was in my early twenties.

Coming back out in the first floor hallway, there was a tall wooden crate standing against one wall. I mean a big damn crate. Angel squealed with joy. "It's here!"

"What's here?"

She looked around excitedly like a puppy sniffing out a treat bag. "I need a crowbar or something." I had one in my office, of course, as one does. Popping the panel helpfully marked OPEN HERE, I was now face to face with the sculpted bronze visage of our namesake goddess.

I sighed. Twice. "Angel, darling, why do we have a six foot statue of Athena?"

Having made short work of the rest of the crate, Angel was busy screwing the two halves of the spear shaft together and setting it in place in the goddess' upraised right hand. "She's closer to seven, really, counting the base plate and plinth over here. Solid bronze. And why? Partly because I paid about eleven grand of company money for her. But mainly because the company is named after her and you didn't even have her picture on the wall."

I bit my tongue. Literally. See, a wise man has to know when to shut up.

Chapter 31

"The AK talks, the bullshit runs, I wish I had time to count all my guns..."
~"Freedom Got an AK," Ice Cube and the Lench Mob

People must figure if something worked once, it will automatically work again. That is why when Cash, Angel, and I were all out to dinner the week after New Year's, another asshole in a suit sat down without so much as a by-your-leave. Better looking and much better tailored than the last one though.

While the girls stared at him angrily, I slowly eyeballed the rest of the place. We were on the back deck at that same Nashville barbecue place, two seats away from where Cash and I had told Fast Eddie what was going on. This time it was the run into the NFL playoffs. The Titans were doing well and the place was crowded again, with the winter curtains down and the heaters going. There were two other guys in suits to our front left by the bar trying very hard not to keep an obvious eye on their boss. They stuck out badly since this was not a suit and tie kind of a place. Both had their suit jackets buttoned only at the top button to facilitate a faster pistol draw and were keeping their right hands free. I calmly nodded at both of them. They pointedly ignored me.

I looked over at him. "If this is about Rhodes and Milner, I already got this little dinner presentation."

He nodded. "Yes, it was quite unfortunate what happened to your lecturer. He fell in front of a Metro train in DC a bit ago." His accent was straight-up East Coast patrician. Sounded a lot like James, or even Cash. Guess it was that whole Harvard-Yale-Princeton thing.

Didn't surprise me. As you know, we knew this. "You and your two friends at the bar came here to promise me and mine some of the same?" I noticed Angel's hands had slid off the tabletop and were probably in her purse. If she didn't have her hands on her gun already, I was a monkey's uncle. Cash was twirling a fork idly on the tabletop, but she was working left-handed with her right hand out of sight. *Fuck around and find out my dates aren't just eye candy, asshole.*

"No, no. You do good work and you are in no danger from me so long as you keep doing good work and playing along."

"I really don't take orders all that well, especially from unknown parties." *True.*

"Obviously there were things Big John never told you about how your little operation fits into a wider network."

I shrugged. "That may be. Or you and your friend could both just be standard-issue senior bureaucrats who think you can add to your pensions by trying to shake down various contractors for a few bucks. Anyone with sufficient position knows who Uncle Sam pays to do what and can pick their squeezing accordingly. Kickbacks are an American political tradition."

He half-smiled. "You have a suspicious nature."

I half-nodded in return. "People in our line of work can rarely afford to be trusting. But if you want me and the firm to help you, this does not get us off to a good start. Walking up on people in public is a nice way to get shot. There are channels for this sort of thing, right?"

"Not really. John took most of his orders from another player in the game, one I am not on good terms with."

I shrugged again. "So? If you knew John, you know damn well he wasn't on good terms with a lot of people. His friends and enemies are not necessarily my friends and enemies. Particularly with him having flown west for the last time over a year ago now."

That's old-timey aviator slang for 'died.' It's okay, I don't think he got the reference either.

He maintained his avuncular act. "It isn't complicated. Still, there are lines. There are power blocs behind the scenes of what people see on the evening news or read in their little

Internet headlines. Most of the lines are simple. Rival clubs of defense contractors. Politicians who sold out to one gang or another of rich foreigners, or a bureaucrat having the right regional desk at State or CIA. In return, they get Christmas presents or birthday cards from their overseas friends.

"Another technique is when they cash in as 'endowed chairs of' at universities or think tanks. Pro-Russia, though that got less common after the Ukraine War. Pro-China is guaranteed. Lots of those. Pro-Saudi, pro-Emirates, pro-Qatari, all for oil money. Rarely the Europeans though. They don't pay well since they can't afford to. Anyone on Europe's tit only does it for aesthetics and class snobbery. California tech billionaires are another bloc, only most of them hate each other even more than they hate those outside their club. Then there is the Texas oil money, though they work worldwide, anywhere they can drill. Your friend from east of Dallas is their boy, whether he knows it or not. And where you once had steel or rail monopolies, like the Carnegies, Vanderbilts, or the Rockefellers, you now have entertainment and media conglomerates. The House of the Mouse owns a little bit of everything and they don't need to resort to violence."

Yeah? Tell that to the juvenile talent that gets molested, passed around, and ends up strung out or crazy. Selling your attractive pre-teen offspring to a major media corporation for a shot at child stardom may not be as stressful as robbing drug cartels of their hard-earned cash, but it certainly had its own collection of ugly downfalls over the years. Ask Britney's parents. Better yet, ask the ones who fell off the train before the "rich and famous" part kicked in. Assuming they lived to tell about it. There's always the "Miley Cyrus Was Killed and Replaced" Internet theory.

I wasn't impressed by any of that shit and didn't care to fake it. "So various flavors of globalists, corporatists, and assorted traitors. Sounds like a scummy bunch of people."

He sighed in disdain. "You ex-soldiers and your absolutist codes of honor. You cling to your bullshit grudges and rarely suppress your enthusiasm for violence. People like you are the reasons we need to have meetings to prevent wars in the first place."

I looked over at Angel. She was rolling her eyes. Cash was doing the same. I turned my attention back to him. "Or when your kind decide you can make a tiddly profit getting some excess 18 to 29 year olds from places nobody gives a fuck about killed off in some foreign shithole every year for a couple decades in exchange for a couple of hundred points in stock market gains or keeping oil prices at a profitable point."

He was unfazed. "That creation of wealth benefits the entire world. What are a few deaths against a greater good for all mankind?"

Oh, bullshit. "At the multinational level, trickle-down economics is a mirage. It turns into corruption and sweatshop slavery faster than villages get clean water or a fuel source that isn't firewood. And never mind the human and economic costs of those unwinnable wars."

He sneered again. "Funny, your file doesn't make you out to be a Marxist rabble-rouser."

I shrugged, appearing reasonable. "I'm not. I just don't think that, for just one example, an electronics factory in a major Asian nation should have to be generously equipped with suicide nets to keep those cheerful beneficiaries of globalized capitalism from jumping off the rooftops and killing themselves rather than work another eighteen hour shift."

He waved my argument off dismissively. "Those are acceptable losses for the global good. Whether they die from the open sewers in their Bronze Age villages or move to the city for work until they die there instead, life is cheap. The world is overpopulated as it is. It's terrible for the environment, really. Another degree's increase in average high temperatures will kill us all."

I was really starting not to like this guy. The casual disregard for death was supposedly something we had left behind in the twentieth century, even if the twenty-first wasn't exactly cake, cookies and ice cream either. And he wasn't going to fool me with Davos environmental propaganda.

He continued. "Regardless of your thoughts on life and death, such decisions are not made at your level. A select and illuminated few with the vision and wisdom to deal with such matters have taken it upon themselves to do it since the earliest days of Mankind."

"You are going to sit here and tell me some gang of jackasses who think they're the Illuminati are running the world and then think I am not going to laugh at you."

He laughed. "Their greatest trick was convincing the cattle, ordinary humanity, that they do not really exist."

"And you're their errand boy?"

He smiled calmly. "I am a loyal supporter. In time I will reach higher levels. For now, I serve in this manner as I seek to advance."

Fucking schizo bullshit. "Let's skip past that part for now. My question is what you want with me and mine and what was so important you had to have old Rife stuck with a couple of hits of bad acid and thrown in front of a train. And doing it at rush hour was just fucking rude, man. People gotta get to work."

He sneered at me again. "I refuse to respond to any allegations of wrongdoing."

"Well, I'm not formally alleging shit. I'm just making dinner conversation."

He nodded, still accepting my polite deflection for what it was; a lie. "What I propose and will make, no matter who else disagrees, and by force where needed, is a permanent liaison committee between factions to minimize disputes and maximize profit for all involved."

I sighed. "What that sounds like to me what you are looking to do is the multinational military-industrial version of the 1930s Commission, when Lucky Luciano sat the other bosses down after the Castellammarese War and set himself up as *capo di tutti capi*. And we all know Charlie Lucky ran that to his own personal advantage as long as he could."

He almost seemed offended. "You think I wish to become the boss of bosses?"

I was resisting the temptation to just sneer back at him. "The lust for power is as old as the human heart. Remember, Lucky had the Night of the Sicilian Vespers for everyone who didn't want to sing out of his hymnal."

"The lust for wealth is just as old. I heard you may have found a nice wad of cash lying somewhere."

I shrugged. "So I keep hearing from people who keep inviting themselves to my dinner table. Had I really found that much laying around anywhere, I would already be retired. I am fundamentally a lazy man and would prefer to spend my declining years in peace, quiet and comfort."

He sneered back a little bit. "Come on, you aren't completely stupid, or poor. You had to have found and been into John's notebooks to know what your little organization has tucked away in the banks here and overseas. I don't know everything John knew, that bastard could keep his secrets, but I know enough. And if you don't want all those offshore accounts I do know of to end up on a State Department sanctions list with the money seized and you indicted, you'll play along."

"Not to mention you have your two gun-toting associates over at the bar to try to make me behave and probably one out front and another two in the back parking lot." His face was a tell. "You didn't bring enough boys to cover the other doors, did you? Yeah. You came light. I'm almost insulted. So here's what's going to happen. You're going to take this menu, your boys over there are going to sit down over there and order something so they stop disturbing my calm. That way Angel and I won't have to pull Sam Colt and kill them while Cash here puts half a magazine of hollowpoints into your face. We want to leave a good looking corpse, right?" He was looking a bit more pale now. Now I was actually carrying my Glock tonight, but "pulling Gaston Glock" just didn't have the time honored phrasing of the earlier version.

I know I come across as a large and jovial fellow, a mostly harmless nerd unless you knew me at work, but for some reason certain people take that as a sign I can be safely fucked with. People forget that Jove, aka Jupiter, aka Zeus the Thunderer depending on your flavor of Greco-Roman mythology, would laugh at jokes and drink all day with cheer, but he also liked to throw lightning bolts at people when he got mad. Stop interrupting me at meals. It pisses me off.

"So, to repeat, do you have a good argument for trying to muscle myself and my companions at dinner besides 'I want to be in charge'? Some compelling reasoning that you should be in charge? Because I don't know who the hell you are, or who that guy in Maryland you had shoved in front of a train was, or this Great Game he babbled about was. We're just simple government contractors trying to make a living off what Uncle Sam taught us to do."

He changed tactics. I could see the switch flip in his eyes as he grinned at me like a fellow conspirator. It was as fake as Cash's tits but nowhere near so pleasing to the eye. "Come on, you mean you didn't steal that billion dollars down South? The Mexicans want blood for that. It would be a terrible shame if someone threw your name into the wind, whether you were responsible or not."

Now I was really getting annoyed. "The fact that you have to ask means you don't know if I did it. If I had done it, or any other respectable caper, I surely as Hell awaits me would not tell someone who just invited himself to my dinner table without so much as a 'how do you do?' or 'Good evening.' And the fact you would sell bad information to the Mexicans to frame up me and mine for something we didn't do, dropping us into a street war we didn't begin and don't want, doesn't give me a whole lot of reason to let you leave this room alive either way."

He started going pale again. "Wait, I didn't-"

"You did. You shot your mouth off with a threat you may or may not back up. I can't afford to take a chance with you on that. And if you think we won't shoot you, your two backup dancers over there, and then walk out of here in about five seconds flat leaving Nashville Homicide an interesting crime scene full of confused hipster white kids and drunk football fans, then you just made the last bad decision of your life."

He was shifting in his seat nervously. "I didn't-"

"Again, yes you did. Angel, grab his wallet." Smiling like a shark, she retrieved it. He opened his mouth to protest, but she quickly sank a thumb deep into the pressure point on the side of his neck atop his carotid artery. He got very quiet as his brain promptly starved of fresh oxygen.

Never underestimate a skilled massage therapist's knowledge of human anatomy.

She passed it to me and I opened it, retrieving his driver's license. "So, Mr. Thomas Holden Van Derlin of Potomac, Maryland..." I took a cell phone picture of the license, "we now know who you allegedly are." I tossed the license back and then took a couple pictures of him. "But digital facial recognition is a miraculous thing and we shall find the truth of the matter one way or another. Either that or I could just chop off a finger or two for DNA and fingerprints."

Still groggy from having his brain forcibly deoxygenated, he also still thought he was in control. "You wouldn't dare-"

I kept my voice low and calm, just another dinner conversation. "Now how the fuck do you know what I would or wouldn't dare to do, asshole?" Great. Instead of staying calm I was suddenly possessed by my buddy Bam Bam. "By my standards, I've got Fuck You money and Fuck You guns and I don't see where I work for you. You want to do business, we can do business. You want to play, we can play. But you aren't wired for that. I see it in your eyes. You lack the confidence, and you think you can get by with dialogue you learned watching old mob movies at whatever Ivy League frat house and buggery society whelped you." I looked over at Cash. "No offense, baby."

She smiled delicately. "None taken, sir. She then pulled a large black fixed-blade knife out of her purse and laid it on the table, discreetly covering it with the menu as if she were contemplating dessert. Cash then turned to our unwanted guest. "If he doesn't cut you, I will. I haven't bled anyone with this one yet, so I am feeling the urge anyway."

I paused for a moment and looked over at her, trying really hard not to show my surprise. Knifing people was not usually Cash's thing. Looking again, the hilt style definitely marked it as something from Spartan Blades outside Fort Bragg, but it wasn't mine. It was the wrong color, though it spoke to her good taste. It was most of four hundred dollars and she usually only spent that sort of money on shoes. She looked back at me with absolutely perfect innocence in face and voice. "Do I get to cut him now, sir?"

Angel looked at her, looked at me and back at her. The look on her face was eloquent. Angel was a wise old soul and she prided herself on being the moderating influence when my mean streak showed or when Cash's multiple wild sides got a little out of hand. I looked over at Angel and shrugged. "Dear, I believe she may have a point to go with the edge. I don't think this guy is a terrible amount of use to us alive." And really, Van Derlin wasn't. He was too uppity to talk, but too chickenshit to fight. And we couldn't sit here all night either.

Angel's eyebrow went up. "Are we sure this is a good idea?"

I shrugged again. "This guy started it. We were eating dinner."

Cash's grin turned from saintly to a deep shade of evil as her hypnotically altered brain's *Do I Get To Go Crazy Now?* switch visibly flipped to *Yes*. "Does this mean I get to finish it?"

I looked over at her. "And I thought you were another of the reasonable ones."

Cash didn't take her eyes off her target. "She was the reasonable one. I'm not her. Me? No. I'm not feeling reasonable. Reasonable has definitely left the table. What I'm feeling like now is slowly, gently and methodically filleting this threat to my family and letting everyone else watch as a warning. I know we don't have the time to make it appropriately prolonged and artistic, but if a couple fingers would please you, it would greatly amuse me. May I, sir?"

I looked Van Derlin in the eye, as calmly as I could manage. "That is up to him." Going pale, our guest was looking a lot less optimistic about life than he had a few minutes ago.

Realistically, I had to concede that there were a dozen other tables and fifty people within a ten yard radius. We weren't going to blades here. I looked back at Cash and Angel. "Okay, we'll skip the fingers. It would be fun, but there are too many witnesses. Ladies, why don't you go close out our tab and meet me out by the truck in a few. Don't let his friends stop you." I gazed over toward the bar where his two assholes were trying not to watch us. My unspoken message was *Get an angle on those two and drop them fast if shit goes sideways.*

Angel looked over their way. "Roger that. Come on, beautiful."

Cash put her knife back in her purse. As she stood, she leaned over, seductively draping herself on to Van Derlin as if hugging our guest good night. She whispered to him, loud enough for us to hear, "You got really fucking lucky, you prick. If I see you again, not even Sir can save you from a quite protracted and bloody end. And oh, how I will enjoy it." He shuddered in a quite non-happy manner.

Those two then headed for the exit. Angel had a spare set of keys for my truck in her purse in case they needed to move on without me. I'd catch up. Across the street to the west and through the golf course, coming out on the north edge probably. I also had the thought that we needed to seriously do something about the location settings on this damn phone. I was getting annoyed with this 'Government People Following Me' shit.

The back exit of the restaurant was a ramp from the deck uphill to the small parking lot. That was a choke point, with the downhill end of the ramp, the hall to the restrooms and the small outdoor bar all converging within six feet of each other. That small space was congested with people getting drinks, watching the game on the flatscreen behind the bar, other people trying to get into the bathrooms... and our new friend's two security guys were right there in the middle of it. I still had my eyes on him, looking at the security guys for half a second every five or so as the girls passed them, but then there was a loud, "MOTHERFUCKER! WHAT THE FUCK?"

I looked back over, saw Angel and Cash were two-thirds of the way up the ramp to parking, but that was when the screaming really began in the crowd. Lots of distinctly male pain noises were followed by the spectators scattering. *Hmmmm, that's a lot of fucking blood over there. Where did that come from?* I had three guesses. *Hmmmm, don't think I am going to get out that way...*

I took a deep breath, drained the last of my Coke and took an extra second to go back over my other departure options. Decision made, I told Van Derlin, "I sincerely hope I never see you again except through gunsights" and swung under the curtain and over the deck railing down into the small drainage canal that separated the restaurant from the parking lot. Scrambling up the other side and moving faster than I like to anymore, I caught up to the girls at the truck and we got the fuck out of there.

As I made the left turn around the traffic circle onto 46th, I threw my phone to Angel. "All the phones need to be off and bagged. Obviously someone with enough clearance can locate the Blacks, so they're officially non-secure until we figure out why. And we need to sweep this truck for bugs first chance we fucking get." She reached into the center console for one of the copper cloth Faraday bags, and secured both my phones plus hers.

Angel nodded as she worked on them. "IT's got everything we need for that, though we might not want to go straight to the office to meet them."

"Agreed. We might want to lay up somewhere to make sure there's no more blood. Speaking of blood, what the fuck happened back there?"

Cash seemed a touch annoyed. "Sorry, sir, I couldn't get a clean angle at his femoral artery, so I just brushed the edge above his knee from behind and sliced into his hamstring. Cut him pretty good before he even felt it or noticed the blood. He won't be chasing anyone for a while."

Goddamn, that was ruthless. "Cash, was that really necessary on the way out?"

"No, but it suited me to do so. Besides, Hybris was the Greek demon-goddess of pride, violence, and outrageous action. She was the demon of *hubris*, or the destructive pride that brings Nemesis, the retribution of the gods. Those assholes needed a little Nemesis."

"You Princetonians and your classical erudition."

"That was why I bought that knife rather than merely borrowing something out of your office cabinet or from the house. I like being outrageous sometimes. Hybris suits me way more than your Ares, your Chris Reeve, or one of the antique Randalls."

Angel sighed. "Babe, that wasn't really necessary. That could have gone way worse than it did. Plus, you really overextended to the right on the draw stroke. Enthusiasm was good, but technique matters. I know it's cool and flashy, but you brought a little too much blade for the job. I used my little Emerson and only stabbed the one on the left a little. He'll live."

I had to laugh. "Goddamn, Stateside knife credit for everybody."

Angel leaned across the center console to get her head on my shoulder. "Baby, when it's three on three and we're trying to break contact, you don't have to do all the work yourself."

Cash piped up from the back. "For what I spent on this, it was going to get used."

Angel giggled a bit, with an edge of adrenaline hysteria. "Okay, I know what we're working on in the gym next. Knife work instead of yoga day."

I shook my head. "I'm just thinking it might be a while before we can show our faces in there to eat again and I really liked the brisket."

They both laughed. "We'll get you a new smoker for your birthday and we'll eat at home."

Besides her Black phone, which was now securely bagged, Cash had a second cell phone in her purse. It was an older Samsung Galaxy she'd bought for cash at a pawn shop, then signed up with one of those 'pay as you go' cell phone services normally found at small gas stations where English is a second language. It was the sort of arrangement used by felons, illegal aliens, or people with really low credit scores. She never turned it on unless she needed it, which was almost never.

Since she now had the only usable phone, we texted one of Morgan's burner lines and he promptly called back. We arranged to meet him in a playground parking lot behind a Methodist church out in one of the southwest suburbs. He showed up inside an hour with a full array of communications security gear and radio scanners. Twenty minutes later, he gave us a thumbs-up. The truck was clean for bugs or trackers, so the Black phones were obviously the problem. I'd been tracked by mine twice now. This annoyed me.

I looked over at Morgan. "Okay, we recall all the Blacks, They get stripped to bare metal and we get somebody really good to look at the coding. Someone's obviously got the ability to track them by location, so there's a hole in them somewhere. That includes the four still out with the Board."

He nodded, acknowledging both the request and its importance. "I'll send the immediate compromise code, then get guys on planes to go recover them first thing in the morning."

"Charter flights if needs be, particularly getting to Eric's corner of North Buttfuck."

Morgan shook his head. "That's only two hours past Paducah. It's faster to drive it, so long as you catch the Ohio River bridge at the right time. I'll handle that myself."

Cash grinned. "I haven't really blown the Shelby out lately. Want a ride?"

***

Surprisingly, Thomas Holden Van Derlin was his real name. His family had made a reasonable killing in steelmaking and auto parts in the World War II boom years. They were the Chicago Van Derlins in some old social columns to differentiate them from the older New York Knickerbocker branch of the family. Apparently the family had finally sold the company in the Eighties and the jobs had all gone to Mexico. That move had gotten his dad murdered by a former employee. The health insurance had been canceled for all the now ex-employees and a kid then died of something awful, so the distraught father had showed up on the front porch at the Lake Shore Drive mansion with a cheap sawed-off 12 gauge. Jury acquitted him, too. Eh, not saying I *approve*, but I *understand*. So that piece of the pie was inherited by this particular scumbag. He had taken his money, gone to the right schools, then spent a career in the Foreign Service schmoozing with degenerate Europeans and oil-wealthy Arabs. He'd topped out as a deputy Secretary of State a few administrations ago. He was a World Economic Forum attendee, with quotes in *The Economist* and *Foreign Affairs*. He was apparently one of the guys standing three rows back in the group pictures at Davos who does all the real work for the political and economic celebrities up front.

Meanwhile, fixing our compromised communications was at the top of the to-do list. This was not something about which to scream at That Bomber Maker's tech support. For all I knew they were part of the problem.

One of the coders who'd helped build the Blacks for B's Defense division in northern Virginia had bragged a little too much about the accomplishment on LinkedIn, so Morgan reached out and made them an offer. We then had to get on a plane for a rural corner of the southeast North Carolina coast. I'd debated taking a different plane from the usual Lear in case somebody was on our scent, but at that point I decided I'd rather have a loyal pilot and a plane I knew rather than ride with fuck knows who. I trusted Matt. It was Morgan, Angel, myself, and then Ben as a backup shooter. We took my definitely compromised Black, Angel's which was an unknown, and Big John's that had been sitting in a locked safe turned off since he died.

We landed outside Wilmington at Cape Fear Regional and told Matt we'd call for a pickup when we were done. His boss needed him and the plane back for some business of his own. The one time I really wanted the bird to sit and be warmed up ready for me to move, it couldn't be done. It kinda pissed me off. I resolved to argue with Cash again about actually buying one.

It being a long walk from the jetport to where we were going, we rented a Kia SUV in a shade of blue that fit the beach area mood. Passing the weirdly named town of Bolivia that looked like it had been built ten minutes ago for relocated Yankees, we ended up out on the edge of a long stretch of sand and pinewoods just above the South Carolina state line. Our hostess was a chunky Goth chick, maybe mid-thirties. She took my phone first, her purple fingernails clicking on the glass as she banged away on the screen with frightening speed. Administrative menus I had never seen before opened. She *hmmmm*'d and mumbled *That's interesting* a few times. Finally she looked up at me and said, "Look, I'm going to be at this a while. Just leave me the phones and," she pointed at Morgan, "let me keep the one who appears to know what he's doing. No offense, but I don't have the mental bandwidth to tutor basic and diagnose advanced at the same time, so… get lost for a few hours. It's thirty or forty-five minutes back down to Calabash Inlet. Go get some seafood and relax or something so I can work on this without too many questions."

For three days, we waited damn near like mourners outside the Holy Sepulcher. We'd eat, come back, get told to fuck off again, wander off, get a motel room to sleep, wake up, and eat again. We drove the hour up to Fayetteville to see a couple old friends at Fort Bragg and tour the multiple museums. We came back after that long day away and got told to fuck off then too. If Morgan didn't look so intent on the project as well, I'd make jokes about it being a goddamned hostage situation. But the local food was good and we needed an answer. Nothing to do but wait.

Finally, we made the trip back from another lunch in Calabash and knocked at her door. I was still picking bits of shrimp out of my back teeth to be honest. They'd been right off the boat. Her look of haggard exhaustion snapped my line of thought back. She was still sipping coffee and I don't think she'd slept at all as she finally ushered us in. Morgan was out cold on her couch with a cat asleep on top of him. She waved us past him and we went back to her office/ laboratory. Multiple monitors were bolted to walls or arrayed on workbenches. She had most of an electronics shop set up back here. Shit, I wondered what it would cost to hire her under Archive and move all this shit to the Hole.

She looked at me, eyes bloodshot and vacant. "You want the good news or the bad news?"

I shrugged. "Bad news first."

Extending a finger at one of the screens, she issued her verdict. "I think your whole fucking network of these things is compromised. I literally wrote a bunch of this code myself five years ago, at least a lot of the proprietary secure bits that weren't in the off the shelf Android package we licensed from Google, and there is a ton of shit added on later. I'd call it a virus, but that doesn't do it justice. It's more like cancer of the GPS." She sipped more coffee dramatically. She was tougher than I was. If I do three days awake these days, I am not lucid after the first two. I'm not forty anymore.

"Software cancer? Is that a thing?"

"Maybe not, but again, calling it a virus doesn't cover it. There's a major, major software exploit in the location software. It took me two days to find it because it's buried in an encrypted folder that's not even in the same piece of the OS. First, the location mode, which you can turn on and off like any other Android based system, can now be turned on remotely. Second, it can be done without the icon popping up that it's on. So your location function is now on and you don't know it. Third, if you look at that block of code there from the other folder, when that remote control is active, that streams the phone's location to an unknown recipient. Ten digit precision on the military grid reference system. See, using three towers and Angle of Arrival calculations off those, the carrier alone can locate you down to a thousand meters. If somebody is into the carrier at the sys-admin level they can do it too. Then this additional exploit turns on 'locationinfo-r10' whether you want it or not. There are actual GPS chips in these things, and that has you down to-"

I finished for her. "Nearly the meter, yeah." I knew all about MGRS grids and GPS math. I'd been a land nav instructor several times, among a hundred other odd military jobs in the last thirty years.

She nodded. "So somebody who knows what phone they're looking for can remotely ping the SIM card through the domestic cell network, get its location to the nearest tower, then finesse that locator function to get you located exactly enough to eat a Hellfire if they wanted."

Or have weird people representing some 'deep state' clique walking up to me and mine at dinner in public locations where I can be easily cornered but where there's also too many witnesses for me to give in to my rumored propensity for irrational quantities of gratuitous violence. In my defense that reputation is largely bullshit. I try to keep my violence rational.

I sighed. This was not good. This was the Mount McKinley of not good. "What else is wrong with them besides the location software?"

She shrugged. "I have copies of the original operating system software and the updates, at least up until the time my fibro got really bad and I left Big B on disability. The call and text sides of the software look okay, but I'm rushing, so don't bet the farm on that. The exploit only looks like it was for location data. It just wasn't configured to send anything else. That doesn't mean there isn't something else I haven't found yet."

I took a real deep breath and gently asked, "Would more time give you a chance to find more shit wrong on these? You're the best asset we have right now."

She shook her head. "I gotta confess, I'm diagnosed bipolar. Even on my meds, I got kinda manic working on this and now I'm on the downhill slide. Once I get you out the door, I'm going to crash and not really be good for anything for a week, not until I can recover some." I actually felt bad for her. I'd seen some of these same physical and mental issues in other people and I knew the physiological price she'd paid to get us even this much.

She continued unabated. "The crypto keys seem secure, so end to end it's probably okay. Whoever it was probably never got the phone calls or the texts. They just know to look for the phone's network IDs, the MAC addresses and SIM card numbers, the things that make these stand out from normal people's phones. Hell, the government knew all that data about the individual phones when they gave them to you."

That was depressing. *The electronic leash for the dogs of war.*

She misinterpreted my pensive look as criticism and got defensive. "Look, I am not the smartest person in the world on this shit. There's one of me and I had three days. Whoever did the original exploit probably had a team of coders and it probably took months."

I shrugged. "But you're who we could get and you found this when no one else did, or when it was missed the first time. We did check these fucking things when we got them, but we aren't set up to work on these things at the software level."

She threw up her hands in annoyance. "It might not have even been there the first time you went over them. All three phones have the problem, even that one you'd said was turned off for over a year. These things do update. Maybe the whole network is compromised, not just the phones given to you guys."

"Fuck."

Angel was across the room on a burner phone. She called Matt and got him coming back our way to get us. Then while she and Ben worked on trying to get Morgan on his feet and functional, I gave our hostess one of the Archive Associates business cards that did not have my real name on it. I also handed her an envelope with twenty-five grand in it as a tip above and beyond whatever Morgan paid her. She grinned appreciatively at that. It made for goodbye hugs all around and I told her we'd definitely be in touch. This problem was a long way from fixed.

Chapter 32

"But I learned a thing or two from Charlie, doncha know, you better stay away from Copperhead Road..."
~ Steve Earle

It was pretty fucking obvious by now that the firm, well, both halves of it, had enemies out there in the tall grass that we knew nothing about. I figure there were only so many ways they could come at us. Legal, financial, or physical. I mean sure, there was also the possibility of news leaks intended to create public slander and scandal, but we knew too much for that to really work. We could out-leak anyone who wanted to throw us under the bus.

Legal, we were mostly covered for now. If we had fucked up there, we'd be up to our asses in real Feds and wouldn't be getting these lone weirdoes coming at us. Financial? We had money in places they would be hard pressed to get at it. Way more than we once did, too. I did resolve to make up a bunch of bags, as in 'here's six month's pay, in cash, be careful with it' bags in case we had to have some of the non-essential staff scatter in an emergency. We didn't have a lot of non-essential staff though. At wartime footing we'd actually want more people around, not less. The additional duties involved in going to 24-7 operations eats up a lot of people fast. It's called a 'troops to tasks matrix.'

Physically? We could always lock down the mountain. Yeah, some people knew where it was and in an age of satellite recon you could eventually find anything. And how we responded from there depended on who came calling. Local cops? Feds? Somebody's black-clad assassination outfit of generic contractor types? The Army with a heavy combat engineer section? I actually considered that the worst case scenario just on resources. Now I wasn't going to go to war against the actual US Army if I could help it. We'd eventually lose. On the other hand, if some asshole wanted to throw fifty or a hundred Blackwater wannabes with ARs and such at the Hole, well, they would regret that pretty quickly. I supposed it was time to speed up my timetable for making the mountain more defensible.

First priority was the air system. If we couldn't breathe, we couldn't do anything else. It never had been completed to full nuclear war standards, such as those as were in the 1950s. Right now if someone went around the hillside to the air intakes and chucked in enough tear gas grenades, it would pose a problem. I knew a guy who could figure that out for us pretty efficiently and upgrade as needed. Frank was another one of my sci-fi fandom acquaintances. After a hitch in the Marines and a lot of time at Georgia Tech, he'd spent twenty years as a facilities engineer for the Centers for Disease Control laboratory complex outside Atlanta. If he knew how to keep Ebola and the plague in, he could figure out how to keep tear gas or worse out. It was a technical problem that just required throwing a lot of money at it.

Second, we needed food, water, and various other consumable supplies for a siege. That was easily done in an age of Costco and Sam's Club. It was time to accelerate the shopping and then finish refilling the water tanks. At the same time, check the diesel tanks and their fuel supply. Getting those last two generators running would be a good idea too.

Third priority, keeping people the fuck off our lawn. Yes, we had a lot of light armaments. In an effort to make our 400 acres a little more defensible, I wanted bigger stuff. Now legally, I could easily buy a few Civil War style muzzleloading cannon manufactured for the reenactor crowd. Those are every bit as deadly now as when "Double canister at ten yards!" from a couple hundred 12-pounders violently ended any hope of the Confederates breaking the Federal line on Cemetery Ridge. Still, those weren't my first choice. But there is an art to working muzzleloading cannon well and I was rusty at it. The rate of fire is slow and if you have to fight in the rain it becomes a real problem. Get into anything newer than that, you then run into legal hassles. I hate legal hassles.

Fortunately, there were solutions to that as well. Owing to our curious not-government, not-civilian, not-criminal status, sometimes we could arrange random hookups and loot drops out of Uncle Sam's closets. It wasn't always easy and we got told no a lot, but sometimes things were either available for purchase or just fell off trucks. Usually we used those chances on communications equipment and crypto software. I didn't waste the effort on night vision or other things that could be obtained just as easily direct from the manufacturers for enough cash. This time it was going to be guns. Big ones. We had the money, especially now, so I wanted to be ready just in case. Alien invasions, angry cartel gangs, Dallas Part 2, whatever. I wanted mortars, recoilless rifles, or maybe a couple small howitzers.

Really, I wanted the sort of hookup that Bam Bam's fairy godfathers had, the strings that got pulled to stock that mysterious safehouse mansion of theirs outside Dallas with top-line SOCOM issue stuff, but I didn't have that kind of clout. I had the money, especially now, but still not the right connections. Meanwhile the enemies circling us weren't going to wait for me to learn the secret handshakes for *H und K* or Fabrique Nationale in South Carolina to send me an eighteen wheeler of the good-good shit. So I turned to the black, or at least the gray, market and called a guy.

I was pretty sure Izzy had gotten his nickname for his resemblance to the original rhythm guitar player for Guns n' Roses. Tall, skinny, and cadaver pale. He had stringy black hair under a newsboy hat, almost always wore sunglasses even at two in the morning, and usually looked high as fuck. But Izzy had been the courier who delivered our dozen Black phones when we went to secure commo a few years ago. That almost counted as a strike against him now, the way people had been abusing them. A year later, I'd passed him in a hallway at Langley when following Big John into a meeting. He was so cleaned up that I almost didn't recognize him when he waved at me. Another friend of mine working freelance had run into him in the Kurdish sector of Syria six months after that. But whoever Izzy really was, he was apparently the guy with the hookup for stuff coming out the back door of the CIA's clandestine weapons warehouses. I had some guesses where those were, but it wasn't really my immediate concern. Now when you called him on his scrambled line, it was flea market rules. You got what he had more than what you necessarily really wanted. Izzy mainly sold off whatever unwanted trash the Agency was trying to get rid of at any given moment.

Let me explain. Factory fresh 'Made In The USA' stuff, or at least decent surplus, goes out as overt military aid or foreign sales through offices at the Pentagon, everything from bandages to jet bombers. Then the CIA does covert military aid, passing out non-American stuff or old American stuff that has changed hands enough times it has plausible deniability. In the Eighties, they went to the Israelis and bought Russian AK-47s captured in the '67 or '73 wars, then donated them to the Afghanis fighting the Russians. They then bought Israeli Galil rifles and donated them to places in Latin America where a Democrat-controlled Congress wouldn't let us donate our M-16s because of 'human rights violations' against the Communist guerillas the Soviets were supplying. Well, there were also lots of genuine atrocities too, but I digress. Shit like that.

But then there were all the pallets of shit in the middle. Some of it was things too traceable to give away, like gear that still screamed 'Property of US Government.' Then there were numerous batches of nearly useless old shit. Sometimes he had the guns but the ammo hadn't been made in forty years, or sometimes the ammo was here but the guns were still in a warehouse in the southern Sudan or some fucking place. And *that* was the stuff he would try dumping anywhere he could find some fool with more money than sense. It was a game to him. He'd sell ammo without guns to outlaw bikers, but the guns without ammo to the Mexican gangs. He'd bankrupted a Nazi militia in Colorado by selling them five hundred worn-out spare barrels for a Czech light machine gun that hadn't been used since the Korean War, but never followed through with the guns themselves.

Yeah, there was a slight chance Izzy would burn us, but I doubted it. He was too deep into dark shit to flip over and show his face in a courtroom narc'ing on us for criminal charges in the States. And on certain nights if the moon was right, he might even have something I could use.

Using my desk phone, not the Black, I hit his speed dial button and the tone sounded, telling me the scrambler was good. It only rang twice before he answered. "Yo."

"IIey, Izzy. It's Prof."

"'Sup, man?"

"Looking for some stuff."

"You' always lookin' for stuff. You' gon' make a great episode of *Hoarders* someday." He sounded higher than usual. I could never figure out if it was an act or not. I'd hate to think the Agency was letting a guy with a fresh arm full of heroin run their illegal arms sales. That would just be shocking and beyond the pale. Please excuse my sarcasm.

I found myself quickly mimicking his street slang accent. "Well, you' in the business of selling stuff, you don' want me wasting yo' time, right?"

"Yeah, man, so whachu' need?" Sometimes he sounded more like Eazy-E than Izzy Stradlin.

"Couple of good mortars with ammo, then some RPGs or recoilless rifles. And three dozen or so cases of 7.62mm NATO link for the MGs I've already got."

"The MG ammo is easy. But shit, everyone wants RPGs man, here and overseas, and we ain't got none to sell you. We're having to buy new off the Eastern European factories just to get them where we need them in time. Ukraine soaked up more than even they made. Recoilless rifles, yeah, might not be new, but those, nobody want' those. You want big mortars or little ones?"

"Would prefer US 81 millimeter or a clone of, but I'll take what I can get in that size class. At least two, preferably four. 60mm if I have to, but not 120s or 160s, that's uselessly big."

"Shit, yeah, will do some looking. What's your budget for all this?"

"Quarter mil or so. Half at most. And don't take that as a license to fuck me. Will take the rest of the tab in ammo. I always need ammo."

"Fuckin' big spender. You never used to have good money back when Big John was sitting on you. You runnin' drugs or pimpin' hoes these days?"

"Just in the bizness of doin' bizness." I'd picked up that expression a long time ago.

"Yeah, yeah, so you say."

"Nah, f'real, I won real big in Vegas bettin' on the Kentucky Derby." Why let the truth get in the way of a good story?

"That was..." I could almost hear him count on his fingers. "Six months ago?"

"I didn't need the mortars six months ago."

"Like hell. What you need 'em for now then, *Professor???*"

"Real estate dispute with the neighbors and I'm looking to settle *way* out of court, y'dig?"

He laughed. "Man, you are full of shit. Anyway, I got a truck coming along I-40 in a week or two, I can throw some extra shit on there for you, say I get you a half mil worth and I take good care of you. Cash money deal, no checks, no plastic. Gold coins, maybe." I suppressed a chuckle. Ought to give him ten kilos of gold bars to fuck with.

"What else you need?"

"Depends what you send me for recoilless rifles, I guess."

"Gotta make some calls, check the warehouse."

"What else you got?"

"Man, you know it varies."

"Fuck it, you know what I'm into and you know what my budget is. Surprise me a little."

"My man. Text ya when the meet will be."

Chapter 33

"You got to carry weapons 'cause you always carry cash.
There's lots of shady characters and lots of dirty deals..."
~ Glenn Frey, "Smuggler's Blues"

Nashville, once again being an Interstate hub where three of them intersect and having a very large rail yard besides, has a variety of trucking facilities, warehouses, and so forth. Some of those warehouses can be rented for rather short periods of time, a place for an eighteen-wheeler load coming from Somewhere to be broken down then reorganized into other loads going Somewhere Else. Izzy had rented one of these for the night. This was a little too much hardware to pass around in a grocery store parking lot like it was stuff your mom bought on Craigslist.

I had half a dozen guys I'd hired from the guard shack roster with promises of overtime money to do the toting and fetching, divided between a rented van to move the people and a 26' box truck we'd rented to move the stuff. We came light; jeans, T-shirts, safety-toed work boots in case of accidents with heavy crates, and concealed handguns.

Compared to my usual pre-mission jitters, the actual meetup was smooth and casual. Both of our crews got to the warehouse before the truck actually showed. As usual, Izzy had a motley crew of thugs to drag pallets and lift crates for him. I was certain there were a few concealed pistols on their side too. Plenty of conspicuous jailhouse tats and meth teeth, but I didn't see any overt weapons. But Izzy's guys also brought a large cooler of beer to keep everyone happy and hydrated. His guys did what they had to do with no real issues, so did mine. After about the first half hour, I wasn't too terribly worried.

That isn't to say we came unprepared for worse. I liked Izzy as much as I like most people, wait, stop laughing, dammit! Still, I sure as shit didn't trust him. That's why I had

Jimmy, Tommy, Ben and a couple other guys sitting in a second van a block away from the warehouse, dressed to impress and with a fat load of firepower as if it were a bad night in Baghdad at the height of the war. Their orders were simple. If Izzy fucked us over, in the attempted robbery or murder sense, their orders were to move in fast then kill Izzy and everyone he had brought with him. Pretty simple.

Izzy himself was in a good mood. He really did seem to love his work and I did have to respect that. "Got your mortars. Four Korean copies of our old M29 eighty-one mil, the late models with the hard-chrome bores. They still made them into the 1990s and these are nearly new. You mostly got ammo compatibility forward and backward, manuals are in the box. A pretty good stack of ammo, both Korean, ours and British. HE, willie pete, a few regular illlum, and a bunch of the British version of our IR illum rounds. I know you got night vision capability."

Translating that into English, we had conventional high explosive rounds, white phosphorus that made thick white smoke and also lit things on fire, some "star shell" parachute flares to light up the night, and a specialized parachute flare whose chemical flame only provided illumination in the infrared spectrum so it aided night vision equipment, not the naked eye. That was a lovely innovation made a few years before I left the Army. I nodded at Freddie and he moved over to check them. Among other things, he'd been a heavy weapons instructor for Special Forces candidates, so he knew way more about mortars than I did. I'd been a Bravo, not a Chuck. "Just what the doctor ordered. What else you got?"

"Couldn't do you much on RPGs, like I said, same with much else in that class. Demand outweighs supply. Since you were okay with recoilless rifles, I got you four old Chinese 82mm ones, their lightweight paratrooper model. We found a bunch of 'em in Africa, still packed for shipping, but there wasn't any ammo. That's really hard to come by since even the Chinese haven't made it in most of forty years. Found some ammo that's at least compatible out of a depot in Bulgaria, but there's only three dozen rounds per gun. About half and half fragmentation rounds and antitank. Old Soviet stuff. It's older than we are, and I am still surprised it didn't end up in the Ukraine wars. Shit's been sealed and it should all be okay. We tested some of the batch out west before we logged it into stock, but it's definitely not fresh."

"Well, that could get interesting." I was fairly certain he wouldn't intentionally sell me anything that he knew would blow me up instead of the target. That would cut into his repeat business. Izzy always liked my money and that was the major reason why I sort of trusted him not to fuck me over. Still, there's a sliding scale between how big the ammo is and how long it can be stored. Over the years I'd fired .45 ammo packed for WWII (Remington, 1942) and .30-'06 literally left over from the first one (Frankford Arsenal, 1918), but some stuff that's more chemically and mechanically complicated doesn't do as well on the shelf.

"The big 106mm ones, either the old American ones or the Taiwanese copies, I can get you those if these aren't enough, but I'd have to bring them from offshore special since nobody here wants them. I think I have some left in a warehouse in Kuwait that I picked up in a trade with the Israelis."

"Nah, these should do." Realistically I just needed a couple dozen rounds to break the back of anyone who got too close after the mortars. If anyone ever showed up. This could be just a waste of money and effort on my part. "And the MG ammo?"

"Austrian surplus; Hirtenberger made, NATO standard linked. Easy to do. Now I cut you some slack on the Chinese 82s, so for the MGs, I brought you sixty crates of 800 rounds each." Huh. That was nice of him. "Then there were these motherfuckers. You wanted weird." He pointed at a pile of five or six green plastic Hardigg cases, what Uncle Sam bought for shipping delicate and expensive stuff. "Came back off a plane from a FOB, uh, somewhere sandy and it shouldn't have. Was on the wrong pallet and it was supposed to stay there. Probably still on the Rangers' unit property book and they may be looking for them, y'know?"

"And because it screams Property of Uncle Sam, you can't get rid of it easy."

"Yeah, not e'rrybody got your taste or your Get Out Of Jail Free cards, man."

Shit. I didn't know if I had my kind out Get Out Of Jail Free cards. We were just good at staying off the radar and not getting caught. I figured if I ever had to actually use this shit, regular cops or the ATF were the least of my problems. I sighed. "What's in the boxes, Izzy?"

"Two Barrett fifty cals if I remember right, and I brought you two crates of Swedish Mk211 too."

Okay, he had me with the Mk211 ammo. A wonder-bang product from those allegedly peace-loving social democrats in Norway, it was tungsten-cored armor piercing ammo that both caught fire and exploded. It was a more modern and much cooler version of our classic AP-Incendiary load from WWII that I also had, um, *some* of. Uncle Sam's cost was reportedly over thirty bucks a shot just because it was so damn hard to make. Two cans to the crate; 480 rounds total. But as for the other cases? Izzy was either high again or trying to pull a fast one on me. That bottom one was NOT a Barrett shipping case. I knew what those looked like. It looked familiar, but I hadn't messed with official weapons shipments and unit load-outs in depth for most of two decades. "Shall we bust it open and look?"

Izzy shrugged. "Okay, oh, but before I forget again, I got you a present. This one's on me." Reaching on top of the machine gun ammo crates, he handed me a faded green canvas case with a familiar outline. I unzipped it and out came a Model 1928A1 Thompson. A '41 Auto Ordnance, with badly worn finish but all the original United States Property and Army ordnance inspection stamps still intact.

Damn. Still, worth at least thirty grand with the right ATF registration paperwork and nearly worthless without it unless you were like me and in a position not to give a shit. I love Thompsons.

I admit, it emotionally got me. "Izzy, I am touched. I really am. Where did you find it?"

"Eh, there was half a crate of 'em in the back of a Company warehouse way down south. Probably been there since the Bay of Pigs for all I fuckin' know. But I know you like old guns and military history, so I was gonna send you one for Christmas. But last Christmas I kinda forgot, so was going to do it this year instead. But this way you get it early."

"Thank you very much. It really is appreciated."

He nodded. Meanwhile my guys were cramming everything off Izzy's truck into our truck. Those Hardigg cases I wanted to look in were half-buried in machine gun ammo crates already. Fuck it. I'd look later. I'd mostly gotten what I wanted out of this deal and the Thompson was better than buying me dinner or sending flowers if Izzy did subtly fuck me anyway.

It wasn't even midnight yet. Time to get everyone and everything back to the Hole. We'd just leave the truck in the bay until tomorrow, then pick up Angel and head home.

Chapter 34

"Then, with victory within ten paces of his muzzle, the silly savage jerked his trigger instead of squeezing it..."
~ *Apocryphal account describing an attempted assassination in colonial Africa*

For us, the next day was mostly spent getting the weapons and ammunition out of the box truck and dispersed. Anything more explosive than machine gun ammo went out to the root cellar. I put Freddie to work planning his picking and drilling of mortar crews, then figuring out how to teach the Chinese recoilless rifles without expending all the scarce ammo in training. Fortunately a couple of the guard shack kids had been 11C school-trained mortarmen and they were now going to be the mortar section leaders.

I then turned my attention to those mysterious green cases Izzy had dumped on me. Yes, the first two boxes were what he claimed they were. I now had two Barrett M107 .50 caliber sniper rifles with their expensive Leopold scopes and four cans of the good Grade A Mk211 ammo. It was loose-packed; the Grade B went in machine gun links, mostly for the Navy. For them it was a small boat killer. Yeah, I was pretty sure the Rangers were annoyed those were missing. It's okay. Ronnie Barrett would happily make them some more. I sure as hell wasn't going to give them back.

I did task Morgan to completely sterilizing the serial numbers off them with an electric drill, just as we had with the old M16A1s we'd refitted into the raid team carbines. Surface grinding won't do the job; there are various chemical and imagery tricks to bring up damaged serial numbers from the metal beneath since stamping leaves traces you can't see. You have to cut a slot all the way through to remove all traces, then patch it with delicate welding. The scopes were numbered too, which would also take some detail work to remove when one of us had the time.

The next case was some sort of big radio I didn't recognize. The one after that was a different big radio I didn't recognize. That one had a collapsible satellite dish; interesting but not my problem. I told Angel to have Petey send a couple guys up for them. If he couldn't figure them out or if we just didn't want them, I'd just do the Rangers a favor. I figured I'd drag them out to the woods near the McKenna MOUT site on the back side of Fort Benning, then call the 75th's staff duty desk from a burner phone. Let them deal with them; we collected too much odd, weird shit as it was. Izzy was right, I tended to hoard interesting things in my mountain fortress like a dragon. Then since we would be going all that way anyway, the girls and I could make a weekend of it and enjoy Atlanta on the way back home after I dragged them through the new Infantry and Armor Museums on Benning and the Civil War Naval Museum downtown on the river.

As we headed out, I noticed the last and largest of the green crates was ratchet-strapped down in the bed of my truck. I hadn't put it there. When in doubt, ask Angel.

"Morgan said it was trash, but you'd want to reuse the crate."

Oh. Whatever. The Hardigg cases were very nice and worth a couple hundred dollars empty, so I'd just chuck it in the barn out back of the house until I had an immediate need to repurpose it. I didn't care. I certainly had the space next to the old Hummvees and my tractor.

Cash picked that moment to join us. "I'm declaring a cheat night on diet mode, so it's dinner out and I'm buying, sir."

"Glad to have you out of your cave and joining us. Nashville?"

The girls nodded. "Nashville." They then looked at each other. "Italian?" They both nodded.

Most of an hour later, we pulled off Charlotte Pike, parking between the restaurant and the former Golden Dome arcade that was now a bank branch. I looked at the crate. Nobody was going to reasonably mess with four heavy ratchet straps to get into it, not in the middle of a public parking lot. Thinking nothing else of it, we went into dinner. Forty-five minutes later, we wandered back out into twilight, with to-go bags from the market side and on the verge of carbohydrate comas.

And that was when some asshole decided to shoot at us from the parking lot across the street to the east. My ears automatically reported *Five five six; semiauto.* The first two rounds blew nice holes in the passenger side of my windshield. Fortunately there was a nice chunky SUV between us and them so we had some immediate cover. I finished shoving the girls into the cab of the truck, then a familiar breeze blew past my ear and my left arm took what felt like, by way of comparison, a fair stinging whack from a kendo stick across the bicep and shoulder. Shit.

I'd worn Mikey's old Swenson Colt since it was Friday and I was in the mood. Sure as shit, the one day I dress with a stylish gun rather than a work piece. I drew it anyway and emptied nine Winchester Ranger SXTs in his direction, at least driving him back down into cover. Three more rounds cracked into my truck, punching sheet metal but missing me.

Motherfucker. My shirt sleeve was cut, but the gouge in my arm hadn't even started to bleed. I was *pissed.* I had made it most of fifty fucking years untouched by bullets. I had been punched, kicked, choked out, clubbed, burned, stabbed, slashed and even blown out of a moving truck by an IED once in that Dallas fuckup, but never shot And this piece of shit, whoever he or she was, had just fucked up my perfect goddamn record. Oh, now I was insanely pissed off. I didn't want this asshole dead, I wanted them to suffer. They could die later. A good bit later.

Never use a small caliber weapon when a larger one is immediately available. I threw my empty .45 onto the passenger seat, telling Cash to reload it from the spares in the center console. There were another half-dozen eight round Wilson magazines in there. I then popped open the nylon rifle case on the back seat floor, sliding my favorite old recce-style AR carbine out. I knew I had a round in the chamber, the 40-round PMag in it and a few more 30s in the case. If I couldn't settle it with that, it wouldn't be settled today. Eventually the cops were gonna show up and interrupt this shit whether this fuckhead and I were done with each other or not. Better to get it done then.

I dropped down into a good prone firing position, scanning underneath the cars. I didn't have the bipod on the gun, but was using the modified floorplate of the extra-long Magpul magazine. Forget what your drill sergeant told you thirty years ago; that does not induce malfunctions with quality equipment. Always get steadier if you can.

I banged the zoom lever on the scope to around 6x with the heel of my hand and focused. My arm hurt, but it was a "fell off the swingset on the playground" kinda hurt. Yeah, some of that was adrenaline, but I could ignore it. I scanned and took a second to get my breathing right. The shooter was still hiding behind what looked like a blue Honda, but... there he was, hunkered down and doing a bad job of it. A nice piece of leg was exposed right... there. Just because you are hiding your head and upper body doesn't mean you can't get something else blown off. I zoomed all the way to 10x. Less than a hundred meters and I was zeroed at 100. Holding about an inch low for the shorter range, I took a couple deep breaths, then on the pause squeezed the match-grade trigger. *Aim small, miss small.* It was a clean shot, putting 70 grains of Barnes hunting bullet through his right ankle. There was an audible clatter as his rifle hit blacktop and his screaming was, wow.

I couldn't resist. "That really sounds like it hurts, man. Sorry! Well, not sorry!"

Naturally he didn't take this with charm or grace. "Fuck you, man!"

I couldn't fault him for being pissed at me, but I was willing to let him hop out of here on his one good foot. "Yeah, well, you might just wanna get a TQ on that ankle first before you bleed to death."

"Then I am gonna kill you then fuck your women. Both of them! You hear me? Both!" Yeah, he was too mad to leave. *Guess I had to finish this then.*

He had rolled to my left, onto his back. Couldn't quite get the head, but I was busy lining up the shot to put one through his now-exposed left shoulder when he mouthed off. *Oh, no you just didn't.*

I didn't want to hit the tire he was behind. That would lower the car, make a smaller gap to shoot him through, and make my life generally more difficult. I scooted a little to my left, trying to get a shot through the shoulder and collarbone down into the heart and lungs to end this shit, but couldn't get a fatal angle. Fuck it, shoot what you got. I then squeezed the trigger again. More screaming. "Dude, I highly, *highly* recommend leaving them out of it!"

Too late. They'd heard. I could hear Angel and Cash diving back out of the truck, then past me up into the back before rummaging in that last packing case. They were pissed and I could hear *Ratchet-ass shit-talking little fuckboy, who the fuck he think he talkin' to, got something for his bitch ass...gonna wish he was never born...Where are the earplugs...*at a nearly normal volume with the electronic muffs on. But I expected to hear the familiar *cha-chak!* sound of an AR charging handle. Both girls knew how to use those. There was one more in the truck, plus they had their usual pistols. Instead, I heard a hollow *thooonk* like tapping on a drain pipe and then a metallic *clack* like your front door's deadbolt. It sounded familiar but I couldn't place it...*come on, name that tune...oh, fuck.* "Girls? Girls! GIRLS!!!!!"

Angel stepped around the rear driver's side corner of my truck with a long green tube over her right shoulder, squinting through the smaller black tube of its optical sight.

She was screeching in a truly accelerated level of pissed the fuck off. "FUCK ME? FUCK US? NO, FUCK *YOU*! BEND OVER, ASSHOLE! HERE IT COMES!"

Over the years I have been repeatedly commended on my composure under fire. I have been shot at a good bit through three decades in the trade, admittedly most of it was unevenly distributed into the particularly eventful 2003 and 2006. I don't get stressed. I don't panic. I very rarely get mad. See, I just have an ability to convince myself it's just like training, nothing worth getting upset over, it's cool. Everything's cool. Nothing unexpected, do the job. This exceeded that. Even more than the fact I'd finally gotten sort of shot for the first time, the sight of my girlfriend with a loaded Goose over her shoulder punctured my usual bubble of carefully calculated denial. My inner monologue derailed.

Oh, so that's what was in that packing case.

Oh, shit. This was really happening.

Mommy!!!!!

I looked behind her and out of habit yelled, "BACKBLAST AREA CLEAR!!!!"

Mostly clear.

Sorta clear. That wall was too damn close.

Shit.

She was then tracking left to flank the next car over and get a better shot when...*Boom. All of the fucking boom.* We were all way too close when she jerked the trigger. It was like getting every inch of me getting 'tapped' by a baseball bat at once.

Okay, the Swedish-made (yeah, peace-loving Scandinavian social democrat weapon-mongers again) 84mm Carl Gustav (aka the Goose, the Charlie G, etc) M3 man-portable recoilless rifle was ridiculous overkill for this particular situation. I don't give a rusted fuck what Harold wrote in *Schlock Mercenary;* yes, there is such a thing as overkill. This was just...oh, God it hurt.

See, recoilless rifles aren't really recoilless, they just vent and redirect the energy of the shot, mostly to the rear in a spreading angle like a boat wake. Physics says it has to go somewhere. The backblast area was supposed to be clear for a hundred feet (varying degrees of really hazardous) and preferably most of a football field (varying degrees of merely unpleasant) depending how closely you hewed to Army range safety regulations. That concrete wall ten yards behind her to the left had reflected some of the concussion. Remember that sound waves are literally compressed air and those bounce, this time back into us. Around us, several cars had their alarms wailing and horns honking. Others just had cracked windows from the overpressure. Explosive concussion is a bitch.

Running, well, more like stumbling, over to look at her target, he was just sort of a weird red smear of uncooked hamburger with a few severed bits for garnish. Like an intact hand and forearm. Half a head. One leg. Well, so much for interrogation and intelligence value. I looked at his rifle, but it was some fairly generic AR and it was in several pieces. Not worth grabbing.

Angel looked disappointed, too jacked on adrenaline and aggression to feel the concussion too much. "WHERE WAS THE BOOM! THERE WAS SUPPOSED TO BE AN EARTH-SHATTERING KA-BOOM!!!"

"THAT WASN'T ENOUGH FOR YOU?!" I was yelling a bit. Even with Peltors on, I was slightly deafened. For big stuff like .50 cals or the Goose, a good technique is to wear earplugs under your electronic muffs to give your ears the extra layer of protection. That way your ears don't randomly screech with tinnitus when you're my age.

"THE CAR IS STILL THERE!" I love that girl, but she watches too many war movies. Explosions don't work like that in the real world.

I sighed. Fuck, it even felt like my eyeballs were bruised. "Sweetheart, you fired a flechette round at him. It's like a really big shotgun full of nails. It won't do shit to a car." And it hadn't. Several dozen flechettes were stuck in the car's sheet metal like darts in a cork board. Good luck writing that shit up for the insurance company, whoever you were.

"Oh."

"And if you had used high explosive, we were close enough it wouldn't have done us any favors either. There is a minimum safe range for HE."

"Oh."

I wasn't out of questions and comments yet. "And *where the fuck* did you even learn how to use that damn thing?"

"YouTube; the 82nd Airborne had a range video. We just looked it up while you were busy talking shit and wasting time. Cash even got your brass. Now come on, baby, we're in a fucking hurry."

Yeah, eventually witnesses are gonna stand up and the cops are going to show. We live in an age where shit gets uploaded fast; we were gonna be on WorldStarHipHop and 4chan in about twenty minutes.

Thankfully it takes a lot to fuck up a Chevy. I wasn't worried about escaping. But first, I grabbed the hand then threw it in a couple plastic grocery bags from the never-ending pile of trash behind my driver's seat. Even in death, he could still give up fingerprints. Angel didn't even flinch. Cash, still the cultured Ivy League girl somewhere inside, faintly curled her lip as if to say *That's just disgusting, sir.* I had some cracked glass and bullet holes, but the truck cranked on the first try and we hauled ass out of that parking lot. We passed a cop going the other way with his lights on, but he was still heading for the scene of the incident and didn't know he was looking for us yet. Emphasis on *yet.* We needed to get the truck the hell out of sight and submerge for a while.

As we skidded out, Angel looked a bit pensive. "You know, you should have gotten the head for the dental records."

I sighed. "One, half of it was gone. Two, way messier. Three, we don't have a forensic dental pathologist or access to the right records. Fingerprints will do."

"Can the cops ID him off the head? And thereby ID us?"

"They'll probably just fingerprint his other hand when they find it, well, if they find it. I'm way more worried about being on fifty cell phone videos. We're gonna be the lead story on the ten o'clock news."

In case I need to spell this out by this point in the story, Angel's name isn't Angel and her "real" name isn't even her real name. What's on her birth certificate is several Chinese elements long. You couldn't track her to my house, her parents' house, or the Hole by it. Her driver's license was three addresses old. And you already know Cash's license was a government-crafted fake. Sadly, I was the only one whose real name and actual address was on the driver's license on me. How depressingly normal of me. I resolved to do something about that in the future. It was a weakness.

Now my truck hadn't been in my name in a few years. It was registered as a company vehicle for Archival Associates. As I have mentioned before, the paper trail for AA dies in a rented post office box. Merely seeing the plate in surveillance footage, assuming there was any, and running it through the Tennessee motor vehicle records wasn't going to get them an address to which they could quickly chase me. But I sure as shit wasn't going to run straight for home or the office either. Where to go hide for a few minutes as the last light of the setting sun faded...

Anyone who's been doing this shit for a while has mentally rehearsed some, "do I run this way or this way, this way or this way" routes away from home territory, or from one spot in the territory to another spot. With the Interstates I have mentioned before, Nashville has such heavy traffic most hours of the day and night that you can be gone with the crowd in seconds and because it's Tennessee, you can be out into the countryside away from red lights and traffic cameras rather fast. So I got on I-65 South, with the intent of then looping back east and then north on the older surface roads paralleling the 840 bypass, passing by Castle Gwyn and the Tennessee Renaissance Festival site. Eventually I planned to get up into Hendersonville northeast of downtown, then sort of bend back toward home. It helped that we were running along with the evening rush hour in a very commonplace model of truck.

I looked down at my arm. It was cut and oozing bloody stuff like a badly skinned knee. Iit still hurt, more so now that I didn't have a gunfight to distract me, but it was functional. I had a couple medical bags in the truck just for road accidents, so when we pulled off, I'd bandage up.

Uh, wait a second. There was another hole in my shoulder that looked like a large blackhead. Well, that was at least a bullet fragment.

And why the fuck was there blood on my leg?

This wasn't good.

Angel reached into the lower center console compartment and pulled out a portable police scanner, loaded with the radio frequencies and in some cases scrambler codes, for the local departments. If they came up with a description for us, let alone names, I wanted the warning that we were being hunted. Cash was working her burner phone, reporting to the office what had happened and telling them to up security across the board.

I was very carefully not mentioning the inconvenient fact I was bleeding in several places.

"Cash, you doing okay back there, sweetheart?"

"Can I shoot that thing next time?" *I'll take that as a yes.*

I smiled. "Sure, dear. I will try to find us some more ammunition for it."

Angel looked over at me and back at her. "She and I shot 'rock, scissors, paper' to see who got to do it. I won."

Cash sort of giggled. "It's okay, slut, I will just think of something really awful to do to you when we get home and can finally relax."

"Don't threaten me with a good time, bitch!" Angel shot back.

Sigh. "Girls, going home might not be a great idea right now. We're going there long enough to grab Odin and the cats, set the good alarms and then Angel, you're moving into the Hole with Cash for a while. Whoever took a whack at us is going to try again and they are definitely going to know where we live."

Cash instantly threw a flag on the play. "No way, sir. If she's getting locked down for safekeeping, you're coming too."

Angel nodded. "We better bring anything else we need for a month."

Shit, better just move the gun safes and anything else I was attached to. One of the back bedrooms had forty thousand dollars worth of vintage *GI Joe* stuff in it and I wouldn't want to guess what some of the antique books or original WWII uniforms would take to replace if I even could.

"Okay, so we go to the office, get some heavier weapons, some more help, THEN go get our stuff."

Cash nodded. "I want a Thompson. They're sexy."

Sigh. "They're also heavy as shit and take some practice to shoot well. How about a nice full-trick AR? You know how to run one of those."

I watched her nod in the rear view mirror. "Also acceptable."

"Also, neither of you are going to the house."

They both stared at me, daggers in their expression.

"We're just going out and stripping the house, which is a known target. I can do that with the security guys and some other gunmen. You two need to get down under hard cover in Cash's room and stay there for a while."

Cash grinned mischievously. "Sir, wait a moment. I have the only bedroom in the Hole. If Angel is in with me, where are you going to stay?"

I merely looked at her in the rear view mirror.

Her smile remained impish. "I am deliberately acting up to entertain you, sir. You know I'd never genuinely misbehave."

"I know, love. You're one of the two best girls on the planet." Something else occurred to me. "Now I do have to ask. Why the fuck was there an 84mm recoilless rifle in the back of my truck?"

Angel and Cash both did their best to look innocent. It wasn't working. Finally Angel giggled. "Well, we'd looked in those crates before you did and saw the Goose. It was too cool to give it back to the Army, so we thought we'd get it home, hide it in the barn, and then gift-wrap it for you for Christmas since it's not like you can exactly buy them over the counter."

That answer somehow managed to be the most Angel thing I could think of. Since we now had a happy and calm moment, unfortunately I had to ruin it. "Uh, Angel, I'm gonna need you to drive in a minute. We gotta stop in a couple minutes and I gotta bandage a couple of these holes."

***

It was most of five hours to circumnavigate Nashville counter-clockwise, using side roads and making plenty of halts. Angel drove the first two hours while she insisted I rest for a little bit. I'd been hit at least three times, so I agreed. Meanwhile, Cash actually fell asleep in the back. Finally, in the gray predawn, we rolled down the rural side road and pulled up to the gate. I stuck my ID in the box and beeped my PIN code. I don't think I had ever been so happy to be heading down that driveway. But coming around the last corner into the parking lot, all of a sudden my dashboard lit up with warning lights. My oil pressure dropped to zero, the temperature gauge went from its normal 210 degrees to hitting the peg, and a combo plate of *stuff* started coming out from under the hood. White smoke, black smoke, hissing steam... then there was a final screech of tortured metal and the truck ground to a halt as the engine blew out and locked up. I did my best to get it on the side of the entrance road as not to block everyone else from getting in or out.

Shit.

Angel and I got out. I was moving much slower than usual. Getting shot a little does that to you at my age, I guess. I clicked a flashlight on and looked at the resulting mess. At least it wasn't leaking fuel. Well, yet.

Angel looked at the truck and shrugged. "It can be rebuilt, sir."

Cash yawned, stretched, and joined us. I gave her a quick hug. "Hey, sleepyhead."

She looked a bit mortified. "I'm sorry. I suppose nervous energy got the best of me."

Angel held her close. "It's okay. You didn't miss anything as we were sneaking around."

Cash looked at the truck. "Oh...shit." That was low-key hilarious. Unless she was in one of her moods, she almost never actually used cuss words outside the bedroom. "Realizing I know almost nothing about actually doing auto mechanics, that looks expensive."

I shrugged. "It will take a while and you're right, take a fair bit of money. Fortunately I can afford it. Still, except for that eleven-fourteen Hummvee in the barn, I don't own anything else to so much as drive to work in the morning."

Angel laid a reassuring hand on me. "Don't worry. We'll get something else, but I'll have this hauled off and make sure it gets fixed."

"I don't have time, Steve doesn't have time, and I don't want to tie up garage bay space here with it while we're still on a wartime footing. I'll just buy another one for now. Fuck it, it's only money. Meanwhile this is a new engine at least."

"True, sir, but I have a lot of good memories of this truck. Maybe your friends in Alabama would like the job." As usual, she had a point. Through one of my college buddies and various convention acquaintances like the Tennessee Valley Interplanetary Society, I knew a lot of gearheads back in the woods down around Huntsville. NASA brats out of Marshall Space Flight Center, part-time rocket scientists, and assorted general rednecks. Guys and girls with home machine shops and free time who'd love a paying rebuild project and who would also keep their mouths shut.

"Not a bad idea. Well done."

"That's one of the dozens of reasons you need me, sir."

I nodded, because she was right. As calmly as I could manage, and kinda limping, I pulled my rifle case out from behind the seat, grabbed the plastic wrapped hand, and kicked the driver's door shut. Angel was looking at the Goose in its case, but it was a couple football fields up to the door. I'd send a couple of Jake's guys down with one of the big four-wheelers to tow the truck up to the garage door and we'd finish cleaning it out there.

Chapter 35

As of this moment, we are at war…"
~Commander William Adama, the Colonial Fleet

My first stop was going to be Intel because of what was going on. I also needed to apprise the old men on the Board what was going on. There was no reason to believe whoever was behind all this wouldn't take a shot at them either. Except for Eric, they weren't the sort to want any part of this shit. Eric, on the other hand, would be home choosing which dozen guns to have ready and then be sitting up all night wishing a motherfucker would.

***

After getting the bandage on my arm changed, and my leg looked at, I'd left the girls downstairs and made a run back to my house to secure the animals. We took the Yukon with the Whitestone in it because nothing else with enough space was handy at that hour of the morning. No, I didn't go it alone, and not just because of my wounds. Fortunately it was only four cats and a dog, down from an all-time high of... uh, a lot more than that. I looked around, mentally categorizing stripping the place, and sighed at the amount of work involved. I am not a minimalist person. Marie Kondo would walk into my house and probably ritually kill herself out on the porch rather than try to de-clutter it.

I rejoined the girls in time to get a fitful morning's sleep. The cats didn't care, Rock being too lazy to care about four more interlopers, but Odin was quite confused by the change in environment. I'm sure it smelled like another planet to him, but once Angel and Cash calmed him down with ear scritches and tummy rubs, he eventually curled up at the foot of the bed and began to snore. That calmed me down too.

I was up again before they were. I didn't really dress for work so much as throw on some old Army physical training shorts, a gray T-shirt that said STARFLEET ACADEMY ALUMNI ASSOCIATION, and a spare pair of flip-flops. I figured I'd let the girls sleep as I grabbed my first Dew of the day and pondered my various to-do items.

With my wheels obviously being known and also out of action, I needed another truck. Another Silverado would be okay, they were nearly ubiquitous here, but a different color would be a good idea. I liked the dark green ones, but naturally Chevy hadn't made those in a decade. I logged onto the outside Internet connection and in about two minutes of dealing with a large used car dealer's blue and yellow web site, I had the one I wanted. This one was a metallic dark red and a year old with just under ten thousand miles. It was even at one of the local locations, no need to ship it in. Cool. I still didn't have time to go deal with it. I was preoccupied with little things like people trying to kill me. I don't take that kindly.

Since the truck was going to be registered to Archival Associates like my current one, I told Angel to bang out a company purchase order, figure out the total price and get a cashier's check for it from the bank. Even though we had more than enough downstairs, you can't literally pay cash-cash for a car from most dealerships without them looking at you funny; the 'anything over ten thousand in actual cash and we have to notify the IRS that you're suspicious' rule applies.

Now little local used car lots where the price is on the windshield and it's under ten grand? Sure. But, like storage-rental places, half of them also exist as fronts for the laundering of drug money. Watch really closely sometime and the same cars will often move from car lot to car lot around a certain area, being traded along with cash for quantities of illegal items.

Angel took Jake and two of Jake's guard shack minions for security when she left to fetch the truck. Me, I went back to work. I wasn't that worried about her going out. Not with three guys rolling heavy backing her up. How heavy? Welcome to Nashville. Not everything in a guitar case is really a guitar.

***

Since Odin and the cats were safe under the mountain, the next task was to get my other stuff out of harm's way. I called Steve, he made a couple calls, and with his CDL we rented an 18 wheeler with a 53' van trailer. With careful use of the ramp, lift gate, and a lot of help, we had my place emptied of anything that really mattered in half a day. Books, a lot of antiques, the gun safes, the good furniture, and so on. It was a good thing I had given up on saltwater aquariums. They don't move for shit.

Not knowing if or when I was going to go back home, I had him return the tractor but kept the trailer on a thirty day lease to store everything. Idly, I wondered if we needed to buy a truck like that for these kinds of emergencies. When I decided yes and that I wanted to call it Optimus Prime, I managed to then convince myself I was being stupid.

It was nearly dinner when the guard shack upstairs buzzed me, letting me know "my" new truck was at the gate. I went upstairs and headed outside to go have a look at it. As I walked out the door, it was just coming into the parking lot. It looked just as nice as the pics, with that dealer-prep shine to it. Great. But to my surprise, Jake was driving, with one of his minions riding shotgun. They got out and walked over to meet me. Looking around, no Angel. The guys I'd sent to make sure my girlfriend accomplished this errand safely were both wordlessly looking at me with the same *We're sorry* look you get when you arrive home to find your dog had shit on the rug.

I sighed. I knew this project had gone too smoothly. Taking another deep breath, I calmly asked, "Jake, where's Angel?" He still didn't say a word; he merely pointed back down the entrance road. *Something* was coming loud and fast. *That makes sense.* "Oh."

Tires squealed a bit at the last curve as a gunslinger in black screamed into the parking lot. It was a late model Camaro of some high end variety, I confess I don't obsess over muscle cars the way I used to in junior high. The driver's side window was down, the stereo was blasting and I saw Angel whooping with glee as she hit the emergency brake and *Tokyo Drift*-skidded it into some empty spaces, effectively triple-parking it. My eyeball is not finely calibrated for car speed, but I'm still thinking she had it up to about ninety before she tapped the brakes. The security guy in the passenger seat still had his eyes closed in terror. She was grinning like Christmas morning as I walked around to her side. I sighed again. "Did a little shopping for yourself, dear?"

She was still laughing. "I didn't put it on the company tab; this was all me. You know I make good money, thanks to you, but almost never spend it." She had a point. The same banged-up Toyota whatever the fuck it was she'd been driving since ten minutes after we'd met was still in the driveway back at the house. She rode everywhere with me and rarely drove anymore. I think the Camaro was going to change that a good bit.

"Eh, I won't complain. Let me guess, you walked in and it was just sitting there?"

The look on her face told me I nailed it. "Yeah, it was somebody's trade-in and I love the color. I just had to have it. I really want a '69, not a used '19, but you just don't find those on lots." Mentally I made a note of that fact. Maybe Christmas some year. Maybe a performance driving school for her birthday. I'd think about it. She even brought me to-go sushi from a pretty good place off Gallatin Pike.

Meanwhile the intel crew downstairs had been busy. We had a hit on the fingerprints and naturally it was in the DOD database. Manuel Castro, age 37, born Miami, Florida. Former member of the 3rd Ranger Battalion out of Fort Benning. After jump school and the first phase of the Ranger Assessment and Selection Program, he did one ninety-day trip each to Syria and Afghanistan, then Ranger School. Reenlisted, promoted, Iraq, Syria, promoted again then Syria again. He was on the fast track when he apparently fell off the rails.

First, there was an across-post transfer to 2nd Battalion, 29th Infantry, which before it was reflagged out of existence had been one of the skeleton units that taught classes and ran ranges for the Infantry School. It was also a real comedown from Regiment, which meant he'd gotten kicked out of the battalion. "Released For Standards" was their term of art, though really, getting kicked out was kinda easy. He could have just been injured. But six months later he lost a stripe and there was a discharge, "other than honorable". That meant he had fucked up again fairly badly at the 29th, but not enough for anyone to bother turning it into serious court martial shit. He ended up living up the road in the Atlanta suburbs, then did six years in a Georgia state pen for armed robbery and three counts of possession with intent to distribute. Been out for three years now.

So why was this guy shooting at me in a parking lot in Nashville? Easy guess, someone paid him to. The question was who. Well, I figure that was also pretty fucking obvious. Van Derlin had that auto parts fortune regardless of what other money he'd stolen. The other obvious thing was I got really lucky. A Ranger Batt boy should have been perfectly capable of killing me and the girls at that distance, unless he was trying so hard to miss them that he missed me too. Maybe his sights were off. Maybe my extremely overworked guardian angel had stepped in again. Moot point though, since Manuel was mostly a big baggie of meat chunks in the Metro Nashville morgue.

This wasn't going to be the end of this shit. There were call rosters full of guys like Manuel out there and plenty of other bigger fish in that pond. If that asshole outside DC was willing to pay enough, he could find half a dozen ex-SOF dudes in Russian, French, American, or other flavors out on the contractor circuit and have *them* hit my house one night. I was good, but nowhere near that good. I wasn't going to walk away from that. Shit, if this guy was connected enough, he could get an actual American unit to raid my house. That would be law enforcement, not military, but I wasn't exactly in a hurry to deal with a SWAT team either. Fighting those dudes when they wouldn't honestly know why? Nah. Or an armed UAV on a 'training flight' could have a 'weapons malfunction' and pop my whole house. I would really be pissed if my library and collections burned up with me.

Me dying really didn't bother me as a concept. When it was my day to go, it was my day to go. Fate is what it is and I already knew where I was supposed to be buried, right down to the numbered grave plot that was being held for me. Dave, Kara, and Cash could keep the team together and in the fight whether I was alive or dead. But anyone killing me wasn't liable to spare Angel or anyone else at home. Sure as hell they would take out Odin. He may be old, one-eyed, and mostly harmless, but they wouldn't want me having that warning bark. And again, collateral damage to a whole lot of my stuff. That would count as historical vandalism and I hate that.

***

The next morning, we had a full sit-down meeting of the department heads and I filled them in on the assassination attempt. I offered to lay off anyone who didn't want any part of life during wartime. The desk side of the company hadn't been recruited, selected, or trained to play in a Stateside combat environment and I wasn't going to ask people with wives and kids to be in the middle of this and risk being cacked on the way to work in the morning. Or worse, having their wives or kids targeted. Old school Mafia rules forbade that, but I don't know how far this asshole was reading out of The Five Families' handbook of classical underworld etiquette. The world is not what it was. And yeah, I made them poll all their people in person and not just blindly announce that "My people are in." This wasn't an *esprit de corps* situation. Meanwhile, Cash was down in the vault with Angel. They were working off a payroll roster making up the 'You're now on paid leave' bags we'd once merely joked about in case we did have to scatter some people. Six months' pay, in cash, in a brown paper lunch bag. We weren't exact about it either. You made just under five grand a month? We rounded up to the nearest thousand. We didn't have time to break it down to exact change.

The next week or two blurred as the company continued our shift to a wartime footing. In the middle of all this foolishness, the guard shack buzzed downstairs. There was a truck at the end of the driveway wanting to be let in through the gate. They insisted they had the correct address for a delivery. This was not a 'me' kind of problem. This was a Jake problem. Dealing with 'sergeant of the guard' issues was part of what I paid him for. He took the call and walked out of the office.

Fifteen minutes later Jake called back down. "Boss, we got a box truck and three Chinese guys down here who insist they have a delivery for you. And they know your name."

I laughed, and asked "Which one?"

Jake wasn't laughing. "Your real one."

I stopped laughing. *Oh, fuck, that's interesting.* "What kind of Chinese guys?"

"Truck says Yin Lung Food Service. Washington state plates on it. They aren't being too cooperative when we're telling them to open up the back of the truck and let us look in it before we let it in." *Yin Lung*. I thought about it. As noted, I don't speak a whole lot of Chinese. *Lung* I knew. I checked Google Translate real fast because my ADHD brain thought of something. Yeah, *Yin* meant what I suspected. *Silver Dragon*. Sneaky little fuckers couldn't resist the joke. And that is how we got the rest of our former Japanese war surplus gold bars back, newly refined and recast in standard London Good Delivery form with a whole lot of documentation.

***

At times like this, you eventually hope that your preparations were enough to mollify Fate and she would then wander off to fuck somebody else instead. Nope, not this time. Sure as hell, my house eventually got hit. As you know, I'd stripped out most everything and none of the animals were home, but it was still a goddamned annoyance to get the call from one of my neighbors that my house was on fire. I got there after the local volunteer fire department was already on scene and decisively engaged with two hoses off its bigger truck.

The bedroom end of the house was a total loss. It had already burned down flat to the top of the foundation, with enough of the floor gone I was looking down into the hole. Some of the kitchen end of the house looked marginally salvageable if they could get the interior walls to stop burning. I doubt I'd bother trying. This was probably now a job for a front end loader and a couple dump trucks. Time to start from scratch. Angel's old car was still in the driveway and was torched as well.

The fire captain was an old Army buddy who'd also stayed in the area and of course he asked the usual questions. Despite coming over to the house to shoot in the yard occasionally, he wasn't exactly in on my secrets. That was fine, as almost no one was. Even my secrets have secrets.

"So, *real name*, what the hell happened?"

I sighed. I knew damn well what happened but I wasn't going to let on. "You're the fire professional, Jeff. You tell me."

"Well, it looks like someone busted out a few of your windows and threw in a bunch of gallon jugs of gasoline with road flares taped to them. We found one in your front bushes that hadn't gotten lit. Who'd you piss off this time?"

I shrugged. "No idea. I was just about to start repainting the inside, so it's a good thing I got a bunch of stuff moved out of the way beforehand. All the animals were at the sitter."

He scowled at me, just as he did twenty years ago when I'd drag one broken or shot-up Humvee after another into his maintenance section and ask him to shit me another miraculous fix on short notice so a mission would go out on time. "It's a good thing I knew this place wasn't worth shit as an insurance burn, or I'd normally think owner arson."

"Definitely wasn't that. You know how lazy I can be."

That actually got a chuckle out of him. "Yeah, you're too lazy to move which is why you're still here all these years. Still. You might want to think about a change of scenery, man. Somebody didn't like you enough to put a fair bit of effort into burning you out."

And then the sheriff's department showed up. This was sufficient entertainment for them to get me a marked deputy's Ford 4x4 and an unmarked sedan. It had been a long time since I knew half their office, so they had several very pointed questions. They were also acting like it was an insurance burn until Jeff pretty much vouched for me and they realized we had mutual friends. I didn't even want to think about dealing with the insurance company. I definitely didn't have time or the patience for that kind of shit.

Chapter 36

"You do what I do long enough, there won't be a soul left to salvage."
~ James Bond. Well, one of them.

Obviously it was going to be a revenge matter. And rather than going tit for tat, I resolved to up the ante dramatically. Misusing a quote from the late Otto Skorzeny, aim for the head. Fortunately, the head had enough ego to have revealed himself to me. Now T. Holden Van Derlin, of the Chicago Van Derlins, had to be reduced to room temperature.

Any qualms I had about having this guy killed went out the window when I saw the recon photos of his house. It was in the swankiest of swank Maryland suburbs, just outside the Beltway and just north of the Potomac River in the extremely expensive acreage between Burning Tree's golf course and the Congressional Country Club. I would describe it as the disgusting half-breed offspring of a French chateau and an Italian Renaissance villa, its trimwork dripping with baroque frippery of imitation gold. It was an architectural atrocity, a repulsive crime against the laws of God and man. Las Vegas lounge singers would turn it down. Russian mobsters would be embarrassed to live there. Nobody with that lack of taste could be shown the barest hint of mercy. And there was not a lot of mercy in my heart these days.

The meeting for this was about as acrimonious as we ever had. That is to say 'not very', but there were way more conflicting opinions than usual for us as the company's key players crammed into my office.

Me? I opened the meeting with my traditional "Big shit up front." I was adamant that I wanted Van Derlin dead. Fucking dead. With a bullet gouge in my leg, a piece of one pulled out of my shoulder, and a little chunk of tricep cut out too, I was in no shape to do it myself right this second, but still I wanted to do it myself. Preferably with an axe, though I had an extremely nice katana in the office sword rack. I wanted his skull on my bookshelf. Or maybe cast into a nice clear acrylic resin to preserve it before I then left it in the first floor men's room urinal for a couple years.

Dave had borrowed one of my Mountain Dews. He crushed the empty and threw it at me to underscore his point. "Yes, I hereby vote to kill him. No, you are not doing this your fucking self."

I looked at him. I was still pissed at this whole situation. "He tried having me killed and he burned my fucking house down."

Morgan scoffed. "Dude, your house sucked. He did you a favor."

I turned toward him. "Fuck you, Morgan. Do you know how much I hate moving?"

Angel smacked him for me. "I lived there too. I liked it."

Dave cut back in. "You're the high profile target. You stay here and stay the fuck out of the way, let the wounds heal up, and that keeps their eyes looking for you while we then sneak the crew of hitters in and do the job. Your going is both sloppy and unprofessional. I'm not letting you do it."

Morgan looked at me and looked at Dave. He pointed at Dave and piped up, "What he said."

Kara raised her hand tentatively. "Not that I have any moral objections to killing people who deserve it, and this guy does, but might it be better to let him live a while and run intel collection on him and any of his associates so we get a more complete picture of who and what we're dealing with?"

I sighed. "Were we going on a completely logical basis here, sure. But now I'm guessing there's a whole other layer to the political and economic ecosystem out there. We're a small fluffy animal in a jungle of things that would probably love to either cage us up to work for them or eat us for lunch. I don't find either of those outcomes acceptable.

Acknowledging this is my anger talking, I'd rather kill him now just to make everyone else in his orbit back the fuck off."

Kara thought about it. "Will that start some shit we can't finish?"

I shrugged. The uncertainty was a cold, heavy emptiness in my chest, but I told the truth anyway. "I don't know. I really don't. If push comes to shove, we can knock guys like him off onesies-twosies all day. They have names, they have addresses. They usually live in nice neighborhoods too."

Angel shook her head. "I saw him, I listened to his bullshit. He thinks there are some group of secret powers running the world and he works for them. He's crazy. Just shoot him and be done with it."

Cash said "For what it's worth, I vote we take him out in a cornfield someplace, pour five gallons of gasoline on him, and then drop a match. I'd never been shot at before and I have decided I don't like it very much."

I nodded. "Forceful. Decisive. I like it. But then if we're going to go to the trouble of snatching him alive, we might as well keep him for a while and torture a bunch of information out him before we make him disappear."

Cash nodded. "I'm okay with that too."

Dave shook his head, as did Morgan. "The problem is you have to know where to start asking questions, and be able to confirm the answers. Properly executed forceful interrogation is mostly training people not to lie, and for that to work you then have to have an idea of what the truth looks like. Unfortunately, we're clueless so far. A clean kill to see what then floats up afterward is as good an option as we have."

"Yeah, I know. Still, I do wish there was a way to get some of the information out of his head before we fuckin' cut it off."

Dave groaned. "This is not *Highlander.* Not even one of the bad sequels. We are not cutting his head off, and you don't get magic powers from it."

***

For a guy who talked such mad shit about becoming the off the books 'mob boss' of the factions, whoever the fuck those guys really were, Van Derlin did not pay as much attention to his personal security as a Lucky Luciano wannabe should have. He liked to drive himself around in his fancy goddamned car and tell everyone he thought was in the know what a big shot he was. Most of the time he only bothered with one security goon. Well, there are reasons some legit big shots were rolling around the States in armored Yukons or Escalades with four-man fire teams and another team in a backup truck like it was the bad old days in Baghdad. Really, I might have to start living that way unless this shit got nipped in the bud quickly.

It was a lovely, quiet morning when my messengers went a-calling. Forgive me for not mentioning who did the job or some of the tactical details. I won't be retired for some years to come and we may have to use some of these tricks again. But the primary weakness through which we entered his life was that he habitually left his house between seven and a quarter after, en route to a restaurant breakfast and then his office at a prestigious DC law firm where he probably did fuck-all during the day except harass the staff.

He was going to be a bit late.

A M18A1 Claymore mine is the size of a large paperback book, eight and a half by five inches of molded green plastic less than two inches thick. On its convex plastic front are molded the iconic words FRONT TOWARD ENEMY. We had several crates of them containing half a dozen each. They were a little old, the packing date was 1974, but the foil inner bags were still sealed and we blew up a couple others from that crate of six to convince ourselves they still worked reliably.

While there are numerous ways for the skilled to make one cleverly explode, the easiest is the standard Basic Training method; using its included electrically-activated blasting cap on its one hundred feet of wire (M41 assembly) and handheld electric generator (M57), aka the, "clacker" for its clicking noise when squeezed. That fires off a pound and a quarter of C-4 plastic explosive and sends a cloud of 1/8" steel ball bearings on their way at about 3900 feet per second. Seven hundred or so of them, if the manual can be trusted. Think of sixty-ish 12 gauge shotguns going off at once and you get the general idea.

The wire easily reached from under the driver's seat of his car, behind the seats, through the weather-stripping of the closed passenger door, across his garage floor and through the slightly ajar garage window to where the team sat behind the hedges with the clacker. Pointing upward, with layers of car roof, garage ceiling and garage roof, it would hopefully contain most of the ball bearings and limit collateral damage. When the car started, the team was to visually verify through the window he was alone, then get the fuck down and blow the Claymore.

The backup plan, if he had company and precision was needed instead, was one of the suppressed .22s per man, it in turn being backed up with other ordnance. We weren't going to blow up any household help, boyfriends, girlfriends, or innocent bystanders and only any henchmen who got in the way or wanted a fight. That's why you hire surgeons to do surgery, not butchers.

As it was told to me, like many important figures, he was a creature of both habit and routine. At 7:09 AM, the M57 went *clack clack clack*, the generated electrical charge reached down the wire to the cap, and he ascended to Glory rapidly. He was announced into the Hereafter for his final judgment with a good-sized bang when that pound and a quarter of C-4 went off. The first two guys snatched up the thirty-odd feet of wire they actually used, ears ringing a bit even with plugs and muffs. A second pair raided upstairs to his office and grabbed his home computer, in and out of the house in two minutes and the four went through the backyards and woods to where they had secured their getaway vehicle. They went down River Road to the Potomac shore and then were across the Chain Bridge into Virginia in a total of fifteen minutes.

Twenty hours later, we were in my office at The Hole and I was getting the whole story. The story was barely being touched by even the local DC stations. One called it a 'propane gas tank explosion in an upscale Maryland neighborhood.' Perhaps the knowledge of how vulnerable some of them were to selective targeting and removal wasn't something our socioeconomic 'betters' wanted publicized. Otherwise people might get the right idea and start knocking off more of the parasitic bastards.

In hindsight, it was a simple thing to have ordered done. Part of me wondered if a similar order would be given for me one day. The thought made me slightly pensive. "Wonder what the last thing to go through his mind was?"

The guys smirked. "A few hundred ball bearings and a chunk of his own asshole, boss."

Even I had to laugh at that. Yeah, I'm probably going to Hell one day, but it'll be crowded.

As the four man hit crew left, Morgan took custody of Van Derlin's desk computer and headed downstairs with it to start digging in the hard drive. That left Dave, Kara, and Angel looking at me.

Finally Angel asked the question on everyone's mind. "Now what happens?"

I sighed. "I don't know. We just keep our eyes and ears open, and get by one more day at a time until we find out."

Afterword

"I'm an Indian outlaw..."
~Tim McGraw

Most everyone in this book is based on someone I know. Easy to keep the cast straight that way; it's a trick I learned from John Ringo and Tom Kratman. I later learned Larry Hama of Marvel Comics fame (*GI Joe, The Nth Man, Wolverine*) does it too. Tom nearly killed 'me' in a novel once, since training accidents are as bad as combat. He also hadn't continued that series so 'I' was stuck in a Houston hospital doing physical therapy for over a decade in that other world until Tom handed that baton off to Justin Watson for Book 4. The idea then trickled down through the Baen Books fandom as many of us got inspired and began to write our own work, also using our friends as characters.

Then fellow Iraq vet Seth Anderson Bailey nearly killed me in a fictional firefight in Dallas in 2016's *Edge of the City*. That incident is known to some in this book as 'the East Dallas Massacre.' Now is this a Jeb Shaw novel? No. Does it occur in kinda the same fictional universe, with only a text message handshake on it between brothers in arms? Yeah. That's why I advertised his stuff at several points. So go buy and read Seth's stuff, even if me does grammar gooder than him do.

That was a joke.

I find a touch of humor necessary to brace for what's coming.

The first problem I have with using people I know is that a lot of them prefer their privacy. Hell, I prefer my privacy. Writing a first-person shooter of a story where someone else's fictional version of me had to be built upon was often an uncomfortable experience. Then for various reasons, ranging from day-job security clearances to some clandestine sexual perversions, the inspirations for the other characters usually have to remain mostly anonymous. Angel is a pseudonym, though she is quite real. Dave has become Dave. Kara has to go by Kara, and the lovely young lady who inspired Cash and helped me write her parts doesn't want her real name out there either. She really was *summa cum laude* in the Ivies, both undergraduate and her MBA. I am very proud of her for that. All the actors know who they are and have my thanks for making my life easier. Knowing a lot of interesting people made this book happen. Debi's really real too, except for the 'cartoonish' chest. Really only "Mad Jack" Chen and the Singapore gang were wholly created. The late Big John, Matt the charter pilot, and Fast Eddie Netherton at least count as composites.

And like any other form of theater, it took more than just the on-stage cast as other writer friends from the veteran community pitched in. Norwich grad school classmate Chris "Mogs" DiNote read an early first draft barely half this size and then nagged me to finish it. He got his cameo in gratitude. Other writer friends merely offered technical advice. Retired SEAL officer Mike Massa, after letting me borrow the Maguire AFB to O'Hare story I mentioned, then helped with bank security matters while Aaron Haskins merely explained pocket squares. Then I loaned one of my M1 Garands to John "PowerPoint Ranger" Holmes of Cannon Publishing at the Libertycon range day. We got talking before I knew who he was. He wanted to look at the manuscript and he actually liked it.

"It's totally not my style, but it works for you. screw it, let's do this." Thanks, John. Now I really had to finish the damn thing. That task, the editing, and the cover art took a couple months, including a full rewrite of one chapter that did make it much better while also adding more violence. If only he were not a heretic regarding the Oxford comma. This thing may publish with them *wrong.** That said, he DID come up with the title. I never named the firm in my original draft except for the Archive Associates offshoot- Athenaeum was his idea.

Editor's note. I'm right, dammit. And I out rank you both in the Army and as the editor. ~J.F.

We won't even get into the months of delays caused by a last-minute trip through the Department of Defense security review system. That took time, and we'd already sold a bunch of copies on pre-sale. That office was really helpful though, even if I'm not supposed to personally thank any of them.

Returning to my point, however. The other, bigger, problem with using people you know is sometimes tragedy strikes in the real world before the fictional one. In my abiding grief, I will pull the backstage curtain on one part of the cast. My buddy since the Lightfighter.net days over fifteen years back, Justin Sanders, the self-proclaimed wagon-burning savage who inspired Morgan, lost a longtime battle against his numerous inner demons. He walked out into his backyard and shot himself in the head on New Year's Eve 2019.

Justin was a full blood Dene Indian, Alaska-born but Indiana-raised. He said the Dene were basically Apaches who preferred frostbite to heat stroke, even if archaeological evidence says the reverse may be true. Justin was rarely one to ruin a good story with the truth. He was a crypto and IT nut, something I carried over to Morgan. He definitely had his vices. He had an extensive past history of drug use and loved "phat-assed white girls- thank you Columbus!" Justin may have left us, but Morgan will live on into the sequel since he inspired much of it without trying too hard.

That leads to the final note. Justin also left behind a wife, three kids, and a lot of heartbroken friends. A whole lot of us have our problems. I probed some of mine in this book over several years as my moods swung and my personal problems stacked. I was often emotionally incapable of working on this manuscript for months at a time. I took so long to finish this that the Fullerton Hotel in Singapore used the coronavirus pandemic lockdown to remodel all their restaurants. The Lighthouse Bar, the Italian restaurant upstairs, and the Japanese buffet downstairs are all gone now. I'm letting that section stay as is. Artistic license and I'm on a deadline.

Seeing how Justin's death affected everyone in our social circle kept me from following him at a point or two when my brain tried to kill me. So before you make a final decision, remember your problems may be over, but they will just splatter we who remain behind. We'll miss you. There are resources out there to help keep you on this mortal coil. Please use them.

If you or a loved one is having trouble dealing with life due to service related issues, please call the VA Crisis Hotline. It's staffed 24/7, usually with people who have been through the same trials and fires that you have. Life can always get better and you still have a mission. ~ Sergeant First Class (R) John F. Holmes. Owner / Editor, Cannon Publishing.

For even more great Military Science Fiction check out:

www.cannonpublishing.us

If you enjoyed this book, please check out Irregular Scout Team One by J.F. Holmes and The Thin Dead Line by Shane Gries. Two parallel series look at small team action and mechanized infantry fighting during the outbreak of a worldwide apocalyptic pandemic.

What's a soldier to do when the war is over? When he's only known conflict his whole life? Since time immemorial the solution has been to find another war, this time for pay. Whoever has the credits and wins the high bid gets the experienced fighter. Sometimes, though, the credits aren't enough to over the price.

Empires rise, but Empires also fall. The Terran Union has spent five centuries under the control of the alien Grausians, like a barbarian tribe under the thumb of Rome. Now, after almost two decades of civil war and succession struggles, the formerly subject races have settled back in their ancient territories to lick their wounds and rearm, leaving hundreds of settled planets to exist in a political vacuum. Into that space steps the free companies, mercenary units that fight for gold, honor, power and glory. Veterans who can't get the wars out of their souls, new recruits looking for adventure, corporations with their own agenda.

457

An ancient enemy invades Earth, returning to claim their home world. The men and women of the U.S. Military find themselves matching technology against magic as cities burn and armies clash.

www.ingramcontent.com/pod-product-compliance
Lightning Source LLC
Chambersburg PA
CBHW070830260626
47170CB00007B/2325